The Best British Mysteries

The Best British Mysteries

Edited by

MAXIM JAKUBOWSKI

This edition published in Great Britain in 2004 by
Allison & Busby Limited
Bon Marche Centre
241-251 Ferndale Road
London SW9 8BJ
http://www.allisonandbusby.com

A catalogue record for this book is available from
the British Library.

ISBN 0 7490 8300 X

Typeset in Plantin by The Old Tin Dog Design Co.
Brighton

Printed and bound in Great Britain by
Bookmarque Ltd, Croydon, Surrey

Contents

Introduction

British crime and mystery writing is popular all over the world. And how could it not be? After all, these are the shores that saw the talents of Conan Doyle, Agatha Christie, Dorothy L. Sayers and so many others flourish. In addition, let us not forget that we even helped educate Raymond Chandler. A further badge of both infamy and notoriety was Jack the Ripper, the first recorded serial killer. At least, he was British; he was ours!

From the Golden Age of classic mystery writing onwards, British talent has conquered the imagination of readers in all countries, and modern days have been no exception, with such accomplished authors as P.D. James, Ruth Rendell, Reginald Hill, Colin Dexter, Minette Walters, Ian Rankin, John Connolly and countless others dominating bestseller lists and, in many cases, mounting a bloody take-over of television screens and darkened cinemas.

Further, the art of the mystery short story is one that British craftsmen have always excelled in. Hence the present book.

Puzzles, slice of life, short action pieces and vignettes are the cornerstone of storytelling and never more so than in crime and mystery writing. They are published in magazines, sometimes in newspapers, in anthologies, more and more these days online and they are a sure indication of the health of the field. Both the British Crime Writers' Association and the Mystery Writers of America reward the short story genre annually, alongside novels, but there has never been an anthology series devoted exclusively to the British crime story until now (although there is an American counterpart). The publishers and I hope this innovative project will please readers with its selection of the best of the past year and the encouragement of readers will allow us to make it an annual event.

And our opening salvo is, I immodestly think, a winner. You will find some of the biggest names currently active in British crime writing together with new voices and talents you might be unaware of as yet, and the breadth of subject matter, emotions, thrills and spills has no equal. Stella Duffy's opening tale won the CWA Short Story Dagger, while Marion Arnott's story was on the award's shortlist, but many of the stories highlighted here only appeared in the USA and thus did not qualify, although their overall quality is as impressive.

I've cast my web wide and trawled material published in far from obvious places like Australian women's magazines, radio and TV listings publications, a Welsh Arts Council funded magazine and even on the Internet, as well as some of the leading genre magazines and anthologies. Something for every criminal taste!

If you enjoy this collection, the biggest compliment you can pay us beyond your hard-earned cash is to move on and read full-length books by some of the authors featured here. They all are well worth the journey.

Enjoy!

Maxim Jakubowski

Martha Grace

Stella Duffy

Martha Grace is what in the old days would have been termed a 'fine figure of a woman'. Martha Grace is big-boned and strong. Martha Grace could cross a city, climb a mountain range, swim an ocean – and still not break into a sweat. She has wide thighs and heavy breasts and child-bearing hips, though in her fifty-eight years there has been no call for labour-easing width. Martha Grace has a low-slung belly, gently downed, soft as clean, brushed cotton. Martha Grace lives alone and grows herbs and flowers and strange foreign vegetables in her marked-out garden. She plants by the light of the full moon. When she walks down the street people move out of her way, children giggle behind nervous hands, adults cast sidelong glances and wonder. When she leaves a room people whisper 'dyke' and 'witch', though Martha Grace is neither. Martha Grace loves alone, pleasuring her own sweetly rolling flesh, clean oiled skin soft beneath her wide mouth. Martha Grace could do with getting out more.

Tim Culver is sixteen. He is big for his age and loved. Football star, athlete, and clever too. Tim Culver could have his pick of any girl in the class. And several of their mothers. One or two of their older brothers. If he was that way inclined. Which he isn't. Certainly not. Tim Culver isn't that kind of boy. Tim Culver is just too clean. And good. And right. And ripe. Good enough for girls, too clean for boys. Tim Culver, for a bet, turns up at Martha Grace's house on a quiet Saturday afternoon, friends giggling round the corner, wide smirk on his handsome not-yet-grown face. He offers himself as an odd-job man. And then comes back to her house almost every weekend for the next three years. He says it is to help her out. She's a single woman, she's not that bad, a bit strange maybe, but no worse than his grandma in the years before she died. And she's not that old, really. Or that fat. Just big. Different from the women he's used to. She talks to him different-ly. And, anyway, Martha Grace pays well. In two hours at her house he can earn twice what he'd make mowing the lawn for his father, painting houses with his big brother. She doesn't know he's using her, thinks she's paying him the going rate. God knows, she never talks to anyone to compare it. It's fine, he knows what he's doing, Tim Culver is in charge, takes no jokes at his own expense. And after a few false starts, failed attempts at schoolboy mockery, the laughing stops, the other kids wish they'd thought to try the mad old bitch for some cash. Tim Culver earns more than any of them in half the time. But then, he always has been the golden boy.

For Tim, this was just meant to be a one-off. Visit the crazy fat lady, prove his courage to his friends and then leave, laughing in her face. He does leave laughing. And comes back hungry the next day, wanting more. It takes no time at all to become routine. The knock at the door, the boy standing there, insolent smile and ready cock, hands held out to offer, 'Got any jobs that need doing?'

And Martha did find him work. That first day. No matter how greedy his grin, how firm his young flesh, no matter what else she could see waiting on her doorstep that young Tim Culver couldn't even guess at. Mow the lawn. Clean out the pond. Mend the broken fence. Then maybe she thought that he should come inside, clean up, rest awhile, as she fixed him a drink, found her purse, offered a fresh clean note. And herself.

At first, Tim Culver wasn't sure he understood her correctly.

'So, Tim, have you had sex yet?'

Why would the fat woman be asking him that? What did she know about sex? And did she mean as in today, or as in ever? Tim Culver blustered, he didn't know how to answer her, of course he's had sex. The first in his class, and – so the girls said – the best. Tim Culver was not just a shag-merchant like the rest of them. He might fuck a different girl from one Saturday to the next, but he prided himself on knowing a bit about what he was doing. Every girl remembered Tim Culver. Martha Grace remembered Tim Culver. She'd been watching him. That was the thing about being the mad lady, fat lady, crazy old woman. They watched her all the time, laughed at her. They didn't notice that she was also watching them.

Tim Culver says yes, he has had sex. Of course he's had sex. What does she think he is? Does she think he's a poof? Mad old dyke, what the fuck does she think he is?

Martha Grace explains that she doesn't yet know what he is.

That's why he's here. That's why she's asked him into her house. So she can find out. Tim Culver knows a challenge when it's thrown his way.

When Tim Culver and Martha Grace fuck, it is like no other time with no other woman. Tim Culver has fucked other women, other girls, plenty of them. He is a local hero, after all. Not for him all talk and no action. When Tim Culver says he has been there, done that, you know he really means it. But with Martha Grace it is different. For a start there is not fucker and fuckee. And she does talk to him, encourages him, welcomes him, incites him. Martha Grace makes Tim Culver more of the man he would have himself be. Laid out against her undulating flesh, Tim Culver's young toned body is hero-strong, he is capable of any feat of daring, the gentlest acts of kindness. Tim Culver and Martha Grace are making love. Tim Culver drops deep into her soft skin and wide body and is more than happy to lose himself there, give himself away.

Before he leaves, she feeds him. Fresh bread she baked that morning, kneading the dough beneath her fat hands as she kneaded his flesh just minutes ago. She spreads thick yellow butter on the soft bread and layers creamy honey on top, sweet from her hands to his mouth. Then back to her mouth as they kiss and she wipes crumbs from his shirt front. She is tidier than he is, does not like to see him make a mess. Could not normally bear the thought of breadcrumbs on her pristine floor. But that Tim Culver is delicious, and the moisture in her mouth at the sight of him, drives away all thoughts of sweeping and scrubbing and cleaning. At least until he has gone, at least until she is alone again. For now, Martha Grace is all abandon. Fresh and warm in a sluttish kitchen. After another half-hour in the heat by the stove, Tim Culver has to go. His friends will wonder what has happened to him. His mother will be expecting him for dinner. He has to shower, get dressed again, go out. He has young people to meet and a pretty redhead to pick up at eight-thirty. Tim Culver leaves with a crisp twenty in his pocket and fingers the note, volunteering to come back next Saturday. Martha Grace thinks, stares at the boy, half smiles with a slow incline of her head, she imagines there will be some task for him to do. Two p.m. Sharp. Don't be late. Tim Culver nods, he doesn't usually take orders. But then, this feels more like an offer. One his aching body won't let him refuse.

She watches him walk away, turns back to look at the mess of her kitchen. Martha Grace spends the next three hours cleaning up. Scrubbing down the floor, the table. Changing the sheets, wiping surfaces, picking up after herself. When she sits down to her own supper she thinks about the boy out for the night, spending her money on the little redhead. She sighs, he could buy the girl a perfectly adequate meal with that money. If such a girl would ever eat a whole meal anyway. Poor little painfully thin babies that they are. Living shiny magazine half-lives of self-denial and want. Martha Grace chooses neither. Before she goes to sleep, Martha notes down the visit and the payment in her accounts book. She has not paid the boy for sex. That would have been wrong. She paid him for the work he'd done. The lawn, the fence, the pond. The sex was simply an extra.

Extra-regular. On Saturday afternoons, after winter football practice, after summer runs, late from long holiday mornings sleeping off the after-effects of teenage Friday nights, Tim Culver walks to the crazy lady's house. Pushes open the gate he oiled last weekend, walks past the rosemary and comfrey and yarrow he pruned in early spring, takes out the fresh-cut key she has given him, lets himself in to the dark hallway he will paint next holiday and walks upstairs. Martha Grace is waiting for him. She has work for Tim Culver to do.

Martha Grace waits in her high, soft bed. She is naked. Her long grey hair falls around her shoulders. Usually it is pulled back tightly so that even Martha's cheekbones protrude from the flesh of her round cheeks, now the hair covers the upper half of her voluminous breasts, deep red and wide, the nipples raised beneath the scratch of her grey hair. Tim Culver nods at Martha Grace, almost smiles, walks past the end of her bed to the bathroom. The door is left open so Martha Grace can watch him from her bed. He takes off his sweaty clothes, peels them from skin still hot and damp, then lowers himself into the bath she has ready for him. Dried rose petals float on the surface of the water, rosemary, camomile and other herbs he doesn't recognize. Tim Culver sinks beneath the water and rises up again, all clean and ready for bed.

In bed. Tim Culver sinks into her body. Sighs in relief and pleasure. He has been a regular visitor to her home and her flesh for almost three years now. The place where he lies with Martha

Grace's soft, fat body is as much home to him as his mother's table or the room he shares with an old friend now that he has moved away. Tim Culver has graduated from high school fucks to almost-romances with college girls. Pretty, thin, clever, bright and shiny college girls. Lots of them. Tim Culver is a good-looking boy and clearly well-worth the bodies these girls are offering. This is the time of post-feminism. They want to fuck him because he is good-looking and charming and will make a great story tomorrow in the lunchtime canteen. And Tim is perfectly happy for this to be the case. The girls may revel in the glories of their fiercely free sexuality, Tim just wants to get laid every night. Everyone's happy. And the girls are definitely happy. It's not just that Tim Culver is good-looking and clever and fit. And he really, really knows what he's doing. Which is more than can be said of most of the football team. Tim Culver is a young man of depth and experience. And, of course, it is good for Tim to be seen fucking at this rate. To be this much the all-round popular guy. But as he lies awake next to another fine, thin, lithe, little body he recognizes a yearning in his skin. He is tired of fucking girls who ache in every bone of their arched-back bodies to be told they are the best. Tired of screwing young women who constantly demand that he praise their emaciated ribs, their skeletal cheekbones, their tight and wiry arms. Weary of the near relationships with would-be-poet girls who want to torment him with their deep insights into pain and suffering and sex and music. Tim Culver is exhausted by the college girls he fucks.

They are not soft, these young women at college, and they need so much attention. Even when they don't say so out loud, they need so much attention. Tim learned this in his first week away from home. Half asleep and his back turned to the blonde of the evening, her soft sobs drew him from the rest he so needed. No there was nothing wrong, yes it had been fine, he'd been great, she'd come, of course it was all OK. She wasn't crying, not really, it was just … and this in a small voice, not the voice she'd come with, or the voice she'd picked him up with, or the voice she'd use to retell the best parts of the story tomorrow, but … was she all right? Did he like her? Was she pretty enough? Thin enough? Good enough? Only this one had dared to speak aloud, but he'd felt it seeping out of all the others. Every single one of them, eighteen-, nineteen-year-old girls, each one oozing please-praise-me from their emaciated, emancipated pores. But not Martha Grace.

With Martha Grace Tim can rest. Maybe Martha Grace needs him, Tim cannot tell for certain. She likes him, he knows that. Certainly she wants him, hungers for him. As he now knows, he hungers for her. But if she needs him, it is only Tim that she needs. His body, his presence, his cock. She does not need his approval, his blessing, his constant, unending hymn of there-there. And maybe that is because he has none to give. She is fat. And old. And weird. What could he approve of? What is there to approve of? Nothing at all. They both know that. And so it is that, when Tim comes home to Martha, there is rest along with exertion. There is ease in the fucking. Martha Grace knows who she is, what she is. She demands nothing extra of him. What sanctions of beauty and thinness, or perfection could he give her anyway? She has none of those and so, as Tim acknowledges to himself in surprise and pleasure, she is easier to be with than the bone-stabbing stick-figure girls at school. And softer. And wider. And more comfortable. It is better in that house, that bed, against that heavy body. Martha Grace is not eighteen and a part of Tim Culver sits up shocked and amused – he realizes he loves her for it. The rest of Tim Culver falls asleep, his heavy head on her fat breast. Martha Grace smells the other women in his hair.

One day Tim Culver brings Martha Grace a new treat. He knows of her appetite for food and drink and him, he understands he cravings and her ever-hungry mouth. He loves her ever-hungry mouth. He brings gifts from the big city, delicatessen offerings, imported chocolates and preserves. Wines and liquors. He has the money. He is not a poor student. Martha Grace sees to that. This time the home-from-college boy brings her a new gift. Martha Grace has tried marijuana years ago: it didn't suit her, she liked to feel in control, didn't understand the desire to take a drug that made one lose control, the opposite of her wanting. She has told Tim this, explained about her past experiences, how she came to be the woman she is today. She has shared with Tim each and every little step that took her from the wide open world to wide woman in a closed house. And he has nodded and understood. Or appeared to do so. At the very least he has listened and that is new and precious to Martha. So she is willing to trust him. Scared but willing. And this time Tim brings home cocaine. Martha is shocked and secretly delighted. But she is the older woman, he still just a student, she must retain some degree of adult composure. She tells him to put it away, take it back to school, throw it out. Tells him off, delivers a sharp rebuke, a reprimand and then sends him to bed. Her bed. Tim walks upstairs smiling. He leaves the thin wrap on the hall table. Martha Grace watches him walk away, feels the smirk from the back of his head, threatens a slap, which she knows he wants anyway. Her hand reaches out for the wrap. Such a small thing and so much fuss. She pictures the naked boy upstairs. Man. Young man. In her bed. Hears again the fuss she knows it would cause. Hears again as he calls her, taunting from the room above. She is hungry and wanting. Her soft hand closes around the narrow strip of folded paper and she follows his trail of clothes upstairs, clucking like a disparaging mother hen at the lack of tidiness, folding, putting away. Getting into bed, putting to rights.

Tim Culver lays out a long thin line on Martha Grace's heavy stomach. It wobbles as she breathes in, breathes out, the small ridge of cocaine mountain sited on her skin, creamy white avalanche grains tumbling with her sigh. He inhales cocaine and the clean, fleshy smell of Martha. And both are inspirations for him. Now her turn. She rolls the boy over onto his stomach, lays out an uncertain line from his low waist to the soft hairs at the curve of his arse. She is slow and deliberate, new to this, does not want to get it wrong. Tim is finding it hard to stay face down, wants to burrow himself into the flesh of Martha Grace, not the unyielding mattress. She lays her considerable weight out along his legs, hers dangling off the end of the bed, breasts to buttocks and inhales coke and boy and, not for the first time in her life, the thick iron smell of bloody desire. Then she reaches up to stretch herself out against him full length, all of her pressing down into all of him. The weight of her flesh against his back and legs has Tim Culver reaching for breath. He wonders if this is what it is like for all the little girls he fucks at college. He a tall, strong young man and they small, brittle beneath him. At some point in the sex he always likes to lie on top. To feel himself above the young women, all of him stretched out against the twisted paper and bones of the young-girl skin, narrow baby-woman hips jutting sharply into his abdomen, reminding him of what he has back at home, Martha waiting for the weekend return. He likes it when, breath forced from the thin lungs beneath him, they whisper the fuck in half-caught breaths. Tim has always been told it feels good, the heaviness, the warmth, the strong body laid out and crushing down, lip to lip, cock to cunt, tip to toe. He hopes it is like this for the narrow young women he lies on top of. Tim Culver likes this. He is surprised by the feeling, wonders if it is just the coke or the addition of physical pressure, Martha's wide weight gravity-heavy against his back, pushing his body down, spreading him out. Is wondering still when she slides her hand in between his legs and up to his cock. Is wondering no longer when he comes five minutes later, Martha still on his back, mouth to his neck, teeth to his tanned skin. Her strength, his weight, like no other female body he has felt. He thinks then for a brief moment about the gay boys he knows (barely, acquaintances), wonders if this is what it is like for them too. But wonders only briefly; momentary sex-sense identification with the thin young women is a far-enough stretch for a nineteen-year-old small-town boy.

They did not take cocaine together again. Martha liked it, but Martha would rather be truly in control than amphetamine-convinced by the semblance of control. Besides that, she had, as usual, prepared a post-sex snack for that afternoon. Glass of sweet dessert wine and rich cherry cake, the cherries individually pitted by her own fair, fat hands the evening before, left to soak in sloe gin all night, waiting for Tim's mouth to taste them, just as she was. But after the drugs and the sex and then some more of the bitter powder, neither had an appetite for food. They had each other and cocaine and then Tim left. Martha didn't eat until the evening, and alone, and cold. Coke headache dulling the tip of her left temple. She could cope with abandon. She could certainly enjoy a longer fuck, a seemingly insatiable desire from the young man of her fantasies come true. She could, on certain and specified occasions, even put up with a ceding of power. But she would not again willingly submit to self-inflicted loss of appetite. That was just foolish.

It went on. Three months more, then six, another three. Seasons back to where they started. Tim Culver and Martha Grace. The mask of garden chores and DIY tasks, then the fucking and the feeding and the financial recompense. Then even, one late afternoon in winter, dark enough outside for both to kid themselves they had finally spent a night together, an admission of love. It comes first from Tim. Surprising himself. He's held it in all this time, found it hard to believe it was true, but knows the miracle fact as it falls from his gratified mouth: 'Martha, I love you.'

Martha Grace smiles and nods. 'Tim, I love you.'

Not 'back'. Or 'too'. Just love.

A month more. Tim Culver and Martha Grace loving. In love. Weekend adoration and perfect.

And then Martha thinks she will maybe pay him a visit. Tim always comes to her. She will go to his college. Surprise him. Take a picnic, all his favourite foods and her. Martha Grace's love in a basket. She packs a pie – tender beef and slow-cooked sweet onion, the chunky beef slightly bloody in the middle, just the way Tim likes it. New bread pitted with dark green olives, Tim's favourite. Fresh shortbread and strawberry tarts with imported out-of-season berries. A Thermos of mulled wine, the herbs and spices from her own blend from the dark cupboard beneath her stairs. She dresses carefully and wears lipstick, culled from the back of a drawer and an intentionally forgotten time of made-up past. Walks into town, camomile-washed hair flowing about her shoulders, head held high, best coat, pretty shoes – party shoes. Travels on the curious bus, catches a cab to the college.

And all the time Martha Grace knows better. Feels at the lowest slung centre of her belly the terror of what is to come. Doesn't know how she can do this even as she does it. Wants to turn back with every step, every mile. Knows in her head it cannot be, in her stomach it will not work. But her stupid fat heart sends her stumbling forwards anyway. She climbs down from the bus and walks to the coffee shop he has mentioned. Where he sits with his friends, passing long slow afternoons of caffeine and chocolate and drawled confidences. He is not there and Martha Grace sits alone at a corner table for an hour. Another. And then Tim Culver arrives. With a gaggle of laughing others. He is brash and young. Sits backwards across the saddle of his chair. Makes loud noises, jokes, creates a rippling guffaw of youthful enjoyment all around him. He does not notice Martha Grace sat all alone in the corner, a pale crumble of dried cappuccino froth at the corner of her mouth. But eventually one of his friends does. Points her out quietly to another. There are sniggers, sideways glances. Martha

Grace could not be more aware of her prominence. But she still sits, knowing better and hoping for more. Then Tim sees her, his attention finally drawn from the wonder of himself to the absurdity of the fat woman in the corner. And Tim looks up, directly at Martha Grace, right into her pale grey eyes and he stands and walks towards her and his friends are staring after him, whooping and hollering, catcalls and cheers, and then he has stopped by her table and he sits beside Martha Grace and reaches towards her and touches the line of her lips, moves in, licks away the dried milk crust. He stands again, bows a serious little bow, and walks back to his table of friends. Who stand and cheer and push forward the young girls to kiss, pretty girls, thin girls. Tim Culver has kissed Martha Grace in public and it has made him a hero. And he made a fool of Martha Grace. She tries to leave the café, tries to walk out unnoticed, but her bulk is stuck in the corner arrangement of too-small chairs and shin-splittingly low table, her feet clatter against a leaning tray, her heavy arms and shaking hands cannot hold the hamper properly, it falls to her feet and the food rolls out. Pie breaks open, chunks of bloody meat spill across the floor, strawberries that were cool and fresh are now hot and sweating, squashed beneath her painfully pretty shoes as she runs from the room, every action a humiliation, every second another pain. Eventually Martha Grace turns her great bulk at the coffee-shop door and walks away down the street, biting the absurd lipstick from her stupid, stupid lips as she goes, desperate to break into a lumbering run, forcing her idiotic self to move slowly and deliberately through the pain. All the way down the long street, surrounded by strangers and tourists and scrabbling children underfoot, she feels Tim's eyes boring into the searing blush on the back of her neck.

Neither mentions the visit. The next weekend comes and goes. Martha is a little cool, somewhat distant. Tim hesitant, uncertain. Wondering whether to feel shame or guilt and then determining on neither when he sees Martha's fear that he might mention what has occurred. Both skirt around their usual routine, there are no jobs to be done, no passion to linger over, the sex is quick and not easy. Tim dresses in a hurry, Martha stays cat-curled in bed, face half-hidden beneath her pillow, she points to the notes on her dresser, Tim takes only half the cash. Pride hurt, vanity exposed,

Martha promises herself she will get over it. Pick herself up, get on. Tim need never know how hurt she felt. How stupid she knows herself to have been. The weekend after will be better, she'll prepare a surprise for him, make a real treat, an offering to get things back to where they had been before. Then Martha Grace will be herself again.

Saturday morning and Martha Grace is preparing a special dish for Tim. She knows his taste. He likes berry fruits, loves chocolate like any young boy though, unlike most, Martha Grace has taught him the joy of real chocolate, dark and shocking. She will make him a deep tart of black berries and melted chunks of bitter chocolate, imported from France, ninety per cent cocoa solids. She starts early in the day. Purest white flour mixed in the air as she sifts it with organic cocoa so perfect that her pastry is almost black. Then the fruit – blackberries, boysenberries, loganberries, blackcurrants – just simmered with fruit sugar and pure water over the lowest of heat for almost two hours until they are thick syrup and pulp. She skims the scum from the surface, at the very end throws in another handful. This fruit she does not name. These are the other berries she was taught to pick by her mother, in the fresh morning before sunlight has bruised the delicate skin. She leaves the thick fruit mix to cool. Melts the chocolate. Glistening rich black in the shallow pan. When it is viscous and runs slowly from the back of her walnut spoon, she drops in warmed essences – almond, vanilla and a third distilled flavour, stored still, a leftover from her grandmother's days, just in case, for a time of who-knows-and-maybe, hidden at the back of the dark cupboard beneath her stairs. She leaves the pan over hot water, bubbling softly in the cool of her morning kitchen. Lays the pastry out on the marble slab. Rolls it to paper fine. Folds it in on itself and starts again. Seven times more. Then she fits it to the baking dish, fluted edges, heavy base. She bakes the pastry blind and removes from her oven a crisp, dark shell. Pours in warm, thick, liquid chocolate, sprinkles over a handful of flaked and toasted almonds, watches them sink into the quicksand black. Her mouth is watering with the heady rich aroma. She knows better than to lick her fingers. Tim Culver likes to lick her fingers. When the chocolate is almost cool, she beats three egg yolks and more sugar into the fruit mixture, pours it slowly over the chocolate, lifts the tart dish and ever so gently places it in the heated oven. She sits for ten minutes, twenty, thirty. She does not wash the dishes while she waits, or wipe flour from her hands, chocolate from her apron. She sits and waits and watches the clock. She cries, one slow fat tear every fifteen seconds. When there are one hundred and sixty tears the tart is done. She takes it from the oven and leaves it to cool. She goes to bed, folds into her own flesh and rocks herself to sleep.

When she wakes, Martha checks the tart. It is cool and dark, lifts easily from the case. She sets it on a wide white plate and places it in the refrigerator beside a jug of thick cream. Then she begins to clean. The kitchen, the utensils, the shelves, the oven, the workbench, the floor. Takes herself to the bathroom, strips and places the clothes in a rubbish bag. Scrubs her body under a cold running shower, sand soap and nailbrush. Every inch, every fold of flesh and skin. Martha Grace is red-raw clean. The clothes are burnt early that afternoon along with a pile of liquid maple leaves at the bottom of her garden, black skirt, red shirt and the garden matter in a seasonal orange rush. Later she rakes over the hot embers, places her hand close to the centre, draws it back just too late, a blister already forming in the centre of her palm. It will do for a reminder. Martha Grace always draws back just too late.

Tim Culver knocks on her door at precisely three forty-five. She has spent a further hour preparing her body for his arrival, oiling and brushing and stroking. She is dressed in a soft black silk that flows over her curves and bulges, hiding some, accentuating others. She has let down her coarse grey hair, reddened her full lips, and has the faintest line of shadow around her pale grey eyes. Tim Culver smiles. Martha Grace is beautiful. He walks into the hall, hands her the thirty red roses he carried behind his back all the way down the street in case she was looking. She was looking. She laughs in delight at the gift, he kisses her and apologies and explanations spill from his mouth. They stumble up the stairs, carrying each other quickly to bed, words unimportant, truth and embarrassment and shame and guilt all gone, just the skin and the fucking and the wide fat flesh. They are so in love and Tim cries out, whimpering with delight at the touch of her yielding skin on his mouth, his chest, his cock. And Martha Grace shuts out all thoughts of past and present, crying only for now.

When they are done, she takes Tim Culver downstairs. Martha Grace in a light red robe, Tim Culver wrapped in a blanket against the seasonal chill. The curtains are drawn, blinds pulled, lights lowered. She sits the boy at her kitchen table and pours him a glass of wine. And another. She asks him about drugs and Tim is shocked and delighted, yes he does happen to have a wrap in the back pocket of his jeans. Don't worry, stay there, drink another glass. Martha will fetch the wrap. She brings it back to him, lays out the lines, takes in just one half to his every two. He does not question this, is simply pleased she wants to join him in this excess. There is more wine and wanting, cocaine and kissing, fucking on the kitchen table, falling to the just-scrubbed floor. Even with cocaine, the wine and the sex have made him hungry. Martha has a treat. A special tart she baked herself this morning. Pastry and everything. She reaches into the cool refrigerator and brings out her offering. His eyes grow wider at the sight of the plate, pupils dilate still further with spreading saliva in his hungry mouth. She cuts Tim a generous slice, spoons thick cream over it and reaches for a fork. The boy holds out his hand, but she pushes it away. She wants to feed him. He wants to be fed.

Tim Culver takes it in. The richness, the darkness, the bitter chocolate and the tart fruit and the cool cream. Tim Culver takes it in and opens his mouth for more. Eyes closed the better to savour the texture, the flavours, the glory of this woman spending all morning cooking for him, after what has happened, after how he has behaved. She must love him so much. She must love him as much as he loves her. He opens his eyes to kiss Martha Grace and sees her smiling across at him, another forkful offered, tears spilling down her fat cheeks. He pushes aside the fork and kisses the cheeks, sucks up her tears, promises adoration and apology and forever. Tim Culver is right about forever.

She feeds him half the black tart. He drinks another glass. Leaves a slurred message on a friend's telephone to say he is out with a girl, a babe, a doll. He is having too good a time. He probably won't make it tonight. He expects to stay over tonight. He says this looking at Martha, waiting to see her happiness at the thought that he will stay in her bed, will sleep beside her tonight. Martha Grace smiles with appropriate gratitude and Tim turns his phone off. Martha Grace did not want him to use hers. She said it would not do for any of his friends to call back on her number. Tim is touched she is thinking of his reputation even now.

She pours more wine. Tim does not see that he is drinking the whole bottle, Martha not at all. He inhales more coke. They fuck again. This time it is less simple. He cannot come. He cuts himself another slice of the tart, eats half, puts it down, gulps a mouthful of wine, licks his finger to wipe sticky crumbs of white powder from the wooden table. Tim Culver is confused. He is tired but wide awake. He is hungry but full. He is slowing-down drunk but wired too. He is in love with Martha Grace, but despises both of them for it. He is alive, but only just.

Tim Culver dies of a heart attack. His young healthy heart cannot stand the strain of wine and drugs and fucking – and the special treat Martha had prepared. She pulls his jeans and shirt back on him, moves his body while it is still warm and pliable, lays him on a sheet of spread-out rubbish bags by her back door. She carries him out down the path by her back garden. He is big, but she is bigger, and necessity has made her strong. It is dark. There is no one to see her stumble through the gate, down the alleyway. No one to see her leave the half-dressed body in the dark street. No one to see her gloved hands place the emptied wine bottles by his feet. By the time Martha Grace kisses his lips they are already cold. He smells of chocolate and wine and sex.

She goes home and for the second time that day, scrubs her kitchen clean. Then she sleeps alone. She will wash in the morning. For now, the scent of Tim Culver in her sheets, her hair, her heavy flesh, will be enough to keep her warm through the night.

Tim Culver was found the next morning. Cocaine and so much alcohol in his blood. His heart run to a standstill by the excess of youth. There was no point looking for anyone else to blame. No one saw him stumble into the street. No one noticed Martha Grace lumber away. His friends confirmed he'd been with a girl that night. At least, the police said girl to his parents, whispered whore among themselves. Just another small-town boy turned bad by the lights and the nights of the bright city. Maybe further education isn't all it's cracked up to be.

No one would ever think that Tim Culver's healthy, spent, virile young body could ever have had anything to do with an old witch like Martha Grace. As the whole town knows, the fat bitch is a dyke anyway.

A season or two later and Martha Grace is herself again. Back to where she was before Tim Culver. Back to who she was before Tim Culver. Lives alone, speaks rarely to strangers, pleases only herself. Pleasures only herself. And lives happily enough most of the time. Remembering to cry only when she recalls a time that once reached beyond enough.

Saint Nicked

Ian Rankin

The man dressed as Santa Claus took to his heels and ran, arms held out to stop the branches scratching his face. It was night, but the moon had appeared from its hiding place behind the clouds. The man's shadow stretched in front of him, snared by the car's headlights. He dodged left, deeper into the woods, hoping he would soon outrun the bright beams. There was laughter at his back, the laughter of men who were not yet pursuing him, men who knew his flight was doomed.

'Come back, Santa! Where do you think you're going?'

'You're not exactly in camouflage! Got Rudolph tied to a tree, ready for a quick getaway?'

More laughter, then the first voice again: 'Here we come, ready or not...'

He didn't pause to look back. His red jacket was heavy, its thick lining padding out a frame that was stocky to begin with. Funny thing was, he'd been stick-thin until his thirties. Made up for it since, though. Chips, chocolate and beer. He knew he could ditch the costume, but that would leave a trail for them to follow. They were right: no way he was going to outrun them. He was already down to a light trot, a stitch developing in his side. The baggy red trousers kept snagging on low branches and bracken. When he paused at last, catching his breath, he heard whistling. *Jingle Bells*, it sounded like. The light over to his right was wavering: his pursuers had brought torches. He could hear their boots crunching over the ground. They weren't running. Their steps were steady and purposeful. He started moving again. His plan: to get away. There was a road junction somewhere not far off. Maybe a passing car would save him. The sweat was icy on his neck, steam rising from his body, reminding him of the last horse home in the 2.30.

'You're going to get a kick in the fairy lights for this!' one of the voices called out.

'There won't be enough of you left to fill a Christmas stocking!'

yelled the other.

They were still 100, maybe 200 yards behind him. He started picking his way over the ground, trying to muffle any sound. Something scratched his face. He wiped a thumb across his cheek, feeling the prickle of blood. The stitch was getting worse. His heart pounding in his ears, so loud he feared they would hear it. As the pain grew worse, he remembered someone telling him once that the secret to beating a stitch was touching your toes. He paused, bent down, but his hands didn't even make it to his knees. He fell into a crouch instead, resting his forehead against cold bark. There was a piney smell in the air, like those air fresheners you could get for the car. His clenched fists were pushing against the frozen ground. There was something jagged there beneath his knuckles: a thin slice of stone. He prised it from the earth, held it as he would a weapon. But it wasn't a weapon, and never would be. Instead, he got an idea, and started working its edge against the tree-trunk.

The movement behind him had stopped, torch-light scanning the night. For the moment they had lost him. He couldn't make out what they were saying: either they were too far away, or keeping their voices low. If they stayed where they were, they would hear him scratching. Sure enough, the beam from at least one torch was arcing towards him. He had a sudden, ludicrous image from films he'd devoured as a kid: he was escaping from Colditz; he'd tunnelled out, and now the searchlights were tracking him, the Nazis in pursuit. *The Great Escape*: that's the one they'd always shown at Christmas. He wondered if it would be shown this year, and whether he'd be around to see it…

'Is that you, Santa?' The voice was closer. But he'd finished now, and was back on his feet, moving away from the light, sweat stinging his eyes. It was the smoking that had taken its toll. Time was, he wasn't a bad runner. At school, he'd sometimes come runner-up in races. OK, so that had been 40 years ago, but were his pursuers any fitter? Maybe they would be tiring, thinking of giving up. Was he worth all this effort to them, when the snug warmth of the BMW was waiting…?

Of course! The BMW! He could circle back, nick the car from beneath their noses. If only he could keep going. But his sides were burning, his legs buckling. And the truth was, he didn't even know which direction he was headed. He'd been doing anything but run in a straight line. The car could be anywhere. Chances were, he was heading further into the middle of nowhere. Even if he got away, he might end up freezing to death on the hills. There were pockets of habitation out here: he'd spotted the lights during the drive south. But they were within shouting distance of the road-side, and he felt suddenly he was a long way from any road. He was an achingly long way from home.

He knew now that he would give them what they wanted, but only on his terms. It had to be on his terms, not theirs. And he did-n't want a kicking. Didn't deserve it. He'd done everything just the way he'd been told...well, almost everything.

His head felt light, but his body was a dead weight. It was like wading through waist-deep water, and he was slowing again. Did he want to escape, to end up alone in this wilderness? The sky was darkening again, clouds closing over the land. Sleet might be on its way. How could it be that he was floating and drowning, both at the same time?

And falling to his knees.

Stretching out, as if on crisp sheets. His eyes closing...

And then the glare of the searchlights. The guards with their torches. Hands pulling at him, grabbing him by the hair. The sil-ver wig came away. He'd forgotten he'd been wearing it.

'Sleeping on the job, Santa?'

They had him now, both of them. He didn't care. He didn't feel well enough to care.

'Tell us where it is.'

'I...' His chest felt ablaze, as if he'd fallen asleep too close to the fire. He started pulling at the front of his costume, trying to shed it.

'Just tell us where it is.'

'I...' He knew that if he told them, they might leave him here. Or punish him. He knew he had to play for time. Blood pounded through his ears, deafening him.

'No more fun and games.'

'Scratched it,' he blurted out.

'What's that?'

He tried to swallow. 'Scratched it on a tree.'

'Which tree?'

'I'll...show you.'

They were trying to pull him to his feet, but he was too heavy, altogether too large for them. Which was how he'd broken away from them in the first place.

'Just tell us!'

He tried shaking his head. 'Show you.'

They dropped him then, arguing with one another.

'He's having us on,' the taller one said.

The stocky one shrugged. 'Tells us or shows us, what's the difference?'

'Difference is...' But the tall one didn't seem to have an answer. He sniffed instead. 'He's caused us enough grief as it is.'

'Agreed, which is why I want this over with.'

'So why don't I persuade him?' The tall man slapped his torch against the palm of his hand.

'What do you say, Santa?' The stocky one shone his own torch against Santa's face. The eyes were open, but staring. The face seemed to be going slack. The stocky man knelt down.

'Don't tell me...' the tall man groaned.

'Looks like.' The stocky man made a few checks, and stood up again. 'Heart gave out.'

'Don't tell me...'

'I just did tell you.'

'So what do we do now?'

The stocky man waved his torch around. 'Said he'd scratched the answer on one of the trees. Can't be too far. Let's start looking...'

But after 20 minutes, they'd found nothing, and reconvened at Santa's cooling body. 'So what now?'

'We'll come back tomorrow. The tree's not going anywhere. Plenty of daylight tomorrow.'

'And him?' The torch picked out the prone figure.

'What about him?'

'We can't just leave him. Think about it...'

The stocky man nodded. 'You're right. Can't have the kids finding out Santa's not around any more.' He tucked his torch under his arm. 'You take the feet...'

★　★　★

Detective Inspector John Rebus was in a bad place, doing a bad thing, at his least favourite time of year.

Which is to say that he was Christmas shopping in Glasgow. It had been his girlfriend's idea: everyone, she'd explained, knew that Glasgow boasted better shops than Edinburgh. Which was why he found himself traipsing around busy stores on the last Saturday before Christmas, carrying more and more bags as Jean consulted the neatly typed list she'd brought with her. Each purchase had been selected carefully beforehand, something Rebus was forced to admire. He, after all, shopped from what some would call instinct and others desperation. What he couldn't work out was why the process took so long: even though Jean knew what she was looking for, and where to find it, they still spent half an hour in each shop. Sometimes – when she was buying something for him – he had to stand outside, shuffling his chilled toes and trying not to look like a man with an impatient wait ahead of him.

It was when they stopped for lunch that Jean, noticing his slumped shoulders, patted his cheek.

'A good impersonation of the condemned man,' she told him. 'You're not exactly entering into the spirit.'

'I'm not the festive sort.'

'I'm beginning to realize.' She smiled. 'The words 'retail' and 'therapy' don't coincide in your world, do they? Maybe we should go our separate ways this afternoon.'

Rebus nodded slowly. 'That would let me buy a few things for you...without you knowing.'

She studied him, seeing through the lie. 'Consider yourself off the hook,' she said. 'Do you want to meet up later?'

Rebus nodded again. 'Give me a bell when you're finished.'

They parted outside the restaurant, Jean pecking his cheek. Rebus watched her go. Fifty yards down Buchanan Street, she disappeared into an arcade of small, expensive-looking shops. Rebus let his nose guide him to the Horseshoe Bar, where he sat at a corner table, nursing a first and then a second whiskey, perusing a newspaper. Thursday's theft from the First Minister's residence in Edinburgh was still causing plenty of amusement. Rebus had already heard two hardened Glaswegian accents joking about it at the bar.

'Looks like Christmas came early, eh?'

'*Only Santa was the one on the receiving end...*'

It was all grist to the mill, and rightly so. Doubtless Rebus would have laughed had a man dressed as Father Christmas walked into a reception in Glasgow and wandered out again with a priceless necklace tucked beneath his costume. No ordinary piece of jewellery, but once the property of Mary, Queen of Scots, brought into the light just one day each year so it could be shown off at a party. With the First Minister of the recently devolved Scottish Parliament as victim, Rebus's police station had been a hive of activity, which was why he intended enjoying what was left of today. Finishing his drink, he asked at the bar for a *Yellow Pages*, jotting down the addresses of local record shops. He was going to find a small gift for himself, a rarity or some new album, something he could play on the big day. Something to take his mind off Christmas. The third shop he tried was a secondhand-vinyl specialist, and Rebus was its only customer. The proprietor had frizzy, greying hair tied in a ponytail, and was wearing a Frank Zappa T-shirt that had shrunk in the wash at some point in the 1970s. As Rebus consulted the racks, the man asked if he was looking for anything.

'I'll know it when I see it,' Rebus told him. On an overcast day, it was easy enough to start a conversation. Five minutes in, Rebus realized he knew the man from somewhere. He pointed a finger. 'You were in a band yourself once.'

The man grinned, showing gaps between his teeth. 'That's some memory you've got.'

'You played bass for the Parachute Game.' The man held up his hands in surrender. 'Ted Handsome?' Rebus guessed, eyes narrowed in concentration.

The man nodded. 'The name's Hanson, actually. Ted Hanson.'

'I had a couple of your albums.'

'Almost as many as we made.'

Rebus nodded slowly. The Parachute Game had appeared on the Scottish scene in the mid-70s, supporting headliners such as Nazareth and Alex Harvey. Then things had gone quiet...

'Your singer did a runner, didn't he?'

Hanson shrugged. 'Bad timing...'

Rebus remembered: the band had crept into the lower reaches of the top 30 with a single from their second album. Their first headlining tour was looming. And then their singer had walked out. Jack...no, Jake, that was it.

'Jake Wheeler,' he said out loud.

'Poor Jake,' Ted Hanson said. He was thoughtful for a moment, then checked his watch. 'You look like a drinking man, am I right?'

'You've got a good eye.'

'Then I reckon this could be my early-closing day.'

Rebus didn't like to say, but he got the feeling Ted had a few of those each week...

They hit a couple of bars, talking music, bands from the 'old days'. Hanson had a fund of stories. He'd started the shop with stock ransacked from his own collection.

'And my flat still looks like a vinyl museum.'

'I'd like to see that,' Rebus said with a smile. So they jumped in a taxi, heading for Hillhead. Rebus called Jean on his mobile, said he might be late going back to Edinburgh. She sounded tired and unbothered. Hanson's Victorian tenement flat was as promised. Albums lay slumped against every wall. Boxes of them sat on tables, singles spilling out from homemade shelves that had warped under the weight.

'A little piece of heaven,' Rebus said.

'Try telling that to my ex-wife.' Hanson handed him a can of beer.

They spent a couple of hours on the sofa, staring into the space between the loudspeakers and listening to a shared musical heritage. Finally, Rebus plucked up the courage to ask about Jake Wheeler.

'You must have been gutted when he walked out.'

'He had his reasons.'

'What were they?'

Hanson offered a shrug. 'Come to think of it, he never said.'

'There were rumours about drugs...'

'Rock stars and drugs? Surely not.'

'A good way to meet some very bad people.' Rebus knew of these rumours, too: gangsters, dealers. But Hanson just shrugged again.

'Jake never resurfaced?' Rebus asked.

Hanson shook his head. Then he smiled. 'You said you had a couple of our albums, John...' He sprang to his feet, rummaged in a box by the door. 'Bet this isn't one of them.' He held out the album to Rebus.

'I did own it once upon a time,' Rebus mused, recognizing the cover. *The Oldest Tree*, recorded by the remaining trio after Wheeler had walked out. 'Lost it at a party, week after I'd brought it.' Examining the cover – swirly, late-hippy pencil drawings of dells and hills, a broad oak tree at the centre – Rebus remembered something. 'You drew this?'

Hanson nodded. 'I had more than a few pretensions back then.'

'It's good.' Rebus studied the drawing. 'I mean it.'

Hanson sat down again. 'Back at the shop, you said you were after something special. Could this be it?'

Rebus smiled. 'Could be. How much do you want?'

'Compliments of the season.'

Rebus raised an eyebrow. 'I couldn't…'

'Yes, you could. It's not like it's worth anything.'

'Well, OK then, thanks. Maybe I can do you a favour some day in return.'

'How's that then?'

Rebus had lifted a business card out of his wallet. He handed it over. 'I'm in CID, Ted. Never know when you might need a friend…'

Studying the record sleeve again, Rebus failed to notice the look of fear and panic that flitted across his new friend's face.

* * *

Sunday morning, Neil Bryant woke up and knew something was wrong. He was the stockier of the two men who'd spent much of the previous evening chasing an overweight, unfit Santa to his death. He was also supposed to be the brains of the outfit, which was why he was so annoyed. He was annoyed because he'd asked Malky Bunker – his tall, skinny partner in crime – to wake him up. It was past ten, and still no sign of Malky. So much for his dawn wake-up call. He phoned Malky and gave him a good roasting.

Twenty minutes later, the BMW pulled up at Bryant's door. Malky's hair was tousled, face creased from sleep. He was yawning.

'You got rid of the deceased?' Bryant asked. Milky nodded. Good enough: the fewer details Bryant knew, the better. They drove out of Glasgow, heading east and south. Different route from last night, and a map neither of them knew how to read.

'Be easier if we drove into Edinburgh and out again,' Malky suggested.

'We're late as it is,' Bryant snapped. The thing was, as you headed towards the Border country, it all started to look the same. Plenty of forests and crossroads. It was early afternoon before they started to recognize a few landmarks. Passing a couple of flatbed trucks, Bryant sensed they were getting warm.

'Working on a Sunday,' Malky commented, glancing out at another truck.

'Run-up to Christmas,' Bryant explained. Then his heart sank as he saw what the trucks were carrying.

'This has got to be it,' Malky was saying.

'Aye,' Bryant agreed, voice toneless.

Malky was parking the car, only now realizing the forest they'd run through the previous night was not a forest. It had been denuded by chainsaws, half its trees missing. Not a forest: a plantation. A fresh consignment of Christmas firs, heading north to Edinburgh.

The two men looked at one another, then sprinted from the car. There were still trees left, plenty of them. Maybe, if they were lucky…maybe Santa's tree would still be there.

Two hours and countless arguments later, they were back in the car, heater going full blast. The foreman had threatened to call the police. They'd threatened violence if he did.

'They're all the same,' he'd shouted, meaning the trees.

'Just call us particular,' Bryant had snarled back.

'What are we going to do?' Malky asked now. 'We go back there without the necklace, our goose is well and truly stuffed.'

Bryant looked at him, then got out of the car, marching towards the nervous-looking foreman.

'Where are they headed?' he demanded.

'The trees?' The foreman watched Bryant nod. 'Edinburgh,' he said.

'Where in Edinburgh?'

'All over.' The foreman shrugged. 'Probably be sold within the day.'

'Addresses,' Bryant said, his face inches away from the older man's. 'I need addresses.'

*   *   *

Rebus and Jean ate Sunday lunch at a hotel in Portobello, surrounded by families who were pulling crackers and wearing lopsided paper crowns.

'Basic training for the big day,' Rebus commented, excusing himself from the table as his mobile started ringing. It was his boss, Detective Chief Superintendent Gill Templer.

'Enjoying a lazy Sunday?' she enquired.

'Up until now.'

'We're looking at fences, John.' Meaning people who might be able to shift an item as hot as the necklace. 'You know Sash Hooper, don't you? Wondered if you might pay him a visit.'

'Today?'

'Sooner the better.'

Rebus glanced back in Jean's direction. She was stirring her coffee, no room for dessert. Rebus had promised to go and buy a Christmas tree.

'Fine,' he said into the mouthpiece. 'So where can I find Sash?'

'Skating on thin ice, as usual,' Gill Templer said.

*   *   *

Ever the entrepreneur, Sash – real name Sacha, courtesy of a mother with a thing for French crooners – had opened an outdoor skating rink on Leith Links.

'Just trying to make an honest dollar,' he told Rebus, as they walked around the rinks perimeter. 'Licences in place and everything.' He watched two teenagers as they shuffled across the slushy ice, the rink's only customers. Then he stared accusingly at the sun, cursing its liquefying powers. Music blared from a faulty loudspeaker: Abba, *Dancing Queen*.

'No interest in stolen antiquities, then?'

'All in the past, Mr Rebus.' Hooper was a big man with clenched fists. What was left of his hair was jet black, tightly curled. His thick moustache was black too. He wore sunglasses, through which Rebus could just make out his small, greedy eyes.

'And if anyone came to you with an offer...'

'The three wise men could knock on my door tonight, Mr Rebus, and I'd give them the brush off.' Hooper shrugged a show of innocence.

Rebus looked all around. 'Not rushed off your feet, are you?'

'The day's young. Besides, Kiddie Wonderland's doing all right.' He nodded at the double-decker bus, decorated with fake snow and tinsel. Mums and young children were queuing up for entry. Rebus had passed the bus when he'd first arrived. It promised 'a visit you'll never forget – one gift per child.' *Santa's grotto on wheels* had been Hooper's explanation, rubbing his hands together. The interior looked to have been decorated with white cotton and sheets of coloured crepe paper. The queuing parents appeared dubious, but Kiddie Wonderland was the only show in Leith. Still, to Rebus's mind, there was something missing.

'No Santa,' he said, nodding towards the bus.

'Soon as you're gone, there will be.' Hooper patted his own stomach.

Rebus stared at him. 'You realize some of these kids could be traumatized for life?' Hooper didn't reply. 'Let me know if Christmas brings you anything nice, Sash.'

Hooper was rehearsing his 'ho, ho, ho's' as Rebus walked back to the car.

He knew that there was a place on Dalkeith Road that sold Christmas trees. It was a derelict builders' yard, empty all year round except for the run-up to 25 December. When he arrived, two men were doing a good impression of taking the place apart, studying each tree before dismissing it, while the proprietor watched bemused, arms folded. One man shook his head at the other, and the pair stormed out.

'I got a call half an hour back,' the proprietor told Rebus. 'They did the same thing to a friend of mine.'

'Takes all sorts,' Rebus said. But he watched the men get into their rusty BMW and drive off. The elder and shorter of the two – his face was familiar. Rebus frowned in concentration, bought the first five-foot fir offered to him, and took it out to his car. It stretched from boot to passenger seat. He still couldn't put a name to the face, and it bothered him all the way to St Leonard's police station, where he made his report to Gill Templer.

'Could do with clearing this one up, John,' she said.

Rebus nodded. She would have the brass on her back, because the First Minister was on theirs.

'We can but try, Gill,' he offered, making to leave. He was driving out of the car park when he saw a face he recognized, and this time the name came easily. It was Ted Hanson. Rebus stopped and wound down his window. 'This is a surprise, Ted.'

'I was in town, thought I'd look you up.' Hanson looked cold.

'How did you find me?'

'Asked a policeman,' Hanson said with a smile. 'Any chance of a cuppa?'

They were only five minutes from Rebus's tenement flat. He made two mugs of instant coffee while Hanson flicked through his record collection.

'A pale imitation of yours, Ted,' Rebus apologized.

'A lot of the same albums.' Hanson waved a copy of Wishbone Ash's *Argus*. 'Great cover.'

'It's not the same with CDs, is it?'

Hanson wrinkled his nose. 'Nothing like.'

Rebus handed over the coffee and sat down. 'What are you doing here, Ted?' he asked.

'Just wanted to get out of the shop…out of Glasgow.' Hanson blew across the surface of the mug, then took a sip. 'Sorry, John: got any sugar?'

'I'll fetch some.' Rebus got to his feet again.

'Mind if I use your loo meantime?'

'Be my guest.' Rebus pointed the way, then retreated to the kitchen. Music was playing in the living room: the Incredible String Band. Rebus returned and placed the sugar beside Hanson's mug. Something was going on. He had a few questions for his new friend. After a couple of minutes, he walked back into the hall, knocked on the bathroom door. No answer. He turned the handle. There was no one inside. Ted Hanson had done a runner.

'Curiouser and curiouser,' Rebus muttered to himself. He looked down on to the street from his living room window; no sign of anyone. Then he stared at his record collection. It took him a couple of minutes to decide what was missing.

The last Parachute Game album, the one Hanson himself had given him. Rebus sat in his chair, thinking hard. Then he called Jean.

'Not found a tree yet?' she asked.

'It's on its way. Jean, could you do me a favour?'

'What?'

'Something I'd like for Christmas…'

★ ★ ★

Christmas itself was fine. He'd no complaints about Christmas. There was the slow run-up to Hogmanay, Gill Templer growing less festive as the necklace failed to turn up. New Year's Day, Rebus nursed his accessory of choice: a thumping head. He managed to forego any resolutions, apart from the usual one to stop drinking.

His Christmas present finally arrived on 4 January, having been posted in Austin, Texas, on 24 December. Jean handed it over, having taken the trouble to wrap it in second-hand paper.

'You shouldn't have,' he said. Then he kissed her, and took the album home for a listen. The lyrics were on the inside of the gatefold sleeve. The songs tended to the elegiac, each seeming to refer to Jake Wheeler. Ted Hanson had taken over vocal duties, and though he didn't make too bad a fist of it, Rebus could see why the band had folded. Without Wheeler there was something missing, something irreplaceable. Listening to the title track, Rebus studied the drawing on the front of the sleeve – Ted Hanson's drawing. An old oak tree with the initials JW carved on it, enclosed in a heart, pierced by an arrow that wasn't quite an arrow. Holding the sleeve to the light, Rebus saw that it was a syringe.

And there below the oldest tree, Hanson sung, *You took your last farewell of me…*But was it the bassist talking, or something else? Rebus rubbed a hand across his forehead, and concentrated on other songs, the other lyrics. Then he turned back to the sleeve. So detailed…it couldn't just be imagined. It had to be a real place. He picked up his phone, called Jean's number. She worked at the museum. There were things she could find out.

Such as: the location of Scotland's oldest tree.

On the morning of the sixth, he let the office know he'd be late.

'That's got to be a record-breaker: the five-day hangover.'

Rebus didn't bother arguing. Instead, he drove to Glasgow, parking on the street outside Ted Hanson's shop. Hanson was just opening up; looked tired and in need of a shave.

'Amazing what you can find on the internet these days,' Rebus said. Hanson turned, saw what Rebus was holding: a near-mint copy of *The Oldest Tree*. 'Here's what I think,' Rebus went on, taking a step forward. 'I think Jake's dead. Maybe natural causes, maybe not. Rock stars have a way of hanging around with the wrong people. They get into situations.' He tapped the album sleeve. 'I know where this is now. Is that where he's buried?'

The ghost of a smile passed across Hanson's face. 'That's what you think?'

'It's why you had to get the album back from me, once you knew what I did for a living.'

Hanson bowed his head. 'You're right.' Then he looked up again, eyes gleaming. 'That's exactly why I had to get the album back.' He paused, seemed to take a deep breath. 'But you're wrong. You couldn't be more wrong...'

Rebus frowned, thinking he'd misheard.

'I'll show you,' Hanson said. 'And by the way, happy new year...'

* * *

The drive took them over an hour, north out of Glasgow, the scenery stretching, rising, becoming wilderness. They passed lochs and mountains, the sky a vast, bruised skein.

'All your detective work,' Hanson said, slouched in the passenger seat, 'did you notice where the record was recorded?' Rebus shook his head. Hanson just nodded, then told Rebus to pull over. They were on a stretch of road that would fill with caravans in the summer, but for now seemed desolate. Below them lay a valley, and across the valley a farmhouse. Hanson pointed towards it. 'Owned by our producer at the time. We set up all the gear, did the album in under a month. Braepath Farm, it was called back then.'

Rebus had spotted something. On the hillside behind the farmhouse, the tree from the album sleeve. The tree Jean had told him was the oldest in Scotland: the Braepath Oak. And behind it, a small stone bothy, little more than a shelter for shepherds, outside which a man was splitting logs, watched by his sheepdog.

'Jake fell apart,' Hanson was saying, voice low. 'Maybe it was the company he was keeping, or the industry we were supposed to be part of. He just wanted to be left alone. I promised him I'd respect that. The drawing…it was just a way of showing he'd always be part of the band, whatever happened.' Hanson paused, clearing his throat. Rebus watched the distant figure as it picked up the kindling, taking it indoors. Long-haired, ragged-clothed: too far away to really be sure, but Rebus knew all the same.

'He's been out here ever since?' he asked.

Hanson nodded. His eyes glistened.

'And you've never…?'

'He knows where I am if he wants me.' He angled his head. 'So now you know, John. Up to you what you do about it.'

Rebus nodded, put the car into gear and started a three-point turn.

'Know what I'd like, Ted?' he said. 'I'd like you to sign that album for me. Will you do that?'

'With pleasure,' Hanson said with a smile.

*   *   *

Back at St Leonard's, Rebus was passing the front desk when he saw the duty sergeant emerging from the comms room, shaking his head in disbelief. 'I'm not that late,' Rebus said.

'It's not that, John. It's mother Hubbard.'

Now Rebus knew: Edwina Hubbard from down the road. Two or three times a week she would call to report some imagined mischief.

'What is it this time?' Rebus asked. 'The peeping postman or the disappearing dustbins?'

'Christmas trees,' the sergeant said. 'Being collected and taken away.'

'And did you explain to her that it happens every year, courtesy of our caring, sharing council.'

The sergeant nodded. 'Thing is, she says they're early. And using a double-decker bus.'

'A bus?' Rebus laughed. 'Firs, please.'

The sergeant laughed, too, turning to retreat into the comms room. 'It gets better,' he said. 'The bus is covered in Christmas decorations…'

Rebus was still laughing as he climbed the stairs. After the morning he'd had, he needed something to cheer him up. Then he froze. A Christmas bus…Kiddie Wonderland. Collecting Christmas trees…Two men running around Edinburgh, looking for a tree… The name flashed from brain to mouth.

'Neil Bryant!' Rebus took the stairs two at a time, sat down at a computer and typed in Bryant's name. Ex-bouncer, convictions for violence. Clever with it. The other man, the taller one, had looked like bouncer material, too. And hadn't Sash Hooper run a nightclub a few years back? Sash…ready to take an unlikely turn as Santa on the bus.

'Santa,' Rebus hissed. Then he was back downstairs and in the comms room, grabbing the sergeant's arm.

'The bus with the trees,' he said. 'Where did she see it?'

★　　★　　★

Rink.

The bus was full of trees, both decks. But finally they'd found one with that single word scratched on its trunk.

Rink.

The way Bryant had explained it to Sash Hooper, they needed the bus so they could collect as many trees as possible, as quickly as possible. Eventually, Hooper had seen the wisdom of the plan. He had got a buyer for the necklace, but the sale had to be quick.

Rink.

Well, it didn't take a genius, did it? They'd turned the bus round and headed for Leith Links. The costume had been Bryant's idea, too, when he'd heard that the First Minister was throwing a party. Send someone in there dressed as Santa, they could walk out with anything they liked. He'd gone to Sash with the idea, and Sash had suggested Benn Welsh, a pretty good housebreaker in his time, now down on his luck. Benny had been good as gold – until he'd found out how much the necklace was worth. After which he'd tried upping out. Wasn't going to hand it over until they had a deal.

★　　★　　★

Three of them now – Sash, Malky and Bryant – slipping and sliding across the ice. Looking for the telltale dark patch, finding it. Benny had cut himself a hole, stuffed the necklace in, then poured in some water, letting it freeze over again. Sash had his penknife out. It took a while, the day darkening around them.

'Give me the knife,' Malky said, chipping away with it.

'Watch the blade doesn't snap,' Sash Hooper warned, as if the knife were somehow more precious than the necklace. Eventually, all three men clambered to their feet. Hooper holding the necklace, examining it. A string of shimmering diamonds, embracing a vast, blood-red ruby. He actually gasped. They came off the ice and back on to solid earth. They were almost in the shadow of the bus before they noticed Rebus. And he wasn't alone.

Two uniforms could be seen through the upper-deck windows. Two more were downstairs. Another was outside, circling the bus.

'Nice little stocking-filler,' Rebus said, motioning towards the necklace.

'You got a warrant?' Hooper asked.

'Do I look as if I need one?'

'You can't just go tramping all over my bus. That's private property.' Hooper was attempting to slide the necklace into his pocket.

Malky tugged at Bryant's sleeve. His eyes had widened. They were on the policeman who'd been circling the bus, the policeman who was now turning the handle which would open the bus's luggage compartment. Bryant saw his friend's look, and his own mouth dropped in dismay.

'Malky, for the love of God, tell me you didn't.'

Hooper was still concentrating on protesting his innocence. He knew this was the most important speech he would ever make. He felt that if he could just get the words right, then maybe...

'DI Rebus,' the constable was saying. 'Something here you should take a look at...'

And Hooper turned his eyes, and saw what everyone else was seeing. Benny Welsh, still dressed in the telltale red suit, lying at peace on the floor of the luggage bay.

Rebus turned to face the three men.

'I'm guessing that means you're Saint Nicked,' he said.

Alice Opens the Box

Denise Mina

If Alice had anything left to give, she'd give it. She'd given her life for Moira already and she'd given it happily. They'd never let her out after what she'd done for her, but she wanted to give more. She looked up. The grey woman was watching her through the glass, a silver badge flashing on her chest. When Alice looked up, the guard looked down at her papers. Alice saw that look all the time, but today, day of days, it cut deep, kicking the breath out of her. She crossed her legs and covered her face, folding in on herself.

The guard watched Alice through the glass, wrapping her hands around her skinny, withered face, coughing or something, bucking from the chest. The guard was glad that she wasn't going in the car. Most of them in here were just unfortunate, but it would sicken her even to touch a woman like that. No one wanted to go with her, no one wanted to talk to her. Alice didn't want to talk to anyone else anyway, she had said about three words in the seven months she'd been here. She had never cried, that's what they said about her, not one tear, even in the hospital. Women prisoners will cry because their tea is cold. The guard looked at her again. Alice had stopped coughing and was sitting calmly, a blank look in her eyes, a hand smoothing her greying hair.

Alice had cigarettes. They were the only thing she had left that was worth anything. She had six from a ration of ten for the day, had them in her pocket and she'd give them to Moira when they got there, as a sign between themselves that she loved her. And she did love her. She wanted to throw her hands out and wrap them around her, hold her tight and not let go.

The guard looked up and saw Alice lift a knee and throw her arm around it, as if she was going to pull her own leg off. She had a skirt on and the guard could see the crotch of her pants, the red and blue skin on her inner thighs. She was sickening. It was as if she wanted to be sickening. The buzzer shrieked and Hannan spoke through the intercom.

'Hannan and Arrowsmith. Here for Alice Paterson.'

The guard let them into the office.

'There, she's there,' she said pointing through the glass.

Hannan and Arrowsmith looked in at her, crossing their arms, contemptuous.

'Did you two run over the governor's dog or something?'

Hannan snorted. 'We're getting brownie points.'

'Yeah,' said Arrowsmith, 'and we're the only two on today who haven't got kids.'

'That poor baby,' the guard shook her head.

'Aye,' said Arrowsmith, 'died after just six hours. As if she knew who her mother was.'

Alice saw them watching her and talking. Whatever they were saying, she knew it wasn't good. They all hated her; even before Moira they wouldn't look at her. The two guards disappeared from the office and the grey metal door in front of her buzzed alive. Hannan pushed it open and stepped back.

'Let's go, Alice.'

Arrowsmith was standing in the corridor, nodding and pursing her lips.

They were rougher than they need have been. She'd nearly dropped the box on to a table and they were pissed off with her for that. Hannan held her upper arm tightly and shoved her towards the car, digging her nails into the skin. Alice felt disgust in the stiffness of Hannan's fingers, in the way she kept her body distant. No one wanted to be here. Neither of them would look at her in the eye. They spoke in single words. 'In,' said Hannan, capping her head as she pushed her into the back seat of the car.

It was hard to hold the box in both hands and get herself into the seat. The side of the box was too deep for her to hold it with one hand. Alice wanted to put it down on the seat, but knew it would make them hate her more. She held it underneath and bumped her arse along the seat, her hand feeling the contents slide to the side, a gentle shift in weight.

Arrowsmith followed her into the back seat, soft thigh pressing hard against Alice, shutting the door behind her. Hannan got into the car through the other door. Like mirror images they slid their belts on, clipping them next to Alice's hips. The driver locked the doors. Arrowsmith passed a belt over Alice's lap, making her lift the box as she handed it across. Hannan took it, clipped it shut. 'Go,' said Hannan to the driver.

They watched the gate open. A wall of grey slatted metal rolled upwards, splinters of sun glinting off the surface. Beyond the gate lay another barrier, a solid metal wall. An electrical impulse shook it awake and it slid back. Alice hadn't seen outside the gates since the last day of the trial. It was green outside, big hills in the distance. Cars passed them as they waited to join the road, clean and dirty cars.

'How long will it take to get there?' asked Alice.

Hannan looked at her. Alice was not known for being chatty. It was the longest sentence she had said since she came in.

'Half-hour,' said Hannan and turned away to look out of the window.

The heater was on full in the car, a hot whingeing breath. Alice looked out of the window, resting her hands on the box, feeling under the lip of the lid with the tips of her fingers. Screw nuts, small, but she could still get hold of them. She looked at the box and smiled. She'd been planning this. She was going to see Moira once more, whatever the consequences, and she was going to give her the fags. They were all she had left.

She looked at the guards. Hannan was watching the road, Arrowsmith was doing the same on the other side. They couldn't bear to look at her and it was a good thing. The driver was watching the road, not checking the mirror as often as he should. His eyes were ringed with brown skin, tired and sickly. Keeping her elbow down and her hands still, Alice turned the metal screw below the lid with her fingertips. It was stuck, wouldn't move. She pressed it hard, keeping her arms slack, pressing on it, stopping when they turned their heads towards her, when their eyes might fall on her hands. She breathed in, keeping her breathing steady. Finally, just as her fingers were about to spasm, she felt the screw give.

The driver slowed for a roundabout and a woman crossed in front of them. She wore a dirty anorak and carried a shopping bag. She looked annoyed and her bare legs were slapped red by the cold wind. Alice watched the woman pass, turning her head to let her eyes linger. Lucky cow, lucky cow. Going shopping for messages, mince and tatties and a mag with puzzles or some fag papers. Lucky, lucky and not even knowing. Alice had a coat like that, with a hood and deep pockets. She wore it for the four winters before the police came to their door. That coat got rained on and snowed on, she wore it against the wind and too long into the summers. It was pink with purple squares and white fur around the hood. She never cleaned it, that she remembered. Never got round to it. It was clean when she bought it in Oxfam and then, suddenly, four years later she looked at it and it was too dirty to clean.

Her fingers turned slowly, undoing the screw. She pulled at the edge of the lid. Sensing movement on the lip, she slid her hand along the wood to the far edge and began to press another screw. The four winters were hard and unkind, the four winters when she did what she shouldn't have. She knew she'd done wrong, knew what she was doing was wrong but it all happened slowly and she couldn't see how it might have been different. She did love him. Charlie. Even the name made her feel hot, sent a flush up her neck. She lived to see his face and would lie in bed at night, staring at the ceiling, amazed that he was with her.

When she first saw him, sitting in the corner of the pub, he was surrounded by laughing men, laughing himself. He lifted a hand, brushing hair from his eyes and she saw gold glinting from his pinkie. A long time afterwards, sitting on the stained sofa, watching him eat a curry off his knee, she realized that laughing along with a crowd was as unusual for him as it was for her. He wasn't comfortable in company, wanted to be alone, to have peace and quiet. It was important to him. She was lucky he moved in, that he forgave her the kids. It was hard to keep them quiet. She thought it was their ages, three to seven, but all she wanted was for them to keep quiet. It didn't seem too much to ask.

The car juddered to a stop at a set of lights, throwing them all forwards on their seats. The box slipped along her thighs, banking against the front seats, dropping at the corner. They all heard the contents hit the side. Hannan and Arrowsmith looked at her, appalled. Arrowsmith lifted the box carefully into her hands again.

'Do you want me to take it?' Hannan said it like a threat, as if Alice couldn't even be trusted to hold something. It wasn't her fault, the car had stopped sharp, but they hated her already and couldn't hide it. She liked the men better. They didn't judge so much. The women were cows. Fat cows who couldn't get a man. Charlie.

Alice shut her eyes. Charlie in the bath in Lomond Street, wet hair, rubbing his face with a flannel. She could see the muscles in his back when he moved his arms. He was thin, Charlie, always slim. He said he was going bald. *No, you're not. It's thick at the back*. She opened her fingers on the back of his head, pushing them up through the thick yellow hair, feeling the sharp ends run through her fingers. *Shut those fucking kids up*. He was a wonder to her. She would look at him when he was watching telly, wondering at him being here with her, despite the kids, despite herself and everything she lacked. She couldn't even cook nice.

She finished the corner screw and moved her hand slowly over to the next one. Charlie was in Perth now. They weren't allowed to phone or write to each other and she could see that it was a good thing. While he was there she couldn't see straight, honestly couldn't see that what they had done was wrong. She just wanted them to be quiet. When Charlie was near he filled her eyes, she couldn't see past him. Even when the police came to the door and lifted the floor boards and found the kids. They were crying. They climbed out themselves, she watched them. She'd looked at Charlie and knew it wasn't so bad. She just wanted them to keep quiet. She kept explaining to them, if they kept quiet she wouldn't need to punish them, wouldn't need to take the belt to them or wet them in the cold bath or put them in the dark place. She didn't enjoy doing it, but they needed to learn to keep quiet or she'd be alone again, in that flat again, for years with no one to talk to, for years with no one. *Shut those fucking kids up*.

She didn't mind sitting in the box in the court, being looked at as long as Charlie was there beside her. She was big with Moira then, her stomach swollen in a big round ball. They were taking Moira away, whatever happened in the court, the social worker said. Because of the cuts on the other kids, because they'd gone bad. But Moira would always be her child, the social worker said. They were made of the same stuff. And Moira might find her when she was eighteen, she'd have the right to look for her. She'd know who her mother was.

In the court a man said she sacrificed her kids for her man. Those unhappy children, he said, unhappy children who suffered her for a mother. What a thing to say. She was doing her best. He'd leave if they didn't keep quiet. She dressed them and let them watch telly, it wasn't much to ask them to keep quiet. James, her oldest, agreed with her. He kept them quiet when he could, made the smaller ones stop running when Charlie was home. James was small for seven. Deep down she knew the man in the wig was right. The jury looked at her and she knew they thought it too. Charlie and James and her, three against all of them. The man in the wig was right. The screw on the box was done and she moved her hand over to the final one.

'We'll be there in a couple of minutes,' said the driver.

Hannan and Arrowsmith looked at her, reading her face and seeing nothing. They looked away.

'Now, we're going to cuff you in a minute, Alice,' said Hannan, trying to be kind, 'I'm sorry but that's how it has to be. Governor's orders.'

Alice's fingers worked and worked, turning the last, the very last chance she had to see Moira. The car slowed as it turned into the drive, passed through the high metal gates and crunched through deep red gravel. Alice slid her hands into her pocket, wrapped her fingers around the fags, breaking them because she was so overwhelmed. With the other hand she wrenched the lid off the box, breaking the wood, the loud crack filling the car. The car stopped suddenly. The driver turned to look, shocked and disgusted. She couldn't see because her eyes were hot and brimming over. Hannan and Arrowsmith's faces blended together. *Stop it, you fucking mental bitch.* Alice pressed the fags into the box shouting, *Moira, sorry, sorry, Moira, sorry.*

Christ, stop her. They pulled the box out of her hands, dragged her out of the car and cuffed her hands behind her back. Alice looked up and, among a field of gravestones, saw an angel in white stone, wings outstretched as if she was just taking off, heading home. She kept her eyes on it while they fussed around her, sat the box on the back seat, tried to fit the broken lid back on.

She hadn't shed a tear in hospital. She knew she was doing right. She pressed and pressed the face until the chest stopped moving. Pressed the face into her own tender breast, hurting herself while the breathing stopped. Moira. As she laid her face down in the cot, her body was still raw from her, her stomach still swollen.

Hannan was crying, looking into the car at the box and crying like kids do, with her chin all tight and her hands limp by her sides. Behind Alice, Arrowsmith was panting hard, yanking the hands up her back, hurting her shoulders.

'How can ye?' she said over and over. 'How can ye?'

'Who is Moira?' shouted Hannan. 'Who's Moira?'

The man in the court said she sacrificed her kids for her man. Now, it was different, now it was better, now it was her for the kids. She looked into the car. The small white box had the broken lid sitting on it, snapped fags around it on the seat and on the floor. Inside the box, precious white box, lay Moira, black hair, skin of milk, blue lips. Moira, the happy child who would never suffer Alice for a mother.

Slaughter in the Strand

Edward Marston

England, 1912

Herbert Syme had never travelled in a First Class carriage before but nothing else would suffice. It was, in a sense, the most important day of his life and it deserved to be marked by the unaccustomed display of extravagance. Impecunious librarians like Herbert were never allowed to pose as First Class passengers on a train to London. Indeed, they could hardly afford to travel by rail at all on a regular basis. Herbert always rode the six miles to work on his ancient bicycle, weaving past the countless potholes, cursing his way up steep hills, hoping that the rain would hold off and that no fierce dogs would give chase. Today, it was different. Instead of arriving at the library, breathless, soaked to the skin and, not infrequently, with the legs of his trousers expertly shredded by canine teeth, he was sitting in a luxurious compartment among the elite of society.

The fact that he was an outsider made it even more exhilarating. Habitual denizens of the privileged area were less than welcoming. They saw Herbert Syme for what he really was, a tall, slim, stooping man in his forties with a shabby suit and a self-effacing manner. The whiff of failure was unmistakable. What was this interloper doing in their midst? Murmurs of resentment buzzed in Herbert's ears. The rustling of newspapers was another audible display of class warfare. They were professional men and he was trespassing on their territory. They wanted him out. The elderly lady in the compartment was more vocal in her criticism. After repeatedly clicking her tongue in disapproval, she had the temerity to ask Herbert if he possessed the appropriate ticket.

The librarian withstood it all without a tremor. While his companions took refuge behind their copies of *The Times*, Herbert took out the letter that had transformed his dull existence. It was short and businesslike but that did not lessen its impact. He read the words again, fired anew by their implication.

Dear Mr Syme,

Thank you for submitting your novel to us. It has found favour with all who have read the book. Subject to certain changes, we will consider publishing it. To that end we request that you come to this office on Wednesday, May 16th at 3 p.m. precisely to discuss the matter with Mr Roehampton. Please confirm that you are able to attend at this time.

Yours sincerely,

Miss Lavinia Finch (Secretary)

There it was – his passport to fame and fortune. Other passengers might be going on routine visits to the capital but Herbert Syme was most certainly not. Thanks to the letter from Roehampton and Buckley Ltd., he was in transit between misery and joy. Long years of toil and derision lay behind him. Success had at last beckoned. Putting the magical missive into his pocket, he reflected on its contents. His novel had found favour at a prestigious publishing house. Instead of spending his days stacking the work of other writers on the shelves of his branch library, he would take his place alongside them as an equal. Herbert Syme would be read, admired and envied. Everyone's perception of him would alter dramatically. Publication was truly a form of rebirth.

'May I see your ticket, please, sir?'

'What?' Herbert came out of his reverie to find the uniformed ticket inspector standing over him. 'Oh, yes. Of course.'

Newspapers were lowered and each pair of eyes was trained on Herbert as he extracted his ticket and offered it to the inspector. Everyone in the compartment wanted him to be forcibly ejected. They longed for his humiliation. To their utter disgust, the inspector clipped the ticket and handed it back politely to its owner.

'Thank you, sir,' he said.

Herbert was elated by the man's deference. It was something to which he would swiftly adjust. From now on, it would be a case of First Class all the way.

*   *   *

The sheer size, noise and bustle of London were overwhelming at first. Herbert had never seen so many people or so much traffic. Garish advertisements competed for his attention on walls, passing vehicles and in shop windows. It was bewildering. Crossing the Strand was an ordeal in itself, the long thoroughfare positively swarming with automobiles, omnibuses, lorries, horses and carts, mounted policemen, rattling handcarts, stray dogs, hurtling cyclists and darting pedestrians. When he eventually got to the correct side of the road, Herbert took a deep breath to compose himself. He needed to be at his most assured for the critical interview with Edmund T. Roehampton. The fact that he would be dealing with one of the partners in the firm, and not with a mere underling, augured well. His novel would finally see the light of day – *subject to certain changes*. Whatever those changes might be, Herbert vowed that he would willingly agree to them. A publisher was entitled to make minor adjustments and add refinements.

When he located the premises of Roehampton and Buckley, Ltd., he met with his first disappointment. Such a leading publishing house, he assumed, would have palatial offices that signalled its lofty position. Instead, it appeared to operate out of three rooms above a shoe shop. Mindful of the request for punctuality, Herbert checked his pocket watch, cleared his throat, rehearsed his greeting to Mr Roehampton and climbed the stairs. When he entered the outer office, he heard Big Ben booming in the distance. A second disappointment awaited.

The middle-aged woman seated at the desk looked over her pince-nez at him.

'May I help you, sir?' she said.

'Er, yes,' he replied, finding that his collar was suddenly too tight for him. 'I have an appointment with Mr Roehampton at three o'clock.'

'What name might that be, sir?'

'Syme. Herbert Syme.' His confidence returned. 'I'm an author.'

'Ah, yes,' she said, her tone softening. 'Mr Syme. I remember now. I'm Miss Finch. It was I who wrote to you to arrange the

appointment. Welcome to London, Mr Syme. Mr Roehampton
will deal with you as soon as he returns from his luncheon.'

'Luncheon?'

'He and Mr Buckley always eat at their club on a Wednesday.'

'I see.'

'Do take a seat. Mr Roehampton will be back within the hour.'

Within the hour! So much for punctuality. It had taken Herbert
all morning simply to reach London. To arrive in the Strand at the
stipulated time had required a huge effort on the part of the provincial author. During the wayward journey from the station to the
offices of Roehampton and Buckley, Ltd., his provincialism had
been cruelly exposed. His instincts were blunted, his accent jarred,
his lack of sophistication was excruciating. He was made to feel like
a country mouse in a metropolitan jungle. All that would soon van-
ish, he reminded himself. He was going to be a published author. As
he sank down on the chair beside the door, he consoled himself with
the fact that that he had made it to the top of Mount Olympus,
albeit situated above a shoe shop in the Strand. It was only right that
a mortal should await the arrival of Zeus from his luncheon.

Miss Lavinia Finch offered little decorative interest to the
observer. A spare, severe woman of almost exotic ugliness, she bus-
ied herself at her typewriter, striking the keys with a random bru-
tality that made the machine groan in pain. She ignored the visitor completely. Herbert did not mind. His gaze was fixed on the
oak bookcase that ran from floor to ceiling behind the secretary.
The firm's output was stacked with a neatness that gladdened the
heart of a librarian. He feasted his eyes on the impressive array of
volumes, thrilled that he would be joining them in time and deciding that he, too, when funds permitted, would acquire just such a
bookcase in which to exhibit his work. Herbert was so caught up
in his contemplation of literature that he did not notice how swiftly an hour passed. The chimes of Big Ben were still reverberating
when Edmund T. Roehampton breezed in through the door.

A third disappointment jerked Herbert to his feet. Expecting
the Zeus of the publishing world to be a huge man with a commanding presence, he was surprised to see a dapper figure strut-
ting into the room. Roehampton was a self-appointed dandy but
the fashionable attire, the dazzling waistcoat and the gleaming
shoes could not disguise the fact that he was a small man with a

large paunch and a face like a whiskered donkey. Seeing his visitor, he doffed his top hat, pulled the cigar from between his teeth and manufactured a cold smile.

'Ah!' he declared. 'You must be Syme.'

'That's right, sir. Herbert Syme. The author of –'

'Well, don't just stand there, man,' continued Roehampton, interrupting him. 'Come into my office. We must talk. Crucial decisions have to be made.' He opened the door to his inner sanctum and paused. 'Any calls, Miss Finch?'

'None, Mr Roehampton,' she said.

'Good.'

'But you do have an appointment at four-thirty with Mr Agnew.'

'Syme and I will be through by then.'

He went into his office and Herbert followed him, uncertain whether to be reassured or alarmed by the news that a bare half-an-hour had been allotted to him. Had he come so far to be given such short shrift? Roehampton waved him to a seat, put his top hat on a peg then took the leather-backed chair behind the desk. Raised up on a dais, it made him seem much bigger than he was. Herbert relaxed. The office was much more like the place he had envisaged. Large and well appointed, it had serried ranks of books on display as well as framed sepia photographs of the firm's major authors. Herbert wondered how long it would be before his own portrait graced the William Morris wallpaper.

Roehampton drew on his cigar and studied Herbert carefully.

'How is Yorkshire?' he asked abruptly.

Herbert was thrown. 'Yorkshire, sir?'

'That's where you come from, isn't it?'

'No, Mr Roehampton. Derbyshire. I come from Derbyshire.'

'I knew it up was up there somewhere,' said the other dismissively, opening a drawer to take out a manuscript. He slapped it down on the desk. 'Well, Syme, here it is. Your novel.'

'I'm so grateful that you are prepared to publish it, Mr Roehampton.'

'Subject to certain changes.'

'Yes, yes. Of course,' agreed Herbert. 'Anything you say.'

'Then let's get down to brass tacks,' said the publisher, exhaling a cloud of acrid smoke. 'Interesting plot. Well drawn characters.

Good dialogue. A novel with pace.' He gave a complimentary nod. 'You're a born writer, Syme.'

Herbert swelled with pride. 'Thank you, sir.'

'But you still need to be weaned.'

'I await your suggestions, Mr Roehampton.'

'Oh, they're not suggestions,' warned the other. 'They're essential improvements. Mr Buckley and I could never put our names on a book with which we were not entirely and unreservedly satisfied.'

'And what does Mr Buckley think of *Murder in Matlock*?' wondered Herbert. 'Your letter said that it had found favour with all who had read it.'

'Yes. With Miss Finch and with myself. We are your audience.' He heaved a sigh. 'Mr Buckley, alas, is not a reader. The perusal of the luncheon menu at our club is all that he can manage in the way of sustained reading. What he brings to the firm is money and business acumen. What I bring,' he added, thrusting a thumb into his waistcoat pocket, 'is true literary expertise and a knack of unearthing new talent.'

'I'm delighted to be included in that new talent, Mr Roehampton.'

'We shall see, Syme. We shall see. Now, to business.' He consulted the notes written on the title page of the manuscript. 'Omissions,' he announced. 'Let us first deal with your omissions.'

Herbert was baffled. 'I was not aware that I'd omitted anything.'

'Yours, sir, is a novel of sensation.'

'I see it more as a searching exploration of the nature of evil.'

'It amounts to the same thing, man. *Murder in Matlock* inhabits the world of crime and that imposes certain demands upon an author.'

'Such as?'

'To begin with, you must have a Sinister Oriental. A murder story is untrue to its nature if it does not have at least one – and preferably more than one – Sinister Oriental.'

'But there are no Orientals, sinister or otherwise, in Matlock.'

'Invent some, man,' said Roehampton with exasperation. 'Import some. Bring in a Chinese army of occupation, if need be.'

'That would upset the balance of the narrative.'

'It will help to sell the book and that is all that concerns me.'

Herbert was deflated. 'If you say so, Mr Roehampton.'

'As to your villain, his name must be changed.'

'Why? What's wrong with Lionel Jagg?'

'Far too English,' explained the publisher. 'We need a wicked foreigner. Do you know why Wilkie Collins chose to christen the villain of *The Woman in White* with an Italian name? It was because he felt no Englishman capable of the skullduggery to which Count Fosco sank. I applaud the thinking behind that decision, Syme. Follow suit. Lionel Jagg commits crimes far too horrible for any true-born Englishman even to contemplate. Henceforth, he will be Count Orsini.'

'An Italian count in Matlock?' wailed Herbert. 'It's unheard of.'

'Anything can happen in Yorkshire.'

'Derbyshire, Mr Roehampton. Derbyshire.'

'Yorkshire or Derbyshire. Both are equally barbarous places.'

'That's unjust.'

'Let us move on. Criminals must be exposed early on to the reader. Lionel Jagg concealed his villainy too well. Count Orsini must be more blatant. Equip him with a limp and one eye. They are clear indications of villainy. A hare lip is also useful in this context. And he needs an accomplice, just as evil as himself.'

'Not another Sinister Oriental, surely?'

'No, no. Don't overplay that hand. A Wily Pathan will fit the bill here.'

Herbert was aghast. 'Wily Pathans in *Derbyshire*?'

'Metaphorically speaking, they are everywhere. They are the bane of the British Empire and we must remind our readers of that fact. Now, sir, to the most frightful omission of all. A hero. Your novel must have a Great Detective.'

'But it has one, Mr Roehampton. Inspector Ned Lubbock.'

'Wrong name, wrong character, wrong nationality,' insisted the publisher, stubbing out his cigar in the ashtray with decisive force. 'Lubbock is nothing but a country bumpkin from Derbyshire.'

'Yorkshire,' corrected the other.

'There – I *knew* the novel was set in Yorkshire!'

'In Derbyshire. Inspector Lubbock is a Yorkshireman, working in Matlock. I thought I made that abundantly clear.'

'What's abundantly clear to me, Syme, is that you need to be more aware of the market you are hoping to reach. The common reader does not want a bumbling detective from a remote northern fastness. He expects style, charm and intellectual brilliance. In short, sir, the Great Detective must be French.'

'Why?' groaned Herbert.

'Because there is a tradition to maintain,' asserted the other. 'Vidocq, Eugene Sue, Gaboriau. They all had French detectives and not simply because they themselves hailed from France. Consider the case of Edgar Allan Poe, the American author. What is the name of his sleuth? Chevalier Auguste Dupin. It's inconceivable that someone called Ned Lubbock should solve *The Murders in the Rue Morgue.*'

'It's just as ludicrous to have a French detective hailing from Yorkshire.'

'Change his birthplace to Paris.'

Herbert descended to sarcasm. 'The Rue Morgue, perhaps?'

'And give the fellow more substance,' said Roehampton, sweeping his protest aside. 'This is the age of the Scientific Detective, the man with a supreme intelligence. Think of Sherlock Holmes. Think of Monsieur Lecoq. Think of The Thinking Machine.'

All that Herbert Syme had thought about for years was publication. Elevation to the ranks of those he idolized most would solve everything. It would rescue him from a humdrum life in a small provincial library where he was mocked, undervalued and taken for granted. Five years had gone into the creation of the novel that would be his salvation. In that time, he had grown to love Inspector Ned Lubbock, to marvel at his invention of the dastardly Lionel Jagg and to take a special delight in the meticulous evocation of his native Derbyshire. His hopes were dashed. Edmund T. Roehampton was mangling his novel out of all recognition. He felt the grief of a mother whose only child is being slowly strangled in front of her. Anger began to take root.

'Inspector Jacques Legrand,' decreed Roehampton. 'That name has more of a ring to it. He uses scientific methods of detection and outwits the villains with his superior brainpower. Needless to say – and I must repair another omission of yours – he must be a Master of Disguise. Just like Hamilton Cleek – the Man of the Forty Faces.'

Herbert struck back. 'And what does this preposterous French detective disguise himself *as*?' he asked, his Derbyshire vowels thickening in the process. 'An Italian Count or a Wily Pathan? Or maybe he can pretend to be the commander of an invading Chinese army. And where do his changes of apparel come from? I should warn you that there are no costume hire shops in the Peak District.'

'I'm glad that you mentioned that, Syme.'

'Does that mean I've got *something* right at last?'

'Far from it. Your location is a disaster.'

'You're going to take Derbyshire away from me as well?' cried Herbert.

'I have to, man. Shift the story to London and we enlarge its possibilities.'

Heavier sarcasm. 'In which part of the capital is Matlock to be found?'

'Nowhere, fortunately,' said Roehampton with a complacent chuckle. 'Unlike your home town, we do have more than our share of Sinister Orientals here so that's one problem solved. My shirts are washed at a Chinese laundry and they are obsequiously polite to me but there's still something ineradicably *sinister* about them.'

'They're foreigners, that's all. In Peking, you would appear sinister to them.'

'That's beside the point. Your novel is not set in China.'

'No,' said Herbert, desperation taking hold. 'It's firmly rooted in Derbyshire. How can a book called *Murder in Matlock* be set in the city of London?'

'By a simple slash of the pen. Here,' said the publisher grandly, indicating the title page of the manuscript. 'I crossed out your effort and inserted my own. I venture to suggest that it will have more purchase on the reader's curiosity.'

Herbert was shaking with fury. 'You've stolen my title as well?'

'Improved upon it, Syme. That is all.'

'In what way?'

'See for yourself,' advised the other, pushing the manuscript across to him. 'Ignore the blots. My pen always leaks. Just imagine those words emblazoned across the title-page of your novel. *Slaughter in the Strand.*'

'But there's no mention of the Strand in the book.'

'There is now, Syme. I've also included some other elements you failed to include. As well as being a killer, Count Orsini must

63

be a Prince of Thieves just like Arsene Lupin. You see?' he said, eyes glinting. 'The Franco-Italian touch once more. Inspector Legrand must solve the crime by playing with a piece of string while sitting in the corner of a restaurant. Notice the hint of Baroness Orczy there? The Old Man in the Corner. It adds to the international flavour of the novel. On which subject, I must point out another fatal omission.'

Herbert gritted his teeth. 'Go on,' he growled.

'There are no German spies in the book. We must have spies for the Kaiser. Remember Le Queux, a true English patriot as well as a brilliant writer. He's warned us time and again about the menace of the Prussian eagle. Yes, Syme,' he concluded, sitting back with a grin, 'those are the few changes I require. Make them and your book may stand a chance in a busy marketplace.'

'Except that it won't be *my* book,' snarled Herbert.

'What do you mean?'

'I mean, Mr Roehampton, that you have been hurling names at me that I neither like nor strive to emulate. Vidocq, Sue, Gaboriau, Baroness Orczy, William Le Queux. They merely skate on the surface of crime. I tried to deal with the subject in depth,' argued Herbert, rising to his feet. 'If you want an international flavour, listen to the names of those who inspired me to write *Murder in Matlock*. Dostoevsky gave me my villain. Balzac supplied me with my insight into the lower depths of society. Maupassant taught me subtlety. Goethe schooled my style. You wave Wilkie Collins at me but a far greater English writer suggested the infanticide with which my novel begins – George Eliot, the author of *Adam Bede*. My debt to them is there for all to see. I'll not have it obliterated.'

Roehampton blinked. 'Am I to understand that you reject my emendations?'

'I refuse to put my name to the rubbish you've concocted.'

'Ah, yes,' said the publisher, rubbing his hands. 'That brings me to my final point. Whatever form the novel finally takes, we cannot possibly put your name on it.'

'Why not?'

'Be realistic, man. Syme rhymes with Slime. The critics would seize on that like vultures. Herbert Syme sounds like, well, what, in all honesty, you are, a struggling librarian from a Yorkshire backwater.'

'Derbyshire!' roared Herbert. 'Matlock is in Derbyshire!'

'That point is immaterial in a novel called *Slaughter in the Strand*.'

'I loathe the title.'

'It will grow on you in time,' said Roehampton persuasively. 'So will your new pseudonym. Out goes Herbert Syme and in comes – wait for it – Marcus van Dorn. It has a bewitching sense of mystery about it. Marcus van Dorn. Come now. Isn't that a name to sew excitement in the breast of every reader?'

Herbert exploded. 'But it's not *my* name!'

'It is now, Syme.'

'You can't do this to me, Mr Roehampton.'

'I'm a publisher. I can do anything.'

It was horribly true. Herbert's great expectations withered before his eyes. He was not, after all, going to be an author. If this was how publishers behaved, he was doomed. Life would become intolerable. All the people to whom he had boasted of his success would ridicule him unmercifully. He would have to return to the library with his tail between his legs. Every time he put one of Roehampton and Buckley's books on a shelf, the wound would be reopened. It was galling. Publication was not rebirth at all. It was akin to the infanticide with which his novel had so sensitively dealt.

The villain of the piece was none other than a man whom he had revered from afar. Edmund T. Roehampton had not only hacked his book to pieces, he had altered its title and deprived the author of his identity. It was the ultimate blow to Herbert's pride. His gaze fell on his precious manuscript, disfigured by ink blots and scribbled notes, then it shifted slowly to the gleaming paper knife. A wild thought came into his mind.

'Well,' said Roehampton, 'do you want the book published or not?'

'Only if it's my novel.'

'Make the changes I want or it will never get into print.'

Herbert stood firm. 'I'll not alter a single word.'

'Then take this useless manuscript and go back to Yorkshire.'

'Derbyshire!'

It was the final insult. As Roehampton reached for the manuscript, Herbert grabbed the paper knife and stabbed his hand. The publisher yelled in pain but there was worse to come. Pushed to the limit, Herbert dived across the desk and stabbed him repeatedly in the chest, avenging the murder of his novel with a vigour he did not know he possessed. Alerted by her employer's yell, Miss Finch came bustling into the office. When she saw the blood gushing down Roehampton's flashy waistcoat, she had a fit of hysteria and screamed madly. Herbert was on her within seconds. Lavinia Finch was an accomplice. She had not only typed out the guileful letter to him, she had read the finest novel ever to come out of Matlock and pretended to admire it. She had deceived Herbert just as much as her employer and deserved to die beside him. He stabbed away until her screams turned to a hideous gurgling. Both victims were soon dead.

* * *

Herbert Syme had travelled in a First Class carriage on the most significant journey of his life but his return ticket would not be used. A horse-drawn police van was his mode of transport now. As he sat in handcuffs behind bars, he reflected that he had, after all, achieved one ambition. His name would certainly be seen in print now. Every newspaper in Britain would carry the banner headline – *Slaughter in the Strand*. A treacherous publisher may have provided that title but its author would not be Marcus van Dorn. It would be Herbert Syme, the most notorious criminal ever to come out of Matlock in Derbyshire. He liked that. It was a form of poetic justice.

24 Hours From Tulsa

Martin Edwards

Which way now?

Lomas is heading due west, but he hasn't a clue where he's going. It doesn't help that this is a route he knows well, far too well. He was up here a few weeks back, early in autumn, the low sun of evening half-blinding him, mile after mile. He was driving on auto-pilot. His eyes can't take the strain as easily as they did once upon a time. Today there's no sun, scarcely a glimmer of brightness to break up the clouds. Ten minutes ago the weather girl on Radio Leeds was warning about the threat of storms.

He ignores the turn-off, tells himself to keep straight on. His head is aching. Carter was right in one thing at least.

'You're not as young as you used to be.'

Hills rise on either side of the road. A sign claims this is the highest motorway in the country. Lomas's instinct is never to believe what he's told; a lifetime of flogging ice to Eskimos has taught him that if nothing else. But if the sign had said it's the worst motorway in Britain, that he'd accept without a second thought. The landscape is lonely, and he thinks it drab, nothing like the Lakes beyond the Kendal exit. Over to the left, not so many miles beyond the brow of moorland, that's where Brady and Hindley buried their bodies. Were all of them ever found? Lomas can't recall. He's never kept up with the news and now it's too late to break the habit of a lifetime.

Traffic slows, the lanes narrow. Lorries are tailing back along the inside lane. A ribbon of cones stretches out in the distance, far as the eye can see. The next ten miles are sure to be a crawl. All those Mancunian commuters, making an early start. Lomas groans loudly, almost theatrically, even though there's nobody to hear, even though the delay shouldn't bother him a bit. He keeps reminding himself that time doesn't matter any more, but although it's true, he can't bite back the profanities when some pony-tailed kid with a death wish and a rust-bucket of an old

Cavalier cuts in just ahead of him.

The day is fading and he switches on the lights. Time was when driving up and down the country was a pleasure, sheer bliss. Not this nose-to-tail grind, knowing that a cow with a laptop and a long face is checking on your every move. Once he could – digress. There are always opportunities, when you're out on the road. Bound to be. Lomas smiles to himself. He's been tempted and fallen, many a time. Only natural.

Selling has gone much the same way. Lomas blames the internet. He's a Luddite and proud of it. Tapping into a computer all day long is for kids, not a grown man who's been around the block a few times. But people don't buy the same way as they used to. They are busy, busy, busy, or so they say. Busy doing nothing, by and large. But that doesn't help when you have targets to meet.

The phone rings. The set is hands-free, a security measure the company insists on, though he's always had a sneaking preference for cradling a mobile against his neck. He grips the wheel tighter, doesn't press *Answer*. The trilling keeps on – bloody William Tell, he should have changed the tone years ago – so he ups the volume on the tape. *New York, New York*. He's always liked Sinatra, can't be doing with all this modern rap-crap.

At last they give up. *1 missed call*. He presses the arrow button and the office number flashes in silent reproach. Well, they can forget it. Tomorrow he'll be off the payroll. He's called in for the last time.

The tape's wound to an end. With practised ease, he slides another cassette out of its box and into the slot, keeping his left hand on the wheel. *Sixties Love Songs – Volume 14*. Never mind about love, it's melodic stuff he likes, even more now than when he was a youngster going out to the clubs. Tuneful, relaxing. Music to watch cones go by.

Trumpets cry out and a man's voice wails. Orbison, maybe? A song he's heard a thousand times, there in the background, part of the soundtrack of his life.

Something happened. To me.

This strikes a chord. Lomas has never listened to the words before. But what else is there to do, sitting on the outskirts of a dark wet conurbation, bumper-to-bumper in a three-mile queue?

Something's happened, all right. Talk about chickens coming home to roost.

'You should have seen it coming.' Hayley, doing her more-in-sor-row-than-in-anger bit. Was she talking about the job or her new lover?

Funny, he thinks about her more now that she's going, now he knows that she's screwing someone else. All those years, the boot was on the other foot, and he found her so boring he could have screamed. Never mind, it's the kids he'll really miss. Or at least, the kids as they were. Tim in the days when they went to watch the match together, Tim before he started stashing dirty mags in the drawer under his bed. Sally-Ann when she wore pretty little party dresses and white cotton socks, when she didn't smoke and have a stud in her nose.

I won't be home any more.

You can say that again. So Lomas presses *Repeat*. The traffic's starting to pick up speed. The worst is over, at least in one way.

He presses the accelerator and the car leaps ahead. One time of day, his dearest wish was to drive a Lexus. He fought for it, stood on the shoulders of others to make his figures stack up. He deserved success and – leave aside the occasional weekend in Paris – this was his real prize.

The leather seats are rather grubby, sure. He's not paid for a valeting since the middle of summer. Not so long ago the company changed cars every three years. It made sense: saving on repairs and cashing in while there was still a good price to be had, but then the men in suits decreed otherwise and the garage bills have been coming in to the accounts department ever since. Typical finance mentality. No vision.

He's been behind this same wheel for five years, almost to the day, too long really, but it's still a super car. He's loved it as much as he's loved anything for as far back as he can remember. The engine doesn't roar, it purrs, the sat. nav. is terrific. A bit out of date, maybe, it doesn't know they've re-numbered the ring road, it's the 60 now, not the 62. Who cares? That's a detail.

Lomas remembers when he used to listen to the computer's voice, clipped and precise, and imagine that she was alive: a woman talking to him, a slave devoted to the task of making sure he headed in the right direction. He could forgive the occasional slip, when she said 'Norwich' instead of 'Northwich', that sort of thing, the kind of mistake that anyone could make. To err isn't only human. He's always liked listening to her, sometimes he'd keep pressing

Voice, have her repeat the same phrases over and over again. Easy to picture a woman talking like that. Cool and elegant, someone who was sure to respond whenever he pressed her buttons.

Sad? Not at all, just a harmless fantasy. Carter is wrong as usual. He hasn't lost it.

Today, though, she's keeping quiet. He's finished with her. *Cancel Guidance*. Somehow he's taken the wrong route after all, and pressing *Detour* won't ever bring him back on the right road.

A madman in a Range Rover that has come from nowhere, maybe zipping down off the slip road, swerves right in front of him, heading off into the twilight in the outside lane. Lomas flashes his lights, then treats the bastard to full beam until he disappears out of sight. Hopefully there'll be a speed cop lurking under the bridge down past Burtonwood. Shit, Lomas thinks, if I hadn't touched my brake, I'd have been up his backside. People like that shouldn't be allowed on the roads. You hear a lot about road rage, but it's understandable. This country's full of people who deserve to be dead, yet all too often it's the innocent who get killed. How can anyone in their right mind believe in God?

'Answer me that,' Lomas says. 'Answer me that.'

Roy Orbison doesn't offer any reply, he just keeps on singing about the day his life changed. Actually, it's not the Big O, is it? Silly mistake, no wonder the quiz team at the Waterman's Arms never makes it to the premier league. Gene Pitney, that's who it is, wailing away. Wallowing in self-Pitney.

Lomas chuckles. No way has he lost it, Carter's a fool.

Yes, yes, Gene Pitney. Wasn't this his greatest hit? The words aren't bad, they tell a story. People don't write songs like they used to, the garbage Tim and Sally-Ann fill their heads with, you can't even make out the words. Probably just as well.

Roadworks ahead. Just for a change. A 50 mile an hour limit coming up, speed cameras in action. You can't get away with anything in this day and age. We're living in a police state and we don't even realise it. A sign brags about the number of offences recorded. It's not the same as people convicted, though. Lomas has heard reps saying there is a get-out-of-jail free card you can play. When the summons drops through the letterbox, tell them you don't know who was driving the car at the time. Some famous people have pulled that one to get off the hook. Lomas has never had the need, but he's always kept it in the back of his mind. How would it work, though? No chance he'd ever let Hayley loose with his pride and joy, never mind Tim or Sally-Ann.

Doesn't matter, anyway. The M6 junction is half a mile distant, it's time to peel off, see if things are any better over the Thelwall Viaduct. There's a first time for everything.

I'm just not the same any more.

Echoes of bloody Hayley. No, no, no. Hayley was wrong, he hasn't changed. It's the world that's changed. *No way* he's losing it. His temper, now, okay, that's a different matter. He's not super-human, never claimed to be. Of course he gets angry now and then. Who wouldn't, these days?

Two bridges at Thelwall, one in each direction, eight lanes with generous margins and still it's a nightmare. Never anything different, it's notorious the length and breadth of England. A combination of circumstances: the rise of the viaduct slows the HGVs and the coming-together of traffic from all the intersecting motorways means that the slightest hiccup in the flow of vehicles slows everything down to a standstill. At least the place doesn't have a name for suicides. Runcorn Bridge, that's something else. Losers keep jumping off or threatening to. For some reason it gives them pleasure to do themselves in during the rush hour. Result: tail-backs full of fuming drivers, telling their passengers that some people have no bloody consideration.

Lomas thinks, if I wanted to end it all, that isn't how I'd do it. Not leaping down into a watery grave.

On top of the viaduct, grinding along at ten miles an hour. Flecks of rain smear his windscreen. That's all he needs. Far below is the ship canal, but all he can see is the lights of the trucks and vans in front of him. He's hobbling along on the inside, because it's time to come off the motorway. Tiredness kills, so the signs always say. Time to take a break.

There's a truckstop with a McDonald's, straddling the junction of the 6 and the 56. He eases his way on to the roundabout: first left, first right and he's there. Parking isn't a problem. Switching off the tape, Lomas wonders for a moment about the drive-thru, but he can't face it. Maybe it isn't a good idea to drive on an empty stomach, but he's been short of good ideas lately. His eyelids were drooping on that last stretch, a black coffee wouldn't go amiss.

Outside the motel, a woman is checking her face in a compact mirror. Her thick red hair rings a bell. Wasn't she here a few weeks back? That time, he almost stopped to say hello, then thought better of it. He regrets it now. Maybe see if she's still around after he's freshened up? He throws her a glance on his way to the greasy spoon. Their eyes meet, but he carries on. A couple of blokes in jeans give him a furtive look as they sneak into the men's room. The shop's shut, so is the barber's, but the café lights are dazzling. The prices are dirt cheap, although frankly money's no object tonight. He gives in to temptation and buys an all day breakfast. Why not? High cholesterol is the least of his worries.

The place is full of screens of one kind or another. Traffic info – nothing good's happening on the roads tonight, but what's new? CNN is covering some crisis in a foreign land. The President is talking about surgical strikes, but Lomas is hardly listening. Lights flash on the video game machines. A couple of truckers are talking soccer, another's pretending not to notice that the fat girl behind the counter's giving him the eye. It's a whole world, out on the road and here in the service areas. Most folk don't realise.

After he's finished, he goes for a pee and to wash his face. The men in jeans can't be seen, but he can hear whispering from the cubicles. Lomas sighs and shakes his head. He's never been one for prejudice, but he's never figured out why perverts have to congregate in places like this. Haven't they got homes of their own?

He's feeling better: the slap of caffeine has done him good. It's still early and he isn't in a hurry. His pace as he sets off back to the car park is deliberate, ponderous even. Two-to-one says she's slung her hook.

Good job he isn't a betting man: she's still there, sheltering under the covered walkway by the corner of the lodge. The rain is beating down much harder, he can see it bouncing off the tarmac.

'Horrible night, isn't it?'

He can still do it. Forget Hayley's complaining, forget Carter's judgmental shaking of the head. He can still sell. Best of all, he can still sell himself. Just look at her. The moment she heard his voice, smooth as treacle, she brightened. Four little words and she's putty in his hands. She'd been yearning for him to speak, he's sure of it. Walking past when he arrived was a good move. She's been waiting anxiously this last twenty minutes.

'Terrible.'

Local accent. Late thirties, at a guess. The PVC coat is cheap, her legs are bare. What's unemployment like round here? Lomas has no idea, but it doesn't make any difference, we can all do with a bit of extra cash any time.

'Cigarette?'

'Thanks.'

He lights it for her. They stand side by side, gazing out at the bright lights of the McDonald's. Companionable, almost.

He can feel her coat flapping against his legs. He moves closer to her, inhales her scent. Ladled on with a trowel, but that's what you expect at a place like this.

'That's a lovely perfume.'

She turns to face him and smiles. Her teeth are yellow, but Lomas's motto is one he picked up years ago on the road. You don't stop to admire the mantelpiece, as long as you're poking the fire.

'You're a very generous man, Mr...'

'Call me Tom.'

'Okay, Tom. I'm Melissa.'

A likely story. All part of the game, of course. Lomas would put her down as a Dawn or a Tracey. Suddenly, he tires of the conversational waltz. After all, they are both aware of what this is all about. He tosses away his cigarette and nods at the motel.

'Come on, then.'

She gives him a hard look. He thinks maybe there was a flicker of disappointment in her pale grey eyes, as if her preference is for men with a bit of class. Maybe she's spotted that his suit's a bit shinier than it ought to be. Well, beggars can't be choosers. He marches to the door, then looks back over his shoulder.

'Are you coming or aren't you?'

She hesitates, then shrugs agreement and trots along after him. As he pays the desk clerk in cash upfront, she loiters at the back of the lobby, running her finger along the leaves of the plastic rubber plant.

All these rooms in all these places are exactly the same. It's a strength of the motel brand. As a salesman, Lomas can see the point. People pretend to enjoy surprises, but the truth is that they fear the unexpected.

Her price is ludicrous in the circumstances, frankly, but Lomas hardly cares. He doesn't try to haggle. She's already seen the notes in his wallet when he paid for the room. He tosses the notes on to a bed and starts to unbutton his shirt. She stashes the money into her bag, then slips out of her skirt and blouse with a minimum, an absolute minimum, of finesse.

'Are you a rep?' she asks.

He pulls down his trousers. This isn't the moment for meaningless conversation. Meaningless sex, he thinks, that's what this is all about.

'Sales and marketing director, actually.'

'I'm impressed,' she says. Is there a hint of mockery there? Did he ask for it, was his tone pompous? He's never thought of himself as self-important. Never.

'For the time being.'

She unhooks her bra. Her breasts are a disappointment: no better than bloody Hayley's. Something in his expression catches her eye and she speaks more sharply.

'Got the push, have you?'

In the act of taking off his tie, he pauses. *Freezes*, to tell the truth.

'What makes you say that?'

His tone has roughened, but she isn't scared. It's not easy to be scared of a man in his socks and underpants.

'Lot of fellers in the same boat, that's all. I met this guy the other week. He was in computers, he was telling me he was going to get made redundant. Something about a downturn in the economy. Came from Tulse Hill, he did. Wherever that is. Somewhere down south, I suppose. Nowhere round here, that's for sure.'

Twenty-Four Hours from Tulse Hill? Perhaps not. The heating is up in the room, he feels almost feverish. There's a pounding in his head. Why is England so much less glamorous than the States? You never hear crooners performing *By The Time I Get To Faversham* or *Do You Know The Way To Saffron Walden?* We always love most the things we can never get, the things and places that are out of reach. And now that bloody song is starting up in his head again.

I lost control.

'I have thirty men out in the field.' The words are skidding into each other. He sounds as though he's been drinking. 'Thirty, count them. Every single one reports to me.'

'Keep your hair on, love.' He sees alarm flickering in her eyes.

'It's no disgrace, losing your job. Just like it's no disgrace, seeking a bit of comfort on a cold miserable night.'

She's become ingratiating. God, he really doesn't like pleading women.

'Carter's a fool. They'll be sorry, I tell you straight.' He's moving towards her.

She sits on the edge of the bed, pulling down her knickers. Breathing hard, she beckons him forward. She isn't excited, she's afraid.

'Come on, then. I'll help you forget all that.'

'I don't need help.'

'Look, love, all of us need help.' Legs apart, hands on her knees. Not looking into his eyes.

'I don't need help.' He's shouting now and as she cringes in front of him, he loops his tie around her neck, pulling it tight.

I hate to do this to you.

What happens in the next few moments isn't clean or pretty. It isn't what he'd expected. No, that isn't right, he has no expectations. All he can do is keep pulling tighter, yanking her hair to stop her struggling, until it is done. Over. Finished.

No need to look at what he's done. It doesn't excite him. Killing someone hasn't turned him on at all. Death disgusts him, it always has. He threw up at his grandfather's funeral. When it comes to his own victim, he's no different. He feels numb, wholly without sensation. Time to get dressed.

A girl is sitting at the desk. Shift change, presumably. The man who took his money is nowhere to be seen. Lomas gives her a curt nod and strides out into the car park.

Behind the wheel again, he revs up far too hard. Quite unnecessary in a Lexus, it isn't that sort of car. He jabs the audio button hard with his thumb. More music. He needs to fill his head with sound, blot out the roaring in his brain.

The rain's teeming down. The wipers work overtime as he heads south. This road isn't the busiest in Britain; in Lomas's book, the prize must go to the M25, Spaghetti Junction's a close second. Even so, the stretch south of junction 20 is grim at the best of times.

Soon the weather will be even worse. Fog, snow, black ice. Lomas has driven all over England in all sorts of conditions, and he's never enjoyed it less. The motorways of Britain are falling apart, no wonder you hit roadworks every five minutes and the Highways Agency is constantly saying sorry for any delay. This country depends on transport, but the railways are a joke, the bus network in tatters, the roads a disgrace. Motorists are public enemy number one, taxed up to the ears and treated as criminals because it's easier for the police than catching the real villains. We've lost our pride, our self-belief.

As for me, Lomas thinks, I've lost everything. My job, my wife, my kids. My liberty.

I can never go home again.

Gene's dead right. There's nothing more that can be done. No healing, no absolution.

Even though it's getting late, traffic's still heavy. As juggernauts rumble by, the spray hits his screen and for a moment or two he can't see a thing. Perhaps that's the way it ought to be.

Never, never, never.

He moves into the outside lane. A sign anticipates a lane closure, but he no longer cares. In the distance, he can see lights flooding the night sky. Red stop lights and the flashing blue of the forces of law and order. He ought to slow down, but there is no longer any point.

He puts his foot down hard, hears the engine roar as if in approval and closes his eyes. Waiting for what will happen next.

Seduced

Jerry Sykes

Time and the vanity frame of TV had altered Frankie Stamp's appearance – his bloated pink face resembled a kid's fist raised in righteous anger, and his brittle grey hair floated around his head like some kind of private raincloud – but the cast of his mouth still refused to hold a smile.

As the interviewer flicked a conspiratorial glance at the camera and then asked Stamp how much of his character in the film had been based on his own experiences, Stamp turned and shot the home audience a look of dark indifference, his lips curled into a smile; it was a smile without a trace of humour, it was a smile that was no smile at all.

Jim Cole stared back at the screen with disbelief on his face. He shook his head and leaned forward in his seat, pushed his spectacles back up the length of his nose.

It had been three decades since he had last seen Stamp – last seen him in motion, frozen images of him had often appeared in newspapers and magazines since his release from prison – three decades in which he had all but forgotten the snap of casual violence that Stamp held in his limbs like a child holds the gift of laughter in its face. Three decades since that cold December afternoon when he had stood with his fellow officers and watched as Stamp had been sentenced to fifteen-to-life for the attempted murder of a barman at the Twisted Globe, the barman caught with the skim from the 'insurance premium' that Stamp had called to collect still in his pocket. Stamp had taken the barman into the cellar and beaten him with a half-full aluminium barrel until the barman had soiled himself and the smell had turned Stamp from the broken frame at his feet and pushed him back up the wooden stairs.

Following the trial a couple of tabloids had suggested that another more serious charge of murder had been dropped after the murder weapon, a rusted WWII revolver, had been stolen from an evidence locker in the basement of Kentish Town police station.

The gun had been rammed into the ear of an Italian baker that had tried to hustle Stamp's girlfriend in a nightclub, rammed deep into his ear before the trigger had been pulled. The gun had still been stuck in the Italian's ear when the corpse had been found the following morning, broken and tossed into a rusted garage behind the parade of shops that housed the baker's.

Of course the police had denied the tale, denied that Stamp had been a suspect in the case, but in communities keen to see the establishment beaten, the fiction became the truth and the truth became folklore; and the folklore elevated Stamp from a marginal figure on the underworld into some kind of noble and gallant hero to stand alongside the Krays and the Great Train Robbers.

Jim Cole lit a cigarette and continued to stare at the TV, the interviewer now asking Stamp about the truth behind the rumours surrounding the murder. Stamp just looked back at him in silent contempt, slid his gaze across to the camera once more to check that the home audience was still out there, and then rode the silence until the interviewer lost his nerve and hustled a chef with flecks of food in his beard across the screen.

* * *

Cole took a sip of beer and looked across the bar to where a small kid sat on the carpet under a table eating a packet of crisps. The kid belonged to the landlord's daughter and wandered around the pub all day while his mother was out at work. Cole reckoned the kid to be about three or four but already he had the deep chest rattle of a chain smoker. Cole let out a sigh and turned back to the bar.

'You see Frankie Stamp on TV this morning?'

The barman rested his arms on the bar. 'Frankie Stamp? I hear he's a film star now, huh?'

'That's what it looks like,' said Cole. He took another sip of beer, moved around on his stool a little.

'You were on the squad that put him down,' said Maguire. 'No?'

Cole hiked his shoulders. 'Sure. Set him on the trail to stardom seems like.'

'Strange times indeed. You kill a man in cold blood and end up in the movies.'

'Can't be right,' said Cole, lost in thought for a moment. 'It can't be right.' He blinked and took another sip of beer, lit a cigarette. 'The world seems to have forgotten about that poor kid at the Twisted Globe. All it seems to care about is the Italian, the baker. And there's no proof that Stamp even did that killing.'

Maguire pointed a thick finger at Cole's face, grinned. 'You were a copper. Since when did the truth get in the way of anythin' interestin'?'

Cole shot him a half-smile and tipped the remainder of his beer into his mouth, pushed the glass across the bar. 'Just fill the glass, Maguire,' he said, and wiped his mouth with the back of his hand.

Maguire pulled another beer from the tap and put it on the bar in front of Cole.

'You see the film?' said Maguire.

Cole shook his head, no. 'Last time I went to the pictures, Robert Mitchum was still the tough guy.'

Maguire let out a short laugh. 'I know what you mean there, Jim. I don't think me an' Jen've been to the pictures since before we took over this place,' he said, and twisted his finger in the air to indicate the pub.

Cole stared at the kid under the table, now picking bits of broken crisps from the floor and stuffing them in his mouth. Cole could see tufts of carpet stuck to the boy's lips. 'I don't understand it, all this attention stacked on a killer.'

'It ain't nothin' new,' said Maguire. 'People've been backin' the men in black hats for as long as I can remember.'

*   *   *

Cole shuffled in his seat until he felt comfortable, waited for the film to start.

As he had told Maguire, it had been a long time since Cole had last sat in the stalls of a cinema. Not that he no longer liked films, it was just that it was easier to watch films on TV and video. Cheaper too, he couldn't believe how much he'd just had to fork out, the price of a couple of video rentals at least.

One other thing about TV, you waited around long enough and you got to see just about any film you wanted. And since his retirement, Cole had seen plenty of films on TV, plenty of other stuff too, sitting around with nothing much else happening, nowhere else to go.

For a time, Cole had wandered along to the cop pubs and been greeted like he was still in the job, still spoke in the same tongue. But after a couple of months, it was like the word was out that he had in fact retired and had no place at the bar with the true cops, and the drinks had stopped appearing, the invites to celebrations folded and slipped back into pockets.

Cole had persevered, conned himself that it was an age thing, but after a couple of nights when he had sat on the fringes of a group of detectives and listened in wonder to the hard conversations, puzzled over the boundaries of copper and villain that appeared to have shifted seismically in the short time since his retirement, he had held his head high and walked away from the job for the last time.

The adverts seemed to go on forever, and the feature rolled around with Cole still in the toilet and he had to struggle past a couple of teens with buckets of popcorn on their laps to get back to his seat as the titles snapped across the screen in violent neon.

He had seen *NYPD Blue* enough times to follow the jagged camerawork, but the opening scenes of the film seemed to have been shot from a camera strapped to the tail of a dog as it chased another dog down the street, weaving in and out of pedestrian legs and passing traffic. A couple of cops chasing a kid down the street, green banknotes flapping from the pockets of his jacket.

And the music, like there was also a tin can tied to the dog's tail.

Cole eased back into his seat to watch the film, but after fifteen minutes he had the sense that he had seen it all before. Not the film itself, but behind all the flashing lights and modern music there was something cheap and familiar about the whole thing. A couple of times Cole recognised pieces from other movies, TV shows – a car chase, the spin of a gun, the manner in which someone would hitch off an overcoat as he entered a room expecting one of his sidekicks to catch it – and he would smile at the memories that surrounded the originals, solid images pinned down in time.

The film rattled along to a fast soundtrack more like a pop video or a cartoon and Cole soon tired of it, started to amuse himself between scenes that featured Stamp in building a list of stolen goods – films and TV shows the film had lifted from: *Bullitt*, *The Sweeney*, *Callan*, something with Michael Caine in it (*Get Carter* or *Mona Lisa*, perhaps both), *GoodFellas*. The list seemed to be endless and Cole soon tired of that as well, shuffled in his seat to ease the numbness in the back of his legs.

Stamp had the part of some kind of drug baron and club owner, not a large part, a few lines at most, but the role gave him a rogueish charm that he had not had in real life. And to its credit, the film did not make too much of Stamp's appearance, although Cole picked up on what he took to be a couple of references to the killing of the Italian baker. In one scene, one of the barmen in Stamp's club had been shot in the shoulder when he had been caught in bed with the wife of one of the club's regulars. The shot had left him with a comic deafness in one ear and later in the film, each time Stamp spoke to him he would have to cup his hand around the ear and lean in towards Stamp's unsmiling face, a look of pain stretched across his features. In a second scene, Stamp had concluded a meeting in his office by pushing himself back from his desk, rubbing his hand over his stomach and announcing, 'Any of you guys hungry? I could murder a pizza.' Balloons of laughter had burst throughout the cinema at that one, loud and insistent.

From the reactions that the audience gave Stamp it was clear that he was held in high regard, a hero for our times, a man who had fought the law and won.

But less than an hour into the film Cole had seen enough and he pushed along the row of seats and left the cinema with knots of frustration burning in his stomach. He bought a pack of cigarettes and stood in the lobby smoking and staring out at the fat drops of rain that fell from the canvas awning onto the cracked pavement beneath.

On the wall facing the ticket booth, a glass-fronted frame held copies of reviews of the films running at the cinema and Cole squinted through the reflections from the overhead lights on the glass to find if the acceptance of Stamp as cult figure held credence across the spectrum of magazines and newspapers.

Before he could read the first of the reviews, Cole felt his gaze pull to the right and focus on a photograph of Stamp and a woman in her late-thirties. There was something about the serious set of the woman's mouth, the look of steel determination in her face that triggered memories, memories that spun just out of his reach, on the tip of his mind.

Cole took a step to the side and stood in front of the photograph, stared through the glass.

After a couple of moments, time began to crumble and fall from the photograph and Cole found himself looking at a thirteen-year-old girl in pink National Health glasses, her dark brown hair pulled back into pigtails tied with ribbons. Her name was Molly Robinson and she was the daughter of one of Cole's fellow CID officers at Kentish Town station. She had been a serious child that would tell her father off for attempting to lure her from her studies – telling her to rest a little, take a break and have some fun.

The woman had her hand in Stamp's and looked at him with a combination of love and admiration. Cole lifted his hand and ran his finger along the caption at the bottom of the photograph: '... and his new wife Molly ...'

Cole closed his eyes and squeezed the lids tight, shook his head. No, this is not possible, he told himself, this is not happening. She had been such a serious girl, held no interest in her father's job whatsoever. Walked out of the room when he told lurid and humorous stories from the station. Cole stared at the photograph once more, touched the glass with his fingers and searched for the flaw that would expose the photograph for the hoax that it must have been.

* * *

The house looked tired and worn, a number of tiles had fallen from the roof like broken teeth and a pane of glass on the first floor had been cracked and repaired with cardboard and Sellotape, the cardboard darkening in the dampness. Cole blinked and for a moment he saw a drunk being carried home between a couple of sober colleagues, makeshift repairs holding his spectacles together. He blinked again and the house reappeared.

Cole pushed open the gate and walked the length of the path to the door, rapped on the door with the back of his hand. He turned and looked off down the street. A couple of kids in school uniform pulling on bottles of alcopops stood and stared back at him, an old man in a suit, feral contempt in their faces.

'Jim?'

Cole turned to see the door open a fraction and Megan Robinson's face poked through the gap, her hands gripped on the doorframe. A puzzled smile ghosted across her face.

Cole reached out his hands. 'Megan, is that you? How're you doin'? It's good to see you.'

Megan frowned. 'I thought it was you,' she said, and headed back into the house.

Cole shrugged and followed her, shut the door behind him. She led him into the kitchen and asked if he wanted a cup of tea by waving the kettle at him. He nodded and took a seat at the table.

'What brings you around here?' said Megan. 'Haven't seen you in a while.'

'No,' said Cole, and felt the heat of embarrassment rise in his face. Bill Robinson had been his best friend and back when he and Bill were still on the force, Cole and his wife had been regular visitors to the Robinson house. The four of them had even taken a couple of holidays together, weekends in Brighton and Southend. He couldn't remember the last time he had seen Megan.

'Retirement treating you okay?' Megan lifted mugs from a cupboard and set them on the counter, dropped a spoon into one of the mugs.

Cole shrugged, smiled. 'It's kind of difficult having nothin' to do all day, you know.'

'That's what Bill said. Not that he had much time to be bored, no time to do nothing.' Bill Robinson had died from a heart attack three months after retiring from the force after twenty-five years.

'No, that must've been hard...' said Cole, the words fading on his breath. He had started to feel uncomfortable, had the feeling that he had caught Megan in a combative mood and wanted to be out of there as soon as possible. 'How's Molly?' he said. 'Married yet, or is she still too busy with her studies?'

Megan turned and glared at him. 'Is that supposed to be funny or something?'

Cole leaned back in his seat, faked shock. 'What? What'd I say?'

'You don't *know*?'

'Know what?' said Cole, still holding the shock mask up to his face – this was more difficult than it looked.

Megan took a step closer, pulled a seat from the table and sat down. She offered Cole a cigarette and lit one for herself. 'Molly.

My daughter, our daughter. You don't know that she married Frankie Stamp?'

Cole paused, leaned into the table. 'Frankie Stamp? *The* Frankie Stamp?'

'I hope to God there's not another Frankie Stamp,' said Megan.

Cole pushed his glasses back up his nose and looked out through the window at the shaded clouds that trudged across the sky, back at Megan. He could see the dark reflection of the clouds at the back of her eyes. 'I had no idea,' he said. 'What happened?'

'I don't know, don't know for sure. It was while she was at college, right after Bill died. She was always really close to him and I think his death hit her hard, particularly as she was away from home at the time. In the middle of her exams.' Megan shook her head, took a pull on the cigarette, rolled the tip on the edge of a saucer in the centre of the table.

'And Stamp – how did he fit into all this?' Cole had forgotten about acting shocked, he needed to hear what had happened.

'Bill used to tell Molly that Stamp had been the only one that got away, the only one smart enough to keep out of his reach. I think she began to think of him as some kind of... oh, I don't know, some kind of romantic hero, I suppose. She began to write to him in prison – letters, postcards – and after a month or so, he started to write back, asking her for a photograph or a lock of hair or something, stuff like that. Soon enough, he just kind of took over. She had always loved her father and here was a man that had beaten him, escaped him. A man that could fill the space he'd left behind. And once he came out...' Her voice faded and fell away.

Cole tapped the tip of his cigarette in saucer, listened to the sound of his own breath in the stillness of the kitchen, the rising call of the kettle.

'We had a blazing row,' said Megan after a couple of minutes.

Cole glanced at her, at the far-off look on her face and realised at once that he had fallen out of the loop, that Megan had transferred the conversation to the quiet of her head, triggered memories.

'I told her, I don't want to see no kids with the blood of a murderer in their hearts...' A thin tremor in her voice made her seem scared and vulnerable, made Cole want to escape. It was the part of the job he had hated the most, talking to bereaved relatives and watching the pain and anger and frustration break on their faces.

'You know where she lives now?'

'… in the papers, I don't recognise her…'

Cole reached across the table and touched her on the arm. 'Megan?' he said. 'Megan, you have her address?'

Megan fell back in her seat a little and shook the bitter stare from her face, narrowed her eyes at him. 'Sorry, Joe. Address?'

'You have Molly's address?' said Cole, irritation lapping at the edge of his voice.

*   *   *

Cole left the car in a residents parking space off the High Street and walked back to the front of the red brick building. He stopped and leaned on the railing that ran the length of the parade of shops and scanned the dull facade, the colours of the painted baker's sign on the brick faded through time and the choke of traffic. The late afternoon shadow of a streetlight ran from the lower left hand corner of the building to the top right like a private sundial.

The baker's had closed down soon after the murder of the Italian, soon after its short tenure as the most notorious location in London when children would act out the murder in front of the store, and an estate agent's now occupied the space. Polaroids of brick shapes floated behind thick glass windows and rippled on the breeze each time the door opened.

Cole stuffed his hands deep into his pockets and walked to the end of the parade and turned down the narrow path that led to the cinder road at the back of the shops. He counted the buildings as he walked to the back of the estate agent's, but in his heart he understood that there was little chance that he would not recognise the garage.

Constructed of brick and corrugated iron and tilted to the side with time, the garage looked like the tip of a taller building that had fallen into the ground. The windows on either side were filmed with grease and dust and the wooden door had twisted from the jamb with the tilt.

Cole stepped through the trash at the side of the garage and raised himself on to the tips of his boots and peered in through the dirt-stained glass. The concrete floor of the garage was almost clear, just a few rusted cans of paint in one corner and a stack of yellowed newspapers bundled together with string under the opposite window. Thin beams of light broke through the rotted wood and speared the darkness.

Cole walked to the front of the garage and hefted the rusted padlock in his hand, pulling a couple of the screws that held the hasp to the door loose. He pulled again and the hasp fell into his hand and he dropped it to the floor, kicked it to one side. He glanced up and down the cinder road, pushed his fingers into the gap between the doors and tugged. The door opened a fraction and then jammed against a packed wedge of dirt. Cole kicked at the dirt with his foot and pulled the door back another foot or so, the dried hinges tearing the still air.

Cole stood and looked into the garage for a moment, the chill of remembrance a second skin. He blinked and the blurred after-image of the Italian on the concrete floor ghosted across his retinas, faded in a whorl of red and black and disappeared once more.

He pushed the door closed and turned and walked back to his car.

*　　*　　*

Cole took a detour past his house to pick up a couple of things and then headed out to the address that Megan Robinson had handed to him on a page torn from a battered address book beside the telephone. He didn't have the heart to ask her if she had the address written down somewhere else, if she had just handed over the sole point of contact with her daughter.

It had started to rain on the half-hour drive and as he pulled up to the kerb a curtain of rain sparkled around the house and garden in sodium spectrum colours.

Cole climbed out of the car and pulled the collar of his raincoat up around his neck, pushed open the iron gate and highstepped across the puddles and up to the front door. He checked his watch and then rapped on the door with the side of his fist, stepped into the shadows at the side of the house.

A light went on in the hall and the door eased open a little and a slice of light fell onto the stone path. The scratch of an old man's breath, and then Cole heard the door open another fraction and the sound of cord trouser legs rub across one another. 'What's that?' came a harsh voice. 'Who's out there?'

Stamp: his thin shadow stretched the length of the path, faded and blurred around the head and shoulders.

Fuelled with a burst of adrenaline, Cole jumped in front of the door and reached out and took hold of Stamp's shirt in his fist, pulled and jerked the old man across the threshold of the house. Taken in surprise, Stamp twisted and fell onto the path and landed on his hip with a loud thud, splintered nerves shooting the length of his limbs in an unconscious attempt to dissipate the pain.

Cole rolled Stamp onto his back and pulled the gun from the pocket of his raincoat, stuck the tip of the barrel into the tight skin across the old man's forehead. Stamp knotted his face and blinked at the raindrops that bloated his tears and rippled across his hot face.

'Get up,' said Cole. 'C'mon, let's get out of here. There's someplace I need you to see.'

* * *

'You kept the gun,' said Stamp, the tone of his voice flat and hard. His face was hidden in shade, flickering streetlights painting all but the deep folds in his skin a bright white at random intervals.

'An old cop needs a little insurance,' said Cole, and pushed the gun a little harder into Stamp's temple.

'I thought you must've pitched it in the river by now. You sure that's the same gun? It looks like the same gun.' Stamp started to turn his head. 'Here, let me take a look.'

Cole jabbed at his temple with the gun once more. 'Look where you're going,' he said, and glanced out of the windscreen, then back at Stamp. 'And keep your hands on the wheel.'

Stamp drove in silence for a couple of minutes, took a right without prompt.

'Sure it's the same gun,' said Cole. 'What, you thought it had disappeared for real?'

Stamp shrugged. 'I'd've thought that you'd've had more to lose than me in keeping it,' he said. 'Holding on to it.'

'You reckon?' said Cole. 'That what you think? Even now, even now you're some kind of *movie star*?'

Stamp smiled, the dull sheen of his teeth breaking from the

dark face. 'You see the movie, huh? What'd you think, you like it?'

Cole said nothing, stared past Stamp and out through the kaleidoscope patterns of rain on the glass.

'That bad, huh?' said Stamp. He checked the rearview, then cut across the oncoming traffic and turned into the High Street. He caught sight of the parade of shops up ahead and felt the pressure of the gun ease off a little on his temple.

* * *

Cole had left the door open on his first trip to the garage that afternoon and he pushed Stamp through the door into the darkness, the fall of light from a high window the sole illumination on the scene. Pale shadows echoed the movements of the two men in the garage.

Cole lit a cigarette and then held the lighter out in front of him, the gun in his other hand pointed at Stamp bunched on the floor. He flicked the gun in the direction of the piles of newspaper. 'Pull up a seat.'

Stamp looked at Cole with a mask of bored contempt on his face. He felt no fear for fear had never been a part of his life, and he had tired of Cole and his foolish game. As far as he was concerned, his connection to the garage had ended a long time back. He shook his head and pulled the short stack of papers across the concrete floor and climbed and sat on top of them, rested his arms on his knees and let his hands hang loose.

'You recognise this place?'

Stamp angled his face around the corners of the garage, precise. 'What do you want, Cole?'

Cole took a step closer. 'That smell,' he said, and took a deep breath through his nose. 'The smell of forgotten time, don't you think? Lost time.'

'All I smell is dampness,' said Stamp. 'Dampness and some kind of rodent shit.' He hiked his shoulders, crossed his arms and gripped opposite biceps with his hands. 'And it's getting cold,' he said.

'Don't worry, this won't take long,' said Cole. 'You'll soon be out of here.'

Stamp looked up at Cole, crinkled his eyes in question.

'You remember this place? This is where it all started, your movie career?' said Cole. 'A film star, you're a film star because people think you killed someone. Funny, huh? Killed someone and dumped them in this room, this garage. You remember?'

'Is that what this is about, huh?' Stamp leaned forward on the stack of newspapers. 'You jealous, Cole? You jealous of that fact?'

Cole felt his grip on the pistol tighten, the snap of the muscles in his jaw attempt to pull out a grin on his face.

'You think that if the public knew the truth then it'd be you up on that screen? That it'd be you getting your crack licked by tuppenny celebrities?' Stamp sneered, rubbed at his forehead with the tips of his fingers. 'What's the problem here, Cole? You don't think we paid you enough the first time around, you think you were cheated?'

Cole snapped the lighter closed in his fist, and then jumped forwards and rammed the gun into Stamp's mouth, rode the momentum until Stamp cracked his head on the floor. The gun fell loose and Cole scrambled to pick it up, then rammed it back into Stamp's mouth, cracked teeth. 'Some kind of fuckin' movie star,' screamed Cole, tight bursts of chill breath breaking on his tongue. 'Some kind of fuckin' movie star. Eat lead, movie star.'

★　★　★

Cole pushed the tip of another slice of pizza into his mouth, took a sip of beer. He frowned and looked at the man in the seat across from him at the canteen table.

The director sighed and looked back at Cole. 'I'm still not sure about 'Eat lead', Jim. It's such a movie cliché, a gangster cliché. Something out of the forties or fifties, Bogart and Edward G Robinson, like that. I think we should avoid clichés.'

'People talk in clichés all the time,' said Cole.

'The movie star bit's okay. I'm fine with that, that's great. It's just the "Eat lead" part.'

'But I was there, remember? I know what I said,' said Cole, and his lips parted but the cast of his mouth refused to hold a smile.

Going Through a Phase

Robert Barnard

'Where did I go wrong?' wailed Cynthia Corey to her friend and nominal boss Mary Haycroft, during a quiet spell in the afternoon at the flower shop.

'I'm sure you didn't go wrong at all,' said Mary in her common-sense voice. 'It's just a phase she's going through.'

Cynthia could read her friend's face: the first sentence was totally sincere, but the second was a placebo she had no faith in. Mary had not seen much of Deborah these last few months, but she had seen enough.

Deborah had been such a gorgeous, heart-warming child. The split with Charles – Charles walking out on her to go and live with his new woman, to put the matter more precisely – never seemed to affect her as it had for a time her elder brother: many of her five-year-old classmates at school were in a similar situation, and she loved going to stay with her father and Tina. The settlement and maintenance agreed by their lawyers had been generous, so Cynthia's part-time job in the flower shop had been no more than icing on the cake. Neither Cynthia nor the children wanted for anything. Deborah had been to an excellent private school, had had riding lessons, been to ballet classes, had all the 'in' clothes bought for her when they came in, and replaced when they went out.

But it was the memory of Deborah's earliest years that really ripped Cynthia apart: her joy at her first sight of the sea, her endless games with Jingle when he was a puppy, perhaps above all the picture on her face when she had just demolished a slice of her mother's special chocolate cream gateau – the little rosebud face, smeared all over brown, looking up at her with angelic satisfaction and saying: 'I enjoyed that, Mummy.'

Nowadays she'd be happy to get any sort of look that wasn't instinct with scorn or loathing.

'If only you could get her away from that Jed,' Mary said.

'Jed!' Cynthia spat out. 'What sort of name is that? What's the betting he was christened Thomas or Matthew or Timothy? If he was christened at all.'

Except that Jed never gave the impression of coming from the sort of world where babies were christened Thomas or Timothy. He did not seem to come from any sort of world that Cynthia could acknowledge as related to her own. Deborah was recognisably a refugee from a sane world of jobs and houses with garages and sit-down meals – she was an outsider taking on new rules and styles even as she rejected her old ones. Jed was a native of her new country: ensconced, at home, the genuine product. And quite uniquely horrible.

She remembered Jed's first eruption into her life. It was last summer, when Deborah was only fifteen. Cynthia had begun to worry about her absences from home, her rudeness, her use of make-up (make-up! how long ago it seemed when make-up was all she had to worry about!). Then one Saturday afternoon, as she was cooking in the kitchen, a motor-cycle had come to a squealing halt outside the gate, and two black-geared figures had got off. As the pillion passenger approached down the drive, removing its helmet, she realized with horror that it was Deborah. When the pair banged through the kitchen door she had swallowed, suppressed her rage, and said:

'Aren't you going to introduce me, Debbie?'

Jed had looked at her, ignored her outstretched hand, then turned to Deborah.

'Isn't there anyfink to eat in this dump?'

'I'm making a chocolate gateau. It's Debbie's fav —'

'Got any 'amburgers in the freezer? OK – wiv plenty of onions an' termater sauce.'

It was an order to Cynthia. Deborah sat on the kitchen table and looked at her. Cynthia just said brightly: 'I'll leave you to cater to your friend's wants' and went through to the lounge. Later she washed up the charred frying pan with bits of burnt onion in it. She'd never set her mind to teaching Deborah to cook. Perhaps that's how he likes them, she thought.

Later when she'd heard his name all too often from Deborah she had got down a dictionary of first names from the bookshelves, bought when Nicholas her son was born, and only pored over once since then, when a name was needed for Deborah. 'Jed,' it said:

'Pet form of Jedidiah.' And under 'Jedidiah' it said 'Hebrew: 'friend (beloved) of the Lord.'

'The Lord has a funny taste in friends,' thought Cynthia.

Since then her encounters with Jed had been infrequent but memorable. The most recent had been a fortnight before. She had been upstairs, and had heard the back door being thrown open. Everything the pair did was a demonstration. She had been changing her clothes at the time, and by the time she was ready to go downstairs the dreadful pair had been ensconced in the lounge: Jed's black boots were on the coffee table and his dirty leather gear was soiling the easy chair he sat in. Pop music was blaring from the television set. He began flicking the zapper, an expression of incredulity on his podgy face.

'On'y five —ing channels. You'd fink you wez in the —ing nineteenth century in this —ing 'ouse.'

His vocabulary embraced words that Cynthia had only heard on late-night television, when flicking through channels. Mostly, however, he confined himself to the one obscenity. It was one that made Cynthia wish he'd soften it to 'bloody'. Her heart was in her mouth, but she was determined not to show fear. She crossed the room, seized the remote control from him and cancelled out the din. With a crunch of boots on wood Jed raised himself in his chair, grabbed the zapper back with unnecessary violence, then turned the television back on.

'Tell this old slag to get me somefink to eat. And tell her to give you some —ing cookery lessons, 'coz at the moment you're —ing 'opeless.'

Cynthia had turned, left the room, and then left the house. Though she was not due at the flower shop for another hour, she had gone straight there and poured out her heart to Mary Haycroft in the intervals of customers coming in and out. Then she had spent half an hour in an increasingly desperate phone call to the police. They were much too canny and overstretched in resources to get caught up in a 'domestic'. In fact they clearly resented being treated as social workers. They advised her to get the family involved, if talking the situation over with her daughter had failed ('It never even began,' wailed Cynthia). Surely the girl's father could help? Or was she close to her brother? If not, was there another relative she could be sent away to for a time?

'You mean I should inflict *that* on my mother?' asked Cynthia satirically. In the end the policeman had an urgent call on another line, refused Cynthia's request to find out if Jed had a criminal record, and rang off.

That was the most recent of Cynthia's few encounters with Jed. Mostly she had just watched as Jed's influence on Deborah became more and more complete. There had been the facial studs and ring which disfigured the rosebud face and both disgusted and somehow frightened her: that *her daughter* could mutilate herself in this way! Then there was the crazy dyed and lacquered hair, the filthy cheap clothing that was somehow a uniform, the sinister smell that Cynthia was sure betokened drug-taking.

On her sixteenth birthday Deborah announced that she would no longer be attending school, and that there was nothing her mother could do about it. When Cynthia rang the Queen Elfrida School the headmistress confirmed that there was nothing she could do. She seemed to be having difficulty keeping the joy and relief out of her voice at the news.

Not long after this she caught a glimpse of Debbie in the bathroom preparing to have a shower: there was a livid bruise on her shoulder. A week after Cynthia's phone call to the police she had injuries that she could not conceal: her left eye was purple and her cheek disfigured by a livid bruise.

'We got into a fight with some other bikers in Aylesbury,' she said, shrugging. 'It's nothing.'

Cynthia's blood froze. She foresaw a horrible end for her daughter in a gang bust-up of bikers. On reflection later she decided she didn't believe in the fight. She put the bruises down to Jed.

The only thing she could think of to do was to follow the advice of the policeman she had talked to: call in the family. She ruled out her mother entirely – too old, too out-of-touch, too easily distressed. That left Charles and Debbie's brother Nicholas. The latter, after early upsets and problems at the time of the divorce, had become ultra-conventional, and was now something in the City that Cynthia did not understand, though it seemed to bring in unimaginable sums of money.

'If Deborah thinks she's an adult at sixteen,' he pronounced, in a voice already scented with pomposity, 'what you should do is treat her as one.'

'What do you mean exactly?' asked Cynthia.

'Tell her she only lives in your house on your terms. Tell her what your rules are, and that the moment she breaks them you will have the locks changed – or, better still, get bolts. Say she has to be in by half past ten, or she's locked out for the night. If she's not in school and hasn't got a job, she should take her share in the housework. And the cooking.'

'Oh, not the cooking!'

'You'd be suffering in a good cause. She's treating your house like a low-class hotel. Show her it can't go on.'

'She'd never accept it. It would be the equivalent of throwing her out of her own house.'

'Well, if that's what it takes. It's your house, not hers, and she might as well be in a doss-house. Throwing her out could be the means of bringing her to her senses.'

That remark did put the suggestion in a more positive light, and Cynthia did think over the proposal for several days. In the end she had to face the fact that she would be condemning her own daughter to a life on the streets, one of those pathetic creatures who held out their hands to passers-by. She couldn't do it.

That left Charles. She was very reluctant to ring him, because it would be obvious at once that what they were talking about was failure: her failure with her daughter. Oddly enough though, the moment she heard his voice she felt comforted. And as they talked she found she liked his suggestion.

'I tell you what, I'll ring her up and invite her over. It's months since she came to see us, and she's always enjoyed coming. I can't give you advice sight unseen. Of course heaven knows if I'll have any to give once I *have* seen the problem. I expect Mary is right: it's a phase that will pass.'

His tone was different after Deborah had visited him. Cynthia was surprised that she went at all, but came to the conclusion she was playing off one parent against the other. Charles rang her the next day at the shop, for safety's sake. His tone was aghast.

'My God – it was like meeting a horrible stranger. It was the visit from Hell. She told Tina to f— off, get stuffed – you name it, she said it. Tina sends her sympathy, by the way.'

'Thank Tina from me,' said Cynthia coolly. 'The question is, what are we to do?'

Charles was silent for a moment, perhaps nonplussed by that 'we'.

'I think you're right that she's made herself over to him. I could see and hear all the time she has some other being – *manifesting* itself through her.'

'Jed.'

'Yes, Jed. The answer seems to be: you've got to strike at Jed.'

Cynthia was uncertain what he meant.

'Do you mean somehow discredit him in her eyes?'

'Is that possible?'

'No. Not at the moment.'

'That wasn't what I meant anyway. I thought of something more physical.'

'I'm not a lady wrestler, Charles.'

'No, but there are people for hire. People who would duff him up good and proper, if you'll pardon the cockney, and make it clear in the process why they're doing it, and that he's got to keep away.'

Cynthia considered.

'It would be using his own horrible methods against him.'

'Exactly.'

There was something ruthless about Charles that had not appealed to her before, but did now.

'I don't suppose they advertise in the Yellow Pages...'

'I wouldn't be so sure. Why don't you ask Nicholas?'

'Nicholas? But he's so respectable!'

'Exactly. He works in a top bank. There'd have to be someone there who knows all about security. And he works with very rich men, people who pay to have themselves properly protected.'

'But wouldn't we want ... something a bit more ... dodgy?'

'The rich men would know all about that too. I bet Nick does himself already, though he might pretend he has to consult. "Respectable" these days is different to what it was fifty years ago when we were young, Cynthia.'

'Thirty years ago.'

'Would you like me to give him a call?'

'Oh, *would* you?'

The next evening he called her back.

'Nicholas says try Spires Protection Services in Oxford. He

says they'll do anything short of contract killings.'

'Oh Charles, you know I wouldn't —'

'Short of, I said. You want a thorough job done, otherwise it won't be worth doing at all.'

That was true. But Cynthia felt very troubled – of course she did. She had lived her life wholly within the law – had once been approached to become a magistrate. Now there had entered her life an element that was ... well, her word 'dodgy' didn't begin to cover it. This was something heinous.

It was also something she could not confide in Mary. That worried her very much, symbolising what she was sliding into. In the end, though, something was bound to spark a determination to act. In this case it was three nights in a row in which Deborah did not come home. After the third, with tell-tale signs of a fight on her daughter's face and shoulders, she told her that if it happened again she would get new locks and bolts fitted on the doors and would summon the police if they made any disturbance. Then she shut herself in what had once been Charles's study and rang Spires Protection Service, and accepted their suggestion of an appointment two days later.

The voice on the phone was quiet and smooth, the premises of the company, just off the High, almost ecclesiastical. The manager's office, into which she was shown, was as clean and anonymous as a bank manager's. It did not occur to her that if this was as respectable an organisation as its image tried to suggest, the manager would be advising her of alternative courses of action, warning her that removing one person would not necessarily stop her daughter mixing in the sort of circles she was obviously attracted to.

Instead Mr Purley nodded as she told him the problem, described Jed, gave vivid details of the transformation in her daughter's behaviour.

'It's as if she's been taken over,' she concluded. He did not suggest that perhaps she had been a willing accomplice in the process.

'He needs to be ... warned off, then ... in a fairly ... direct way,' said the quiet, almost self effacing, man.

'That's what I had in mind,' admitted Cynthia.

'And recently your daughter has been coming home at night?'

'The last two. I don't know how long it will last.'

'Then speed is of the essence, as I'm sure you'd agree. What time would you expect him to bring her back?'

'Any time between half past ten and two.'

'And the neighbourhood?'

'Residential. Mostly elderly people, early to bed. And the school round the corner occupies most of the block, with a row of quite nice shops opposite. Quite busy in the daytime, but very quiet at night.'

'Fairly promising then. In any case this young man is, by your evidence, the type likely to find himself in confrontational situations. We would need a van, to load his bike on to – just in case he is in no condition to ride off himself. Would he ride off before your daughter was safely in the house?'

'No – certainly not at the moment. He waits to see she's not been locked out.'

'Ideal. We wouldn't want her to see what happens. Now – two men, a van, maybe a bike for the other chap, to simulate driving away for your daughter's benefit... I think it could be done for fifteen hundred.'

The sum took Cynthia's breath away, but after a second she nodded. Mr. Purley suggested that same night, and he saw her out rather as if they had just arranged a small temporary overdraft.

When she got home Debbie of course was out. The time of waiting was almost unbearable. Anticipation, a mixture of dread and excitement, fought in her mind with conscientious scruple: if it came to the point, how could she justify in court condoning – inciting, in fact – a criminal act? Everything that was happening was so out of her normal sphere. Twilight was about eight-thirty, and once it was dark Cynthia lurked restlessly around in the darkened upstairs of the house looking for signs of the men she had hired. She made a cup of tea, and when she went back upstairs she saw an unobtrusive white van parked on the side-road, outside the school. Going to the front of the house she saw a motorbike arrive, ridden by a looming black shape. Soon there were two such shapes – oblong and right-angled, hideously substantial, and stationed under an overhanging laburnum tree four doors down on the other side of the road. Suddenly Cynthia's tea no longer seemed refreshing.

She had nearly an hour and a half's wait. The tension inside her screwed up to an almost unbearable tightness. Then, close to eleven-thirty, she heard a powerful motorbike in the distance. Overcome by some irresistible impulse she darted downstairs, into the kitchen, out of the back door and round to the side. She heard farewells in the street, the click of the gate, then the front door banging with Deborah's usual obtrusive lack of consideration. She forgot that a forceful shutting of the front door often caused the back door to swing open if it was unlocked.

A motorbike started up. Surely he wasn't going to be allowed to get away. No – Mr Purley had said ....Yes, and there was Jed still on his bike, adjusting his helmet. As she watched another bike loomed out of the darkness and drew up beside him. Then a second shape came from across the road. In a second Jed's helmet was grabbed from him, he was hauled off his bike, and then on to the pavement, shouting and struggling. Cynthia, her heart beating fast with excitement, crept forward, keeping out of the pool of brightness dropped by the street light. She heard muffled cries, then through the iron railings saw the man on the ground being violently kicked, first on the legs and body, then in the unprotected head and face. Then she saw the larger of the two shapes pull him up, throw him backwards across his own bike, and shout in his bleeding ear.

'You never come back here again, do you understand? And you never have anything to do with that girl again. Got it?'

Cynthia thought there was a nod. Then they started again, banging his head against his bike, throwing him to the ground and weighing in with their heavy boots.

Suddenly Cynthia was conscious of a shape beside her. Horrified she saw it was Debbie.

'The back door was open,' she said. 'I wondered where you were.'

For a moment she sounded like the old Debbie. Cynthia turned and looked at her. The rosebud face, or some dim remnant of it, was still there, but there was a sharp gleam in her eyes. The vicious kicking was still going on. For a moment the larger shape straightened up, and in a pale shaft of street lighting Cynthia saw a square, brutal, sensuous-looking face looking at her daughter. Then he took one last kick, and the two men began to drag the unconscious body round to the van. They heard a bump as he was thrown in. Then the bigger man came back to fetch Jed's motorbike. Again he looked in Deborah's direction. This time a definite spark passed between their eyes, and the edges of his mouth turned up cruelly.

'I enjoyed that, Mummy,' said Deborah.

Brand New Boyfriend

Carol Anne Davis

'Isn't he the cutest?' Jen exclaims.

Anita nods and kneels on the carpet, hoping that the shivering little Yorkie will approach her.

'That's not a dog – it's a hamster,' a male voice says.

Anita looks up at the man and feels the giggles start from somewhere behind her ribs, an infrequent feeling. He has no hair in the centre of his head so she giggles some more. Then she pulls up her knee length socks above her skirt hem in the hope that he'll think she's wearing heavy white tights, and tries to put on her most sophisticated face.

'Dad – this is Anita,' Jen says, not looking at either of them.

'So, you in First Year too?' he asks, walking across the room and sitting in one of the huge beige chairs.

Anita swivels around to keep facing him: 'Uh huh. Same class as Jen.'

Jen's dad nods, then reaches down to his far side and brings up an unopened can of lager. 'Used to have a budgie that drank this stuff, didn't we, Jen?' he says.

Jen nods, and picks the tiny grey terrier up. It hides its face between her large blouse-held breasts and whimpers.

'What happened to it?' Anita asks.

'Had to join Alcoholics Anonymous,' he snorts, then winks and toasts her with his beer can. She laughs at the image and because he's being so sweet.

'We gave it to Aunty Marge. It was really Billy's bird but he wasn't looking after it,' Jen says, then kisses the little dog's head.

Anita hasn't seen Jen's big brother Billy yet. She knows that he's seventeen, that he already has a girlfriend who he goes to bed with. Still…

No one speaks. When it's silent at home Mum usually says 'Guess what Anita did?' and Dad raises his fist.

'Is Billy getting to keep Duke?' she asks quickly, mind searching for a new list of topics.

Jen looks over at her Dad and her lips turn downward. He pulls his mouth into a grimace which narrows his eyes. 'Hell, what's one more mouth to feed with your mother the size she is, eh?' Anita uses her hand to smother an astonished guilty laugh. Jen jumps up, a sudden spreading yellow stain on her blouse proof that the puppy needs walking. 'Treat yourselves to an ice cream, love,' he adds.

The heavy coins clink in Anita's school pinafore pocket as they walk to the park.

'Ice-cream my arse. If Billy was here he'd get us cider,' Jen mutters. Her normally low voice lightens as the road fills with tune-chimes, 'Here's the van. We can buy a few fags instead.'

Fags aren't just cigarettes. They are also male homosexuals. Anita sits with the dictionary in her bedroom that Saturday trying to find hand-job and blow-job and sixty-niner and diddy-ride. Gayle, who gets to go to discos all the time and has a clothing allowance says that she's done all four with various boys.

'You given anyone a diddy-ride, yet, Nitwit?'

'Her? She's a titless wonder. The guy's cock would just fall right through.'

And they're right, they're right. There's still nothing to put in the pink first bra that Gran bought Anita for her birthday. Curiously, she turns the dictionary pages to B. No boy has ever unbuttoned her blouse in the way that they do on TV movies, far less asked for a blow-job or anything else. *'An act of fellatio'* the definition says. Poised on the edge of some new discovery, she looks up *'fellatio'* and finds that it's *'oral stimulation of the male genitalia.'* And when she flicks on to find *oral* it says that it's *'relating to the mouth.'*

A pair of lips and those slug-like shapes that boy toddlers urinate through at the side of the road: she can't quite see the connection. And the woman with the grey hair is on duty again when she walks into the library that afternoon. 'You're only thirteen – you can't take that out,' she'd said last month as Anita handed over *'Make It Happy'* from the adult section. Everyone in the queue behind her had stared and stared.

Now Anita puts her head down and hurries past the desk towards Teenage Books then sneaks slowly round to the adult fiction section, and flicks through novel after novel until she comes to the bits where men and women go to bed.

Billy goes to bed with his girlfriend. He uses Mr and Mrs Wearsley's King Size bed. He gives Jen cans of Guinness and lager to buy her silence. Jen shares the bitter liquid with Anita, and they listen, breathless, at the bedroom door.

'What if your parents come back unexpectedly?' Anita whispers.

'They never do. Dad's shift's till ten. Mum works till six then usually goes on for a drink.' She takes a bigger slug from the long can, 'Even if they did come home, they're hardly ever in there. Mum falls asleep in the recliner half the time and Dad kips on the settee.'

Anita listens and listens, long after Jen has walked away to turn egg whites into two toning facemasks. But all she hears is the mattress's rhythmic squeak. And after the lovers come out she sits in the lounge and stares at Karen, and wishes that she could take her place in the big warm bed. It must be brilliant, having a boyfriend who thinks that you're pretty, having a second home where you can stay and stay and stay.

'Want me to make you two up?' Karen asks.

The homemade facemasks forgotten, they watch each other being transformed into regular robo-babes. Anita stares at her friend then looks at herself in the mirror. A strange new confident expression stares back. Billy pops his head around the door and wolfwhistles loudly. Anita takes the lip gloss from the dressing table and strokes it over her lower lip again.

Then she looks at the pink cotton skirt and teddybear embroidered blouse that Mum makes her wear ('You young girls all look so drab these days') and hates the garments with a new hot intensity. Even Jen, who has to buy her clothes from the outsize shop, has high-heeled suede shoes, a matching waistcoat and a button-through denim dress.

Jen's also replaced socks with tights in Smoke Grey, Fudge Brown, Just Sable and Barely Black, but obviously they're much too big for Anita. Maybe when Mum sees how grown up she's looking with her make-up she'll understand...

But Dad's the only one at home when she gets back.

'Where's Mum?'

He looks up from the TV. 'Not around to do your fetching and carrying.' His eyes narrow, 'What's that muck on your face?'

'Blusher, lipstick and eyeshadow. Billy's girlfriend put it on for me.' She tries to meet his gaze, to negotiate reasonably for what she wants like they tell you to do in *Misty* magazine.

'Well take it off now.' His eyes and voice are full of contempt and a barely contained known hatred, 'It makes you look like a tart.'

The next weekend Mum wins ten pounds on an instant, so Anita tries to tackle her on her own.

'Can I have tights if I don't go on that Youth Hostel Trip?' Thirty quid to spend three days in a faraway town with the rest of First Year. Her stomach aches and churns at the prospect. Gayle has told the class that Anita hasn't got a fanny and has warned that the other girls will check.

'We've already been through this a hundred times.' Mum scrubs even harder at a dish. Anita's heart beats faster as she dries a saucepan. 'You know how hashy you are. You'd just get them laddered the first day.'

'I wouldn't. Honest.' She tries to stretch taller than her four foot ten, 'I'd be careful.'

'What's the hurry? I wore socks until I started work at fifteen.'

'But everyone else wears tights, and…'

'Not everyone else's father is on the dole.'

Reluctantly she slides closer to the truth. 'I don't want to go to the Youth Hostel anyway.'

'Because of these trashy girls?'

Dad's already hit her twice for not sticking up for herself. 'No, it's cause the teachers will take us hillwalking and I hate things like that.'

'The school says it's part of your history project, so no one's going to say we let you miss out.'

Mr Wearsley misses out because Mrs Wearsley is too fat to go anywhere. He takes Jen and Anita to the cinema, to the skating, to a home game football match and to the Kentucky Fried Chicken. 'When I was younger I crossed shark-infested waters to bring her the Milk Tray. Now she just sits on her arse to eat them,' he says as Jen's mum shuffles off to get him some more beer.

And Anita knows that she shouldn't grin, but the words are cruelly funny. And she grins even more widely at his casual use of grown up words like *arse*. He knows, then, that despite the socks and lack of breasts she's an unshockable young woman. Her eyes must show that she's learning all the sexual words the dictionary has.

'D'you think we could smoke openly at your house?' she asks

Jen the next day as they shiver in a shop doorway with their indi-vidually-bought-from-the-chip-van filter tips.

'Christ, no.' The February wind makes Jen's full cheeks look especially rosy, 'Dad's just found the belt we hid behind the fridge.'

And until that moment Anita hasn't known that Jen gets hit too: it's not the sort of thing folk seem to discuss in detail. And she knows in that same moment that Mr Wearsley would never ever hit *her*. Even Jen has said as much on a couple of occasions: 'He's always in a better mood when you come round.'

Linda at school starts to get round and then she leaves and everyone says that she's going to have a baby. So even Linda has done it – Linda who has her nose pierced with a silver stud at one side.

'Karen's been on the pill for months so *she* won't get pregnant,' Jen says confidingly.

Billy spends all his time with Karen, so maybe she's especially good at giving blow-jobs. Anita spends longer than ever practicing kissing on the back of her hand.

And at last someone touches her sexually. But it isn't a pop star or Billy – it's Billy's dad. It happens after School Assembly, the day that Jen's first ever period starts. 'Come home with me to get some money, then go out to the shop and buy towels and stuff?' she asks, clutching the three spare tyres that make up her skirt clad stom-ach, 'Mum's at the sweet shop and anyway she just uses tampons and I don't know how they work.' So they take the bus back and find that Mr Wearsley's in till his afternoon shift.

'Bunking off, are you?' he asks, winking from his armchair.

'No I'm going to bed, Dad. I don't feel well,' Jen fills herself a hot water bottle as they've been told to do in the *So Now You're A Woman* book. Mr Wearsley follows them into the kitchen and perches on a stool. Jen puts the stopper in the bottle then drags Anita into the bedroom. 'Go into the third cupboard on the right when he's not looking. There's a tea caddy – Mum keeps her emer-gency money there.'

'But why can't I just ask your Dad for a few quid?'

Jen closes her eyes and grimaces as she holds her belly. 'I don't want him to know.'

And Anita wishes that she could swap places with Jen and claim the blood red pain-filled sign of womanhood. For then the other girl's couldn't say that she didn't have a fanny, and maybe she'd start to grow breasts.

He's still in the kitchen when she walks back.

'What's wrong with the Big Yin, then?'

A disloyal small giggle. 'Got a stomach ache.'

'Stuffing her face ache, more like. Can't walk past a biscuit tin. Just like her mother, she is.'

Anita's dad pinches Anita's lank arms and calls her a Buchenwalder, but Mr Wearsley's suggesting that it's good to be thin.

Now she has to get him out of the room so that she can grab some money for the sanitary towels. She can ask him to fetch the terrier. 'Is Duke around?'

He shows his small white teeth again in a slightly tense smile: 'He was rectangular, last time I looked.'

He's staring and smiling the way he always stares and smiles. She risks an oh-very-funny style groan and raises her eyebrows. After all, he likes her – it's okay to risk speaking back.

He smiles some more. 'You know, you suit that pinafore dress.'

Just as well, cause it's the only one she's got. It goes in the wash every Friday. 'I'd rather have a black skirt like the other girls have.'

To her amazement he pulls out a wallet and takes a twenty quid note from it. 'There you are.'

'Oh no. I didn't mean... I wasn't hinting.' Overwhelmed, she tries to push the money back at him, but he puts his palm over her hand, imprisoning the note.

'Go on, love – treat yourself.' She looks down at his hand. It's small and warm with little black hairs over the knuckles. Probably rather have more on his head, she thinks, and feels a wave of affection and pity, a sort of love.

She looks up, shy now: 'Thanks.'

'Any time.' He moves slightly closer and she breathes in the familiar scent of lager. 'Any chance of a thank you kiss?'

A kiss. She's thought so often about lying under Billy, or that blond boy in Second Year who told the other girls to stop laughing at her red plastic sandals. She's pictured Jarvis Cocker's sexy knowing lips. But it's Mr Wearsley who wants the kiss – Mr Wearsley who must be in his forties, for Jen's Mum has said she was almost an unclaimed treasure who got married late in life.

Anita stands with her hands at her sides as Mr Wearsley's head gets close. She holds her breath as he brushes his mouth against hers then repeats the featherweight contact. He's got feet that are small and neat like hers are. He's wearing those fashionable boot-style shoes.

'Anita?' Jen calls urgently from her room.

'Got to go,' Anita mutters. She runs to Jen's door then just can't bring herself to go in. 'Going to the shops for you now,' she shouts and takes off, clutching the crisp new twenty. Two packs of towels only cost her three quid. Then it's back to Jen's house feeling almost dizzy with the knowledge of what may be happening. Steeling herself to go beyond shyness and kiss him back.

He opens at her ring. 'Come back to talk to Jen's lonely old man?'

She giggles. 'You're not old.' Not compared to her own dad, at least not in attitude. He beckons her into the long hall where she holds up the carrier bag, 'I'll just give Jen this.'

'Fish supper, is it?'

She laughs some more then can't think of another answer. 'Won't be a min.'

But she stays in Jen's room for many mins until Jen's eyes have closed and she starts gently snoring. And still she sits and sits. Another door clicks. Duke the Yorkie yelps. She hears the TV start up in the living room. It's warm and peaceful here, better than school or home or a cigarette-lit shop doorway. She wants to stay.

He's seated when she walks into the lounge. She can't go to him. She just can't. She sits on the floor beside the settee so that the puppy can curl on her lap, then she wonders if that looks childish.

'Mrs Wearsley working today?' she asks.

He sighs. 'Eating away the profits, more like. God knows why she opted for a sweet shop. She's getting too big for her skin.'

They're talking adult to adult now. Anita sucks in her breath. 'Was she that size when you two got married?'

'Big, yeah, but not the size of a house.' He clicks his fingers at the Yorkie, 'You've got an admirer there – he really likes you. You can take him home if you like.' He crosses the room and hunkers down beside her and strokes the fawn fur on Duke's small, round, silken head.

'I wish. But my Dad would have a fit.'

'Not a dog lover, then?'

Doesn't seem to love anyone. She shakes her head.

'Our Jen's never been round your place?'

'They don't like having people round, not even my aunties. Mum says 'Is your own house not good enough for you?' whenever I come round here.'

He puts an arm around her shoulders. She freezes again and flushes redder than any blush cream. *Act like a woman. Touch him back like they do in the movies. Relax, relax, relax.*

'You know that you're welcome here any time?'

'Yeah, Mr Wearsley. Thanks.'

His fingers slide up and down her arm, a surprisingly nice sensation. Maybe they'll find a cure for baldness soon and he'll grow more hair. He moves his free arm towards the sleepy little Yorkie and it timidly licks his palm.

'How would you and Jen like to go to a Dog Show in Birmingham next Sunday? We could make a proper trip of it, stay over in a hotel for a couple of days.'

And she knows immediately that she can't, the calendar screaming out that the trip is getting closer. 'Jen and I have to go on this Youth Hostel thing with the school next Monday to Wednesday.'

'Don't sound so cheerful about it.' His breath warms the side of her face. He keeps stroking her arm.

'I'm not. It's…' He thinks she's womanly, special. How can she admit that the older-looking girls all hate her, that she doesn't fit in? 'I just don't fancy it,' she says casually, then cuddles the yawning terrier some more.

Mr Wearsley pats her shoulder. She can tell that he's staring at her face, all pink in profile. She pulls her socks up and keeps looking at the almost-sleeping dog.

'You can always play hooky,' he says, sliding a hand up to her neck then tracing it down again, 'Come here instead, if you like.'

'Won't Mrs Wearsley mind?' Jen's Mum is usually out but when she's home she's too tired to talk very much.

'Nah, she's off to her sisters in Ipswich all that week.' He laughs his slightly tense laugh, 'Don't mention this to her, mind – she thinks I'm working. She'd make me drive her down if she knew I was off.'

And so, as Jen bleeds into womanhood in the next room, Anita promises to let her folks think that she's still going to the hostel.

He'll then forge the school a note from Mum saying she's had to stay behind for a family funeral instead.

'What about Jen?' she asks, knowing that Jen won't want to be left alone with Gayle and her crowd in a late night dormitory.

'Just let her think that you're going as planned.'

'But she'll be so ...' *Left out and scared and even angry.*

'You're not on the phone, right? She won't be able to check.'

Until now she's hated being the only girl in the class without a phone (except for Mandy Nicholls who has loads of uncles and a definite hygiene problem) but now she's really glad. It's going to be her and Duke and Mr Wearsley, for Billy's living at Karen's house permanently now.

'He hates being home,' says Jen. 'They're always on at him to get a job but he says it's all slave labour on those youth programme schemes.'

'I love being at your house,' Anita says. She wonders if she'll be able to love Mr Wearsley with the creases under his eyes and his balding centre. But men can grow new hair these days: just look at Elton John. And Mum says that people have just got to make the best of things and that there's more to life than looks.

She's going to look good for these special three days, though. Anita leaves the house in her uniform on the day she plans to become a proper woman. She walks shakily up the road towards the hated school bus stop. She carries her supposed youth hostelling clothes in Gran's small tartan case. All of the other girls on the trip will have bum bags and Adidas holdalls, but then she's not going on the trip.

When she's out of sight, Anita takes a different turning then catches a bus into town. She walks self-consciously into the super-market toilets and goes into the cleanest cubicle. There she changes into the black pencil skirt and plunge-neck top that she's bought with the bulk of Mr Wearsley's twenty quid. The bra Gran bought her still sits in unfilled lines where her breasts should be. Carefully Anita pulls balls of cotton wool from her suitcase and stuffs them down the lacy pink cups. Then she starts to put on the make-up that Jen has nicked from Karen over many days.

Done it. When she's finished, she breathes 'Yes' out loud. Grey-lidded eyes stare back at her, ringed with sooty kohl, the lashes mascara-lengthened. Blush-pink cheeks sit at either side of a rouged and lip glossed mouth. Anita rubs a perfume card on her wrists then strokes it gently down her bra-based cleavage. Then she puts on her duffle coat, buttons it up, and takes a bus to the Wearsley's beloved house.

She climbs the tenement stairs very slowly, stopping on each landing to catch her breath. Takes off the duffle coat and puts it in her tartan case, then combs her hair forward and tosses it back again to get the big hair look that Gayle gets in the loos. She checks her appearance in her little pocket mirror: if only the other girls could see her now. But they'll all be driven off in the Youth Hostel bus within the next hour and the only person to see Anita will be Jen's Dad.

Anita Wearsley. Mrs Anita Wearsley. Mr and Mrs William and Anita Wearsley. There's the small problem of the existing Mrs Wearsley, of course, but he's made it clear that they don't get on and that he prefers thin women like Anita, that Jen's mum has let herself go.

Go on – do it. She rings the bell then holds her breath. She so wants him to be pleased with her clothes and make-up. She wants him to wolfwhistle and gaze at her more closely like Billy did. He opens the door, half smiling. Then he... he scowls and stares.

'Thought you'd have been in your school uniform.'

She shifts from one nylon clad leg to the other and looks at him through her lashes the way women do in Billy's naked girlie magazines.

'I got changed.'

'Right. Come in, then. Come in.'

He wipes the back of his hand across his mouth. She smells whisky as she sways on the high heels she's bought from Oxfam. Remembers belatedly to put a slight wiggle into her step.

She hesitates when she's halfway down the hall. 'Are we going into the lounge?'

'We are now.' His voice is the verbal equivalent of sandpaper. He walks in and switches the TV on and pours himself a glass of scotch from the bottle by his chair.

'Can I have one?' she asks, sitting down on the settee and slanting her legs sideways like they do on the telly.

'Can you heck.'

The slight tension that usually inhabits his voice is amplified by at least a hundred. She wonders what's happened to make him so enraged.

Silence. Not good.

'Mrs Wearsley get away all right?'

'Yeah. Lucky she's not going by boat.' He moves his arms out to indicate an enormous stomach, 'We have embarkation. Glug, glug, glug.'

She snorts at the image then can't stop giggling. At last he smiles.

'You want a milk shake or something?'

Her stomach is too cramped-up for anything but alcohol. She shakes her head.

'Where's Duke gone, then?

'He's in the bedroom.'

'Your bedroom?'

He nods: 'I shut him in with his basket. He hasn't been feeling so good.'

'Can I go and see him?'

He nods, and finishes the glass of scotch he was drinking and pours himself another. He picks up the filled glass and the half empty bottle. 'I'll come too.'

He puts a hand on her back as if to steer her down the hall. Her face burns as she walks ahead of him. *Do it, do it, do it.* In a few moments from now she'll be a woman rather than a girl and no one will ever be able to say that she doesn't have a fanny again.

'D'you think he needs a vet?' she asks to fill up the void as they reach the door.

'Reckon he's just pining for a little mate,' Mr Wearsley answers. He gives a low short laugh but it ends on a hiccup instead.

She walks into the King Size bedded room where Mr and Mrs Wearsley and Billy and Karen have blown and sixty-ninered. Mr W still has his fingers on her back. He lets go as she reaches down to pick up the tail-wagging Yorkie. She sits on the bed and holds him in her lap.

'Have you not been well? Do you want to go for a walk? Would you like some medicine?' She looks up as Mr Wearsley pours himself yet another glass. 'Give us a double, then.' She pushes back her shoulders so that the top clings more closely to her padded breasts. Her bare arms come out in goosebumps.

'No, you're only thirteen.'

'I'm mature for my age,' she mutters, flopping back on the bed. Her heart is beating overtime through every cell of her body.

'You aren't usually,' he mutters, and the mattress moves as he crawls up one side.

'Such little breasts,' he mumbles. His hands clasp both well-stuffed cups then move quickly away again. 'What the fuck?' he mutters. Then she feels his fingers moving up her nylon-clad leg. Anita closes her eyes and thinks of Jarvis Cocker. The hand stops at her specially-bought silken panties and the contact stops. 'Look what I've got for you,' he slurs softly, pulling her hand towards his zip.

Reluctantly, Anita opens her eyes. A half-hard fleshy oblong lies drily in her palm. Nervously she licks her lip-glossed lips and the veined shape loses some of its thickness.

'For Christ's sake wash that muck off your face,' Mr Wearsley suddenly yells.

He pushes himself up and off the bed and staggers over to the dressing table, returning with a box of tissues and a jar of cold cream.

He launches himself onto the quilt as Anita backs away up the bed, trying to dodge his flailing arms, trouserless legs and hopelessly hanging soft penis. 'Leave me alone,' she screams, 'You're just like my dad.' And she's striking wildly at his right hand and thinking that this is her worst ever moment when the bedroom door swings open and Jen walks in.

Exit, Pursued

Simon Brett

'Set on there. Never was a war did cease,
E'er bloody hands were wash'd, with such a peace.'
Cymbeline's final couplet echoed around the Globe Theatre.
From the tower above the stage, a trumpet sounded, to spell out
to the stupidest of the groundlings that the play was over. Applause
came from the audience, but the sound was ragged, interspersed
with catcalls, not the full-throated thunder that bespoke success.

Charles Parys was behind the curtain of the tiring-house, waiting to see whether the cast would be called on to take a bow. In his
fifties, cynical, he had witnessed too many first performances to
take rejection by the audience personally. And yet, in the heart of
all actors there always glows a little flicker of hope. *Cymbeline* still
might work. The alchemy that made a play a success or failure was
an arcane and inexplicable art.

He caught the sceptical eye of the actor playing Posthumus
Leonatus, who had just come off the stage. 'Don't think Master
Shakespeare's got a winner this time,' said Robert Hillard, brushing at the fine black velvet of his doublet where it had scuffed
against the powdery paint of the curtain.

'They liked some of it,' said Charles Parys, unwilling to condemn the play out of hand. 'The fights... and the songs... and the
Ghosts.'

'Oh yes, and you coming down from the heavens on an eagle –
that gave them a good laugh. But they really lost interest in the last
bit, with all those explanations, tying up the loose ends of the plot.
Most of this lot'd rather be at the bear-baiting than seeing a proper play. No taste, theatre audiences these days.'

'Are we going out for a bow or not?' shouted the boy Ned
Brackett, the fine vowels he'd used as Imogen giving way to his
natural Cockney in a voice that would soon be too deep to play
more heroines. Robert Hillard tried to catch the boy's eye, but his
glance was deliberately evaded.

All the actors deferred to the book-holder, a harassed, balding man in a rough woollen jerkin. 'Oh yes,' he said. 'Give them one bow. See how they take it.'

The applause when the cast trooped sheepishly back on stage was at best lukewarm, and there were some boos. Most of the audience were already scrambling for the exit, the groundlings held back by stage-keepers, as the gentry passed fastidiously over the debris of nutshells, orange peel and rushes to the safety of their waiting carriages.

In spite of the feeble reception, Robert Hillard strutted and preened for the remainder of the audience. He cut a fine figure in black velvet doublet cut on silver tinsel and trimmed with silver lace. There was a regular crowd of merchants' wives who liked to stay at the end of the plays and ogle the actors. One in particular, a well-rounded, black-eyed mischief-maker, seemed to be staring with unambiguous interest towards Robert Hillard. With an angry swirl of ratty fur cloak, a long-nosed elderly man, who could only be her husband, put an arm around his chattel's shoulder and whisked her away from such riff-raff. As he vanished into the crowd, he turned back and focused a look of sheer venom on his potential rival.

'Do you know that sour-faced pantaloon, Master Parys?' asked Hillard. 'He seemed to be staring at you.'

'I don't think it was at *me*. He did not like the interest his wife was taking in *you*, Master Hillard.'

'Oh yes.' Robert Hillard preened a little more. 'That does happen quite often. It's something I've learned to live with.'

Charles Parys reflected on the strangeness of the situation. The actor standing next to him had all the qualifications to be a ladies' man, except for even the mildest of interest in the ladies. Boys were Robert Hillard's dish of choice.

'But do you know him, Master Parys?'

'I believe he's an ironmonger and locksmith called Ezekiel Goodbody. Said to have made a lot of money and to have invested much of it in the business of entertainment.'

'Ah. So maybe he will be our paymaster soon?'

'I don't think plays are the sort of entertainment he favours.'

Back in the cramped tiring-house was a maelstrom of ribaldry and errant limbs, as too many actors vied to get out of their costumes

and be first to the tavern. Above the chaos shrilled the voice of
Rokesby Lander, the Master of Properties and Apparel. He was a
huge man, swollen like an overfilled wineskin, and, in spite of the cool
May weather, sweating like a cheese in direct sunlight. The story went
that he had been a boy actor and that an unscrupulous theatre manager had castrated him in an unsuccessful attempt to extend his days
of playing female parts.

Lander's words were the same after every performance, and
after every performance the actors ignored them. 'Now don't just
leave your costumes lying on the rushes! Fold them up and shake
them out! Some got wet with the rain, and must be dried before
they're used again! Come on, gentlemen, please!'

Nobody was sure when, if ever, *Cymbeline* would be performed
again, but the costumes, particularly the fine ones, would be worn
in other plays. They were amongst the chief assets of the King's
Men, and Rokesby Lander had to account to the shareholders for
every last lost button. Given the habitual untidiness of actors, his
was not an enviable task.

He came across to Charles, who was struggling to free himself
from the gold-painted pasteboard wings he'd worn as Jupiter. 'Can
I help you there?' the unsexed voice trilled.

Rokesby Lander was always offering to help, and during the
quick change Charles had to make out of his Cloten costume into
his Jupiter one, that help had been very much needed. There was
always an ulterior motive to Lander's offers; his liking for Charles
was more than just professional. Still, Charles himself had never
had a moment's doubt since birth where his own interests lay, and
the Apparel Master's fondness for him had sometimes proved useful in obtaining the odd favour.

Lander lowered his voice – in volume if not in pitch. 'Will you
be going to the tavern for a drink, Charles?'

'When did I not? Thirsty work, a new play.'

'Yes.' Rokesby Lander gestured hopelessly round the clutter of
spangled costumes, left exactly where the actors had stepped out
of them. 'When I've finished this lot, I'll be going down to the Bull.
Maybe see you there…?'

Not if I see you first, thought Charles Parys.

★ ★ ★

Simon Brett

The Bull was no worse than any other tavern South of the Thames, which is to say it was smoky, dingily lit by rush lights, damp from condensation and the sweat of bodies crammed inside. The smells of urine and sour ale fought for dominance, and it was a frequent complaint amongst the customers that the tavern-keeper served the one for the other. Since the Bull's regulars comprised a mix of stinking labourers, conmen, cutpurses and whores, the actors fitted in very well. They frequented the tavern for the simple reason that it was in a crooked alley behind the Globe, but off the main thoroughfares which led the quality back to their relative elegance North of the river.

At five-thirty, particularly after the first performance of a play, most of the King's Men would gather in the Bull to commiserate about what had gone wrong, and gloomily assess the new work's prospects. They would drink for an hour or two. Only the rash or intrepid would stay longer. In May it was twilight by seven, and the Bankside was a rough area in which to loiter after dark.

'Come to the bear-baiting!' shouted a harsh voice as the actors approached the tavern door. 'Tomorrow afternoon at three! See the dogs tear the living flesh from the bears! See the bears crush the dogs like piecrust! Don't bother with these long-winded plays! Come to the Bear Garden in Shoreside Lane! See some proper entertainment!'

The fellow trying to do them out of business was a ferret-faced man in a stained leather tabard on which had been painted a crude black outline of a bear harried by dogs. As the actors muscled forward to chase him from his pitch, he gave a sharp look towards Robert Hillard, before scampering off into the darkness of the surrounding alleys.

Inside the tavern door Charles Parys exchanged banter with the other *Cymbeline* actors while they waited to be served. There seemed to be only two potboys on duty to deal with the heaving mass, a skeletally thin old man, and a lad scarcely into his teens who hobbled dangerously on legs warped by rickets. Between fusillades of insults at each other, the actors hurled oaths and exhortations to the potboys.

Charles was the butt of most of the company gibes. The parts he'd taken in the play ensured that. For the first four Acts he'd played Cloten, the brutish son of *Cymbeline's* Queen, but after that character's decapitation, a headless dummy had been thrust into Cloten's costume, and Charles had had to don the awkward wings, scratchy beard and shining robes of Jupiter. He'd then had to rush up the rickety stairs from the tiring-house to the hut above the stage, whence he'd been launched by uncaring stage-keepers on the back of an eagle. This was a rickety structure of cloth-covered basket-work, which wobbled dangerously on ropes as it was lowered to the stage. The descent of the mighty Jove had thus prompted more laughter than awe. The 'thunder and lightning' specified in the book-holder's copy of the text had been forgotten by the stage-keepers, and the firework which should have gone off when Jupiter hurled his thunderbolt had failed to ignite, with the result that the bolt thudded feebly down on to the stage to a cry from some witty groundling of 'Beware chicken droppings!' It hadn't been Charles Parys's finest hour.

Finally the limping boy brought their order and the actors' robust badinage gave way to a greater priority. Charles took a thankful sip from his cup of ale and, given the speed of the service, wished he'd ordered two. The ale was sour but welcome against his palate.

'Beware chicken droppings!' said a breaking voice at his side. Ned Brackett was dressed once more as a boy, but still retained some of Imogen's mincing elegance. Around his neck sparkled a gold chain with a pendant of inlaid pearls. The boy's voluptuous lips caressed a stick of brown sugar.

'Very amusing,' said Charles. 'So what's the painted bauble you have there?'

'Not painted, Master Parys. It's true gold. Given me by a gentleman of the Court.'

'In return for what favours?'

The boy smiled coquettishly, and gave a suggestive lick to his sugar stick.

'It's no gentleman of the Court!' Robert Hillard staggered angrily across to join them. 'Some jumped-up rascal in a borrowed doublet with a fancy for a young boy's arsehole.'

Ned Brackett fluttered his eyelashes. 'It takes one to know one, Master Hillard.'

'Why, you…!' The actor who had played Posthumus drew his hand back as if to strike the boy, but seemed to think better of it.

Hillard hadn't been in the tavern long enough to get as drunk as he appeared, and Charles realised the man was in the grip of violent emotion. He also realised the aptness of Ned Brackett's words. Against the express orders of Rokesby Lander, Robert Hillard was still dressed in his black and silver doublet. His stage sword hung in its scabbard at his side.

The boy smiled smugly, knowing his power to hurt. 'Now forgive me, Masters. I must go to join more select company.'

And he teetered, emphasising his Imogen walk, across to a tall figure in a purple doublet trimmed with gold. The man was as sallow as a Spaniard; a single pearl depended from one ear lobe. On a ribbon round his neck was a pomander of cloves, but, rather than foppish, he looked menacing. He laid a proprietorial hand on the boy's backside and smiled triumphantly across to Robert Hillard.

Charles Parys could feel the seething beside him; his fellow-actor's body was tensed to spring into violence. Charles laid a hand on the velvet of his arm. 'Don't do anything. He's not worth it, Master Hillard.'

'"The boy disdains me".' A void of misery lay beneath the actor's words.

Charles continued the quotation from the play they had just completed.

"He leaves me, scorns me; briefly die their joys
That place them on the truth of girls and boys."

Hillard remained transfixed by the sardonic, challenging look of the man in purple. The anger still coursed his veins like molten metal, and his hand dropped instinctively to the pommel of his sword. 'A man of the Court!' he shouted. 'Put a monkey in a purple coat, and he'll pass for a man of the Court!'

His antagonist held silence, fondling Ned's bottom with one hand, and with the other fingering the boy's pearl pendant, goading Hillard on to further fury.

'So maybe he is a man of the Court! When the King himself is a lad-lover, what else would you expect? That this fellow is sent out by the King to bring back pretty bum-boys for the royal pleasure!'

The talk in the tavern dropped to silence. With a last, piercing look at Robert Hillard, the man in purple put an insolent hand on Ned Brackett's shoulder and led the boy out into the street.

'You fool, keep quiet!' hissed Charles, as conversations around them slowly came back to life. 'To say that about the King is to risk your life.'

'I say no more than the truth that everyone knows.'

'Master Hillard, it doesn't matter whether it's true or not! There are spies everywhere, and saying stuff like that is foolhardy. It's not just us you put at risk. The King has revoked the licence of other actors' companies for less.'

The younger actor turned away in despair. 'I don't care. I love Ned. I need him. If I can't have him, then nothing else matters.'

'Master Hillard! Master Hillard,' squeaked an approaching voice, shrill with affront. 'You are a wicked man, and deserve a good beating!'

It was Rokesby Lander, sweating more than ever, forcing his bulbous body through the disrespectful crowd that milled around the tavern door.

Hillard turned to look at this new annoyance. 'What is it, you vat of lard?'

'Your costume, Master Hillard. Players are expressly forbidden to leave the theatre wearing apparel owned by the King's Men! It is against the rules!'

'Rule me no rules, Master Tunbelly! Rules are for lesser men. You are now addressing the best actor in London!'

This defiant shout again brought the tavern to stillness. There were plenty of factions supporting other actors who would have challenged Robert Hillard's boast. Careless in his anguish for the loss of the boy Ned, he seemed set on a course of self-destruction.

'I must insist,' Rokesby Lander said primly, 'that you come back with me to the Globe this instant to return your apparel.'

Robert Hillard's hand was again on his sword, and the fat man quailed before the balefulness focused on him. 'A fig for your insisting, Master Doughbucket! I say to you, as Master Shakespeare has written in one of his more successful plays – "Sneck up!"'

And with that, the actor stormed out of the Bull Tavern. The hand tight on his sword handle ensured that the crowd shrank back to let him pass.

Conversation quickly reasserted itself. The Bull Tavern had witnessed too much drama to take much notice of one more flouncing exit.

'Could I buy you a drink, Master Parys?' wheedled Rokesby Lander.

The temptation was strong. The contents of his first cup had scarcely touched the sides of Charles's throat. But to accept the drink would oblige him to at least a polite minimum of Lander's conversation, and Charles didn't think he could face it. 'No, no, I must be on my way shortly.' There were other taverns to stop at between the Globe and his lodgings in Shoreditch. 'But don't let me stop you...'

'I'm in no hurry,' said the eunuch. 'I'll have a drink after we've had a little chat.'

'Oh.' Charles Parys was uncomfortably suspended between tedium and downright rudeness. He made conversation. 'What did you think of the play, Master Lander?'

The fat cheeks puffed out in disparagement. 'Won't see many more performances of that one, I can tell you. As ever with Master Shakespeare – too many words and not enough action. Nor enough special effects to please the groundlings.'

'There was me coming down on the eagle...'

Rokesby Lander giggled girlishly. 'Yes, very funny too. But the public wants more than that these days. More spectacle. Like the masques that Master Jonson and Master Inigo Jones have devised for the Court. Prodigiously fancy costumes they have there, and fine music. What's more, being indoors, they can make magical effects with the lights. I tell you, Master Parys, the theatre of Shakespeare and his like is old-fashioned. The future lies with the masques... oh, and of course with the bear-baiting. The rich men of the future will not be the actors' companies but the owners of Bear Gardens like Master Ezekiel Goodbody.'

Charles couldn't let that go by unchallenged. Not only did such a view offend his opinions, it also threatened his livelihood. 'No, Master Lander, there will always be a place for the kind of theatre that challenges the mind to – '

But his case for the defence got no further. There was a shriek from the tavern doorway, and a seventeen-year-old whore, bare feet muddy beneath her ragged finery, burst in. 'Sirs, come quickly! There has been murder in the streets!'

*   *   *

Charles Parys and Rokesby Lander were among the first to arrive at the scene of crime. A frightened link-boy held a trembling torch over the body. Screams sounded from surprised whores and their clients in nearby alleys. Men shouted for the Watch to come.

Robert Hillard lay in the trickle of sewage that guttered down the middle of a narrow alley. Flames from the torch flickered on the mud, on the running water, on the blade half-drawn from the actor's scabbard, but also on the dark blood that had almost ceased to pump from the wound in his chest. Of the other sword – or whatever weapon had made the fatal thrust – there was no sign.

Charles Parys crouched down at his colleague's side, knowing he was too late. Hillard's eyes were dull in the torchlight, their fire extinguished.

Above him, Charles heard a piping wail from Rokesby Lander. 'Oh, no! Look at the mess it's made of that doublet!'

* * *

Master William Shakespeare looked weary and melancholy. The dome of his head was furrowed, and more of the hair fringing it was white than when Charles Parys had last seen him. 'So?' asked Charles.

'So we will do another performance of *Cymbeline*.'

'That's good news.'

The playwright shrugged. 'I have just come from a meeting with my fellow shareholders. They took a lot of persuading. And do you know what finally convinced them we should give the play another try?' Charles shook his head. 'Your bloody eagle, Master Parys. They said the King's Men had spent so much making the device that it must be used more than once. And doing another performance of *Cymbeline* would be cheaper – though only just – than commissioning a new play by a younger author, also containing the miraculous descent of someone on an eagle.'

There seemed nothing to say that could ease the despair evident in his friend's words. So Charles suggested having a drink.

* * *

The meagre May sunlight was sufficient that morning to justify standing outside the Bull. The stenches were no less than inside, but at least more varied. Shakespeare drank sack, with the air of a man who intended to keep drinking sack all day. Charles Parys stuck to the ale. At three o'clock he had a performance to give in *Philaster* by Beaumont and Fletcher. The play's lines maintained their customary tenuous hold on the sides of his brain.

'You have no thoughts, do you, Master Shakespeare, as to who might have killed Master Hillard?'

The playwright shook his head. He was too deep into his own failure to think about anything else. 'Some jealous man…?'

'Not a husband. Or if it was, he must realise he's got the wrong victim. By now all London knows Robert Hillard's tastes.'

'I did not say a husband. Maybe some other worshipper of Sodom, whose bumboy Hillard had seduced away…?'

'It had happened the other way round. Ned Brackett … you know, Imogen … had just rejected Master Hillard.'

'Then I don't know. But I'd still put it down to the workings of love … or love gone sour. Jealousy is the most powerful of the human emotions.'

'"The green-ey'd monster".'

'Yes, Master Parys. A good line… that I wrote in the days when I still wrote good lines.'

'Oh, come on. For heaven's sake. *Cymbeline* is full of good lines.'

'Not enough of them. Whatever skill I once had, I have lost it. Or the public doesn't want it. They want younger writers. They want Beaumont and Fletcher.'

'Or bear-baiting.'

'They will always want bear-baiting,' said Shakespeare despondently.

'Cheer up. It's not as if you haven't made a good living from the theatre.'

The dark eyes fixed Charles's in a beam of unnerving intensity. 'You think the money matters when I cannot write?'

'It must cushion things a bit.'

'No. It provides no comfort at all when the mind is dead.'

'So…' Charles searched around for something to say, and felt embarrassed by the crassness of what he came up with. 'Are you writing anything at the moment Master Shakespeare?'

'There is something, but it's not working.'

'What?'

'Master Greene wrote a tale called *Pandosto*...' Charles shook his head; the title meant nothing to him. 'Well, it concerns the unreasoning jealousy of a king who believes his wife to be unfaithful, and he thinks he has had her killed for her imagined betrayal, but she's been hidden away and... oh, the usual stuff. Purification... regeneration... the road to self-knowledge... But I think I'm going to have to abandon it. The structure's not working.'

'Why not?'

'Because the play's in two parts and there are sixteen years between them and... oh, don't let me bother you with my technical problems.'

'So time comes into it again?'

'Yes, I'm even thinking of having Time as a character – a Chorus to bridge the sixteen years, but...' He seemed to lose himself in a far country. 'I'm becoming obsessed by time.'

To avoid metaphysical entanglements, Charles Parys resorted to a simpler question. 'Do you have a title for the play?'

'I don't know. *Leontes and Hermione*...? A *Tale for a Winter's Night*, perhaps? As I say, I probably won't finish it, so it won't need a title.'

'Any good parts?' Charles asked diffidently.

'Good parts for a Clown?' For the first time that morning there was a light of wry humour in Shakespeare's eye. 'There is one very good comic part – a peddler, a rogue, a coney-catcher. I've got a name from Ovid and Plutarch that I think will suit him. Autolycus.' He saw the hope he had aroused and immediately extinguished it. 'There is also the part of a lesser Clown. A shepherd, a gull. You could play *him*, Master Parys.'

'Thank you,' came the humbled reply.

'Good day, Master Shakespeare.'

They looked up to see a young woman approaching them. Her face, soon to be ragged from the hardness of life, still wore the glow of youth. The dress looked even more tawdry in the daylight, gold paint cracked and flaking on its seams. She was still barefoot. It was the whore who had sounded the alarm in the Bull a few nights before.

'You are out early, Mistress Dorcas.'

'And you could be *in* early, Master Shakespeare...' she replied unambiguously, '...if you so wish.'

'I'll think about it.'

'And while you think about it, I'm sure you'll buy a poor girl a drink.'

He nodded. 'Tell the potboy to put it on my reckoning.'

Dorcas made a mock-curtsey, and disappeared into the gloom of the tavern. For a moment Shakespeare avoided Charles's eye, then looked up defiantly. 'So, if a man leaves a sour-faced wife minding his affairs in Stratford, may he not take a little pleasure when he is in London?'

'I never said you couldn't. If there's any guilt about, it's your own.'

'It has not always been whores,' said Shakespeare defensively. 'There have been ladies of quality, the occasional pert merchant's wife. A man has needs.'

'You don't need to tell me.' Charles pondered the wobbly state of his own marriage.

The playwright continued his self-justification. 'And Dorcas is a good girl, in spite of her calling.'

'I never said she wasn't.'

'No. And she has made me happy. Though for how much longer...' He looked pessimistically at the dwindling contents in his tankard of sack.

'It's the drink. "Lechery, sir, it provokes, and unprovokes; it provokes the desire, but it takes away the performance."'

Shakespeare smiled glumly. 'Another line from the days when I could write. *Macbeth* was good.'

'Yes...' Charles sighed wistfully, remembering past glories, '...and gave me my best part ever.'

'A Drunken Porter. The part for which you had been rehearsing all your life Master Parys.'

'Well, I wouldn't say – '

'Then all was well with me. I could do no wrong. I'd written a play celebrating the King's Scottish lineage, so I found favour with him, and all the Court were -'

Charles interrupted once again to halt the slide into depression. 'When we next do *Cymbeline*,' he asked brusquely, 'who will play Posthumus Leonatus?'

Shakespeare gave a hopeless shrug. 'It will have to be me. I more or less know the lines. I'm too old for the part, but then you are too old for Cloten, Master Parys.'

'Though not too old for Jupiter.'

'I think it would be a hard task to be too old for Jupiter.' A grin transformed his features. 'Beware chicken droppings!'

Oh dear. Charles Parys knew he was never going to live that one down.

Shakespeare's grin transformed itself into a beam as Dorcas re-emerged from the tavern, bearing a steaming cup of mulled wine. After a night spent on a draughty street corner, she needed something to warm her up.

'So what have you been up to, my little sugarplum?' asked Shakespeare.

'I've been talking to the Watch,' she said proudly.

'What offence have you committed this time? Have you been insulting the gentry again?'

'No, no. The Watch wished to speak to me as a witness.'

Shakespeare looked blank, so Charles Parys explained. 'The young lady saw Robert Hillard stabbed.'

'Well, not so much *saw*, but I was the first person to arrive after he had been stabbed.'

'You didn't see the murderer then?'

'Maybe a flash of someone in a dark coat rushing away, but that was all…'

'Are you sure it was all?' Charles persisted. 'You didn't hear any words… any other sound… anything else that was strange…?'

'Well…' The girl hesitated, afraid that her words might sound foolish. 'There was a smell…'

'A smell?' Shakespeare laughed. 'So do we now identify a murderer by his smell? What was it – brimstone from the gates of hell?'

'No,' said Dorcas sullenly.

'Why not by smell?' asked Charles. 'It might be as good a means of identification as any other. So what was the smell, child?'

Dorcas blushed as she replied. 'It smelt like a bear.'

'A bear?' This struck Shakespeare as even funnier. 'Are you saying that Robert Hillard was murdered by a bear? Not only that, but a bear that could wield a sword?'

Dorcas looked more uncomfortable. 'As I say, it was just a smell.'

'Plenty of bears pass those alleys when they're led from their kennels to the Bear Garden.'

'I know that, Master Shakespeare,' said the girl firmly, 'but not after dark. And I did get a distinct fresh smell of bear.' She punctuated her insistence by downing the rest of her drink. 'I must get to work.'

'You will find men about so early?'

'It's past noon, Master Shakespeare. Even the laziest cock will be ready to crow by now.'

He smiled. She lingered. 'So… will I see you?'

'I'll find you around three. When everyone I might drink with has gone to the theatre… to see the latest great success of Sir Francis Beaumont and Master Fletcher.' He could not keep the bitterness out of his voice.

Dorcas left to trawl the alleyways for business. There was a clatter of the tavern door opening, and a tall, dark figure stalked out. By his clothes Charles recognised the man who had apparently seduced Ned Brackett away from Robert Hillard. In the daylight his purple doublet looked scuffed and worn; he was no genuine member of the Court.

He looked angry. Hard on his heels came Ned. The boy laid his hand on the purple sleeve and was shaken irritably off. The man strode away in a northerly direction. Ned Brackett stood still for an anguished moment, tears welling at his eyes. Then, seeing he was observed by Charles and Shakespeare, he rubbed a hand across his face and hurried off in the opposite direction from his former lover.

'Oh, the potency of dumb-show!' the playwright murmured. 'A whole story told without words. I am sorry that the dumb-show is now thought old-fashioned. Mind you, most of what I do is now thought old-fashioned.' The earlier anxieties continued to gnaw away at him. 'I really thought I was on to something with *Cymbeline*. What really worries me is the fact that the groundlings didn't get behind it. They didn't seem interested even in the battles.'

'It's the problem of nationality,' Charles reassured him. 'Always difficult when you're dealing with the Welsh. Scots, fine. You did that in *Macbeth*. Good play, great murder mystery. But Belarius and that lot in *Cymbeline*… you've hit a real difficulty there. Fine with one Welsh comic character like Fluellen. But when you've got lots of them… and they're meant to be heroic… I'm afraid it's virtually impossible to make the Welsh interesting to the rest of the people in this country.'

'Hm,' said Shakespeare.

'And Milford Haven's never going to sound great in blank verse.'

'No,' Shakespeare agreed. 'Doesn't even scan.'

'Come to the bear-baiting!' The ferret-faced man had resumed his pitch outside the Bull and went into his routine. 'This afternoon at three! See the dogs tear the living flesh from the bears! See the bears crush the dogs…'

'Should we frighten him off?' asked Charles.

'Why bother?' Shakespeare replied. 'We'd only be holding off the evil moment. The bear-baiting will win in the end.'

Before Charles could remonstrate, an unmistakable voice squeaked 'Master Shakespeare!', and the bulbous shape of Rokesby Lander wobbled towards them. Over his arm was draped a familiar black and silver doublet. 'See, the laundresses and the seamstresses have done their best. Your doublet is as good as it was when you first had it made.'

'Your doublet?' echoed Charles.

'Yes,' said Shakespeare. 'The doublet is mine.'

Suddenly the man from the Bear Garden stopped in the middle of his sales pitch. He gave a piercing look towards Shakespeare and Charles, as if memorising their faces. Then he turned sharply on his heel, and scuttled swiftly away.

'What was that about?' asked Shakespeare.

'Couldn't stand the competition? Knew what's happening at the Globe this afternoon will be better than any bear-baiting could be?'

'I doubt it, Master Parys. Perhaps, though. Not one of my doomed plays on today, one by the bright young Beaumont and Fletcher, so maybe it will be better than the bear-baiting.'

There seemed nothing Charles could say that didn't dig Shakespeare deeper into his pit of gloom. He tried a change of subject. 'What's all this about the doublet being yours?'

'It's true,' said Rokesby Lander.

'Certainly is, Master Parys. When I bought New Place in Stratford, I imagined briefly that I was joining the local gentry and had clothes made accordingly. But I found the local gentry neither interested in me nor interesting in themselves, so I rarely wore my finery. Whatever you dress him in, an actor will always be a vagabond at heart.'

'And a man is known by the clothes he wears.'

'Exactly, Master Parys. I am glad you've been paying attention to the lines I've written for you in *Cymbeline*.'

"*Thou villain base,*
Know'st me not by my clothes?"

Softly, Shakespeare took up the cue from Cloten's speech, and gave the reply of Guiderius : "*No, nor thy tailor, rascal,*
Who is thy grandfather: he made those clothes,
Which, as it seems, make thee."

'It is good stuff,' said Charles.

'Huh,' came the cynical response. 'Anyway, so I was in Stratford with these useless clothes and I thought, waste not, want not, and put this doublet – and the hose that went with it – back into the business.'

'Another costume the King's Men did not have to buy.'

'Precisely, Master Lander.' Shakespeare took the garment and looked closely at the almost invisible black stitching of the repair. 'To think this is the mouth through which a man's whole life spilled out...'

Fortunately, the Apparel Master had no time for an 'Alas! poor Yorick' moment. 'That's as maybe.' Gathering up the doublet, Rokesby Lander waddled away. 'I must get this to the tiring-house. See you later, Master Parys. Don't be late for *Philaster*. Or for me,' he added coyly. 'And not too much of the ale. Remember, you have a performance to give this afternoon.'

The advice was good, but Charles still had a temptation to go on drinking. It was a temptation that seemed to arise with ever greater frequency as he grew older. He looked across to his companion, and saw that Shakespeare had once again slumped into gloom.

'I'd like to do something that lasts.' The playwright was almost speaking to himself.

'I'm sure some of the plays will.'

The lack of conviction in Charles's tone must have communicated itself. 'I doubt it, Master Parys.'

'Who knows what posterity will think? If it's not through your work, then maybe your name will live on through your children...'

The melancholy brown eyes fixed on his. 'Do you have children, Charles?'

'A son. Also Charles. An idle boy. Has no talent for anything useful... so maybe he too will become a play-actor. Maybe I will be father to a whole dynasty of play-actors.'

The dome of Shakespeare's brow wrinkled. 'I'll have no dynasty. Not with the name of Shakespeare. My son Hamnet died fourteen years ago. He was only eleven.'

'I'm sorry.'

'Oh, it's just a life. These things happen. So far as the gods are concerned, we're just as flies to wanton boys.'

'"They kill us for their sport."'

The playwright smiled wearily. 'Yes. Dear oh dear. Repeating myself now.'

'That was good, though,' said Charles encouragingly. '*King Lear*. The groundlings loved it when Gloucester's eyes came out. That'll live on.'

'I doubt it.' Shakespeare was still locked in melancholy. 'And no son to carry on my name. Two daughters. Susanna made me a grandfather a couple of years back. But another girl. Elizabeth Hall. Not Shakespeare. The line will die with me. And in my current mood, the sooner that death comes, the better.'

'You are not ready for death.'

'Oh, I am.' Wryly, he quoted a line spoken by Posthumus Leonatus in his latest play. '"Over-roasted rather; ready long ago."' A failed husband, a failed father, a failed playwright... In fifty years the name of Shakespeare will be forgotten.'

Charles Parys knew that this was all too probably true, but it didn't do to say so. Instead, he resorted to the cure-all of actors since time began. Forget that afternoon's performance in *Philaster*. 'Potboy!' he called. 'More drinks over here!'

*   *   *

And more drinks inevitably led to more drinks. Charles knew he had a duty to his profession, but he had a greater duty to keep Shakespeare from slumping further into gloom. As a result, by three o'clock he was in no state to give the best account of himself in Beaumont and Fletcher's *Philaster, or Love Lies A-Bleeding*.

Simon Brett

The play was the usual tragi-comedy of thwarted lovers and mistaken identities. In previous performances Ned Brackett had been highly praised for his acting as Euphrasia, who spends most of the play disguised as the page Bellario; and Robert Hillard had cut a striking figure in the title role. But the actor who'd been drafted in at short notice to take the lead lacked the dead man's charisma and had a very shaky hold on the lines. Also it rained heavily all afternoon, water dripping from the thatched eaves on to the disgruntled groundlings. Even the plays' cast were not immune. The 'heavens', the roofing which should have protected the stage, had sprung many leaks, and new moves were added to those rehearsed as the actors dodged the drips.

The addition of a drunken Charles Parys to this mix did not improve the afternoon's theatrical experience. He was playing three parts – 1st Woodman, A Country Fellow and An Old Captain, but none of them came on till Act IV. As a result, during the first half Charles fell asleep in the tiring-house and, when woken for his cue by a very tetchy book-holder, had bleared vision and a sore head.

He stumbled onstage as 1st Woodman, realising he'd forgotten his bow and arrows. The lines came back to him in a slightly jumbled form, which would not have pleased either Sir Francis Beaumont or Master John Fletcher. Still, he managed to get his laughs on the dirty bits, notably the description of one female character: 'That's a firker, i'faith, boy; there's a wench will ride her haunches as hard after a kennel of hounds as a hunting saddle, and when she comes home, get 'em clapt, and all is well.' The groundlings always liked jokes about venereal disease.

Things got worse, however, when Charles Parys reappeared – with minimal costume change – as the Country Fellow. He got laughs there too, but not for the right reasons. His swordfight with the ill-prepared substitute Philaster had the pair of them skidding over the wet rushes on the stage till both ended up flat on their arses. Though the groundlings loved it, Charles got a severe ticking-off from the book-holder.

And it was a very slurred Old Captain – again in minimally different costume – who marched on with 'Citizens and Pharamond prisoner.' He even failed to get the sure-fire laugh on his response to the 1st Citizen's suggestion of castrating their prisoner: 'No, you shall spare his dowcets, my dear donsels.'

The performance got worse. Charles seemed to have lost his concentration completely, and the other actors had to keep feeding the Old Captain his cues.

But in fact it wasn't the drink that distracted Charles Parys. It was something he had seen happening in the audience, something that made him feel suddenly stone cold sober.

The long-nosed merchant Ezekiel Goodbody was sitting with his black-eyed wife in one of the galleries, safe from the rain. Charles was aware of a movement behind them, and saw a thin figure in painted leather approach. It was the man from the Bear Garden, the one who had vanished so abruptly from outside the tavern that morning. He leant forward to whisper something in Ezekiel Goodbody's ear. Whatever he said brought fury to the merchant's weasel face, a fury that gave way to an expression of pure evil.

Suddenly, everything fell into place for Charles Parys. He knew exactly what had happened to Robert Hillard. And he knew the same fate awaited someone else.

Sweat prickled on his temples as he gabbled through his last speech, which ended, rather appositely:

"then to the tavern,
And bring your wives in muffs. We will have music;
And the red grape shall make us dance and rise, boys."

Never before had *Philaster* witnessed such a quick exit. As Charles hurled himself through the tiring-house, the book-holder's hissed words faded away behind him. 'You'll be up before the shareholders for this, Master Parys! I've never witnessed such an unprofessional performance in the whole of my...'

*　*　*

William Shakespeare was sitting alone at a table in the Bull. On an opened leather carrying-roll was a sheet of paper; an unstoppered ink-bottle stood beside a cup of sack. The quill pen in his hand covered the page at speed, and there was a new luminosity in the dark eyes.

'Master Shakespeare!' cried a panting Charles Parys. 'You are in danger!'

'Ssh! I can be in no danger. I am writing again. *A Winter's Tale*

131

it's called, and it's working! Bless Dorcas! "I have,"' he went on, gleefully quoting *Cymbeline*, '"enjoyed the dearest bodily part of my mistress." Dorcas, for the moment, is sufficient muddy muse for me!'

'Master Shakespeare,' Charles insisted. 'Your life is in serious danger!'

'But my play is in no danger!' As he spoke, feverish with excitement, his hand continued, almost unconsciously, to spill words out on to the page. 'I've nearly finished the Third Act. The scene is: "Bohemia. A desert Country near the Sea." Antigonus has saved the baby Perdita and is about to abandon her there. I just need a good exit for him and the scene will be nearly done.'

'Listen!' Charles slammed his hand down on Shakespeare's. The quill dug into the paper in a splutter of ink.

'Why have you done that?' A dangerous fury came into the brown eyes. 'I cannot be stopped when the ideas are flowing!'

'If you do not listen to me, you will be stopped for ever!'

This did finally engage Shakespeare's attention. 'What do you mean?'

'I know who killed Robert Hillard, and now he is planning to kill you.'

'How do you know this?'

'Have you heard of a locksmith called Ezekiel Goodbody?'

'The one who has put money into the Bear Garden?'

'The very same. He married a pretty young wife a year or so back, and it's the old May and December problem.'

'She has a roving eye?'

'Yes, and she has needs that her husband cannot satisfy. He is mad with jealousy, to the point of killing anyone whom he suspects of making doe-eyes at his wife.'

'So is that why he killed Robert Hillard? If so, he was certainly badly informed. Master Hillard was as much attracted to a pretty young wife as I am to a week-old herring.'

'I know. But it was what Master Hillard looked like that caused his death. Ezekiel Goodbody has a spy, the scoundrel in painted leather we saw outside the tavern this morning.'

'And?'

'And he must have seen someone leaving Mistress Goodbody's chamber wearing the doublet that poor Master Hillard wore as

Posthumus Leonatus.'

'So that is why he was killed?'

'Yes. But by now all London knows that Robert Hillard had no lust for woman's flesh. So the murderer knows he had the wrong victim. But then this morning Master Goodbody's spy was on hand to hear you say that *you* owned the doublet.'

'Oh, my God!' The full gravity of the situation hit Shakespeare. 'So he thinks I am the one who has been colting his wife?' Charles Parys nodded. 'And will try to murder me too?'

'I fear so.'

'Master Parys, how do you know all this?'

'I've been thinking about it a lot. The solution came to me during the performance of *Philaster*. I saw the spy whispering to Master Goodbody.'

Shakespeare looked at him with new admiration. 'I had not thought of you as a follower of clues, a diviner of mysteries.'

Diffidently, Charles Parys spread his hands. 'A small talent I have.'

'If you have the skill to unmask murderers, I would not call that a small talent. I do not understand how you have enough information to reach these conclusions.'

'Just a matter of logic and deduction,' said Charles, with partial truth.

'I still find it strange… But to more immediate concerns. How am I to escape the avenging hand of Ezekiel Goodbody?'

'I have a plan, Master Shakespeare, that will not only save your life, but also see that the villain gets the punishment he deserves.'

*   *   *

'We meet again,' said the Constable.

A potboy instantly brought a cup of ale as the Constable lowered his considerable bulk on to a tiny stool. No payment would ever be requested for the drink. The tavern-keeper knew the wisdom of keeping the right side of the law.

'Good to see you, Master Dewberry,' said Shakespeare. 'I hope you didn't take to heart any of those silly rumours that…?'

'No, no, no, Master Shakespeare. I know people said there was a dissimilarity between me and the Constable in your play, but so far as I am conserved, it was, as the title goes...' He paused and chuckled heavily '...*much ado about nothing*. And the people who make such allocations that I am a fellow who gets words wrong, do nothing but show up their own ignominy. They do not seem to compromise that your character is *Dog*berry and mine is *Dew*berry, so there cannot be any caparison between the two, by any stretch of the invigilation.'

'You're absolutely right,' said Shakespeare, earnestly avoiding Charles's eye. 'Now do you understand Master Parys's plan?'

'I do. And I think it a work of great genitalia. The Watch and I will do what is necessitous, and discharge ourselves like true offenders of the Crown.'

'Good,' said Charles Parys, earnestly avoiding Shakespeare's eye. 'I knew I could rely on you.'

*   *   *

Charles lifted the foul leather drape that hung over the Bull's window to see his plan unfold. William Shakespeare, full of hot sack for courage, had stepped boldly out of the tavern's door and set off on exactly the fatal route that Robert Hillard had followed. The playwright paused at the corner where the flickering torchlight melted to darkness and, sure enough, in that moment a dark figure in a fur cloak leapt towards him. Thin steel gleamed in the dwindling light.

Instantly Dewberry's men leapt from their hiding places, and the Constable himself bellowed out, 'Stop, in the name of the Watch!'

The fur-cloaked figure, still only a dark outline against the greater darkness, turned on his heel and fled, with the ragged, shouting Watch in full pursuit.

William Shakespeare was unhurt, but shaken. Somewhat unsteadily, he made his way back to the safety of the Bull.

*   *   *

Charles Parys had changed from ale to sack, its tartness softened by sugar, warmed by the thrust of a red-hot poker. Shakespeare ordered the same and they settled down to put away a good few of them.

A little later, Ned Brackett came into the tavern and looked around disconsolately.

'Are you looking for your gentleman of the Court?' asked Charles.

'He's no more a gentleman of the Court than you are,' said the boy venomously. 'The chain he gave me is of painted tin, and all I am left with is a nasty discharge in my pizzle that will send me to the apothecary.'

'Who will prescribe you a course of sweating to cure your clap,' said Shakespeare.

'That's something to look forward to.' The boy turned sullenly towards the tavern door. 'Never again will I be taken in by rich apparel. In future I will find out the character of the man inside the clothes.'

'You know,' said Shakespeare as Ned Brackett trailed out, 'maybe *Cymbeline*'s not such a bad play, after all. There's some good stuff in there about appearance and reality.'

'Of course there is,' Charles Parys agreed enthusiastically.

And then Dewberry appeared to report on the success of his mission. Once again, as the Constable sat down, a complimentary cup of ale appeared as if by magic in front of him.

A smile sat smugly on his broad features. 'We have him, sirs, condemned by his own emission. I had hardly to mention the thumbscrews or the bastinado before he freely confused to the murder of Master Hillard. And omitted to the attempted murder of Master Shakespeare. He's now locked in chains of his own man-ufacture – a fitting fate for such an evil melon.'

Charles Parys raised his eyebrows and mouthed, 'Melon?'

'Felon,' Shakespeare mouthed back.

Charles nodded, suppressing a giggle. 'And was he easily caught, Master Dewberry?'

'By no means. He was fast for a man of his age, and ran back to the Bear Garden in Shoreside Lane, which he owns. There he thought to fructate the watch in the perusal of their duties by releasing one of the bears on us. But the beast, remembering the many cruelties of Master Goodbody, turned instead on his master. How it mauled and mammocked him! The beast chased him straight out of the bear-pit and into the expectorant arms of my faithful Watch.'

A blissful, beatific expression had settled on Shakespeare's face. He dipped his quill in the ink bottle, and Charles Parys watched as he wrote : 'EXIT, PURSUED BY A BEAR.'

* * *

Charles was the last of the three to leave. Dewberry had bustled off after a few cups of ale, professing that he must find his wife to 'raise up an object of great impotence.' Dorcas had appeared, and Shakespeare had gone off to spend the night in the arms of his muddy muse, leaving enough money on the table to pay the evening's reckoning twice over.

As Charles Parys sipped at the warm sweetness of a new sugared sack, he wondered how long he'd leave it before persuading Rokesby Lander to lend him the black doublet once again, so that he could pay another – now risk-free – visit to the voluptuous and avid wife of Ezekiel Goodbody.

The Wagon Mound

Val McDermid

Nothing destroys the quality of life so much as insomnia. Ask any parent of a new baby. It only takes a few broken nights to reduce the most calm and competent person to a twitching shadow of their normal proficiency. My wakefulness started when the nightmares began. When I did manage to drop off, the visions my subconscious mind conjured up were guaranteed to wake me, sweating and terrified, within a couple of hours of nodding off. It didn't take long before I began to fear sleep itself, dreading the demons that ripped through the fabric of my previous ease. I tried sleeping pills, I tried alcohol. But nothing worked.

I never dreamed that I'd rediscover the art of sleeping through the night thanks to a legal precedent. In 1961, the Privy Council heard a case concerning a negligent oil spillage from a ship called the *Wagon Mound* in Sydney Harbour. The oil fouled a nearby wharf, and in spite of expert advice that it wouldn't catch fire, when the wharf's owners began welding work, the oil did exactly what it wasn't supposed to. The fire that followed caused enough damage for it to be worth taking to court, where the Privy Council finally decreed that the ship's owners weren't liable because the *type* of harm sustained by the plaintiff was not, as the law required, reasonably foreseeable. When Roger, the terminally boring commercial attaché at the Moscow embassy, launched into the tale the other night in the bar at Proyekt OGI, he could never have imagined that it would change my life so dramatically. But then, lawyers have never been noted for their imagination.

Proximity. That's another legal principle that came up during Roger's lecture. How many intervening stages lie between cause and effect. I think, by then, I was the only one listening, because his disquisition had made me think back to the starting point of my sleepless nights.

Although the seeds were sown when my boss in London decided to invite the bestselling biographer Tom Uttley on a British

Council tour of Russia, I can't be held accountable for that. The first point where I calculate I have to accept responsibility was on the night train from Moscow to St. Petersburg.

I'd been looking after Tom ever since he'd landed at Sheremetyevo Airport two days before. I hadn't seen him smile in all that time. He'd lectured lugubriously at the university, glumly addressed a gathering at the British Council library, done depressing signings at two bookshops, and sulked his way round a reception at the Irish embassy. Even the weather seemed to reflect his mood, grey clouds lowering over Moscow and turning April into autumn. Minding visiting authors is normally the part of my job I like best, but spending time with Tom was about as much fun as having a hole in your shoe in a Russian winter. We'd all been hoping for some glamour from Tom's visit; his Channel Four series on the roots of biography had led us to expect a glowing Adonis with twinkling eyes and a gleaming grin. Instead, we got a glowering black dog.

Over dinner on the first evening, he'd downed his vodka like a seasoned Russian hand, and gloomed like the most depressive Slav in the Caucasus. On the short walk back to his hotel, I asked him if everything was all right. 'No,' he said shortly. 'My wife's just left me.'

Right, I thought. *Don't go there, Sarah.* 'Oh,' I think I said.

The final event of his Moscow visit was a book signing, and afterwards, I took him to dinner to pass the time till midnight, when the train would leave for St Pete's. That was when the floodgates opened. He was miserable, he admitted. He was terrible company. But Rachel had walked out on him after eight years of marriage. There wasn't anyone else, she'd said. It was just that she was bored with him, tired of his celebrity, fed up of feeling inferior intellectually. I pointed out that these reasons seemed somewhat contradictory.

He brightened up at that. And suddenly the sun came out. He acted as if I'd put my finger on something that should make him feel better about the whole thing. He radiated light, and I basked in the warmth of his smile. Before long, we were laughing together, telling our life stories, swapping intimacies. Flirting, I suppose.

We boarded the train a little before midnight, each dumping our bags in our separate first-class compartments. Then Tom produced a bottle of Georgian champagne from his holdall.

'A nightcap?' he suggested.

'Why not?' I was in the mood, cheered beyond reason by the delights of his company. He sat down on the sleeping birth beside me, and it seemed only natural when his arm draped across my shoulders. I remember the smell of him; a dark, masculine smell with an overlay of some spicy cologne with an edge of cinnamon. If I'm honest, I was willing to kiss him before he actually did. I was entirely disarmed by his charm. But I also felt sorry for the pain that had been so obvious over the previous two days. And maybe, just maybe, the inherent *Dr Zhivago* romance of the night train tipped the balance.

I don't usually do this kind of thing. What am I saying? I *never* do this kind of thing. In four years of chasing around after authors, or having them chase me, I'd not given in to temptation once. But Tom penetrated all of my professional defenses, and I moaned under his hands from Moscow to St. Petersburg. By morning, he swore I'd healed his heart. By the time he left St. Pete's three days later, we'd arranged to meet in London, where I was due to attend a meeting in ten days' time. I'd been out of love for a long time; it wasn't hard to fall for a man who was handsome, clever, and amusing, and who seemed to find me irresistible.

Two days later, I got his first email. I'd been checking every waking hour on the hour, wondering and edgy. It turned out I had good reason to be anxious. The email was short and sour: 'Dear Sarah, Rachel and I have decided that we want to try to resolve our difficulties. It'll come as no surprise to you that my marriage is my number-one priority. So I think it best if we don't communicate further. Sorry if this seems cold, but there's no other way to say it. Tom.'

I was stunned. This wasn't cold, it was brutal. A hard jab below the ribs, designed to take my breath away and deflect any possible comeback. I felt the physical shock in the pit of my stomach.

Of course, I blamed myself for my stupidity, my eagerness to believe that a man as charismatic as Tom could fall for me. Good old reliable Sarah, the safe pair of hands who second-guessed authors' needs before they could even voice them. I felt such a fool. A bruised, exploited fool.

Time passed, but there was still a raw place deep inside me. Tom Uttley had taken more from me than a few nights of sexual pleasure; he'd taken away my trust in my judgment. I told nobody about my humiliation. It would have been one pain too many.

Then Lindsay McConnell arrived. An award-winning drama-tist, she'd come to give a series of workshops on radio adaptation. She was impeccably professional, no trouble to take care of. And we hit it off straightaway. On her last night, I took her to my favourite Moscow eating place, a traditional Georgian restaurant tucked away in a courtyard in the Armenian quarter. As the wine slipped down, we gossiped and giggled. Then, in the course of some anecdote, she mentioned Tom Uttley. Just hearing his name made my guts clench. 'You know Tom?' I asked, struggling not to sound too interested.

'Oh God, yes. I was at university with Rachel, his wife. Of course, you had Tom out here last year, didn't you? He said he'd had a really interesting time.'

I bet he did, I thought bitterly. 'How are they now? Tom and Rachel?' I asked with the true masochist's desire for the twist of the knife.

Lindsay looked puzzled. 'What do you mean, how are they now?'

'When Tom was here, Rachel had just left him.'

She frowned. 'Are you sure you're not confusing him with someone else? They're solid as a rock, Tom and Rachel. God knows, if he was mine I'd have murdered him years ago, but Rachel thinks the sun shines out of his arse.'

It was my turn to frown. 'He told me she'd just walked out on him. He was really depressed about it.'

Lindsay shook her head. 'God, how very Tom. He hates tour-ing, you know. He'll do anything to squeeze out a bit of sympathy, make sure he gets premier-league treatment. He just likes to have everyone running around after him, Sarah. I'm telling you, Rachel has never left him. Now I think about it, that week he was in Russia, I went round there for dinner. Me and Rachel and a cou-ple of her colleagues. You know, from *Material Girl.* The magazine she works for. I think if they'd split up, she might have mentioned it, don't you?'

I hoped I wasn't looking as stunned as I felt. I'd never thought of myself as stupid, but that calculating bastard had spun me a line and reeled me in open-mouthed like the dumbest fish in the pond. But of course, because I'm a woman and that's how we're trained to think, I was still blaming myself more than him. I'd clearly been sending out the signals of needy gullibility and he'd just come up with the right line to exploit them.

I was still smarting from what I saw as my self-inflicted wound a few weeks later at the Edinburgh Book Festival, where we British Council types gather like bees to pollen. But at least I'd finally have the chance to share my idiocy with Camilla, my opposite number in Jerusalem. We'd worked together years before in Paris and we'd become bosom buddies. The only reason I hadn't told her about Tom previously was that every time I wrote it down in an email it just looked moronic. It needed a girls' night in with a couple of bottles of decent red before I could let this one spill out.

Late on the second night, after a particularly gruelling Amnesty International event, we sneaked back to the flat we were sharing with a couple of the boys from the Berlin office and started in on the confessional. My story crawled out of me, and I realized yet again how foolish I'd been from the horrified expression on Camilla's face. That and her appalled silence. 'I don't believe it,' she breathed.

'I know, I know,' I groaned. 'How could I have been so stupid?'

'No, no,' she said angrily. 'Not you, Sarah. Tom Uttley.'

'What?'

'That duplicitous bastard Uttley. He pulled exactly the same stunt on Georgie Bullen in Madrid. The identical line about his wife leaving him. She told me about it when I flew in for Semana Negra last month.'

'But I thought Georgie was living with someone?'

'She was,' Camilla said. 'Paco, the stage manager at the opera house. She'd taken Uttley down to Granada to do some lectures there, that's when it happened. Georgie saw the scumbag off on the plane and came straight home and told Paco it was over, she'd met someone else. She threw him out, then two days later she got the killer email from Tom.'

We gazed at each other, mouths open. 'The bastard,' I said. For the first time, anger blotted out my self-pity and pain.

'Piece of shit,' Camilla agreed.

We spent the rest of the bottle and most of the second one thinking of ways to exact revenge on Tom Uttley, but we both knew that there was no way I was going back to Moscow to find a hit man to take him out. The trouble was, we couldn't think of anything that would show him up without making us look like silly credulous girls. Most blokes, no matter how much they might pretend otherwise, would reckon, good on him for working out such a foolproof scam to get his leg over. Most women would reckon we'd got what we deserved for being so naïve.

I was thirty thousand feet above Poland when the answer came to me. The woman in the seat next to me had been reading *Material Girl* and she offered it to me when she'd finished. I looked down the editorial list, curious to see exactly what Rachel Uttley did on the magazine. Her name was near the top of the credits. *Fiction Editor, Rachel Uttley.* A quick look at the contents helped me deduct that as well as the books page, Rachel was responsible for editing the three short stories. There, at the end of the third, was a sentence saying that submissions for publication should be sent to her.

I've always wanted to write. One of the reasons I took this job in the first place was to learn as much as I could from those who do it successfully. I had half a novel on my hard disk, but I reckoned it was time to try a short story.

Two days later, I'd written it. The central character was a biographer who specialised in seducing professional colleagues on foreign trips with a tale about his wife having left him. Then he'd dump them as soon as he'd got home. When one of his victims realizes what he's been up to, she exposes the serial adulterer by sending his wife, a magazine editor, a short story revealing his exploits. And the wife, recognizing her errant husband from the pen portrait, finally does walk out on him.

Before I could have second thoughts, I printed it out and stuffed it in an envelope addressed to Rachel at *Material Girl*. Then I sat back and waited.

For a couple of weeks, nothing happened. Then, one Tuesday morning, I was sitting in the office browsing BBC online news. His name leapt out at me. TOM UTTLEY DIES IN BURGLARY, read the headline in the latest news section. I clicked on the 'more' button.

"Bestselling biographer and TV presenter Tom Uttley was found dead this morning at his home in North London. It is believed he disturbed a burglar. He died from a single stab wound to the stomach. Police say there was evidence of a break-in at the rear of the house.

Uttley was discovered by his wife, Rachel, a journalist. Police are calling for witnesses who may have seen one or two men fleeing the scene in the early hours of the morning."

I had to read the bare words three or four times before they sank in. Suddenly his lies didn't matter anymore. All I could think of was his eyes on mine, the flash of his easy smile, the touch of his hand. The sparkle of wit in his conversation. The life in him that had been snuffed out. The books he would never write.

Over a succession of numb days, I pursued the story via the Internet. Bits and pieces emerged gradually. They'd had an attempted burglary a few months before. Rachel who was a poor sleeper, had taken sleeping pills and stuffed ear plugs in before going to bed. Tom, the police reckoned, had heard the sound of breaking glass and gone downstairs to investigate. The intruder had snatched up a knife from the kitchen worktop and plunged it into his stomach, then fled. Tom had bled to death on the kitchen floor. It had taken him awhile to die, they thought. And Rachel had come down for breakfast to find him stiff and cold on the kitchen floor. Poor bloody Rachel, I thought.

On the fifth day after the news broke, there was a large Manila envelope among my post, franked with the *Material Girl* logo. My story had come winging its way back to me. Inside, there was a handwritten note from Rachel.

Dear Sarah, Thank you so much for you submission. I found your story intriguing and thought provoking. A real eye-opener, in fact. But I felt the ending was rather weak and so I regret we're unable to publish it. However, I like your style. I'd be very interested to see more of your work. Gratefully yours, Rachel Uttley.

That's when I realized what I'd done. Like Oscar Wilde, I'd killed the thing I'd loved.

That's when my sleepless nights started.

And that's why I am so very grateful for Roger and the case they call Wagon Mound (No.1) And for an understanding of proximity. Thanks to him, I've finally realized I'm not the guilty party here. Neither is Rachel.

The guilty party is the one who started the wagon rolling. Lovely, sexy, reckless Tom Uttley.

Mat Coward

'Find the name and address of the person who's renting the PO Box,' said the client, 'and keep it to yourself. Simple, yeah?'

'*Don't* tell you what I've found out?'

'Right.'

'Right,' I said. He'd explained it twice and I still didn't get it. 'I could,' I pointed out, 'simply ask at the post office. They're obliged to tell you, I believe.'

The client – Barry Irving, a man in his fifties with long grey hair and a short grey beard – shook his head. A chain of beads around his neck rattled. 'No, no good. I'm pretty sure she's given the post office false details.'

'All right,' I said, and wrote down *false details* in my notebook. 'And do you have any kind of description of the person you're looking for?'

'It's a woman,' he said.

I wrote down *woman*. 'Well, that's a start.'

He nodded. 'It's a start. Yeah.'

He was looking at me hard. There was a question he wanted to ask me, but he didn't know how to phrase it politely. To save time, I answered it for him. 'I'm twenty-three,' I said. 'I look younger, but I'm actually twenty-three. I've been working as a private detective for one year.'

'OK,' said Irving. 'That's cool. And do you, like, own the agency?'

'Well, the office is rented. As a matter of fact, so is the furniture.' I looked around me. 'Except for the umbrella stand. That belongs to my grandmother.'

He looked at the umbrella stand. He didn't look at it long, because there wasn't much of it. It wasn't a fancy umbrella stand. 'It's very nice,' he said.

'Thank you. I have it on indefinite loan. I'm a sole trader, Mr Irving. Just me.'

He nodded. His beads bounced. 'Cool.'

'Let me make sure I've got things straight,' I said, writing *cool* in my notebook. 'You want me to identify the person who rents PO Box 171 at the Post Office in Cork Street.'

'It's actually behind the post office – that's where you collect the post from. There's an entrance next to the sorting office.'

'All right. You know that this person is a woman – '

'Sure. A woman, definitely.'

' – and that she always collects her mail on Thursday afternoons. But you don't know, or don't wish to tell me, anything else. Like, what your interest in this person is, or what she's up to, or ... anything?'

He thought about that. His beads kept still. 'I don't have to discuss my motivation with you, do I?'

'No, not at all. Provided you're not asking me to break the law, or planning to use the information I provide you with to break the law, then no – you don't have to tell me anything.'

Irving smiled. 'Then that's cool.'

'But it doesn't make my job any easier, I have to say.'

He shrugged and his beads shrugged with him. 'With respect, Mr Walker, that's not really my problem.'

*   *   *

The next day was Wednesday. At 10.15 in the morning, I entered the PO Box office via the door next to the sorting office, and rang the bell marked 'Please Ring For Attention.' After three minutes, a man wearing a turban and a postman's tunic appeared behind the counter. I assumed he was also wearing trousers, but I couldn't see his legs from where I was standing.

'Sorry to keep you waiting,' he said. 'What can I do you for?'

'Actually, I think I'm in the wrong place. I wanted to get a passport application form.'

He leaned across the counter and pointed through the door I'd just come in by. 'Yeah, you need the Post Office proper. This is the sorting office. Go back out, turn left, you'll see there's a little path there. You follow that, turn left again, and there you are.'

'Thanks. Sorry to trouble you.'

'No problem. Enjoy your holiday.'

My recce of the PO Box place had shown me, as I had expected, that it was not somewhere where I would be able to loiter inconspicuously. It was too small, and not busy enough. The boxes themselves weren't on display, so presumably the addressee Rang For Attention, showed some sort of identification, and waited while the post was fetched.

On leaving the office, I didn't take the helpful man's advice about how to find the main post office entrance. I already had a passport. Instead, I scouted out the surrounding area, looking for a spot from which I might observe the comings and goings of the box-holders.

I guessed that the employees' car park immediately behind the PO Box entrance would be quiet enough, except during shift changes. Towards the back of the tarmac area there was a large tree. I didn't know what sort of tree it was – I know regrettably little about trees – but I noticed that there were no vehicles parked immediately beneath it. On inspecting the ground, I discovered why: the tree shed some kind of sticky substance, which would make a mess of a car's windscreen and paintwork. When I returned the following day at 11.30 am, therefore, I made for the sticky tree, and set up my observation point at its base, from where I had a decent view of the door in question, but was reasonably well hidden by surrounding shrubbery.

Mr Irving had said that the target always collected her post on Thursday afternoons – he'd been unable or unwilling to be more precise – and I'd established that the office closed at 5.30pm. I had with me, therefore, a packet of cheese and pickle sandwiches, a large bottle of mineral water, and an empty mineral water bottle. It was a warm summer afternoon so I didn't bother with any protective clothing. Though I did, of course, bring that item known as the private eye's best friend – the umbrella.

If anyone saw me, they'd probably think I was a school kid bunking off school. Except that I don't smoke.

During the first three hours of my observation, seven people entered the PO Box office, presumably to collect their mail. Two of the seven emerged empty-handed. One of the two wore a face filled with fury and muttered angrily to himself as he left. Seven of the seven were men. I took photographs of every comer and goer with my digital camera.

Two more hours passed, during which I yawned forty-three times and urinated once. I was glad I hadn't brought a book, as by now I would have been bored enough to read it, and therefore possibly to miss the arrival of the target. I did consider using my WAP phone to look up sticky trees on the internet, but that's not really what I bought it for.

At 4.37pm, a woman entered the office. She was about sixty, smartly dressed, and wearing sunglasses. Five minutes later, she exited the office, carrying several large envelopes.

I waited until she was on the high street – it's not a good idea for young men to approach old women on secluded pathways – and then I called after her.

'Excuse me!' I jogged up to her as she turned round. I panted a little, for effect, and slapped at my chest a couple of times. I also blushed. The blushing wasn't something I had control over, but it was probably quite helpful even so. 'Excuse me, but I think you dropped this.'

'Me?'

I showed her an A4 buff envelope, which I had stuffed the night before with circulars advertising digital television and invisible hearing aids. 'That is you, I presume – PO Box 171?'

'Oh no, I'm 208.' She showed me one of her envelopes by way of proof. It was addressed to Ms J. Sands, PO Box 208, Cork Street.

'Oh, dear – how embarrassing!' I rolled my eyes and blushed some more.

'Not at all.'

'I just saw the envelope on the floor back there, and I saw you carrying a pile of envelopes, and I just assumed ... Oh well, I suppose I'll just hand it in at the post office.'

'Yes, I should. They'll know what to do with it.'

'Right. Well – sorry to have troubled you.'

She smiled. 'Not at all. It was very kind of you.'

When I got back to my tree, I wrote down Ms Sands' name and box number in my notebook. I ate another sandwich.

I didn't have to wait long for the next female customer to turn up. This one was middle-aged, quite fat, and dressed for jogging. She was wearing sleek-looking running shoes, but I reckoned I could catch her if I had to. In the event, I caught her up without breaking into a sweat. She too denied being PO Box 171, though she didn't volunteer her correct number, nor let me get a clear sight of the sole envelope she was carrying. She wasn't very friendly at all, in fact.

By closing time, those two were the only women I'd seen collecting mail. I wasn't surprised that neither of them had turned out to be the target, since neither of them had been in possession of the large, tartan envelope I had posted to PO Box 171 two days earlier.

I was, on the other hand, a little concerned at the target's apparent absence. It was possible that I'd missed her while I'd been accosting the two false alarms; but if so, she must have been in and out of the sorting office in a hurry. Which, of course, she might well be, if her business there was of a nefarious nature.

I was wondering about this – and also about the more curious aspects of my client's instructions – while I hid in the shrubbery behind the sticky tree, allowing the 5.30 shift change a chance to disperse before I went home. It was fortunate that I took this precaution.

At 5.35pm, a young woman – by far the youngest I'd seen today, and of somewhat distinctive appearance – arrived at the PO Box office door in a hurry. She'd clearly run some distance, and her panting was altogether more convincing than mine had been. She rattled the door, and discovered it locked. She read the notice affixed to the door, which declared the office's opening hours, then she rattled the door again. She looked at her watch. She swore, loudly. She banged at her own head with balled fists, though not very hard. She kicked the door and swore again, even more loudly than before.

From around the side of the building, a postal worker appeared. It was the same turbaned man I'd spoken to the previous day. I was too far away to hear much of the subsequent conversation, beyond the odd word which the woman spoke at full volume, but the gist was not difficult to determine. She pointed at her watch several times, and he shook his head on an equal number of occasions. She raised her hands above her head and looked incredulous. He shrugged. She pointed at the locked door, and he pointed at the sign.

She departed, still shaking her head in disgust or disbelief. He read the sign through once more, nodded to himself, and disappeared back where he'd come from.

By the time all was quiet again and I felt it safe to come out from behind my tree, mount my moped and ride it to the high street, there was no sign of the young woman. Before heading for home, I used my mobile phone to send a text message and an email to my client, Mr Irving. Both asked the same question: 'As far as you know, does the woman I'm looking for have a shaved head and rings through her nose?'

* * *

I didn't know how rigid the target's habit of collecting her mail only on Thursdays might be. Perhaps that was the only day of the week on which she could possibly get to her PO Box. I hoped not, because if it was I was in for a long, dull Friday.

This time, I arrived at the sticky tree very early, before the office opened. In addition to my mineral water, empty bottle, and sandwiches, I had a flask of black tea and several slices of my grandmother's oat surprise. (If you ask her what the surprise is, she replies: 'Nothing. You don't get many surprises with oats'.)

There had been no reply so far to my query concerning the nose rings. I wasn't really expecting one. Mr Irving either didn't know what the target looked like, or else he knew and didn't want to tell me. For whatever reason.

My secret hope was that the young woman with the shaved head would turn up as soon as the office opened, eager to complete her frustrated mission; that she would leave carrying a large tartan envelope full of pamphlets outlining the advantages of thermal underwear; and that I would be able to follow her discreetly on my moped. Having thus discovered her name and address, I would have fulfilled my unorthodox commission.

When the first female caller at the office was the fat jogger from the previous day, I logged her in my notebook, but other than that thought nothing of it. Presumably, quite a lot of people emptied their PO Boxes on a daily basis. In any case, she was followed within seconds by the young woman – I put her at about my age, or a few years older – with the shaven head and the nose rings. I made myself ready to move, which primarily involved swallowing a large but unsurprising mouthful of oats, putting my notebook in my pocket, and picking up my bag.

The two women were inside the building for just over four minutes, and they exited it simultaneously – or at least, as simultaneously as a fat woman and a woman with nose rings *can* exit an ordinary-sized doorway. I crouched, ready to make a run for my moped as soon as they were out of sight. Which was when I noticed that the middle-aged jogger, not the young razorhead, was carrying the tartan envelope.

I had been so certain until then that the young woman was the target, that for a moment I wasn't sure what to do; which woman to trail. However, after a moment's consideration I decided that, when in doubt, one should always follow the thermal underwear.

★   ★   ★

She was on foot, which made it harder to follow her, but easier not to lose her. I mean that it is difficult, when mounted on a moped, to tail a pedestrian without being obvious, but that at least they are not likely to get away from you.

I didn't dare dump the bike, in case she suddenly got into a car or cab, or onto a bus. Or, indeed, onto a moped. In any profession, there are certain mistakes which one makes only once.

As they proceeded down the high street, with me wobbling along behind them, it seemed possible that the two women knew each other; from behind, and at a distance, it was hard to tell whether they were talking as they walked, but they could have been.

After a couple of minutes, the young woman went into a shoe shop, while the middle-aged one kept walking. I'd already made my decision: I was following the fat jogger. She had the tartan envelope, so she must be the holder of Box 171. I could only suppose that the reason she hadn't had the envelope yesterday was because it had been delayed in the post, despite the fact that I'd posted it in the post office attached to the sorting office, and therefore its journey had been one of approximately twenty yards.

The fat jogger turned off the high street after a couple of minutes, and into a residential street consisting mostly of Victorian houses converted into flats. A third of the way along this road she let herself into one such house.

I wrote down the address in my notebook. There were no names on the doorbells, and I couldn't risk speaking to the woman in case she recognised me from the previous day, so I would have to get her name the slow way – by checking the electoral register, and then cross-checking via an internet search.

I was riding off to do just that when I saw the nose-rings girl come out of the shoe shop. Despite her shaven head, and her rather grubby-looking leather jacket, she was quite an attractive young woman. I noticed that she had legs, eyes, a bottom and so on; all those things which, in my opinion, make most women quite attractive. I decided that I might as well follow her, too, just to be thorough. It was the professional thing to do.

It didn't take long. She walked directly to the same house the other woman had entered – and entered it herself, using a key.

Well. Mother and daughter? This was interesting, but strictly speaking none of my business. Mr Irving had hired me to find out the name and address of the woman who rented PO Box 171, Cork Street. I had the address; I would soon have the name. End of job.

When I got back to my office, I worked at the computer for a while, and then phoned the client on his mobile – I didn't have a home number for him – and told him that I had identified the target. I had photographs of her. Would he like to see them? I could bring them round now.

'No, no! Not necessary. You've done what I asked you to do, that's cool. You keep the photos, all right? Keep them in your office.'

'Well, OK. I'll send you my bill, then.'

I could hear birds singing in the background on his end of the line. He was speaking quietly, so I wasn't sure I heard him correctly when he said: 'Are you absolutely sure?'

'Well, yes,' I said. 'I always send a bill.'

'No, like – are you absolutely *sure* you've got the right woman?'

'Mr Irving, I sent her a distinctive envelope, I saw her collect it, I followed her home, I saw her open the front door with a key, and I checked her name on the electoral register and double-checked on the internet. I am sure, Mr Irving. I am competent.' And I *am* older than I look, I didn't add.

'Sure, yeah, that's cool – it's just that you sent me that weird email. I was worried that you were, like, losing your focus.'

'The girl with the shaven head?' I wasn't sure how to tell him about her without actually telling him anything – as per his instructions. 'Forget about her, Mr Irving. False alarm.'

I heard a female voice in Mr Irving's hinterland, competing with the birds. 'OK,' said the client. 'That's cool. Got to go.' He went.

I sat at my desk for a while, trying to work it out.

Mr Irving hired me to collect some information, under strict orders that I was not to tell him what I discovered. This was a first in my experience as a private detective.

If he didn't want my information, then he must already have it. So why was I hired? An unpleasant thought crept up on me. If his intentions towards Diane Eden, the fat jogger, were heinous, then perhaps I was to be his alibi. Through me he could prove – albeit in a somewhat circuitous fashion – that he didn't know her identity.

If so, why would he wish to harm her; what was she to him? The obvious answer – she was a blackmailer. She was a lover or ex-lover, and she was threatening to tell his wife.

It was none of my business. The job was done. All I had to do was send the bill. But a reputable private detective does not turn a blind eye to crime, or potential crime. It would be unprofessional. Besides, I really wanted to know who that shaven-headed girl was.

* * *

That evening on my computer, and the following day on my moped, I checked up on my client. I found that Mr Irving worked as an accountant – not, as his appearance and manner might have suggested, as a rock promoter – and that he lived in an unexceptionally nice house in a quiet street with his wife and dogs. The dogs were named Hendrix and Dylan. They had two children (Mr and Mrs Irving, I mean), both of whom were in their thirties, neither of whom lived with their parents.

My blackmail theory was getting firmer and I was getting nervous. I needed to know what the connection was between the client and the target, and whether it was something I would have to tell the police about.

From the back of a borrowed van, parked near the Irving's home, I took some photos of my client with my digital camera. I returned the van, rode back to my office and printed out the best of the pictures.

At four that afternoon, I rode to Diane Eden's street, and rang her buzzer. The younger woman answered. I didn't know her name, because she wasn't on the electoral register.

'Good afternoon,' I said. 'I'm sorry to trouble you, but I'm a –'

'I don't have a car,' she said.

'Oh. Fine. So – do you need a lift somewhere?'

She sighed and rolled her eyes. I hoped she wouldn't start hitting her head again. 'I don't have a *car,* yeah? So I don't need my car *washed.* Right?'

'Ah. Right. Actually, I'm not a Boy Scout, and I'm older than I look, and I'm a private detective, and I – '

She laughed. 'You're a what?'

I felt a blush starting. It occurred to me that I would be very happy to be old and bald and wrinkly if it meant I no longer blushed. 'I'm a private detective, and I – '

She shook her head and began to close the door. 'We're a bit busy now, kid. Family conference.'

I took the photo of Mr Irving out of my pocket. 'I'm trying to trace this man, here. He's not in any trouble or anything, in fact it's to do with a bequest, and I understand he used to live in this street. You see, I'm a private detective, and I – '

She looked at the photo, looked at me as if I'd just turned into a hobgoblin before her eyes, and shouted behind her into the hall. 'Mum!'

The voice of Diane Eden called back: 'I heard – you'd better bring him in.'

The shaven-headed daughter took hold of my arm and steered me through the first door on the left. We were in the small entrance hall of a small and rather dark flat. The door slammed behind me, revealing the fat jogger herself. She was wearing a tracksuit. She had her right hand in her right trouser pocket. From the outline, it was obvious that the hand was gripping something solid. Solid and dangerous.

'Get in there,' she said, indicating the living-room with a nod of her head.

'Is that a pleased-to-see-me in your pocket,' I said, 'or are you just gun?' I blush when I'm nervous. Until then, I didn't know that I also gabble when I'm terrified.

'Keith Walker – what the hell are you doing here?'

My client sat in a deep armchair at the far side of the room. At first I thought he was tied up, but then I realised this was merely an illusion of body language; he was sitting in the chair *as if* he were tied to it. His eyes met mine briefly, but for the most part they were busy staring at Ms Eden's bulging pocket.

'You know this kid?' she said.

I tried to explain. 'I'm a private detective, and I – '

'You're a what?'

Her daughter said: 'He's older than he looks, apparently.'

'Well he'd have to be, wouldn't he? Otherwise he'd be an egg. So what,' said Ms Eden, jerking her chin at Mr Irving, 'is a private detective doing looking for *him*?'

'Actually,' I said, 'I'm not.'

The daughter poked me in the back with a finger. 'You said you were.'

'So,' said Diane Eden, 'not only are you younger than you look, you're less honest, too.'

Mr Irving groaned, and his beads shook. 'He was working for me.'

'What are you talking about?'

'I hired him so that if you killed me – '

'*Killed* you?'

' – an independent witness would be able to tell the cops what was going on.'

'*Kill* you?' Her grip, it seemed to me, tightened on the hard object in her pocket.

My client sat up a little straighter in his chair. 'Yeah, so think about that, Diane. My man Walker here has photos of you collecting mail from your PO Box. Got them in his office safe, haven't you, Keith?'

'Right,' I said, thinking this was not the moment to mention that my office didn't have a safe.

'I didn't hire you to save my life, Keith, but that's cool. We'll have to talk about a bonus.'

The daughter was staring at her mother. The mother waved her free hand in front of her as if shooing flies. Silly flies. 'You melodramatic old fool, Barry, why would I want to kill you?'

'Well,' said Mr Irving. 'You know. Because, like, you'd been driven mad over the years by bitter jealousy. On account of me dumping you. And, like, if *you* couldn't have me then no one could.'

'*Men*, my God! What do you take me for? I'm not a murderer. I was blackmailing you, that's all.'

His beads rattling softly, my client screwed up his face in puzzlement. 'Blackmailing me? What about?'

Diane Eden pointed at the shaven-headed girl. 'About your illegitimate daughter, of course. I was threatening to tell your wife. Didn't you get my letters?'

'Yeah, but they were a little, you know, obscure.'

'They were *supposed* to be! They were *blackmail* letters.'

He pulled at his beard for a moment. This seemed to calm him. 'But my wife already knows. Always has done. In fact,' he said, smiling at his daughter, 'she's really keen to meet you, sweetheart.'

The daughter stuck both hands in the front pockets of her very tight jeans, and said: 'As if. Sod that.'

'What do you do for a living, love?' said Mr Irving.

'She's been travelling,' said her mother. 'But now she's back, which is why I needed extra money.'

Mr Irving made a sympathetic face. 'Unemployed, huh? That's tough.'

'Am I hell!' The girl took her hands out of her pockets. 'As a matter of fact, I'm a roadie.'

'A roadie?' He leaned forward, his eyes wide. 'What, like, for a band?'

'No, actually,' she sneered. 'Like, for the *Queen*. I set up the thrones before all her big gigs, make sure her corgis have the right colour of dog biscuits in their dressing rooms.'

Mr Irving nodded. His beads danced. 'What sort of band?'

Avoiding eye contact with her mother, the shaven-headed girl said: 'At the moment I'm with a sort of bluesy-punky outfit.'

'Bluesy-punky ... wow, cool.'

She ran her hands over her stubbly scalp. 'Yeah. With a kind of reggae-cum-Bach thing going on in there, too.'

'Right, right,' said Mr Irving, nodding with his whole body now. 'Totally cool.'

'Never mind all that,' said Diane Eden. 'If you didn't know I was blackmailing you, why did you keep sending me padded envelopes full of used fivers?'

Irving shrugged. 'Well, you know – maintenance payments.

Child support. I've always felt bad about abandoning you when you were pregnant, so this was my chance to make it up to my lovely daughter.'

'Maintenance payments? You idiot!' She was jogging round in little circles, kicking bits of furniture and thumping the walls with her free hand. Obviously an hereditary thing. 'You insensitive, unimaginative, brainless little – '

'One good thing,' I put in. 'I don't think you can be done for blackmail if your victim doesn't even know he's being blackmailed. I mean, he wouldn't make much of a prosecution witness, would he?'

I spoke in the hope of quietening things down. It worked, but not very well. The fat jogger looked at me, then looked at my client, and then said, very quietly: 'You know what I'm going to do now, you hopeless little worm? *Worms*, plural, in fact.' She began wrestling to free the hard object from her pocket. The tracksuit was slightly too small for her.

'I knew it!' said Mr Irving.

'Mum!' said the daughter.

'Gun got a she's!' I said, and started blushing again.

The pocket ripped. Diane Eden cursed, and dragged her hand free. She waved the dangerous thing at us. It was a mobile phone. 'I'm going to call my brother, Raymond. You remember Raymond? He's going to sort you out like he should have done years ago.' She started dialling.

'It's *not* a gun,' I said.

'Run!' said Mr Irving. 'Run for it!'

I ran. We ran. We didn't stop for ages. Mr Irving's beads rattled so hard they fell off.

* * *

In a pub, a taxi-ride away, my client and I drank brandy.

'Did you really think she was going to kill you?'

'Well,' said Barry Irving, 'it did cross my mind, when she got in touch. Di was one crazy lady back when I knew her. That was part of the attraction, I guess.'

'But she didn't actually threaten you?'

'I *thought* she was threatening me, in her letters – subtly, you know. Without incriminating herself in writing.'

'Whereas, in fact, she was subtly blackmailing you.'

He laughed. 'Too subtle for me.'

'And my role was to provide you with a means of justice from beyond the grave.'

He nodded. 'Hey, but it had nothing to do with revenge, you know. I was only thinking of my wife. Didn't want her to spend her widowhood wondering what had happened, always looking over her shoulder.'

I drank some brandy. 'All right. I can see why you didn't go to the police, you didn't think you had enough to show them, and anyway you didn't want to involve your wife, but couldn't you have told everything to your lawyer? So that in the event of your sudden death –'

'My lawyer is my wife's brother. Anyway, you're cheaper.'

'So why didn't you want me to tell you the information you hired me to find out?'

Mr Irving smiled. 'Simple, kid – I wanted to reduce to an absolute minimum the possibility of you ringing me at home, my wife answering, and you blurting out that I'd hired a private eye.'

That didn't make sense. 'But if your wife already knew about your daughter ... oh I see. Your wife *didn't* know.'

He spread his hands. 'Don't look so shocked, Keith. Telling the whole truth to the people we love is not always the coolest thing to do. You'll understand that when you're older.'

When you work as a private detective, the ethical standards of your clients are not your concern. You concern yourself with facts and with the law, not with other people's morals. 'Sure,' I said. 'That's cool.'

It was only later, on the bus home, that I realised there was one question I hadn't asked him. Why had he gone round to Diane Eden's flat if he thought she harboured homicidal intentions towards him? By the end of my journey I'd figured out the answer. Barry Irving had known from the start that he was being blackmailed, not threatened with violence. He had gone there to tell her that he wouldn't be paying her any more. That he'd hired a private detective, who had gathered evidence against her, and that he would use it if she didn't disappear out of his life. He knew that my report and photos would always be available to him, should he ever need them.

Nobody had been planning to kill anybody, after all. This was just an ordinary, suburban case of a blackmailer being black-mailed.

But Mr Irving hadn't reckoned on his ex-lover's raw anger. Or on the ominous bulge of her mobile phone. Or, perhaps, on the shock of seeing his daughter for the first time ever. And he certainly hadn't reckoned on me turning up on my moped, and –

My moped.

Hoping to avoid embarrassing confrontations, I waited till dark before I went back to Ms Eden's house to collect it. I needn't have bothered. The shaven-headed girl was sitting on the stoop, smoking a cigarette.

'Hi,' I said. She tilted her chin at me, very slightly, by way of greeting. 'Been an interesting day,' I said.

She shrugged.

I persevered. I have read that women like men who can make conversation. 'Why does your mother always collect her post on Thursday afternoons?'

'*What?*' she said.

'It's not important, I was just wondering – '

'It's her afternoon off. She works as a hairdresser's assistant. Works every hour she can get. She's broke, in case you hadn't noticed.'

'Right.' A silence followed. 'So, I was wondering – '

'Isn't it past your bedtime?'

'You've got a PO Box, too?'

'So?'

'I just wondered why. I mean, I know why your mum had one, but –'

'Sometimes the post gets stolen from the communal hall here.' She smoked for a moment, pulling hard on the cigarette, but letting the smoke escape carelessly through the sides of her mouth. Then she added, as if to herself: 'Least, that's what she told me.'

She stood up, extinguished her cigarette on the doorstep, and turned to go inside. Now or never, I thought.

'I'd really like to see your band some time.'

She looked at me over her shoulder, and said: 'Well, if we're doing any matinees, sonny, I'll send you a ticket.'

I still didn't know her name. I got on my moped and rode home.

The End of Innocence

Anne Perry

The soft wind rippled across the fields and stirred the heavy elms at the far end of the pitch. It was the 5th August, and far too early in the year for a rugby match, but by October all the young men would be in France. Yesterday the Kaiser's army had marched into Belgium, and England was at war. In the next few days the men of all the villages in Northumberland would have joined their regiments, and a local derby would be impossible, a thing of dreams. Joseph was thirty-nine. He would not bear arms, but he would go as chaplain, follow where the men went, wherever that might be.

So this match mattered: it was pride, tradition, the last time it would be played by these men. The world was changing, probably forever. This golden afternoon, however absurd to play rugby now, would sit like a jewel in the memory through the dark days to come.

Everything must be right: the places for the old men, the women and children to sit, tables for the refreshments, a proper area set aside for the carts to park. It was always a match played with passion, even ferocity, but village pride, as well as good manners, demanded that hospitality be the best that could be offered.

He saw young Alan Trubridge walking over towards the goal posts, the sun glistening on his hair. He waved but Alan did not see him. He looked anxious. No doubt he was concerned about his father who was still very fragile since the loss of his leg. He knew more about war than other men because of his profession as a military engineer. He had seen enough death in the Boer War to have a better idea than they of what lay ahead. What words of comfort were there that Joseph, or anyone, could offer? There was only comradeship and the knowledge of loyalty.

Actually Alan's thoughts concerned a debt he was hard-pressed to pay, and about which he could tell no one. His father's dependence was a secret he could share with no one at all, not even Dorothy, in fact especially not her. How could she regard John Trubridge with the old respect if she knew how he had cried out in pain after his terrible surgery, and the morphine he had needed just to make it through the night? Injuries like that were beyond her imagination, or anyone's who had not seen them.

She had not sat up all night with him as Alan had, watching the delirium, the sweats, the dry retching and the agony of body, the shame and the fear.

They had had to let the resident hand go, and have Mabel come in from the village by day, but always leave by nightfall. Alan had managed on his own, cleaning, laundering, mopping up so no one else would know.

John Trubridge was better now, still gaunt, and the shadow of pain was there in his eyes, but his dignity was back, his belief in himself and in some purpose, even on crutches. The addiction to the morphine was gone, but the debt for it remained. Thank God at least he had no idea how much that was. Alan had borrowed it from Will Harrison. Now that war was a reality, he would have to pay it back a little each month out of his army pay, and trust to God he would not be killed before it was settled.

But then everyone was going with that trust for one reason or another. There were even those like Dorothy's twin brother Ernest, who thought they might all be home by Christmas. It would be good if he were right!

He was standing doing nothing, staring at the goal posts. They were perfect. He should move on and check the other end. The sun was hot. Hope it was cooler by this evening for the game. He started to walk over the short, level grass.

Should he wait until Christmas before asking Dorothy to marry him? Was that the fairer thing to do, fairer to her, at least? Would it make parting easier, rather than leaving her betrothed to a soldier, feeling an obligation that might prove restricting? It smacked a little of emotional pressure, as if he were saying 'I'm going to war, be faithful to me, even though I can't offer you anything but letters now and then, probably full of pretty wretched news'.

He could see her standing over on the far side of the pitch, with half a dozen others, the sun on her fair hair, the breeze ruffling her skirts a little and making the soft fabric cling to her body. His heart ached for the beauty of her.

Blanche was standing a couple of yards away, darker, without the laughter or the charm. They had called her 'Prof' at school, not always kindly. Blanche's love for him was an embarrassment he would rather not think about at the moment. Not that she was obvious about it. She had too much dignity for that, but he could not help seeing it in her eyes. Probably most of the village knew how she felt, and that he had only ever loved Dorothy. They were made for each other.

He quickened his pace until he caught up with Joseph.

'Good afternoon, Reverend,' he said with a smile. 'I think everything is just about ready.' He squinted a little as he stared across the grass. 'Should be a good match.'

'I hope it'll be cooler by this evening,' Joseph replied. 'And it is still light until nine o'clock. I can't think of anything better than to have the two villages come here together.'

Alan glanced at him, but Joseph was staring into the sun also, shielding his eyes from the brightness, and perhaps from being observed too closely. The minutes were racing by. How soon this would become only a memory as they walked into the darkness. A curious thing, time! It passed with a relentless, measured thread regardless of anything man could do, and yet all its volume depended upon what you did with it. These bright hours which were now the present would become caught like a fly in amber, never to be forgotten, and never recaptured. He cleared his throat.

Joseph stood quietly as if he knew Alan wanted to speak to him.

'Er... Reverend...' Alan began.

Joseph pushed his hands into his pockets. How could he look so relaxed? He would be leaving in a day or two, just as they all would, and he had a wife and two young daughters. How would they manage without him? He didn't have to go.

Joseph turned from gazing at the young women, moving among the light tables ready for cakes and sandwiches this evening. He smiled. 'You want to see me?'

Alan felt the colour warm in his face. 'Am I so easy to read?'

'I would be in your place,' Joseph replied.

'I want at least to ask her before I go,' Alan explained. 'But is it fair? To her, I mean. Does it place an obligation on her, just to make me feel... I don't know... as if I have someone? I think it might matter terribly... in France.'

'I think it might, ' Joseph agreed. 'But mostly I think you

should ask her, and let her decide.'

'But if I do, then I've already placed her in a position where she has to accept and tie herself, or else refuse,' Alan pointed out. He wanted to ask her so much he could not set his emotions aside. If he didn't ask her before he left, perhaps something would happen to him, and then she'd never know how he felt.

'Alan,' Joseph said firmly. 'Don't take from her the right to make her own decisions. Just don't press her if she won't commit herself, but remember that if you don't ask her, then she cannot say anything at all. Don't rob her of that. She may want more than anything else to tell you how she feels.'

Alan relaxed, the tension slipping away inside him. It seemed so simple. It was what he needed to do. He looked across the green of the pitch and lifted his hand in a wave. Dorothy waved back, smiling.

'Thank you,' he said to Joseph. 'Of course you're right. I'll see you this evening.' And without hesitating any more, he ran across the grass to join Dorothy. They would walk home for lunch together, it was barely two miles.

He nodded to Ernest and Chris Eaves, then he fell in step beside Dorothy, linking his arm in hers, deliberately not catching Blanche's eye. He did not want the discomfort of seeing the loneliness in her. He started to walk.

'I think we'll win this year,' Dorothy said cheerfully, keeping up with him. 'Everyone's got a terrific spirit up. Ernest says we've never been better.'

'It would be a good note to go out on,' he agreed, then instantly regretted it. 'Sorry.'

'Don't worry,' she said quickly, tightening her arm on his. 'No one believes it'll last very long. Ernest says that when the Kaiser sees we mean business, he'll back down. We probably could have had the match by New Year anyway, but it'll be good now, regardless.'

He looked at her face in the sun. Was this the time to ask her? He might press too hard, make her feel as if she owed it to him, for all the wrong reasons. And yet when would he ever be able to ask her and not feel the emotion well up inside him like this and take control.

'Dorothy...'

She turned to him. Did she know?

But before he could say anything more, Ernest came running up from behind them, his face flushed and a look of unmistakable irritation in his eyes. He slowed his pace and fell into step with them.

'All ready?' he asked, looking at Alan. 'We'll beat the socks off them this time. Hope they take it in good part. We'll all be comrades in arms in a few days. By the way, I don't suppose you know anyone who'd like to look after my car for me, do you? Not much use to me for the next few months, and I paid a fortune for it! Overpaid, actually. Bit of daylight robbery if you ask me. But that's Will Harrison all over.' He gave an angry little gesture. 'I should have known better than to buy anything from him. He's an absolute outsider.'

'Never mind,' Dorothy told him, linking her other arm in his. 'You said yourself, it won't be long.'

'We don't know that!' Alan said quickly. 'Best prepare ourselves.'

'Oh, come on!' Ernest said cheerfully. 'We can beat the Kaiser's boys any day. Where's your patriotism, old fellow? Put a bit of heart into it!'

'I just think we shouldn't take it lightly...' Alan began.

'Don't be such a misery!' Ernest chided him. 'We'll win the game this afternoon, and we'll win the war this year! All it takes is guts and a little belief in ourselves.' He turned to Dorothy. 'Isn't that right, Dot?'

'Of course it is,' she agreed, her eyes bright. 'Come on, Alan! We'll be fine. You'll see.'

Alan forced himself to smile at her and nod his head. They reached the village church and he stopped for a moment while they went left, then when they were around the corner and he could not see her any longer, he went right towards his own house.

His father was in the sitting room in his armchair, his eyes closed, the newspapers half folded on the floor beside his foot. In the bright sunlight the lines were cut deep in his face and his skin had a papery quality, as if it might tear if anyone pulled it too hard. Still, the hollow greyness of constant pain was gone, and the hands in his lap were loose, not clenched.

He opened his eyes as Alan came in. He smiled. 'All ready for the match?'

'All ready,' Alan conceded cheerfully. 'Feel like coming? I think just about everyone from both villages is going to be there. Ernest will take you in the car, if you like?'

'I'll think about it,' the older man replied, and Alan did not press him. That was their understood way of saying that he did not feel well enough, or did not want to face the well-meaning questions and the awkwardness of people who are kind, but have no idea what to say to someone who has been ill more profoundly than they can imagine, and endured physical pain they do not know. Somehow the empty trouser leg embarrassed them, they did not know whether to look at it, or look away, say anything, offer to help or not.

'Ready for lunch?' Alan asked. 'Bread and pickle, and the rhubarb pie, so Mabel said. And there's cream.'

'Sounds good.'

Alan looked at his father's face, then at the newspaper on the floor. He was on the brink of asking what was in it, then changed his mind. Let them have at least one meal without thinking about war. It lay behind everything they said, an awareness of the lifetime's familiar objects in the room, the silence in the village street beyond, the drone of bees in the delphiniums in the garden and a dog barking somewhere. It was all so normal, and so immeasurably precious. Why do we value such things so intensely only when they are a danger? No use in asking.

He turned and went into the kitchen to fetch the meal from where Mabel had left it set out on a tray.

They had only just finished eating when Will Harrison appeared. He was a big man with a handsome moustache and hard blue eyes. He greeted John Trubridge cautiously, inquiring after his health, then turned to Alan.

'All ready for this evening?' he said heartily. 'Got to make the day one to remember, eh?' He glanced at the tray, then at some neatly folded papers on the bureau in the corner. He looked at Alan with a bright smile. 'Perhaps we could talk outside, and not keep your father from his work. I know how important it is, sir,' he added.

The older man nodded gravely, but there was a faint flush of pleasure on his face. 'By all means,' he conceded. 'After all, it's a village derby. These things matter.'

Alan followed Will through into the kitchen, then with surprise into the back garden beyond.

'Better private,' Will said conversationally, walking up the lawn towards the plum trees a good fifty feet from the sitting room window.

Alan experienced a curious sinking in the pit of his stomach. He knew when Will spoke that it was going to be about the debt between them.

'Such a lot of money,' Will said lightly, but there was a tension in his body. 'Does your father know how much?'

'No!' Alan moderated his voice. 'No. And I would rather he didn't.'

'Yes,' Will agreed. 'I imagine he would feel very badly. Rather strips one of dignity, not to say the natural desire to keep one's illness private, and the difficulties of it, of course.'

Alan was embarrassed, and in spite of his gratitude for Will's help, annoyed that he should mention it in such a way. It was intrusive. 'I'll pay you back every month, as I can,' he said quickly. 'I'll have my army pay reverted to you.'

'I imagined you'd say that,' Will nodded. 'It's not as if your father were dependent on you. After all, he's a pretty good military engineer. Rather a special man, in fact.'

'Yes,' Alan said decisively. 'Very special, actually.'

Will smiled, but there was no warmth in it. 'Ernest thinks the war is going to be over by Christmas. But then he was always a trifle facile in his opinions.'

'I've heard a few people say that,' Alan replied. 'I'd imagine it's what they want to think.

'The reality's going to be very different.' Will was still looking at him speculatively, as if trying to read his thoughts. 'But even if it doesn't last long, there will be a lot of men killed.'

'Of course,' Alan said sharply.

'And you could be among them,' Will pointed out. 'Hope not, of course, but we have to face reality.'

'Any of us could.' Alan felt a shiver run through him.

'So I'm afraid your army pay month by month isn't going to be sufficient, old chap.' Will shrugged. 'I'll need rather more than that.'

'I haven't got any more…'

'Well you have, actually.'

'No I haven't! I sold everything to pay for the morphine before I came to you. Good heavens, do you think I'd have come to you if I could have raised it any other way?'

Will's eyes were very level.

'Not what I meant. Just a small favour you could do me, and I'd call it evens.'

* * *

That should have been a tremendous relief, and yet looking at the hard glitter in Will's eyes and the set of his heavy shoulders, it was not. Alan felt unmistakably afraid. His mouth was dry when he spoke. 'What?'

'Put a spot of laudanum in your father's night-cap tonight,' Will said very clearly. 'And leave the keys to his safe in the dish on the mantelpiece. Make sure you stay in your room. A spot of laudanum for you too might not be a bad idea.'

Alan was horrified. He knew that there were military papers in his father's safe, things that would make a difference to England's success in the war. A man a yard away from him on the lawn, with the August wind in his face off the fields, was asking him to betray his country! For a minute his breath would not come.

'I can't!' he gasped. 'That's… it's…'

'A very practical solution to your troubles,' Will finished for him with a tight smile. 'Think about it, Alan, but don't take too long. It needs to be tonight. After all, old chap, consider the alternative.' He glanced towards the house. 'I can see that you don't like the idea, but at least it will be nice and private. No one will ever know about it but you and me. The other way… rather messy, you know? You off to France, to live or die… you father left here to face debt and embarrassment. In fact I don't think "humiliation" would be too strong a word. Anyway, give it a bit of thought. I'll see you after the match. Oh… and leave the back window open.' He started to stroll gently down the grass. He pointed to the window nearest the wisteria. 'That one, I think. Make sure you get it right, there's a good fellow. I don't want to be messing around trying one after another. And Alan…'

Alan stopped. His mouth was too dry to speak.

'Don't think of calling Constable Riley over from Hadfield for me. If you do, I shall have to tell him I was coming to see your father, who had left the window open for me...'

'No one would...' Alan started to say.

Will smiled. 'Believe me? Oh, but they would. It all makes excellent sense. A weak man, addicted to morphine, bought it illegally, got addicted to it, into debt! Finally reduced to selling his country to pay for it. He sent for me. I didn't know what he wanted... until too late. Very believable, old chap. And make no mistake, I'll tell them.' He shook his head. 'I have no intention of letting you stitch me up. Try anything like that, and I'll ruin him. Sordid end to a distinguished career.' He opened the kitchen door. 'Don't bother to show me through. I'll find my own way out. See you at the match!' He walked through the sitting room. 'Good afternoon, Mr. Trubridge. Don't suppose you'll be coming to the game this evening, sir. But we'll trounce them, it'll be one to remember.'

Alan did not hear his father's reply. His head was swimming. Minutes ticked by, or perhaps it was only seconds. He knew he must do something, but either course open to him was hideous. He could not sacrifice his father to ruin and despair, nor could he betray his country. Will Harrison had left him no way of escape. He had thought of all the paths by which Alan might evade him, and blocked each one.

He must get away from the house before his father suspected anything. He must not know. With a smile on his face that felt ghastly he went through the kitchen and into the sitting room. 'I'm going to see the Reverend,' he said without meeting his father's eyes. 'Will wants a favour from me, and I need to talk to ... to the Reverend about it. I'll be back for early supper.'

'Yes, of course. Are you all right, Alan?'

He smiled, only a quick glance upwards. 'Yes, of course. I'm fine.'

'It's not the match worrying you, is it?' That was only half a question. 'Dorothy?' His father's voice was gentle. They had never discussed their feelings a great deal. It was sometimes too revealing, usually unnecessary. They understood each other well, and had been close in instinctive knowledge since Alan's mother had died nearly twelve years ago. The sharing of a pleasure, a poem quoted, a piece of music, a good discussion on anything that mattered, philosophy or a rugby match, all said more than bare words. Companionship was its own explanation. He would miss that more than anything else he would leave behind.

With his throat tight he answered. 'Only a bit. I'll speak to her this evening, after the match, I expect. I'll see you later.' And he went out into the street and walked briskly back towards the church and the Manse beyond.

He passed half a dozen people he knew and either waved or called a hasty greeting. He could not entertain any kind of conversation today. He reached the gate and saw Christopher, since early school days his closest friend. He was coming out of the churchyard opposite. If he went to the door he could not avoid him. They knew each other too well to hide anything. It was Alan that Christopher had turned to when Will Harrison had stolen his first love, and then thrown her aside when he was bored. Christopher had never forgiven him for that. None of them had ever seen Eleanor since, or known what had happened to her.

Alan turned away from the gate and walked on briskly, as if he had purpose. Anyone seeing him would assume he was going back to the pitch, presumably he had forgotten something.

Chris was not the only other one to dislike Will. Fred Mundy had no love for him either. He blamed him for some cruel gossip that had circulated for quite some time. Jim Wallace from the Hadfield village had never forgotten the golf match in which he believed Will had cheated him out of first place, and the prize that went with it.

Would this evening's game be a last chance to settle some old enmities before the infinitely greater tide of war made them brothers in arms against a different enemy, one whose wages were not village squabbles, broken dreams or broken hearts, but the terrible reality of broken bodies buried in the mud of a foreign land?

These petty grudges were absurd. Even to think of them at all would be idiotic, were it not that it was a way to keep sane. The future was too big even to look at. Concentration on a single anger was bearable.

He turned and walked back towards the Manse and went straight up to the door and knocked. It was answered by the minister's wife and she was too wise, now of all times, to ask what a young man wanted with the Reverend. She simply showed him into the study and left.

'Sit down, Alan,' Joseph said, frowning a little. His voice was soft, as if he knew trouble before it was spoken. He had a strong, gentle face with very dark eyes. The bookshelves behind him were filled with well-used volumes, every one ready to fall open at his favourite passages. There were far more than scriptures or studies of theology. Even at a glance Alan could see poetry, the Greek legends and stories of classical and renaissance Italy. The largest space not covered by books held a portrait of the poet Danté.

How Joseph would miss this haven of thought and collected beauty of the ages when he left home for the fields of France! And he was going because he believed it was his duty, and to fight for what he loved, in his own way, by sharing the life of the men and giving them what comfort he could. At least he would walk beside them every step of the path. Surely this was the ultimate way he proved that he believed what he preached every Sunday?

'How can I help you Alan?' Joseph's voice cut across the turmoil in his mind. What could he say? He already knew at heart part of the answer. Whatever it cost, he could not leave the keys for Will Harrison. It was impossible.

He looked up. Joseph was waiting. He could not tell him. He must say something else, anything. What?

'Are you concerned about your father?' Joseph asked.

'Yes.' That was the answer. 'Yes. He's going to be... so much on his own. I don't know why I'm telling you. I'm sorry. It's not as if you would be here. There's nothing you can do. I suppose I just don't know how to take care of it. I feel ... helpless.'

Joseph smiled. 'We're all pretty helpless at the moment. There comes a time when there's nothing you can do but trust in God and carry on the best you know how. I know that's not a lot of comfort now. I'm afraid it's all I have.'

'I know,' Alan said ruefully. 'It isn't as easy as I used to think – merely black and white, right or wrong, and that's all there is to it.'

'Is there something else, Alan?'

'No... no thank you. Thank you for listening to me. I expect half the village'll be here in the next day or two. I don't envy you trying to find something to say to them.'

Joseph looked down at the desk. 'It's the same thing for everyone, just trying to find the right way to say it for each.'

171

'I'm glad you're coming with us – except I wish you were staying here too! Sorry. That sounds idiotic.'

Joseph stood up. 'No it doesn't. We're all going to wish we could be in more than one place. But for now, give the game your best effort and don't think of tomorrow yet.' He offered his hand and Alan took it, and made his escape with the burden of decision still just as heavy in his heart.

* * *

Everyone from both villages was there for the match. It was an exquisite evening, the low sun golden on the grass, the wind barely rustling the elms against a stainless sky already glowing with the softness of evening, the warmth of colour deepening in the west, shadows spreading deep. The crowd had gathered all around the edges of the pitch, women and young girls in their pale summer dresses, cottons and silks like so many bright flowers among the plainer shirtsleeves of the men. Children played on their own with hoops and balls, and one little boy was trying unsuccessfully to get a kite up in the still air.

Several groups of older men stood around, talking to each other seriously about the finer points of the game.

Alan gazed around him. He knew the world beyond. He had studied and travelled a little, but what mattered was here. It was these people he loved and who bounded all that was precious. He could see the roof of his own house in the distance, where his father was sitting reading. His mother was buried in the churchyard. Dorothy was over there in the crowd, and Christopher, Joseph and his wife and two daughters, the postmistress, Mabel who cooked for himself and his father and kept the house in order, Blanche and her father the schoolteacher, the shopkeeper, Chris's father the blacksmith, Dr. Kitching.

He must pay attention to the game. It was about to begin. Now of all times he must not let them down. The whistle blew and he plunged in as if victory here were all of life.

It was hard fought, at moments brilliant, at others clumsy beyond belief. Idiotic mistakes were made, and superb tries, men running as if their feet had wings. The scrums were violent, no mercy asked or given.

Just before half time the score was eleven all.

They were in the scrum again, pushing, shoving, scrambling for position, feet everywhere. Alan felt a boot scrape down his leg, tearing the skin. He was hit heavily in the middle of the back and fell forward. There was someone half underneath him. He had no idea where the ball was.

He was shoved from behind and caught by a shoulder in the chest. He fell sideways and saw Will Harrison slip and crash heavily almost underneath him. He tried to stand up and was knocked from the left. Chris was beside him and then gone again. He lunged forward and regained his balance. The ball was gone. Will Harrison's head was in the mud below him, the pale skin of his throat and ear exposed. He hesitated only a moment, thinking of his father, the long nights, the pain, the whole village going to France, then he trod down hard on Will's neck, and turned away. He knew what he had done as he felt the bone crack. Is this what war would be like? Knowing the second it was over, and too late?

Someone had the ball and the scrum broke apart. He staggered to his feet. He must not look back. He lunged forward blindly and his legs bucked underneath him. The ground hit his chest, driving the breath out of his lungs. He must get up, look as if he were playing. Someone tripped over him and fell. He was glad of the boot in his ribs, the weight on top of him. They scrambled up together. It seemed like eternity before the whistle blew and there was a shout that something was wrong.

He turned round and saw the referee go over to where Will was lying motionless on the ground. He bent and looked at him, then rose to his feet. He seemed dazed. He swung around, looking for Dr. Kitching.

Slowly the whole crowd realized it was not just a man slipped or a broken leg. An anxious silence hung over the field as the doctor detached himself from the spectators, ran over and bent down to look. Alan recognized the dark figure of Joseph going over to join the little group. They were speaking together quietly.

It was only a few more moments before Kitching stood up and said that Will was dead. His neck must have been broken in the scrum. It was a terrible accident, but by no means the first of its kind.

Alan had never imagined he could feel so utterly alone. Cain must have felt like this, cast out of all he knew to wander the earth.

But Will would have betrayed them all, these quiet ordinary people Alan loved so much – and ten thousand other towns and villages like them all over the land.

He never doubted for an instant that Will would have said he had come because John Trubridge had sent for him, offering him secrets for money to buy morphine. God knew, enough of it had changed hands between them in the past! The police would believe it! How could they doubt?

Alan couldn't have done that! The betrayal was beyond him.

Dr. Kitching was addressing the crowd, his voice sounding thin in the fading summer evening. The light was already gold on the top of the elms. He was telling them that Will Harrison was dead, and they should all go home. There was nothing more to be done tonight. He apologized, as if somehow it were his fault, then he turned to Joseph.

Alan did as everyone else did, walked quietly, bemused, back along the lane to the village. But unlike others, he walked alone. He hoped anyone seeing him took it for grief. They could never know the burden he carried that hurt inside more than bruises or broken bones, swelling until it filled all of him.

* * *

Will had no family for Joseph to tell, or try to comfort. Of course there would be letters to write, but that could wait until tomorrow. Rugby tragedies did happen. He had known of others, admittedly less serious, many broken bones, head injuries, even one that ended in paralysis. But death was not startling, merely an added burden of sorrow at a time when men and women were expecting far worse to come, and there were too many good-byes to be said.

It was about the time people would have been home from the game, had it run its full course, when there was a knock on the study door and Dr. Kitching came in, his face puckered with deep concern.

'What is it?' Joseph asked immediately, rising to his feet. 'What's happened?'

Kitching sank to the chair on the other side of the desk, his eyes dark with weariness and distress. 'I don't know Joseph. I'm not sure how bad it is. I considered ignoring it altogether, but I don't think I can because there may be others who have received them as well.' He was holding a piece of paper in his hand.

'What is it?' Joseph was puzzled.

'An anonymous letter,' Kitching replied, passing it over. 'It's pretty simple. It just says Will Harrison was killed deliberately – murdered in fact.'

Joseph took the paper from him, surprised to find his hand was not shaking. 'Murder?' he said with disbelief. 'Who would say such a vicious thing? And...' He was about to add 'pointless' until he looked at the paper and saw that Christopher Eaves was accused and the rivalry over Eleanor given as the reason. It was motive enough, in most people's eyes. No one knew what had happened to Eleanor since, and Christopher had never loved anyone else in the same way. He had had a few slight romances but they had never grown to anything serious. The ghost of Eleanor came between him and any new sweetness and certainty. Joseph looked up at Kitching.

'You don't believe it's possible, do you?' Kitching's voice was high and edged with distress.

'No,' Joseph replied with more decision than he truly felt. The whole world was changing. Young men were thinking of death in a way they never had before. They went to answer the calls of duty and loyalty to all they loved, home, family, a set of ideals and a way of life. Some of them looked no further than that, and imagined it would all be over in a few months. Others, perhaps a little older or wiser, knew that no one experienced the violence, the terror and alienation of war without being irrevocably changed. Not everyone would come back, and among those who did, many might be maimed. Was this vicious letter some settling of old scores before the sunset of this golden age? It was a startlingly ugly idea, and he could not rid himself of it. 'Have you any knowledge as to who wrote this?' he asked.

Kitching shook his head. 'None at all. I don't even know if Harrison was killed on purpose or if it was a complete accident. I thought I'd go and look at him again, but I'd appreciate it if you'd come with me. I find this...' He stopped, choked for words to express himself.

Joseph stood up. 'Of course. We'd better go straight away.'

He explained to his wife only that Kitching needed him and he was expecting to be gone a short while. He was aware how precious every hour was, but he had no choice, and she was accustomed to him being sent for on urgent matters he could not share with her. She said nothing except to wish them good-bye, but he was aware that she stood in the lighted doorway and watched them until they turned the corner and were no longer visible.

Kitching took him to his surgery where Will Harrison was lying, and lifted the sheet off his face. Joseph stared down at him. He had been a big man in life, full of confidence, even something of a bully, not a man Joseph liked. But lying here now, naked but for the covering of decency, he looked smaller and oddly vulnerable. Funny because now he was beyond all pain.

'You see?' Kitching said, pointing to the abrasions on the side of Will's neck where the skin had been torn by the rough sole of a boot.

'That could be accidental, surely?' Joseph asked, peering at it and then looking up at Kitching. 'Isn't that how it would be if someone trod on him, without meaning to?'

Kitching pointed delicately to where the tears formed a slightly curving pattern. 'That looks as if someone turned sharply, and that's what broke his neck, instead of only bruising him, or even knocking him unconscious.'

Joseph followed his indication. 'Couldn't that just as easily have been an accident?'

'Possibly, but it looks less like it. Why would anyone turn, unless they had the ball? And from what I could see, no one ran with it from there. In fact, no one ran with it at all, until after Will must have been dead.'

'But this doesn't prove murder, does it?' Joseph argued. 'You can't hang a man on this.'

Kitching pulled the cover over the face again. 'No.' He looked across at Joseph. 'I'd be inclined to ignore it, if I were certain no one else received any letters like the one I have. But I can't be.'

Joseph wanted to say something helpful, but it would have been a lie. The truth was ugly, and unanswerable. 'We'll have to wait until morning. The village is a small place. If there is another one, and the recipient doesn't destroy it, as I think they should, then we'll soon know about it.'

Kitching sighed. 'I agree. Thank you, Joseph. I... I just didn't want to do this alone, I suppose. What a damnable thing, now of all times.' He walked to the door and turned the light out. 'You might as well go home, and get a decent night.'

But there were other letters. By mid-morning the village was buzzing with accusation against Christopher. To begin with he was bewildered, then hurt. By lunchtime he was thoroughly frightened and had no idea which way to turn. He was an ordinary, decent young man who had grown up in the cottage behind the forge. He had been to the village school and believed that he had a secure place in the esteem of his friends, albeit a less privileged one than many of them. Now, without warning, it was shattered.

Alan heard it from Ernest, a little after eleven o'clock. He dismissed it as rubbish. Ernest was quick and graceful, like Dorothy, but he had a sharp tongue and had never been especially fond of Christopher, thinking that he gave himself airs he had no right to.

Then he heard it again from the postmistress. She shook her iron grey curls as she fished behind the curtain for a rubber band. 'I don't know what things are coming to. Nice young man like Christopher. Can't believe it's true, myself. But it's all over the place. You're his friend, Mr. Alan, you're going to have to stand by him and that's no mistake.'

Alan thanked her and walked out into the sun with his heart hammering in his chest.

Even as the thoughts were racing in his mind, he was walking towards the Manse. This time there was no decision to make. He could not say why he had done it, of course. That would defeat the whole object. If he could not think of another reason, then he would have to remain silent, and let people think what they would.

It was desperate, and yet in a strange, sad way it was a kind of relief. His father would be devastated, but perhaps that was always going to happen, whatever course he had taken. Damn Will Harrison. Hope he was in some kind of Hell.

Joseph received him right away.

'They are saying that Will Harrison was murdered,' Alan began as soon as the study door was closed. 'And that Christopher did it.'

'I know,' Joseph replied. 'I am truly sorry. I find it very difficult to believe. And I know that you and Christopher have been friends for years. I will do all I can to get to the bottom of it, I promise you, and to protect Christopher's name as much as I can. Or to stand by him should that prove impossible.'

Alan let out a long sigh, and squared his shoulders. 'Christopher didn't kill Will Harrison. I did.'

Joseph was startled, incredulous. Then his frown eased out into sadness. 'I know you count loyalty very high, Alan, and I admire you for it, but why on earth would you kill Will Harrison?'

'I... I quarrelled with him.'

Disbelief was plain in Joseph's eyes. 'Over what, that you would kill him for it?'

'I can't tell you...'

'Alan...'

'I did! Believe me, Reverend, I am telling you the truth. I saw my chance in the scrum, and I took it.' He closed his eyes, as if it could block out the remembrance which was inside him. 'I put my foot on his neck and I turned it. You can't allow Christopher to take the blame for something I did. That would be intolerable! Surely you, of all people, can see that?'

Joseph smiled ruefully. 'What I can see is a young man of great idealism prepared to sacrifice himself to save his friend, perhaps believing that as the son of a distinguished military hero of the past, he may receive a gentler hearing on the matter than a young man whose father is the village blacksmith, and whose mother was a laundress. I see a childhood friendship grown deeper with manhood, where the stronger protects the more vulnerable, and perhaps pays back debts when the protection and the loyalties were the other way.'

'But I did kill Harrison!' Alan said desperately. 'Maybe I would lie to protect Chris, I don't know, but it isn't necessary. He didn't do anything!' He took a deep breath. 'I came to you first, because I thought you would want to make sure justice was done, but I'll go to Dr. Kitching, and over to Hadfield to the police, if you don't.'

Joseph glanced down at his hands, then up again. 'I'll speak to Dr. Kitching but I won't speak to the police. I can understand your loyalty, Alan, but I don't think you have thought this through very carefully. Consider your father, as well as Christopher.'

Alan felt the blood leave his face. This was the sort of nightmare when every step he took was blocked. Every time he thought he had escaped, he began to run, and the way in front of him was closed off again. He rose to his feet, ashamed to find his legs shaking. What was battle going to be like if he was afraid simply standing here in his minister's study fighting against his own demons?

'Thank you,' he said awkwardly. 'But it won't change anything.' And before Joseph could say more, he went out of the door and closed it behind him softly.

⋆   ⋆   ⋆

He told Dorothy what he had done because she raised the subject when they met in the early afternoon. He could not allow her to believe Christopher guilty, and it seemed she did so.

'You said what?' She stood in the sun in the quiet lane, her eyes wide and angry.

'I told the Reverend it was I who killed Will Harrison, not Christopher,' he repeated.

Her face was flushed, her soft hair blowing a little in the wind. 'For heaven's sake, Alan! What on earth are you thinking of?' She sighed impatiently. 'I know you feel a sort of loyalty to Christopher going back years, and that he looked after you when you were at school, and all that, and this is all very quixotic and I love you for it... but think of our happiness as well!' She bit her lip, aware that perhaps she had presumed too much, not the fact, but the speaking of it aloud, before he had. 'The Reverend didn't believe you, did he?'

'No, he said not...'

'Thank heaven for that! At least he has more sense!' She pushed her hair back off her brow, smiling a little now as relief took hold. 'It's all just silly gossip because people are – upset. Everything's changing so quickly, with the news of war, and knowing all of you are going away. People are jumpy. It's all so difficult, so uncertain. And we'll miss you dreadfully.'

'Not half as much as we'll miss you!' he said with a rush of emotion. 'And all this!' He looked around at the hedges with the last of the wild roses falling, and the ripening fields beyond, the great elms in the distance. It looked exactly like any other late summer.

'I know,' she said gently, taking his arm. 'But you'll be back soon, and everything will wait for you. Just don't say anything more about Will Harrison, and let Christopher take care of himself. It'll all blow over. I know they quarrelled about Eleanor, and no one could blame Chris for that, but he wouldn't kill anyone, and they'll all realize it in a day or two, you'll see.'

Could he tell her that what he had told Joseph was true? He had killed Will Harrison. Would she ever understand that? Could she put herself in his place and imagine the dilemma he had faced, the need to act one way or the other, choose between two wrongs, and do it in the space of a few desperately short hours? There was no time to weigh and measure, seek other alternatives.

'Alan?' She was regarding him quizzically, a half smile on her face. In her clear eyes there was no reflection of the turmoil he felt. She had given an answer to Christopher's problem in that he should face it himself. That excused Alan, and so also her. There was no more to be said. 'Alan, darling, let it go,' she urged. 'We've only got another couple of days. Let's spend them happily. Give us both something to remember when we're apart. It's terrible that Will is dead, but we can't alter it. Don't let it cloud everything else.'

It was true. And neither of them had liked Will. But it could not be dismissed in a few words. However true part of them were, it was infinitely less than the whole.

'Come on!' she said, moving a little forward. 'Let's walk up as far as the stream before supper. It's going to be another perfect evening.'

He went with her, but the golden light held no warmth for him, and in spite of being beside her, he had never felt more alone.

*   *   *

Joseph did not believe Alan when he said he had killed Will Harrison. It seemed too obviously an attempt to save Christopher, born out of old loyalties. It was like Alan. The ties of love had always bound him very tightly, as long as Joseph had known him, and that was over ten years now.

He did not believe Christopher would have killed Will, in spite of the vicious way Will had destroyed his romance with Eleanor. But Joseph had discovered many times that there were darker and more complex sides to even the sunniest people, and sometimes shallower hearts where one had expected pity and strength.

It was a strange lie for Alan to tell, panicky and ill-judged. But then everyone's emotions were raw now. He must be profoundly worried about his father, who was still not strong. His long illness had drained him far more than most people in the village supposed. Joseph had seen the pain in his face, even the despair at times. Only Alan's selfless devotion had pulled him through.

And yet for Alan to have stayed when all the rest of the young men of the villages all over the county were going to war, would have been an even greater burden. John Trubridge was intensely proud. He would have died alone rather than have his son remain at home in safety to look after him. It was perverse, difficult, but Joseph admired him for it. He could not count the times when visiting him he had looked away rather than see his pain, in order to leave him the dignity of pretending it never overcame him.

Joseph sat back in his chair and stared at the ceiling of his study. Who had sent that miserable letter to Kitching? And who else had received one and started the talk in the village? He had not recognized the ugly printing on the page Kitching had shown him, but then whosoever had sent it had taken obvious trouble to disguise the hand. No one would willingly have been identified with such a contemptible thing.

He would like to know who it was. An honourable person knowing anything about Will Harrison's death would have come and said so, face to face. Only cowards made accusations to which they would not sign their names.

There were many men in the scrum who might have felt they had reason to hate Will, but who hated Christopher enough to accuse him without evidence? That was somewhere to begin. It didn't have to be anyone on the pitch, since they didn't claim to have evidence they could substantiate. It could be anybody.

Did they really believe it could be true? Who thought so ill of Christopher they would allow it to warp them into such an act? He thought of all the people he knew, both men and women, probing in the painful places of his memory for the secrets he had learned one way or another, the weaknesses and private sins his profession had made him privy to.

They were so ordinary, the fears of loneliness and failure that beset us all, the embarrassment, the envy, the rejection, the dread of ridicule, the exhaustion of illness, the misery of poverty. So few of them were born of real viciousness, only confusion and a lack of understanding as to what really matters, and that they already had the power to alter things, if only they would use it with faith.

Perhaps whoever wrote that wretched letter already regretted it? It might be that somewhere within a couple of miles someone else was also sitting alone, wishing in despair that they could undo the last day and not set pen to paper. He wished that might be so, and they would be sorry enough to admit it, and confess that the charge was untrue. That would take a lot of courage. But he thought with pity of the path that lay ahead of the person either shipping out to France to face battle beside the man he had betrayed, or staying here safely at home and watching the others go, and knowing it was too late ever to take back the words.

He wished he could find them and try to persuade them tonight, but he had no idea who it was, not even if it were a man or a woman. Their spite would poison both places, and he would find it hard to forgive them for that.

* * *

Alan and Dorothy sat beside the stream watching it rattle over the stones, dimpled in sunlight, shadowed brown and green under the overhanging banks dense with grasses. It was the perfect place to ask anyone to marry, and Alan had intended to ask her this evening, but his mind was filled with Will Harrison, and the terrible decision he had made and carried through. He could not ask anyone to commit themselves to him, with this weight on his soul. He would far rather have been here alone, free to think, to try to explain to himself what he had done.

But whether he did that or not, he must help Christopher. He must find a way of making either Joseph or Dr. Kitching believe him, before they all left and it was too late, and that would be intolerable. He would have to invent another reason that they could accept, otherwise it would have to be the truth.

And yet doing so would expose his father's vulnerability and the magnitude of his debt, the very reason he had killed Will in the first place. There was an irony in that – perhaps even a kind of justice.

Dorothy was looking at him. She was waiting for him to propose to her. He knew it as surely as if she had said so.

His father would rather have died during that hideous operation and the long, agonizing recovery, than know that Alan had killed a man to protect his secret. If he had to tell anyone why he had done it, then lied as to a death, a murder, not just the village but the whole country would know. It would never be forgotten.

'Alan...' Dorothy's voice hardly penetrated his thoughts. 'Alan!' she said more insistently.

He turned to face her.

'Are you still thinking about that wretched anonymous letter?' she asked, with an edge of impatience. 'For goodness sake, forget about it! We've only got tonight and tomorrow left! Think about us for a while. You can't help Christopher. If he killed Will Harrison then justice will catch up with him, and you can't prevent that! If he didn't, then it'll all go away. Alan!'

'He didn't kill him!' he said sharply, angry that she should even consider it, and perhaps angrier still that she should speak so easily of justice as if it were an absolute and she understood it. Judgment was so difficult, far more than he would have imagined even a week ago. It was not always between right and wrong, sometimes it was between two wrongs, and no time to decide which was the worse. Any fool could choose when it was black and white. What about when it was grey and grey?

She was smiling at him now, a million miles away. What would she say if she knew it was he who had killed Will? 'Justice will catch up with you'? Would she understand why? Would she care?

He looked steadily at her fair face, beautiful in the evening light, and he saw expectation in it, certainty of herself and her beliefs. She was waiting for him to tell her he loved her, and she knew he did. He had done since they were both in school. But the words were not there. Will's death had separated them. He was no longer the man she knew. He had turned himself into someone else she could not love. And what was more amazing, he could not feel the same excitement, the warmth and the peace he had felt for her until only yesterday. Now she was a stranger with a beautiful face, and a mind that was as bright and shallow as the stream a couple of yards away.

'I know what you're waiting for me to say, and I can't.' He met her eyes and saw the disbelief in them, and then the anger. 'I have no right to ask you to commit yourself to a man in my position.'

'And if I choose to?' she said roughly, fighting tears.

'You don't, Dorothy,' he answered with a gentleness he had not known he felt. It was not passion, not tenderness, but a kind of remote regret, as if they had parted long ago, it was just that he had not understood it until now. Very slowly he climbed to his feet and looked down at her. 'I've got to go and see if I can do something about Christopher. I'm sorry.'

'Ernest says he probably did it!' she challenged him.

'Ernest wasn't even in the scrum,' he replied. 'But if he was the one who wrote the letters, then I wish to hell that he and I were not in the same regiment. I'd rather not face an enemy with him beside me.'

She blushed crimson. 'That's a terrible thing to say!'

'It was a terrible thing to do,' he returned.

She stood up too, her cheeks flushed, her dress a little rumpled. 'No it isn't! Not if Christopher is guilty, and Ernest thinks he is. So do I.'

Alan found his throat tight. 'And you can make a judgment so easily, and be sure you're right?'

'Yes I can! What's the matter with you? You've changed. Are you afraid of going to war?'

'Yes, of course I am!' he said bitterly. 'Only an idiot thinks it's going to be a big adventure. We won't all come back, you know? It's not death or glory… it'll be boredom, exhaustion, fear, injuries and more boredom.'

'Is that what your father says?' she demanded. 'You shouldn't listen to him so much. It isn't like that any more. Just because he got injured in South Africa and then lost his leg later because of his wound, doesn't mean it's like that for everyone.'

'There's nothing to argue.' He moved a step away. 'Christopher didn't do anything to Will, and I've got to go and see that people don't believe that he did. I can't go away leaving it. I'm sorry.' And without waiting for her to say anything more he turned and walked away rapidly up the bank and across the rough grass towards the lane.

He would have to think of a way of saving Chris, without destroying his father, but the more he turned over every possibility in his mind, the deeper was his feeling of helplessness and despair. He was oblivious of the soft wind in his face carrying the perfume of the hay fields, or the song of the wild birds in the hedgerows. He almost bumped into Blanche before he noticed she was there. She was riding her bicycle and she dismounted immediately. His first reaction was irritation. He did not want to see anyone at all, but least of all her. The effort to mask his feelings and be civil was more than he could manage. He knew his face gave him away.

'Hello, Alan,' she said quietly. 'You look wretched...'

He drew in breath to snap back at her, anything to make her leave him alone. His world was in ruins and he was more deeply afraid of disaster that would destroy all he loved. There was no strength left to be kind. But she spoke before he had time.

'You must be worried sick about Christopher.' She fell in step beside him along the narrow track, pushing the bicycle. 'I don't think we'd normally be so quick to repeat stupid gossip like this, but everyone's frightened because we're facing the unknown, and we can't even do it together. Half of us will be left behind not knowing what's happening to those we love, while the other half go off into a situation none of us has ever faced before. I know people like Ernest are saying it'll all be over by Christmas, but we don't know if that's true. And even if it is, some will be killed. Even if it's only a few, those you love best could be among them.'

It was the most reasonable remark he had heard anyone make so far, and the anger in him melted away. He looked at her face. It was quite calm, but the fear in her eyes was real. She was holding it in only with difficulty.

'Yes,' he admitted. 'I can't... I can't think what to do to show that Chris isn't guilty of anything. I know he still hurts over Eleanor, but he didn't kill Will.'

She walked in silence for a moment or two, thinking hard. 'Don't you think that if anyone killed him on purpose, it would be over something that happened just lately, rather than years ago?' she said finally, as they came to where the lane narrowed as the hawthorn hedge spread wide and low over the verges. 'Why would he wait until now?'

Was it a glimmer of hope? 'He wouldn't!' he agreed quickly. 'Unless it's because we're going to war? And there won't be another chance.'

She turned to look at him with level candour, her glance critical. 'That doesn't make a lot of sense. If they both came back he would deal with it then, if he still cared. And if Will were killed it wouldn't matter. I can't believe Chris would want to do that now, before going, on the chance he might be killed himself.' She pushed the bicycle wheel over a rattle of stones. 'That just isn't the kind of person he is. If it mattered to him that much, he'd have done something years ago. But knowing Chris, he'd far more likely have had a fight when Eleanor went, not keep it until now.' She stopped, as if there were something more to say, but she did not want to go on.

'What?' he asked. It was automatic. If she did not want to tell him then she wouldn't. The moment the word was out he wished he had not spoken. The sooner they reached the village and he could decently leave her, the better.

'Unless he just heard something about Eleanor in the last day or two,' she replied. 'Do you know if he did?'

'No.' He was surprised. 'Not as far as I know, and I think he'd have said.'

'Maybe not, but you'd have seen it in his face,' she pointed out. 'He's pretty transparent.'

'You're right!' he felt a wave of relief. 'Surely people will see that?'

They walked a further dozen yards or so. The light was low and touched with gold, shadowing the lane completely. The evening air was sweet, and there was no sound but their footsteps and the slight squeak of the bicycle wheels.

'You can't take that for granted, Alan,' she said, looking at him quickly, and then away again. 'Most of us aren't thinking so very reasonably now. We're frightened. That does funny things to common sense, and I sometimes think to our better nature as well. Somebody wrote some pretty rotten letters. I don't even know how many, do you?'

The relief vanished. 'No,' he admitted. 'But I know Chris didn't kill Will Harrison.' He avoided meeting her eyes.

'Do you?' There was no inflection in her voice, certainly no challenge. She was asking him. The temptation to tell her the truth was almost overwhelming. At least he would no longer be alone with his monster. But he must not. It would be dangerous, and unfair to her. But he was also weary to the soul with lies.

'Yes, I do.'

Now it was she who kept silent for a space. Far away on the slope of the hill a sheep bleated. Above the woods the starlings were circling.

'Then that means you know the truth,' she said finally.

He waited for her to add that it was his duty to speak it, but she didn't. He had no intention of looking at her. He did not want her eyes reading his feelings. She was too quick, too honest.

They were almost at the corner where the lane opened out and joined the road to the village. Then he would be rid of her. He stopped, without knowing why.

'You can't protect everyone, Alan,' she stopped as well, looking at him now without any pretence at the games people usually played. She was not a lonely and rather plain girl, and he was someone else. He was a young man going to war in a few days, and she was someone who had seen the anguish inside him and not turned away from it.

He did meet her eyes after all, and saw a courage there which was better than laughter or admiration, and just at the moment it was also better than love.

'If you don't tell someone the truth, you may end in protecting no one at all,' she added. 'I would go and see the Reverend, if it were me.'

'I tried,' he said with a twisted little smile. 'He didn't believe me. He thought I was lying to protect Chris.'

She looked down at the ground. She took a very deep breath and let it out slowly. 'I'd have thought the only person you'd lie this hard to protect would be your father.'

The fading sunlight seemed to shimmer around him. He could see every blade of grass at the roadside, the tiny moths fluttering and dipping. Did she know the truth?

'I'd go and see the Reverend if it were me,' she repeated.

There was no escape. She was right, he would only end in getting everyone hurt. If he were the one hurt himself, there would be a kind of cleanness about it, even honour, if nothing else.

'Yes... I think I'll do that. Thanks, Blanche.' He smiled at her. He meant it profoundly, and saw the colour burn up her cheeks. She wasn't pretty, but there was something in her which was more than that, even beautiful. 'Thanks,' he said again, feeling awkward. Then he turned and walked quickly down the road towards the Manse, before he could lose the courage.

*   *   *

187

Joseph walked down the lawn towards the apple tree with Alan beside him. He was not really surprised to see him back. He felt helpless to do anything for him. All day the talk in the village had gone back and forth, one in accusation, one in defence, far too many repeating what they had heard or thought. It saddened him and made him angry, but even his indignation had done nothing to crush it, except within his hearing. He knew perfectly well that it had resumed the moment he was out of earshot. He had changed nothing, except to set himself apart.

Alan was deeply unhappy, but there was a different air about him. He had resolved upon something.

'What is it?' Joseph asked him when they reached the tree, already laden with tiny fruit. It needed another two months at least before they would be ripe. It would be a good crop, if the winds didn't take them.

Alan stared at him, his eyes pleading. 'When I told you that I killed Will Harrison, it was the truth. I just didn't tell you why because it was to hide that that I did it.'

Joseph was stunned. What could Alan Trubridge have to conceal that was worth even injury, let alone killing a man?

'I see,' he said aloud. 'And are you now going to tell me what that reason was?'

'Yes.' Alan's gaze did not waver. 'When my father was ill I got morphine for him. I got a lot of it, over time. More than Dr. Kitching or anyone else would give him. And he was ashamed of it. He believed a soldier should have the courage to bear any amount of pain without recourse to such things. And then afterwards it took him a long time to... to be able to do without it.'

Suddenly a hundred small things became clear to Joseph. Shadows of memory fell into place and became understandable. 'I'm terribly sorry,' he said, and meant it. John Trubridge had been a good friend, a man he admired deeply. 'Was your purchase of it illegal? Is that what Will Harrison knew?'

'Well, I suppose semi-illegal, yes. But I had to borrow the money from Will to get it. I couldn't not...'

'I understand. You don't have to explain. And you owed Will a considerable sum. Alan, for heaven's sake, couldn't you have found another way?'

Alan's face was white with misery. 'I offered to give him my army pay every month until the debt was cleared, but he wanted it now, before we go to France.' He swallowed hard. 'He said he would cancel the whole debt if I left the key to my father's safe on the mantle shelf, and the sitting room window open.'

Joseph was so shocked it took him a moment or two to repeat the words over in his mind and understand what they meant. How could it be true? How could he even contemplate selling his country, let alone blackmailing someone else into helping him? It was inconceivable. And yet even as he denied it, he looked at Alan's face and knew it was true.

'And if you did not?' he asked. He knew the answer to that also, but he had to hear Alan say it.

'Then he would make public my father's illness... and how he faced it,' Alan said simply. 'And if I'd told the police there would have been nothing they could do until he'd got in, then he would have said my father had left the window and the keys for him, for more money for morphine. I couldn't let that happen.'

'No... no, I see that.' Joseph agreed. He could see it. John Trubridge would have been ruined, very possibly even executed for treason. The son who had loved him could not bring that about.

'What should I do?' Alan asked.

'Nothing,' Joseph said immediately. 'Not yet.'

'There's no time,' Alan began.

'I know,' Joseph cut across him. 'The day after tomorrow we shall leave, and none of us will come back the same as we were. The innocence will be gone from us, and some of the belief. We will have seen things around us we haven't even imagined yet. And more than that, deeper and far worse, we will have seen things inside ourselves we didn't dream of.' He lowered his voice. 'And of course some of us will not come back at all. And our women will be different as well. All of them will be afraid for us, and some of them will mourn.' He took a deep breath. 'And I imagine some of those we leave behind will never understand how we have changed, or why.'

'You mean like Dorothy?' Alan asked.

'I don't know. Do I?'

'I think so.'

'Don't judge her too quickly.'

Alan smiled, and Joseph saw in his eyes that the decision was already made. Whatever happened in the future, there was no going back on that at least. It was not a sudden change, only a sudden realization. He was not totally surprised.

'What are you going to do?' Alan asked, the edge of urgency back in him.

'I'm going to see Dr. Kitching. I think you should go home and prepare for travelling. Spend your last day with your father. He'll miss you very much. But keep your own counsel on this matter. Be brave, and kind to him. Let him believe there is nothing wrong except parting. You have the rest of your life in which to make peace with God for what has happened over the last days. From now on you can be whatever you want, if you want it badly enough.'

'But...'

'No "buts",' Joseph answered firmly. 'Go forward doing all you can, and leave the judgment to God. You can't help anyone by telling this story, except as you have to me. It is better for everyone, including Will Harrison, if his death is considered an accident. I shall see to it that Christopher does not continue to be blamed for it, I promise you.'

'Just... go?'

'Harder, perhaps, than confessing and taking the blame now, but of infinitely more service to your fellows,' Joseph said. 'We need you, Alan. You can't afford the luxury of sitting down in a heap of guilt. You must keep going, lengthen your stride, not shorten it. Now go home and be with your father. I'm going to see Dr. Kitching, and then I am going to spend tomorrow with my family too.'

'Yes,' Alan said huskily, but his voice was quite steady. 'Thank you, Reverend.'

'You're welcome. Will you tell my wife I shall be back in half an hour or so. I'll go the back way across the lane.'

'Yes... and thank you.'

'You already said that. Goodnight.'

'Goodnight, Reverend.'

* * *

'An accident?' Kitching said with surprise. 'You walked over here at this time of the evening to tell me that?' Joseph sat down in the big leather armchair. 'Yes, I think it's important the whole village knows that before we all leave.'

Kitching looked at him levelly. 'What made you decide that now?'

Joseph smiled. 'You have your professional confidences, Robert, so do I.'

'Was it anything to do with young Christopher, and Eleanor Cooper?'

'Nothing at all.'

'And it satisfies your conscience?'

'I can think of nothing better. It is not an easy answer, but some questions are too difficult. The questions between right and wrong are simple, it's the ones between one wrong and another that confuse us and test our judgment, and our compassion, and perhaps above all our courage. Let it be, Robert. Will Harrison died as a result of his own actions. Don't make other people suffer more than they already have, and will go on doing.'

'Right you are, Joseph, an accident it was,' Kitching agreed. 'God knows in a little while one death is going to be a small tragedy, by comparison.' He stood up and walked over to the window. 'The longer I live, the more I realize how much I don't understand. For example I can see young Alan Trubridge down there on the bank by the stream, and he's talking to Blanche Elder. I would have sworn he was in love with Dorothy, but that's not what it looks like from here. I've never seen such tenderness in his face.'

Joseph smiled. 'It's not a time for laughter and pretty girls any more. I'm afraid it's the girls with courage and strength who matter now, and will do until this is over, and perhaps long after that. Things are never going to be quite like this again.'

Kitching turned back to the room. 'I know that, Joseph. But there's still one more day of innocence left.'

Joseph stood up. 'And I'm going to spend it at home. Goodnight, Robert, and thank you.'

The Duke's Wife

Peter Robinson

I was absolutely speechless. After everything that has happened, there he stood, bold as brass, telling all the world we were going to be married. *Married!* You would have been speechless too.

Let me give you a little background. My name is Isabella, and until that moment I was all set to enter a convent. I fear I have a wayward and impulsive nature that needs to be kept in check, and the convent I had in mind, the votarists of Saint Clare, was one of strict restraint. Imagine my feelings when, head swimming from the twists and turns of recent events, I heard I was to be married to the Duke!

But there's more, much more.

A short while ago, the Duke realized that he had become lax in his duties, being of too mild and gentle a nature to enforce the laws of the land to their fullest. Of special concern to him, because it ate away at the very institution of marriage itself, was the law that forbade, on pain of death, a man to live with a woman to whom he was not married.

Fearing that the people would revolt if he were to suddenly change course and start enforcing the law rigorously himself, the Duke thought it better to slip away for a while and leave his deputy, Angelo, in charge. Thus, Angelo was invested with all the Duke's powers and charged with clearing up Vienna.

Mistake. Big mistake.

Where do I come into all this, you might be wondering? Well, it so happens that my brother Claudio had plighted his troth to his fiancée Juliet, and they were sleeping together. The problem was that they had kept their marriage contract a secret in the hope that Juliet's family would in time come to favour their union and provide a dowry, and this brought them within the scope of the law against fornication.

Now, Angelo *could* have exercised mercy, realizing that this was a very minor infringement indeed, and that the two were, in all but the outward ceremony itself, legally married, but Angelo is a cold fish and a sadistic, ruthless dictator. He likes to hurt people and make them squirm; it gives him pleasure. Believe me, I *know*.

Finding himself so suddenly and inexplicably condemned to death, Claudio asked me to intercede with Angelo on his behalf and see if I could secure a pardon. This I did, with disastrous results: Angelo told me he was in love with *me*, and he would let Claudio go only if I slept with *him*.

Now, while I do realise that in many people's eyes to give up one's virginity for one's brother's life might not seem too much to ask, you must bear in mind that I was to join the votarists of Saint Clare. I was to be married to God. This was my life, my destiny, and all of that – my very soul itself – would be sacrificed if I gave in to Angelo's base demands.

And don't think I didn't care about Claudio. Don't think for a moment that the thought of complying didn't cross my mind, but I wasn't going to give in to that kind of blackmail. I didn't trust Angelo, anyway. For all I knew, he might take my virginity *and* have Claudio executed as well – which, as it turned out, was exactly what he had in mind!

The whole process was degrading, me pleading passionately for my brother's life, going down on my knees on the cold stone to beg, Angelo making it clear that only by yielding my body up to his will could I save Claudio. Humiliating.

When I told him my decision, Claudio wasn't at all understanding. Of everyone, he should have been the one to see how important my virginity was, but no. He even had the effrontery to suggest that I should reconsider and commit this vile sin to save his life. Claudio was afraid of death, and all he could talk about was his fear of dying when *I* was facing a much greater enemy than death.

I told him he would find his comfort in the bosom of the Lord. He didn't seem to agree.

Where was the wily Duke during all this? You may well ask. As it turns out he was secretly directing events, disguised as a friar, and he was the one who came up with a cunning plan. He might be of a tender and mild disposition, but he has a devious mind, and he likes to play games. Nor does he always stop to think who might get hurt by them.

Angelo had once been betrothed to a woman called Mariana,

but her dowry went down on the same ship as her brother Frederick, and Angelo left her in tears, pretending he had discovered some stain on her honour when it was, in fact, the loss of her dowry that turned him against her. If you needed any more evidence of his worthlessness, that's the kind of person he is.

Now, if I were to go back to Angelo and pretend to agree to his demands, the friar suggested, we could arrange things so that Mariana went to his chamber in my stead, breaking no laws and saving both my virginity and Claudio's life.

It seemed a very good plan, and it worked, though the friar did have to do a little juggling with severed heads later on to convince Angelo that Claudio had indeed been beheaded. Then, for reasons of his own, the friar let me go on believing that Claudio had been executed – I did say he liked to play games, didn't I? – until the final scenes had been played out.

He had Mariana beg for Angelo's life, and the poor woman importuned *me* to beg with her! Thus, I found myself on my knees for a second time, this time pleading for the life of a man I hated, the man who, I thought, had killed my brother even though, he thought, he had enjoyed the treasures of my body.

So is it any wonder I was speechless when in walked Claudio, as alive as you or I, and the Duke announced that I was to be his Duchess?

*   *   *

I could have said no, I suppose, but at the time I was too stunned to say anything, and the next thing I knew, we were married.

Though it took me many months, I got over the shock of it all and adapted myself as best I could to my new life. I hadn't actually taken my vows, so there was no legal problem with the marriage. The Duke took over Vienna again and enforced the law himself, tempered with mercy and charity, and things went back to an even keel. I'm not saying that fornication ceased. That could never happen here. We Viennese are an odd lot, our lives full of secret vices and lies, and anyone with an interest in the human mind and perverse behaviour would have a field day studying us.

Being the Duke's wife had many advantages, I soon found, though I did have some trouble adjusting to his husbandly demands. He wasn't a young man, but he was certainly vigorous, though he needed certain props to help him perform those functions he liked so much. In particular, he liked to dress as a friar and intone Latin vespers when he took me from behind, as was his wont. That, I could deal with, but I drew the line when he asked *me* to dress as a nun. That would have been too much of a travesty for me to take, given everything that had happened.

So time passed, and on the whole I was quite enjoying the life of idleness and luxury. I loved my horses, enjoyed the theatre and the frequent grand balls, and I came to rely on the kind attentions of my maids and the delicious concoctions of my cooks. As I say, the sacrifices were bearable. Once in a while, I had a wistful thought for the life I might have led, but I must confess that when I hosted a magnificent banquet or walked the grounds and gardens of our wonderful palace, the thought of a bare, cold, tiny cloister lost much of its appeal. Mind you, I still attended church regularly and prayed every night, and we gave generously to the votarists of Saint Clare.

*   *   *

You might be interested in knowing what happened to the others. Claudio and Juliet were married, after which they moved to the country. By all accounts, they are happy enough, though we don't see them very often. Angelo and Mariana were also married – it was *her* wish, the Duke's dictate, and in accord with the law – but their story didn't end happily at all. Well, how could it with an evil, sadistic pervert like Angelo for a husband? Mariana is very sweet, but she is *such* a naïf when it comes to men. Even when I was headed for the convent, I had more idea than she did.

So I wasn't at all surprised when she came to me in tears about six months after her marriage.

'Dry your eyes, dear,' I said to her, 'and let's walk in the garden.' It was a beautiful spring day, with a warm gentle breeze wafting the scents of flowers through the mild air.

'I can't go on,' she said.

'What's wrong?'

'It's Angelo.'

'What about him?'

'He doesn't love me anymore.'

He never did love her, I could have said, but I held my tongue. I doubted that was what she wanted to hear at the moment. 'What makes you think that?' I asked.

She looked around, then leaned in towards me and lowered her voice. 'He has other women.'

I could have laughed out loud. Just about every husband in Vienna has other women. I suspect even my own Duke has one from time to time, but if it spares me the friar's costume and the Latin vespers for a night, who am I to complain? But Mariana, I could see, was really upset. 'It's just men, Mariana,' I told her. 'They're like that. They can't help themselves. It's their nature. Every time they see an attractive woman, they just have to conquer her.'

'But am *I* not attractive?'

'That's neither here nor there. You're his *wife*. That's all that counts.'

'Yes, I am his wife, so why does he have to sleep with other women? I'll sleep with him anytime he wants. I'll do *anything* he wants me to, even if it hurts me, even that disgusting thing with the–'

'Mariana! I told you, it's just their nature. You'll have to learn to live with it or your life will be a very unhappy one.'

'But I already *am* unhappy. I can't live with it. I want to die.'

I took her arm. 'Don't be so histrionic, Mariana,' I said. 'You'll get used to it.'

She broke away. 'I won't! Never! I want to die. I'm going to kill myself.'

I sighed. 'Over a man? There must be better reasons. Look, who is this woman he's been seeing?'

Mariana looked at me. Her eyes were so full of pain that my heart cried for her, even though I thought she was being foolish. 'It's not just *one* woman.'

'How many?'

'I don't know.'

'Two, three?'

'I told you. I don't know.'

'You must have some idea. Is it three, four, or five?'

'About three. I think that's about right.'

'So he's been sleeping with three other women?'

'Three a week. Yes.'

'*What?*'

'He has them sent to him. There's a man called Pandarus, a Greek I think, a despicable human being, and Angelo pays him to procure young women. Usually young virgins from the provinces who are new in town and haven't settled into employment. They're so young. They don't … I mean they don't all know what to expect.'

'He forces them?'

Mariana nodded. 'I've heard cries. Screams, sometimes, and he swears they will die terribly if they ever speak of what happened.'

Mariana's story was starting to interest me. I had heard of this Pandarus, though I had never met him, and I knew that he affected a respectable enough surface and was able to move among varying levels of society. Procuring wasn't new to Vienna, even at the highest echelons – nothing to do with sex is new to Vienna – but this Pandarus intrigued me all the same. 'How do you know all this?' I asked.

'A dear friend told me. She had a conversation with one … with one of the girls.'

'And you're certain it is true?'

Mariana nodded. 'One night I lay in wait, hiding in the bushes, and watched. We always had separate quarters, and Angelo maintains the same chamber he used … do you remember the night I went to him in your stead?'

I nodded. It wasn't a memory I cared to dwell on. Not one of my finest moments.

'They come in the darkest of night, and he burns no candles. Everything is just as it was that night.'

'I see,' I said. I had hated Angelo long and deeply enough for what he had inflicted on me that even as we spoke, the beginnings of a plan began to form itself effortlessly in my mind.

'What can I do, dear Isabel? Pray, tell me, what can I do?'

I took her hand. 'Do nothing,' I said. 'At least not for the moment. I know it pains you, but bear with it. I'm certain there's a solution and I promise that your suffering will come to an end ere long.'

Her eyes widened and lit up at that little sliver of hope. 'Really?

You promise? Oh, Isabel, is it possible I can be happy again?'

'We'll see,' I said, busy thinking. 'We'll see.'

★   ★   ★

I was finally satisfied enough with my changed appearance and the peasant clothes I had painstakingly made to venture out into the city streets in the guise of a country girl seeking employment. Through further, cautious questioning of Mariana, I had already determined that Panduras tended to prey on his victims in the busy public square near the coach station, often approaching them the very moment they arrived in the city. He had, I imagined, a skilled eye and knew exactly who was vulnerable to his approach and who best to leave alone. I affected to look lost and weak, and on my second visit, a man came up to me. His clothes and his bearing signified a certain level of wealth and influence in society, and his general manner was that of a gentleman.

'Are you new here?' he asked.

'Me?' I responded shyly, keeping my head down. 'Yes, sir.'

'Where are you from?'

I named a distant village I had once heard one of my husband's ministers mention.

'And what, may I ask, brings you to Vienna?'

'I seek employment, sir.'

'You do, do you? And what skills do you possess?'

'I can cook, sir, and wash, and mend clothes.'

'Valuable skills, indeed. Come, walk with me.'

I couldn't just go with him, not that easily. I had to play the shy country girl. 'I cannot, sir.'

'Cannot? Why not?'

'I don't know, sir. It just seems so … forward. I don't know you.'

'Forward? Walking alongside a perfect gentleman in a public place?' He smiled. He really did have a warm smile, the kind that leads you to trust a person. 'Come, come, don't be silly.'

So I walked beside him. He offered his arm, but I didn't take it. That didn't seem to upset him too much. 'You know, I think I might be able to help you,' he said, stroking his moustache.

'Help me, sir? You mean *you* require my services?'

He laughed. 'Me? Oh, no. Not me. A friend of mine. And I will speak for you.'

'But you don't know me, sir. How can you speak for me? You don't even know my name.'

He stopped walking and put his fingers under my chin, lifting my face. He was taller than I, so I had to look up, though I tried to keep my eyes down under my fluttering lashes. I felt myself blush. 'I am an excellent judge of character,' he said. 'I believe you to be an honest country maiden, and I believe you are exactly what he has in mind.' He let me go and carried on walking. This time I picked up my pace to keep up with him, showing interest. 'He does, however, have one peculiarity I must mention,' he went on.

'What might that be, sir?'

'He prefers to conduct his business at night.'

'That is strange, indeed, sir.'

He shrugged. 'It is a mere trifle.'

'If you say so, sir.' As a mere country girl, I could, of course, have no idea of the ways of city folk.

'So, should you be interested – and he is a most kind, considerate, and bountiful master – you must go to him through his garden at night and he will acquaint you with his needs. You need have no fears. He is an honourable man, and I shall be close by.'

Again, I had to remind myself that I was playing the role of a simple country girl. 'If you think so, sir.'

'Tonight, then?'

I hesitated for just as long as necessary. 'Tonight,' I whispered finally.

'Meet me here,' he said, then he melted into the crowds.

*   *   *

My plan was simple enough. I intended to gain entry to Angelo's chamber under cover of darkness and... Well, I hadn't really thought much past there, except that I planned to confront him and expose him for what he was. If necessary, I would claim that I went to visit my friend Mariana and that he attempted to ravage me, but I doubted it would come to that. One of the many advantages of being the Duke's wife is that subjects tend to fear my husband's power, and I had no doubt that Angelo would give up his nightly escapades if faced with their possible political consequences.

A wife's railing is easy enough to ignore, but the power of the Duke is another matter entirely.

I could not help but feel restless all evening as I waited for the appointed hour. After the usual antics with cassock and vespers, I slipped a sleeping draught into the Duke's nightcap, and he went out like a snuffed candle. When the servants were all in bed, I donned my disguise and slipped out of the house.

The dark streets frightened me, as I had not gone out alone at night before, and I feared lest some drunken peasant or soldier should molest me. In case of just such an incident, I carried a dagger concealed about my person, a present to the Duke from a visiting diplomat. But either the denizens of the night are better behaved than I had imagined, or I was blessed by fortune, for I made my way to the square without any hindrance whatsoever. When I got there, I was surprised at how many people were still out and about at such a late hour, lounging by the fountain, talking and laughing in the light of braziers and flaming torches. I had no idea that such a world of shadows existed, and I found that the discovery oddly excited me.

Pandarus appeared by my side as if by magic, wrapped in dark robes, his head hooded, as was mine.

'Are you ready?' he asked.

I nodded.

'Then come with me.'

I followed him through the narrow alleys and across the broad cobbled courtyards to Angelo's quarters, where we paused at a gate in the high wall surrounding the garden.

'This gate is unlocked,' said Pandarus. 'Cross the garden directly to the chamber before you, where you will find the door unlocked also. Enter, and all will be explained.'

I managed to summon up one last show of nerves. 'I'm not certain, sir. I mean … I do not …'

'There's nothing to fear,' he said softly.

'Will you accompany me, sir?'

'I cannot. My friend prefers to conduct his business in private.'

He stood there while I gathered together all my strength, took a deep breath and opened the gate. There were no lights showing beyond the garden, so I had to walk carefully to make sure I didn't trip and fall. Finally, I reached the door of Angelo's chamber, and it opened when I pushed it gently, hinges creaking a little. By this time, I could make out the varying degrees of shadows, so I was aware of the large canopied bed and of the silhouette standing before me: Angelo.

'Come in, my little pretty one,' he said. 'Make yourself comfortable. Has my friend Pandarus told you what you must do?'

I curtsied. 'Yes, sir. He told me you might have a position for me, but that you only conduct interviews at night.'

Angelo laughed. 'He's a fine dissembler, my Pandarus. But in that, he is not all wrong. I do, indeed, have a *position* for you.'

With this he moved forward towards me, and I felt his lizard-like hand caress my cheek. I should have drawn back, I know, and at that moment told him who I was and why I was there, but something in me, some innate curiosity, compelled me to continue my deception.

Angelo led me slowly to the bed and bade me sit, then he sat beside me and began his caresses again, this time venturing into more private territory than before. I took hold of his hand and moved it away, but he was persistent, growing rougher. Before I knew it, he had me on my back on the bed and his hand was groping under my skirts, rough fingers probing me. I struggled and tried to tell him who I was, but he put his other hand over my mouth to silence me.

All the time he manhandled me thus, he was calling out my name. 'Isabella ... Oh, my beautiful Isabella! Do it for me, Isabella. Please do it for me!' At first, this confused me, for I was certain that he hadn't recognized me. Then I realised with a shock that he *didn't* know who I was, but that this must be what he said to all his nighttime visitors. He called them *all* Isabella.

And then I understood.

The whole thing, the recreation of the exact same conditions as the night I was to visit him in exchange for Claudio's life – the hour, the insistence on absolute darkness. Though Mariana had gone to him in my stead, Angelo either refused to believe this, or thought that by duplicating the trappings he could enjoy the treasures of my body time after time in the darkness of his vile imagination.

As we struggled there on the bed, disgust and outrage overcame any simple desire I harboured for justice, and I knew then what I had been planning to do all along. Angelo's behaviour just made it all that much easier.

I slipped out my dagger and plunged it into his back with as much force as I could muster. He stiffened, as if stung by a wasp, and reared back, hand behind him trying to staunch the flow of blood.

Then I plunged my dagger into his chest and said, 'This is for Mariana!'

He croaked my name: 'Isabella ... My Isabella...'

'Yes, it's me,' I said. 'But I'm *not* yours.' And I plunged the dagger in again. 'This is for me!' I said, and he rolled to the floor, pleading for his life. I knelt over him and plunged the dagger in one more time, into his black heart. 'And this is for not being able to tell us apart in the dark!'

After that, he lay still. I didn't move for several minutes, but knelt there over Angelo's body catching my breath until I was sure that no one had heard. The house remained silent.

Knowing that Pandarus was probably still lurking by the garden gate, I left by the front door and hurried home through the dark streets. Nobody accosted me; I saw not a soul. When I got home, in the light of a candle in my chamber, I saw that my clothing was bloodstained. No matter. I would burn it. As soon as that was done and I was washed clean of Angelo's blood, all would be well. Mariana might shed a tear or two for her miserable, faithless husband, but she would get over him in time and he would never hurt her or anyone else again.

And as for me, as I believe I have already told you, there are many advantages to be gained from being the Duke's wife, not the least of which is the unlikelihood of being suspected of murder.

Judith Cutler

Meena Sangra twisted and tugged at the bright new gold ring. It was too tight to let her scratch the rash developing underneath. But there wasn't time to worry about that. She stooped for another attack on the piles of newspapers. The binder tape cut into yesterday's blisters.

There. The last pile in place, ready for the paperboy. Poor little thing: he didn't look strong enough to carry such a load. And he was so well spoken: she could understand his accent, at least, and he always made sure his nouns agreed with his verbs. She could trust his personal pronouns, too. So many of the people here in Smethwick seemed to find them difficult. 'Us are off down the market,' for instance: what did they mean by that? Her father would never have permitted such sloppiness. He had learned English from a teacher straight from England: he had the purest vowels, the most clipped enunciation, of all their acquaintance. He regretted deeply that even the good girls' school his daughter had attended had English teachers who were not native born – time and again he would mock her accent when she drove with him on his rounds in the old Morris. Meena swallowed hard. Part of her was glad that he wasn't alive to see to what depths she had been brought; half resented his early death, which had reduced her to this.

Putting her hand to the small of her back she straightened. Five past six. Vinod would be expecting his tea by now. And her mother-in-law must be bathed and dressed. Although the routine was less than a week old, it irked already.

Oh, my daughter, that you should have come to this, she heard her father lamenting.

She looked down at the ring. In England, Father had told her, the Christians used to marry 'for better, for worse, for richer, for poorer'. Neither her Hindu nor her civil marriage ceremony had used those precise words, but she understood them very clearly on this cold, wet morning. The words 'worse' and 'poorer' had the heaviest weight.

The marriage broker had given her mother to understand that Vinod was a rich businessman. He had shown her photographs of the home she was to expect, a spacious five-bedroomed house in the Birmingham suburb of Harborne: 'Very, very fine,' he'd insisted. 'A big wide road, lined with trees. The houses have such big gardens, front and back, that you cannot hear the big cars as they rush back and forth. And Mr Sangra has a fine car: look, there it is, in front of the garage. Neighbours? Oh, millionaires to a man. You have to be to live on Lordswood Road.'

Her dying mother was happy to take the broker at his word. And however independent Meena had wanted to be, life in India as a woman not quite young any more, with no family to support her, seemed less attractive than a traditional marriage. In her rush to escape the empty family home, Meena had even agreed to get together a dowry. The broker insisted that it was still the norm for decent Hindu women in England, whatever the law in India might be. What were a few hundred pounds, anyway? Even as she started to realise her capital, she heard her father say, as clearly as if he'd been at her shoulder, *Keep something in reserve, my child.* So she would not sell, but insisted on renting out the old family house. And before she handed the keys over, she took a spade and dug as deep as she could, so deep that no monsoon flood would wash away the earth, and no drought make cracks deep enough to show what she had buried. One day her new husband might be grateful for her forethought.

'Meena! Where are you? Come here at once!'

'Coming, Mother-in-law!' She ran upstairs to the best bedroom, recoiling at the smell of old woman and old woman's urine. Perhaps she would get used to it. Her father had got used to unpleasant smells. He'd conducted post mortems on the long dead, so that one day he could become not just a family doctor but a famous pathologist. He'd come home stinking of the morgue: Meena could almost smell him now. But instead she gagged at the old woman and her chamber pot, and had to dress the former and empty the latter. *There, Father, you'd be pleased I got those right.*

The old woman was fat and arthritic. It didn't take her father to diagnose that. But he had made himself unpopular amongst fat, arthritic old ladies by telling them that the best way to deal with their aches and pains was to get up and walk to market, as fast as they could. Lying in bed made them worse, he'd insisted. Mother-in-law had sniffed when Meena had relayed the advice, clear as if her father had spoken it from beyond the grave.

'Walk to market?' she'd repeated in disbelief. 'That's what *you're* here for: to run to the market.'

Or at least to the shops. Smethwick was well provided with shops selling familiar food: vegetables and spices lit up the eyes and nose with their freshness. She loved shopping. Even when the cold rain drenched down, she could bury her nose in a box full of methi and imagine herself at home. And there were shops selling cosmetics and saris to dazzle the eye and empty the purse. Not that her purse had much in it. It seemed it was the custom in Smethwick for men to dole out housekeeping money a coin or two at a time. She'd have to ask Vinod when she wanted more clothes. It seemed she even had to ask him when she wanted a simple walk along the High Street to Smethwick library. For they were not living in a house on Lordswood Road, Harborne. Not yet. They were living at the back of their shop. And when she asked him when they were moving to the house in the glossy colour photographs, he had hit her. Not very hard. There was no bruise to show on her cheek, but she needed mouthwash for the ulcers that came up. Ask Vinod for extra money? Thank goodness for her father's voice, telling her that ordinary salt dissolved in hot water was as good as anything she could buy from a pharmacist.

When she got used to English money, Vinod told her to make herself useful in the shop. She obeyed. Despite her efforts, it was clear he preferred to keep an eye on her. But one day Mother-in-law had an appointment with the doctor and needed Vinod to drive her. No, the car wasn't the gleaming Jaguar in the photo. To be fair, it wasn't an old Morris, either, but something in between. An Orion, that was it. Blue, with a scrape along one side.

'The girl comes with me!' Mother-in-law had insisted. 'Someone has to help me undress.'

Visibly Vinod agonised: mother or making money? The latter won. *See, Father – I haven't forgotten.*

She still had difficulty distinguishing what the locals said. Everyone had the same whining gabble, whether it was the old white men coming in, whippets at heels, for a couple of ounces of rough tobacco, or the proud Sikh women with more bright Indian gold than she'd seen outside a jeweller's shop. It was one of the old men who asked her, 'Wor'appened to the other one, me love?'

'Other one?' she repeated.

'Ah. The other wench. Not so old as you, but not so pretty, neither. Worked here nigh on a year, dae her, Tom?' He addressed another old man, his upper lip stained by the snuff she now sold him.

'Ah. Then her went away.'

Meena smiled politely, but for the first time wished her husband were here beside her, if only to translate. 'Wench?' she ventured.

The first man slapped his thigh. 'Yow doe half talk funny. Like them folk at the BBC.'

'Wench,' his friend put in with a helpful smile. 'Someone like yourself as might be. And her was here for a bit, and then her went away. Go back to Pakistan, did she?'

Pakistan? What were they talking about? If only they would speak English! It was best to smile as she took their money and carefully counted the right change and say, 'I'm afraid I've no idea. You would have to ask my husband about this wench.'

The old men exchanged a glance. She'd no idea why, no idea what it meant. But the incident made her uneasy.

Mother-in-law was in a terrible mood when she came home. As Meena bent to ease off her sandals, a huge clout knocked her off balance. 'You and your exercise! So much for you and your exercise!'

Meena had no idea what she meant. But she knew her ear was ringing, and that the wrist that she'd landed on was already swelling. *A cold cloth, wrapped tight. That's best for a sprain,* her father told her. So she gathered herself up and headed for the sink.

'Where do you think you're going? You pauper: a slut with a dowry your size, and you think you can go where you want? Come back here!' Mother-in-law's voice thundered round the small room.

'I've hurt my wrist, Mother-in-law.'

'Poor girl. Come here: let me see!' The old woman sounded contrite.

Meena approached, squatting, as before, at her feet. As she laid the damaged hand in the old woman's there was another thunderous blow, this time to the other ear.

By now Meena was crying – shock, pain, anger. Vinod must hear of this. She stumbled into the shop. Vinod was stacking shelves. There was no one else to be seen. By now the pain in her wrist was so bad she knew she had broken a bone. She ought to find a doctor. She blurted it all out to Vinod, who carried on methodically placing one tin of cat food on another, just as if she didn't exist.

When the shelf was complete, he turned to her, and boxed both ears. 'You think my customers want to hear my wife snivelling and wailing like a mad woman? You think that's the way to make my customers happy so that they buy and we can have that house on Lordswood Road, Harborne? You think that? Let me tell you, wife, a woman who wants medical treatment will have to come up with more dowry. Let me assure you of that.'

'But there's the Health Service. It's all free!'

'Not dentists!' And he slapped her so hard across the mouth that she could swear that her teeth moved in their sockets.

★   ★   ★

In their bedroom, she rocked herself backwards and forwards like a sick child. She didn't know which part of her body hurt the most. Sick, dizzy, and bleeding where he had taken her by force, she wept for her father, and the books he had read aloud to her when she had a fever he couldn't cure or a sorrow he couldn't soothe away. Cinderella, that was who she felt like. With her family already calling for their supper.

Grabbing a tea towel, she bound the throbbing, swollen wrist as tightly as she dared. Keeping it tucked as far from their eyes as she could, she picked over dhal and peeled garlic with as little movement as she could manage. She managed to press the chapattis into a semblance of a decent size and thickness. But when she came to lift the big heavy frying pan, she had to admit defeat. Tonight she would have to use one of the lightweight saucepans her mother-in-law despised. Once they had been non-stick, but Mother-in-law insisted on the vigorous use of scouring pads.

As she fried onions and added pinches of dhania and jeera, she tried to blot out what was happening. But it was all too clear. She'd read of countless women who had disappeared after marriages. Sometimes the pitiful remains of their poor charred bodies were found. Sometimes they were not. And it was clear that the police turned the blindest of eyes. Who'd ever heard of the husband or mother-in-law being brought to justice? Not in the whole of India, so far as she knew. Some women did contrive a risky escape: they told of beatings and cruelty like her own. Worse. It was the dowry their husbands wanted, the dowry and a domestic slave. And the police shook their heads in disbelief that their families should have so blatantly broken the law by handing over a dowry in the first place. If the Indian police were so unsympathetic, what could she hope for from these strange English people whose accents she could not penetrate and who didn't even know their personal pronouns?

No, it was to herself that she must look for salvation. Back home she had a house, after all, and the cache buried deep in the herb garden. But that was thousands of miles and an expensive air ticket away. Somehow, somehow, she must save odd pennies of change from her shopping, and hide them until she had enough. Months? Years? Who knew how long it would take.

Keep a low profile, daughter, her father said over her shoulder.

$$\star \quad \star \quad \star$$

After three weeks, she had saved two pound coins and seventy-three pence. And gained a fresh black eye. The blue and purple marks on her wrist had subsided to greyish yellow smears. She was learning how to deal with the nightly rapes, using the breathing system her father had recommended for women in labour too poor for the painkillers they needed. She would smile and scrape before her mother-in-law, and flatter her husband. But she knew that she might as well have been nice to tigers. All the good meals and subservience in the world wouldn't stop them turning on her when the mood took them.

One Tuesday it did.

She was in the shop, stacking packets of cigarettes behind the counter. Vinod was dealing with Lottery tickets. Not daring to turn round, she recognised the voice of the man with the whippet.

Quickly, silently, she passed Vinod the tobacco he'd want.

Vinod might not have registered her efficiency; the old man did.

'Ah, you'm got a good wench there, mate. I was asking her the other day, what happened to the other one? Where's she gone? Back to Pakistan?'

Vinod said dismissively, 'Oh, that young cousin of mine. She's gone back to India. To get married. Very hard-working girl.'

He was talking too fast. Meena knew there was something wrong.

'No better than this wench here. You know how to pick them, all right, Mr Patel. I'll say that for you.'

Vinod barely waited till the door had pinged shut before he gabbled, 'Ah! These stupid old men. Calling us all Pakistanis, and all Mr Patel.'

Appease, appease!

Meena clicked her tongue in disapproval, as was expected, and continued with the cigarettes. She did not want to talk, after all. She wanted to think. So 'wench' meant 'woman'. And as far as she could recall, there'd been no mention in the broker's report about any dependent cousins working in the Sangra business empire. No respectable bachelor would have an unmarried female in his household, not without a wife to chaperone her. Even his mother would not do. Almost absentmindedly she scratched the rash on her ring finger.

She wasn't surprised when Vinod made a swift excuse and left the shop. He was going to speak to his mother. He was going to make sure they told the same story.

Meena took especial trouble with the meals that day: they could have no complaints there. She tried to ask Vinod sensible questions – even suggested, very tentatively, that they might free up floor space in the shop by storing stuff in the cellar.

'Damp,' he said, as swiftly as he'd dismissed the old man.

Soon the tigers decided to strike. At least the old one did.

Meena was kneeling at her feet, cutting her toenails. The nails were thick, twisted into strange shapes. The scissors were clearly inadequate: they needed the sort of strong clippers her father had used on his mother's feet, so long ago she'd almost forgotten. Perhaps the momentary lapse in concentration was to blame. She had pulled on a nail and hurt the old woman. The yells brought Vinod dashing up. Before she knew it, she was on her knees, and Vinod was unbuckling his belt.

*   *   *

When she recovered consciousness she was in pitch darkness. For a moment she thought she'd died. For another, longer moment, she wished she had.

Use your wits, my child, her father told her. *Come on: think! Where are you?*

Rolling on to her knees, she made her fingers explore. Small square tiles – the sort they had in the kitchen. If she crawled slowly forward, she might find – yes, a wall. Systematically working round, she found steps, and the rough wood of a door. No, not dead. Just locked in the cellar. She hauled herself up so that she could sit on the bottom step. Quickly she lay down again. It wasn't just the pain, though she was afraid of fainting again. It was the fear of Vinod finding her somewhere he hadn't thrown her.

Deep breaths. That was it. The sort she used at night when Vinod took her. But something else penetrated the fog of her mind. A smell.

Of course there was a smell. Vinod had explained only a few hours ago that it was damp.

Her father might have been holding her hand: *My child, this is why we have to work quickly. That smell means someone is dead under there.*

There had been an earthquake – just a small one, not terrible enough to bring the world's press in – and she and her father had been amongst those struggling to claw out the living before they too started to give off that strange sweet smell. The same sweet smell she was breathing in now. That first time, with her father, she'd managed not to vomit. Now, holding her nose, breathing through her mouth, she might manage again. She knew it was vital – yes, Father, literally a matter of life and death – that she betray no hint to Vinod or his mother that she suspected something – some*one* – might be buried in the cellar.

Next time Vinod took Mother-in-law to the doctor, Meena bribed the paperboy to watch the shop and dashed down to the cellar, taking a lantern torch out of stock. Yes! The red quarry tiles were very slightly disarranged, over in the far corner. Half of her wanted to lift one to see if what she feared was correct. The other half feared dirt under the fingernails. She fled back upstairs.

As soon as the shop was empty, she prised some money from the Air Ambulance collecting box and replenished the till.

★ ★ ★

When a florid card invited them to a family wedding in Leicester, Meena wondered briefly if they would want her presentable enough to take with them, and that for a week she might be spared any beatings. For a day or so it seemed she might be right. But the old woman's arthritis flared up: she would have to stay behind. And it didn't take Father's whisper in her ear to tell Meena that she would have to stay behind to look after her. Well, a night without Vinod's attentions must be a bonus, even if the old woman would be sulky and vicious-tempered at missing the celebrations.

Once the old woman was snoring, Meena crept down to the cellar. No, she was crazy. She couldn't believe it. Of course she could smell damp.

Damp, yes – and something else. You know what that something else is! Courage, my daughter: evidence – that's what the English police will want.

Meena nodded. Even the Indian police wouldn't argue with a body in a cellar.

Yes, there was a scrap of cotton: her predecessor had been reduced to the cheapest of saris. And a skein of long black hair. Poor woman. Meena didn't want to see any more.

Oh, you coward! You think the police will take the word of an Indian woman without a bone or two to show them?

The thought made her gag. She was concentrating so hard on not vomiting, she didn't hear the door creak open.

'You bitch! You interfering bitch! Well, there's no help for it now! You'll have to stay down here till Vinod comes back. He'll know what do!'

No. Meena wasn't going to stay down here with only a half-exposed skull for company. She hurtled towards the old woman, who stepped back so quickly she lost her footing. There was a dreadful thud as her head hit the step. She slithered down, little by little. Meena was paralysed. She could hear the breath rattling in Mother-in-law's throat: she knew she was dying.

She ought to call an ambulance. The police. She knew she ought. And show them the hair and the sari. But what if they thought she'd killed the old woman? Vinod would certainly swear she had. Blindly, desperately, she pulled up more tiles, dashing into the kitchen for a knife to slice aside the damp earth. Scrabbling, dragging, at long last she got the old woman into the grave only just deep enough for her bulk. The earth she'd displaced? Thank God it was still night, and she could sprinkle it over the back yard, under the old TV and carpet Vinod had dumped there. All the time she worked, she tried to work out what to do next.

If she robbed the till and fled, Vinod would set the police on her. There was no doubt about that. And she knew they'd soon find an errant woman. Interpol. The Indian police. She'd be hounded down and imprisoned for life.

Well, was that any worse than what she'd suffered recently?

Meena washed and dressed very carefully. There was no telltale earth under her fingernails. If she looked tired and pale when she opened the shop for the paperboy on Sunday morning, no one would be surprised. The customers were used to averting eyes from her bruised arms and swollen face. In fact, the shop did its usual brisk business, the whippet man buying extra tobacco to celebrate his birthday. To his amazement, she pressed an extra packet on him.

When Vinod returned, still bleary though it was after midday, she was ready for him. Bringing tea as he took his place – still in his best clothes – at the till, she asked polite questions about the wedding, and replied indifferently to his questions about his mother. It was after three when he decided he ought to see her.

Meena locked the shop and flicked over the Closed sign. The people of Smethwick would just have to wonder why they'd packed up so early.

Vinod was calling and calling, both for his mother and – now – for Meena. She went to the cellar head to wait for him. She had both the lantern torch and the heavy frying pan in her hands.

Keep your voice steady, daughter. Remember, you have to win this argument. Put down that pan. Right out of sight. Your only weapon must be your brain.

She returned the pan to the kitchen.

'So where the hell is she?' Vinod shook her.

'If you calm down I'll show you.' She stood back deferentially to let him go first: he'd see nothing sinister in that.

He stood on the step below her. Yes, with that pan she could have smashed his skull quite easily – are you sure you're right, Father? 'Your mother's down there.' She pointed with the beam of light from the torch. But she pointed to the corner where the young woman was buried. 'Oh, no. I've got it wrong. That's where the other body is, isn't it? No, I wouldn't advise touching me. Or you might well join them.' She pressed a finger into his back. Just as they did on the films. Just as they did on the films, he believed it was a knife. He raised his hands. 'Be quiet and listen. I have enough evidence to have you taken to prison.'

'But Mother – you've killed her!'

'In fact she had a heart attack or something. But it might take time for the pathologist to find that out. Stand still, I tell you.' She drove in her fingernail more firmly. 'I shall be leaving England as soon as I can get a flight. To pay for the flight I need money from you.'

He was ready to turn and bluster. She pressed harder.

'You don't deserve it, but I'm offering you a chance. What is a thousand pounds, five thousand pounds, to spare yourself prison? You'll buy two tickets, in fact, one for me, one for your mother. Different flights, I think. That should buy you a little time. The only time you'll ever hear from me is if I learn you've remarried. Yes, Vinod, you've got to stay here in Smethwick for the rest of your life. No more wives, no more dowries, no more dreams about Lordswood Road, Harborne.'

'But –'

'Is it a deal, Vinod? Because frankly, if it isn't, I don't reckon much for your chances. Not if the police find you locked in here with the bodies of two dead woman.' Another fingernail stab. 'Down the steps.'

It didn't take long for him to agree. While he whimpered and snuffled in darkness, she used his credit card to book tickets. She raided the till for cash and slipped out to buy a new sari and travel bag.

* * *

She toyed with leaving him in darkness forever, but it would look better if the street saw him waving her off in an A1 taxi. The club class flight was comfortable. The pounds sterling she flourished were quite enough to compensate the people who'd been renting her house. She dug at her leisure. In time, she acquired a new passport under new name, and then a visa for the States.

She was waiting for the taxi to take her to the airport when she heard her father's voice again. *My child, this is your last chance. Write that letter to the English police now.*

'But what about our bargain? I promised I wouldn't split.'

And after all he did to you, my daughter, you think you're bound by a promise?

Obedient as always, she reached for pen and paper.

Big City

Bill James

There was an agreement. Rhys and Jill had spelled it out together. They told each other it was for the sake of the children. Rhys told himself that, too. But he knew it was for her own sake. He must not lose Jill. To keep her he had accepted terms. They would be pals, living together with their family. For passion she would go elsewhere. It was painful, she said, but they must accept change. It could happen in a marriage. Look at most of their Cardiff friends! She suggested people were becoming more sexually independent, confident, and generally 'big city', now the London government had given Wales *almost* a Parliament, *almost* independence. The Welsh Assembly, as this cut-price Parliament was called, had housed itself in a waterside building on Cardiff's dockland. Jill said this transformed Wales, made it a *real* country again and brought the city the status of a true, world-scale capital at last. Small-town negativeness, small-town prudishness, narrow moralising, were no longer on. She considered the new attitudes were especially evident in folk from their circle – journalists, politicos, lobbyists: those most in tune with the reborn Wales. She said she still loved Rhys, but was not *in* love with him. She had met someone else.

Although Rhys was hurt, he rejected the difference between love and *in* love. Or at least he did not believe that side of it would last. He must wait it out. Nor did he see why political devolution from London should mean rampant adultery, but he let the point go. And so, the agreement. He considered it a workable pact and not necessarily humiliating. Later, looking back, he was sure nobody could have foreseen so much tragedy.

When the agreement began, Jill used to offer fairly plausible tales beforehand to cover an absence, in case Rhys tried to ring her. She'd say shopping or a drink with Beth Postern. That stopped. It obviously sickened her to lie. She had a wonderful honesty; one of the things he loved her for. Now, she would announce that she'd be out from midday. He did not ask where. Silence was part of the agreement. He noticed she never put on her smartest outfits for these meetings, nor wore jewellery he'd bought her. This meant she refused to rub his nose in it by festooning herself for someone else. He felt grateful. He could not tell her that, though.

In fact it was when Rhys and Jill called the babysitter and went out as a couple to a restaurant or a party that she dressed up and appeared at her most elegant. A room full of people shone if she was among them, shone *because* she was among them. As her husband, Rhys felt pride. Just as much as emotions and sex, her sparkle was the essence of Jill, and could never be withdrawn from him. This helped Rhys accept the agreement. She remained his. He owned that wondrous social side of Jill. He exulted to read the covetousness in men's faces.

Part of the agreement was that if he found somebody else, he should be free to go to her. Rhys felt sure he would never want that. This certainty enraged Jill, possibly increasing her sense of guilt. Too bad. He could not alter. Jill was the only woman for him. Once – only once – she tried to explain what had drawn her to the other man. Apparently, he relayed non-stop ferocious desire for Jill. This was the word she picked, *ferocious*. Rhys was embarrassed by it, not injured. He felt she sounded quaint. Yet she said this man's passion had left her no choice.

When the arrangement was new, he did not allow himself to think much about where the two of them went, and at that stage he would never have secretly tailed her. Although this was certainly not banned by the agreement, it would have seemed shady. He assumed they generally had an early lunch in a restaurant and afterwards … Gross to speculate on that, and probably unhealthy. She liked to be home soon after the girls returned from school.

Rhys and Jill still visited restaurants themselves. Looking brilliant, she would talk and radiate at full power, and anyone watching would surely have supposed them alight with joy in each other, perhaps even lovers, not man and wife. It thrilled him. This was Jill as Rhys's, her jewellery very much in place. Occasionally, they bumped into acquaintances at these places and would perhaps make up a four or even push tables together for a party of six or eight. The more the better for Jill.

On one of these evenings, they came across friends and colleagues at The Celtic Bistro, and, while helping to rearrange the furniture, he felt the back of a hand, a woman's hand judging by size, pressed for a few seconds very firmly against the inside of his left, upper thigh. Very upper. At first, he thought it an accident amid the confusions of aperitifed people reshaping the restaurant. Soon, though, he corrected: The contact was too prolonged. He yearned to believe it had been Jill. Was she telling him in a sudden, uncontrollable, almost shy fashion she was his after all; totally his, not just her public self? Perhaps her affair and therefore the idiotic agreement were dead. Time had righted things?

But, he must not dream. Really, he knew Jill was never near enough to touch him as they shifted the tables and chairs. He decided only Beth could have done it; Beth, strapping young wife of busy, inaugural Welsh Assembly member Jeremy Postern. No apology or joke came from her about the contact, though. That seemed to confirm the incident was intentional. Yet she did not attempt to sit next to him for the meal, and when he talked to her he found no personal message, no readable explanation in her blue-black eyes for knuckles wilfully nudging his nuts. The incident shook Rhys. It made him realise that the notion of 'another woman' could be more than a notion. Perhaps someone else *was* available. To his amazement, this interested him. Was Jill correct, after all, to resent his self-righteous dismissal of the agreement's clause entitling him, also, to sexual liberty? Curiosity about the significance of the act dogged him. Perhaps it was part of a new sophistication: A woman would wait and hint.

Early one evening, when he was having a semi-work drink with Jeremy Postern, other Assembly members, and press friends in The Referendum cocktail bar, Rhys went outside briefly and mobiled Beth. She seemed warm, pleased to hear him, unsurprised. He wondered if they might meet one evening, and she thought they might. They fixed a time. Rhys went back to the bar feeling not excited or victorious but, yes, more *wholesome* than for ages, more manly.

Beth and he seemed to need no preliminaries. It was as if they had been waiting for each other. She went halves with him on a bottle of Dubonnet and the charge for a room overnight in the plush new Capital Hotel in Cardiff Bay, though they would be using it only for a few early evening hours. They made fierce, prolonged love. Yes, it was even *ferocious* prolonged love. Afterwards, while they lay relaxed, he reassured Beth about the care he would take with her reputation, explaining how he had phoned only when certain Jeremy was not at home.

'The smug sod wouldn't care,' Beth replied. She sounded defeated. 'He's too deep in all the superlative Assembly crap for a love life. We go our own ways.'

'You don't like that?'

Hurriedly, she turned towards him: 'Darling, of course I do. I wouldn't be here with you now, otherwise, would I? Aren't you and Jill permissive of each other, too?'

'Good God, no. I couldn't tolerate the idea of her seeing somebody else, screwing somebody else.'

'I adore jealousy in a man,' she said vehemently. 'It means he cares. It's what makes you so damn irresistible, Rhys. *You* wouldn't doze through a marriage. God, but Jill's lucky.'

This encounter revolutionised Rhys, gave him vision. Jesus, might Jill think he did not care because he showed no rage and put up with the agreement? Was this why she had discarded him sexually? But he *did* care. He must show it. He was not like Jeremy – and like many men Rhys knew: by piffling career obsession and bed coolness they forced a wife to seek fulfilment elsewhere. He decided he must watch Jill discreetly when she went to one of her meetings. Although he still loathed the idea of gumshoeing, he had come to loathe apparent indifference even more. He would annihilate this disgusting, arid agreement. But agreements were only words and sentiments. He wanted something solid to smash. He needed a look at the opposition.

Luckily, he could take time off as he wished. He was part of the newly hatched lobbying industry around Mount Stuart Square in Cardiff Bay at the docks, and ran his own hot public-relations firm. Surveillance was sure to be difficult, though. Jill would soon notice his Citroen. And so, next time she said she would be out for the afternoon, he took a company Vauxhall to wait near their Cowbridge, Vale of Glamorgan, house until she left at around noon.

She drove to a side street in Splott, an undazzling region of Cardiff. She parked. Rhys drove on a bit and also parked, then watched through the mirror. Soon, a Toyota arrived and drew in not far from Jill's VW. At once, Rhys sensed this was Lover Boy and turned in the driving seat now to get a proper look through the back window. He kept his face partially obscured by the headrest. A middle-height man left the Toyota and walked twenty yards to Jill. Opened the VW passenger door, and climbed in. For a few minutes they kissed and talked, all excited smiles, arms locked around each other, as if they'd fought their way across ice floes after years of forced separation. Probably they were here every week.

Lover Boy's hair was grey, but cut in a bristly, young-thruster style. Boy? Palely aglow with the tired beams of Indian summer, he must be at least ten years older than Rhys. It hurt. She could prefer someone this age? He had a round, pushy face with heavy eyebrows. Although he could have had them trimmed, he must have felt they were part of his image, proving verve. Image was vital in this jumped up metropolis. His face was full now of … full of what Rhys longed to dismiss as raw, lucky-old-me triumph. This was someone in his fifties at least, all set for a nice afternoon with a beautiful woman of thirty-four. Horrified, though, Rhys found he could not honestly describe what he saw like that. His view was imperfect, but he glimpsed … well, damn it, yes, he glimpsed *love* there – maybe ferocious, maybe just intense, but in any case enough to terrify him. He sensed the power of their relationship, almost admired it, certainly envied him, the spry jerk. God, Beth had it so right and Rhys could switch on the jealousy. He was delighted at how well he hated. He might tell Beth about this whole unpleasant sequence.

The man's clothes were like some 1970s sports commentator's – three-quarter-length sheepskin coat and a crimson scarf. Still, he was presentable. Naturally. To think otherwise would be a rotten insult to Jill. And it would be mad to feel jealous if the rival were pathetic.

The lovers left the VW and began to walk. They turned into the main road. Rhys went after them on foot, staying well back. He saw Jill take the man's arm for a while, as though feeling anonymous in this unfashionable spot. But then she suddenly let go and put a little gap between them. She probably realised that, down market or not, people who knew her could be driving through. To be observed at all would be bad, but walking arm-in-arm was an utter giveaway. They kept the distance between them until vanishing into a rough–looking eatery. Never would Rhys have taken a woman to such a place, and certainly not a woman like Jill, even in run-of-the-mill clothes. At first, he thought Lover Boy must be short of money. But no, it was clearly part of the cleverness. This pair were unlikely to meet anyone they knew in such a dump, and especially not Jill. Secrecy above hygiene. After about ten minutes, Rhys walked past on the other side of the street and looked in. They were at a table near the window, too bloody tied up in themselves to notice anyone else.

He was sick with distance and rage and helplessness. The agreement came to seem contemptible. Bloodless. He returned to his car intending to wait until they appeared, then drive behind them to their next destination, presumably a room somewhere. But he found he could not face this. The old tenderness towards Jill, the old reluctance to snoop on her, ravaged him, made any further dogging impossible. Briefly, he contemplated vandalising the Toyota. In the Citroen boot he had a tyre lever which could have made an impression. But he was not driving the Citroen and, in any case, that was a crazy, infantile thought – vehicle-breaking by daylight in a well-peopled street. Instead he walked to the Toyota and glanced inside. On top of the dashboard was an opened envelope showing a name and address. It seemed Lover Boy must be G. Lowther and lived in the Pontcanna district of the city. This comparatively chic spot was home to many loud people from independent television companies, presently coining it with innumerable worthy films about Welsh identity. Rhys thought this lad looked like a Geraint rather than a Glyn or a Gwyn. He couldn't have said why. Perhaps G. was on the technical side, or Rhys might have recognised him through work.

Rhys went back to the office and, as he sometimes did, stayed late. There were papers to deal with after his spell away. Some routines had to continue. But, obviously, his mind was badly troubled and he did not operate well. Would he ever operate well again if he stuck with the emptiness and degradation of the agreement? He finished, went out to the Citroen in the yard, and decided to drive home via Pontcanna. When he eventually reached Cowbridge, he was surprised to find Jill still up. She seemed desolated.

'Jeremy Postern rang,' she said.

'Some sparkling speech he wants puffed? Am I to call him back? At this hour?'

'He rang *me*,' she said.

'Oh, yes?'

'Beth told him you and she have an affair going.'

'Why the hell would she do that?'

'To make him jealous, I expect. Compel him to want her.'

'But he couldn't care less, Jill.'

'You fool. He's frantic at the thought of losing Beth. He asked me what he can do about it, he and I.'

'Just like Jeremy.'

'Maybe. Anyway, I won't tolerate this. Rhys, I'm leaving you. Tonight. Now. For keeps. I've sent the girls by taxi to my mother's.'

'But, Jill, darling, why?' he cried. 'It was only the agreement.'

'The agreement is finished.'

'It is?'

She wept. 'It's not needed. Gaston and I ended things today. It all came to seem ludicrous, barren, mean. The relationship just dropped dead while we walked to a restaurant. We both sensed it, though neither of us understood why.'

'Oh, a restaurant where?' Rhys asked.

'I intended a new start.'

'But this is wonderful!'

'Not now. Impossible. It's unfair of me, maybe, but I can't stay since hearing of you and Beth. Unbearable. I'm going.' Jill went out to her car. He walked urgently after her, and saw that the VW had suitcases on the rear seat. She climbed in, keyed the ignition, and music sounded from the radio. He stood by the side of the car, the driver's door open. She seemed to remember something and went hurriedly back into the house. She left the engine running, as if to tell him she had not changed her mind. He waited. The music ended and a local news bulletin began on the radio. It reported the discovery of a so-far-unidentified middle-aged man dead on the ground of a Pontcanna street. He had been killed by head wounds. Jill returned with another small case, which she placed in the back. She climbed into the VW again and reached out for the door, which still stood open. She said: 'Rhys, how in God's name could you betray me with someone like Beth Postern?'

'But it was Beth who taught me to hold on to you, love.'

Jill pulled the door to and drove off. She did not wave.

Enough was Enough

Martina Cole

Shona looked at the two little boys asleep on the back seat of the car and she smiled to herself. Such good-looking boys, everyone said so. Blond-haired and blue-eyed, both had sturdy bodies and friendly smiles. They were very confident little people who assumed they were welcome anywhere and who settled down within minutes in a strange environment.

But then, why wouldn't they? Both adored, both loved so very much by each of their parents.

She saw her older son Tom's leg quiver as he slept and guessed he was finally out of it at last. He fought *everything,* especially sleep.

She yawned. She was tired herself. It had been a long day and an even longer night.

All that fighting and arguing had taken it out of her.

She glanced at herself in the mirror above the dashboard. Adjusted it so that she could see herself properly. Long blonde hair that saw the benefit of the hairdresser more often than it was needed and a full-lipped wide mouth that made her look sexier than she really was.

Wide-spaced blue eyes, so like her sons' and the creased forehead of a woman who had a lot on her mind.

She relaxed her face and stared at herself for long moments.

She glanced at her husband as he moaned and ignored him completely.

He was always moaning lately. She had a feeling it was because he was much more interested in being with the woman from the swingers' party than being with her or the boys.

She closed her eyes and laid her head back against the car seat. It was comfortable and she could easily sleep now, but she forced herself to stay awake.

Joseph had stopped his noise and she was glad of that much at least. It took a lot to shut that man up.

She remembered when they had first met and the memory reminded her of how much she had loved her husband once. How much he had loved her.

When they drove along then, there had been no moaning about her and the kids. He would suddenly slip his hand from the gear stick and trail it up her skirt. Making her hot for him, the sheer pleasure from the feel of his fingers on her skin was overwhelming. She would feel his mouth go dry and she would close her eyes and let the feelings of embarrassment tinged with shame wash over her as his fingers parted her legs and she would open herself to him.

He had enjoyed her discomfort as much as he had enjoyed the pleasure he gave her.

She still felt hot at the thought of it. The same confused emotions washed over her and she wanted him to do it again, one last time.

But she knew it wouldn't happen.

His fingers were trailing up other skirts, making other women come while he drove.

She felt the sting of her tears and swallowed them down.

Why wasn't she enough for him?

Why did he need other people?

She studied him again, her handsome husband. All her friends had been so jealous when she had bagged him. She had asked him once what had attracted him to her and he had laughed at her. He had laughed at her a lot in those days. Still did, come to think of it. Only then it had been with pleasure and with love not with ridicule and contempt as it was now.

He had answered that it had been the way she seemed so remote; it had been her remoteness that had attracted him. He had honestly not understood why this answer had upset her so much.

He was cruel, really. He didn't like women as much as he thought he did.

When Tom had been born he had dropped her off at the hospital and taken the car to be valeted. Her waters had broken on the front passenger seat and he had been like a demented maniac at the thought of the cleaning bill.

She remembered feeling upset at the time, hurt that he could care more about the car than her or their child. But that was Joseph all over.

She giggled at the memory of his face when he had come back

hours later to see his son emerge from inside her. He said he couldn't believe that his child was hanging out of his wife's body.

He had been so amazed that even the midwife had laughed.

When he talked about it afterwards at dinner parties he always made it sound as though *he* had done all the work, that *she* had just been peripheral to the whole procedure, and people had believed him. It was a way he had.

He was a fucking bully; at least that is how she described him in her mind. He was nothing more than an emotional bully who came across as all sweetness and light to everyone, except, of course, to his wife and children. The life and soul of the party, but a terror when you got him home.

Her head was aching now from all the thinking.

That had always been her problem, even as a child she had lived too much inside her head. School reports reported her as dreamy, inattentive. Living in her own world.

Well, so what? Who wanted to live in this one all the time? Not her, that was for sure.

She watched his hands move around. Once, she had loved those hands as much as she had loved him. Those hands had given her so much pleasure. She had tingled just thinking of him coming home to her. (That was in the days when he had still come home to her, of course!) Now someone else tingled at the thought of his fingers and his mouth. Someone else ran to replace lipstick on bruised lips and rearrange breasts in bras that were as uncomfortable as they were impractical.

Those bras she had worn for him were all too big for her now; perhaps she should give them to the new woman in his life. Her breasts had all but disappeared since the boys had arrived, but she still looked good. She was *determined* to look good even if he rarely saw her.

The first time he had taken her to one of *those* parties she had been amazed at some of the women there. Big women overweight and underdressed. Tits and arses hanging out for all the world to see. Joseph had loved it. She saw his eyes popping out of his head at the antics of the people there.

But they were ugly people, ugly inside and out.

He didn't think so, though, he thought they were great. Funny, in touch with their sexual personalities was how he had described them.

Fucking exhibitionists was how she thought of them privately.

But she had gone along with it as she had gone along with everything he wanted. It was how you kept someone like Joseph beside you. By doing what *he* wanted instead of what *you* wanted.

Like the handcuff escapades and the pretend rapes.

She wondered what he thought about the handcuffs now.

He was obsessed with sex. Any kind of sex.

Now it was sex with perfect strangers.

She had quite liked having sex with the woman, though. She had wondered at that, it had happened in a bedroom without everyone watching and looking on. She had been trying to escape the sight of her husband on the floor with all those people. Had sneaked into a bedroom and been followed in there by the pretty, dark-haired woman with the smooth hands and the even smoother tongue. It was as if she had disappeared into her own body for the first time in years.

She shook the memory away, disgusted with herself for her feelings.

That was what he had reduced her to. A lonely, sad person who had got off on someone being *nice* to her, because the woman *had* been nice to her. Had told her she knew how she was feeling and how only another woman could understand her predicament.

They had sought each other out after that.

It had annoyed Joseph because she had connected with someone and according to him that was not what the parties were all about.

They were about anonymity.

It was weird taking the kids to school and seeing neighbours who had fucked her husband acting normally and talking about the children and the washing machine and how hard it was to find a good au pair these days.

Fucking surreal.

She was swearing in her head a lot these days. Effing and blinding all the time.

It was creeping into her everyday language as well.

Even her mother had remarked on it. Her pinched mouth had expressed sorrow that her daughter, *who had everything,* could talk in such a disgusting manner.

Good job she couldn't listen to what went on inside her head, it would blow her away completely.

She would love to be a fly on the wall when this latest debacle became public knowledge. She would get the blame, of course, she got the blame for everything.

Her eyes wanted to cry and she was bravely stemming the flow of tears. Tears got you nowhere and gained you nothing. She should know, she had cried enough of them.

The first time Joseph had stayed out all night she had cried. Innocent to the ways of the world then, she had been frantic. Believed something had happened to him, a car crash or something. Wrong!

He had looked at her crying as if she was something he had dragged in on the bottom of his shoes.

He had shaken his head as she had screamed and created. Laughed at her bloated face and blotchy skin. Informed her how stupid she looked, a grown woman expecting her husband of three years to remain faithful.

Was that when she had changed towards him?

She peered at him once more. His handsome profile as he sat in the driving seat of their Mercedes making her heart jolt because he still had that power over her. The power to make her want him.

He was talking away, but she was not listening to him.

He talked about the kids now! Oh yeah, *now* he wanted to talk about the kids. Now it was too fucking late! Usually he found them a boring topic of conversation.

Now suddenly it was important for him to see them grow up, see them become men.

She watched his lips move, but the words were not making sense to her any more, but she could hear the desperation in his voice. She was enjoying his fear, she could almost smell it.

But then desperate times meant desperate measures she supposed.

And this was one desperate and terrified man. At last she had his undivided attention, maybe she should have done something like this years ago.

She had finally had enough and he knew it.

He had taken her and degraded her, he had used her and abused her. He had given her two children and had then promptly dismissed them from his life along with her.

Now they were all *so* important.

She had gone along with anything he wanted to keep him by her side and nothing had worked.

He had thrown it all back in her face.

Enough was enough, as her mother used to say.

Enough was enough.

*   *   *

The policeman looked into the car and shook his head in despair.

The two little boys looked asleep, as did the woman. In fact she was smiling as if she was having a wonderful dream.

But the man who was handcuffed to the steering wheel looked as if he had been through hell. His head was cut and bruised, there had been violence and it had obviously been directed at him. His wrists were torn and bloodied from his attempts to slip them from the handcuffs. He had fought for his life, all right.

He had managed to smash his head through the side window of the Mercedes; it must have taken some effort.

But it had made no difference. The garage had filled up with fumes and it had just taken him longer to die.

He stepped out of the large garage and looked down the sweeping drive to the electric gates that told intruders this was private property so keep out, and waited for the pathologist and the ambulance to arrive.

It was a lovely day, bright and sunny. He could hear the sounds of summer, buzzing flies and birds singing in the trees. It really was an idyllic setting.

The imposing house with its gables and its moneyed air looked lonely in the brightness of the morning.

Bereft of life, it seemed to be looking out at the world with a weary expression.

The policeman thought of his wife at home with the kids and his homely face broke into a small smile.

Suddenly, he wanted to see them this very second. Make sure they were all OK.

But instead he waited as he was expected to.

Stephen Gallagher

'So,' he said to me. 'What does an honest week's work feel like?'

'You should give it a try sometime,' I said, looking out of the car window as tattoo parlour followed titty bar on the way down Airline Drive.

'Yeah,' he said, slowing for a bakery truck that had just pulled out ahead of us. 'Make four dollars an hour and join you back there in the Ozone Motel. Like that's gonna happen. How about I set you down at this corner?'

'Anyone sees that, it's going to look weird,' I said. 'Let me out right in front.'

So when we reached the gas station he turned onto the concrete apron, and as we slowed to a stop by one of the fuel islands he said, 'Watch yourself. Look respectful when you get out.'

'What are you staring at?'

'That shirt,' he said. 'Jesus. Talk about playing the part.'

I opened the door and stepped down and looked back into the Cherokee to say, 'Thank you for the ride, sir.'

'Just keep your nose clean,' he said, and he was starting to move off even before I'd got the door closed. Like this was a place you might pass through if you had to, but where you'd never choose to linger. He made a big loop around the islands and then rejoined Airline Drive to head back the way he'd come.

He wasn't necessarily wrong. Airline Drive ran through an end of town that had seen great days, and these weren't them. You'd find no family restaurants or miniature golf here. This was the bargain-basement retail zone for fast food, fireworks and fornication. And soon it would start getting dark.

I crossed the gas station's forecourt to enter the store. Half a dozen automobiles were lined up outside the repair shop that operated around the back, mostly fitting discount tires and mufflers. Some of those vehicles were top-of-the-range, collected from their owners in smart downtown offices and delivered back to them at the end of the working day.

The store was the usual three aisles of late-night needs plus a donut display and a coffee machine. The whole thing was run from the far end by a solitary employee. Behind the counter right now was a shaven-headed black man of brick-wall bulk, wearing the yellow Penry's uniform shirt unbuttoned over a singlet. I hadn't seen him before, but even before I could open my mouth he said, 'You the new guy?'

'John Lafcadio,' I said.

'Oberon Luce,' he said, and stuck out his hand. I shook it.

'Oberon?' I said, not sure that I'd heard it right.

'What of it, *Lafcadio*?' he said.

'Nothing,' I said.

'Least I don't got my parole officer drivin' me to my job.'

I glanced at the desk. Not only were there three cameras covering the forecourt, there was a microphone pickup out there as well. 'Who says he's my parole officer?' I said.

'You one of the Jailbirds for Jesus or not?'

'I guess,' I said.

'Well, there you go.'

I joined him behind the counter for the handover. As I was signing in I said, 'How's it been?'

'Quiet,' he said. 'Coffee machine's on the spazz and the donuts are still yesterday's. The man from the magazine place came to fill up the racks and left some free dirty books. Don't let Old Jake see them less you want to watch your new boss having a coronary.'

There wasn't much more to the handover than that. The takings from Luce's shift went into the back office, where he dropped them through a one-way slot into a safe set in the concrete floor. Most of the sales were on charge accounts and credit cards, so there wasn't a lot of cash business. The owner called by twice a day to collect the money and check it against the record. Any shortfall came out of the cashier's wages. Two shortfalls, and you were out.

I'd be starting my shift with a clean roll and a twenty-five dollar float. Old Jake Penry might be a businessman and lay preacher willing to offer ex-convicts a job and a measure of trust to help them get rehabilitated, but Old Jake Penry wasn't stupid with it.

Oberon Luce disappeared around the side of the building and reappeared a couple of minutes later behind the wheel of an ageing

Ford Fairlane. Less than a minute after that he was gone, carried away in the steady Airline Drive traffic.

Over the next half-hour I kept an eye on forecourt sales and tidied up some of the stock in the store. I tapped one of the donuts against the glass in the case; any staler, and it could have been rinsed off and sold as a bagel. A couple of people came in and bought phone cards. A beer truck driver asked for directions. Someone out at the pumps was having trouble with the card swiper and I had to get on the mike and tell him how to do it. Then I had to tell him where to find his receipt slip because he was looking in the wrong place.

While that was happening I heard the connecting door to the repair shop swing open, and looked at the in-store surveillance monitor to see one of the mechanics heading for the coffee machine. I saw him stop and read the handwritten notice on the front of it, and then from over the shelving I heard him curse.

I called out, 'Don't you have your own supply back there?'

'We got our own hot water, but that's no good when the coffee can's empty,' he said, emerging into sight from the end of one of the aisles.

'I can sell you a jar.'

'Not at Old Jake's prices.' He was young, with a shock of dark curly hair that sat on top of his head like alfalfa spilling out of a wrap. The embroidered name on his coverall read *Dave* in scarlet thread. He took a Coke from the chiller cabinet and slapped coins down on the counter.

'Just remember,' he said with a glance up at the camera. 'Wherever you are, whatever you're doing, God is always watching you.'

Then he hooked a finger under the ringpull, lifted one foot from the floor, and cut a rasping fart in the same instant that he popped the tab.

'That sure scratched the inner itch,' he said, and strolled back through into the workshop.

*   *   *

Business was steady through the evening, and in the first lull I went and took the front panel off the coffee machine to see if there was anything I might be able to do with it. Someone came in while I was getting the wingnuts unscrewed.

'Right with you,' I called out, and I set the panel down and went back to the counter. There was a tall man waiting for me, straight-backed, slight paunch over his belt, shock of white hair. It was Jake Penry. He must have reached over the counter because he was holding about a hundred dollar's worth of cheap single-use cameras that had been packaged as a hanging strip. If you wanted to buy one, you tore it off the bottom. He obviously meant this by way of a demonstration.

He said, 'I could be out that door with all of these and the money from the cash drawer by now.'

'The cash drawer's locked and you'd have found me in the way,' I said.

'Think you could take me on, son?'

Well, I had at least a two-decade advantage but it didn't seem wise to be pointing it out.

'Just trying to save you some money, boss,' I said. 'The coffeemaker's down again. I watched the service engineer fixing the same fault on Monday. What did he bill you, fifty dollars for the callout? And all he did was clean the filter.'

He narrowed his eyes in that pissed-off-amused way of people who don't like to climb down over anything and aren't used to the need for it.

'Is that right?' he said.

'Yes, sir, it is,' I said.

'Is there any situation you couldn't talk your way out of?' he said.

'I had the misfortune to meet a judge who seemed to think so,' I told him.

While this had been going on, Dave the mechanic had come through from the repair shop with the day's worksheets. Taking them from him, Penry said, 'I want to see your time cards for last week, Dave.'

'Whenever you like, Mister Penry,' Dave said.

'Now sounds good to me.'

Old Jake headed through to the back, and Dave gave me a meaningful look while calling after him, 'I'm right behind you, sir.'

Then he lowered his voice and added, 'Smooching ass with the rest of them.'

'I see the gratitude starts to wear a little thin with time,' I said.

'Screw gratitude,' Dave said. 'Jailbirds for Jesus fills this place with cheap labour and gives him a ticket into heaven. For Jake that's a win-win situation.'

Shortly after that, the repair shop closed down for the night. When the half-dozen mechanics had all set off for home, Dunleavy, the repair shop manager, rolled down the shutters and came through into my section to set up the night alarm. I had to look the other way as he tapped the four-number keycode into a wall panel behind the counter.

When he'd gone, that was it. I was alone. My shift would finish at six a.m., when I'd hand over to my replacement and then walk down to the bus stop for a ride back to the Ozone Motel. There I'd sleep for about four hours until the noise from housekeeping disturbed me.

When it was fully dark I brought all the loose stuff inside and made bundles of the day's unsold newspapers, and then I switched off half the store lights and locked the doors. From now on, all transactions would be through the security window. If you wanted something that wouldn't fit into my sliding drawer, you wouldn't get it.

I found where Oberon Luce had put the free dirty magazines, and took a couple of the more normal-looking ones. Then I settled in for the night. I had the security screens on my eyeline, the microphone within reach, and all the fuel reset buttons to hand; unless somebody wanted a carton of milk or a magazine I'd have no reason to move between now and the end of my shift, unless it was to scratch or pee.

From my limited experience so far, the weeknights were never too busy. They were, however, something of a weirdo parade.

It took less than half an hour to get started.

*　　*　　*

I couldn't have told you what kind of car it was, just that it was black, and riding low, and bulging with a drum-machine sound. Add-on custom parts had changed its shape beyond recognition, and the alterations had been carried out with little talent or skill. The windows were tinted, so I couldn't see who was in it.

Then the noise level rocketed as the doors opened and a couple of boys got out. One went to the fuel pump and the other walked over toward me. At this hour, for a cash sale, you paid first.

Knuckle-draggers. The boy crossing the forecourt was fat and soft with a scarf knotted on his head, a fantasy apache. He stared at me as he approached.

'I don't know you,' he said.

'That's okay,' I said, which stumped him for an answer and effectively ended the exchange. He put down five dollars, peeling it slowly from a thick wad of bills and watching for my reaction. I didn't give one. I just went ahead and set up the amount on the pump.

Big wad of bills. The peacock strut of the uncreditworthy.

While they were filling up I could see that there were three of them. They favoured the kind of music that annoys you at stop lights. At that age, you don't think about ear damage. If it's too loud, you're too old.

When they'd got their five dollars' worth, they climbed back into the car but they didn't drive off. They just sat there with the doors open and the speakers blasting out. Someone came on in an SUV, swiped, filled up, picked up their slip and drove away, and still the boys sat there.

After a couple of minutes I pulled the mike over to me and said, 'Can you take the party somewhere else, please, boys.'

Nothing happened. They probably hadn't even heard. I wasn't about to go out to them; they didn't scare me, but why be stupid? I switched off the forecourt lights instead.

When they looked toward me, I pointed. *Now go.* They couldn't mistake the message. Then I switched all the lights back on.

It took a moment for the tubes to gink back into life and when they did, one of the boys – a different one – was walking over. He was doing a white boy's idea of a jungle cat stroll. It should have been funny, but it was kind of off-centred and sinister.

He stopped in front of the glass and looked past me into the store.

'Give me some of those flowers,' he said, pointing, his voice crackly from the pickup mike. I looked around.

'Which kind?' I said.

'The white ones.'

For his mother, or what? It was an unlikely purchase, aside from the fact that the blooms had been on sale for several days and were past their best. But I put the lock on the drawer and went to get them.

If he thought I'd open the door to hand them out, he could think again. But that wasn't his plan. When I told him the price, he said, 'Now I've changed my mind.'

I said nothing. Just put the flowers under the counter and out of sight. If he'd been hoping to get me running up and down for his amusement, he'd have to be disappointed.

'I'll have some of those blue things instead,' he said, pointing again.

'What blue things?'

'On that shelf at the end.'

'Those are baby wipes.'

'I'll have two.'

By now I really wasn't in the mood.

'No,' I said.

He seemed genuinely surprised. This wasn't the script he had in his mind.

'What do you mean?' he said.

'You've given us the joke. I'll be laughing all night. Now quit while you're ahead and make your exit.'

He opened his mouth to speak, but then he closed it again and his face set.

Then, deliberately, he drew aside his printed wool coat to reveal the handle of a 9mm automatic pistol thrust into the waistband of his pants. Letting the coat fall back, he stuck up his thumb and pointed his forefinger, mimicking the shape of a gun and pointing it at my face before making a pretend-pow, grinning, and turning to walk away.

I let him go. Watched him get into the car. Saw the ostentatious, rubber-squealing departure that I knew had to be coming.

Then I got out from behind the counter and went to the store's pay phone.

The first number I called was transferred to a service after seven rings. So then I called the police switchboard.

'I need the officer of the watch,' I told the woman who answered. 'It's an urgent operational matter.'

'Is it an emergency?'

'It could develop into one.'

'Please hang up and dial 911.'

'I'm a police officer,' I said. 'Just put me through.'

'Your name, sir.'

'I'm working undercover. I don't want to give you my name on an open line.'

'One moment, please.'

I waited. After a few moments I heard, 'Major Devereaux speaking. How can I help you?'

I told him where I was, and gave him a description of the car and its license number.

I said, 'When it left here it was heading east on Airline Drive. Three white males in their early twenties. One of them's carrying a concealed weapon and an attitude. He made a point of showing me the gun. I got the impression they may be intending to use it tonight. And judging from how coked-up they were, probably soon.'

'Can you stay on the line, please?'

'I don't think I can. I'm in a situation, here. I explained it to your operator.'

I didn't think they'd be back, but you never knew. I'd messed up the movie in their heads. Bit players like me were supposed to lie stunned and humiliated in their wake, and I'd failed to play along.

The moment I hung up the phone, it rang.

I hadn't been expecting this. I hesitated, and then I picked it up.

'Hey,' said a voice from what sounded like a cellular phone in a moving car.

'Who's this?'

'You've got a short memory. Turn off the workshop alarms.'

'What?'

'You heard me. Turn off the alarms and have the door open ready. I'll explain when I get there. You see anything more of Old Jake?'

I had him now. It was Dave the Mechanic. My memory was fine, I just needed a little more than 'Hey' for it to work on.

I said, 'Not since the start of my shift. What's this about?' and as I was saying this I could hear a voice in the background at the other end saying, *There it is.*

'Gotta go now,' he said. 'Don't forget what I told you.'

'I don't know the code.'

'Everybody knows the code,' he said, 'it's obvious,' and then the signal broke up and I didn't get whatever came next, just the words *Dunleavy* and *favourite movie*.

Once again, I hung up the phone. It didn't ring this time.

The forecourt was empty right now, but something seemed to hang over the place and it wasn't good.

All the same, this was the kind of development I'd been sent in to wait for.

I went to the alarm panel. It was a piece of old crap. Three of the keypad buttons were grimy and the rest were clean. The 1, the 2, the zero.

Three digits for a four-digit code. I could only think of one movie that fit and so I tried the obvious, *2001*. The configuration of the panel lights changed for about a second, and then went back the way they'd been.

Was that it? Had I done it? There seemed to be only one way to find out. I went over with the spare key and opened the connecting door into the workshop.

No bells rang when I switched the lights on and went through. Nothing happened at all.

Well, Dunleavy a sci-fi freak. You never can tell.

Once in the repair bays, I rolled up the shutter as instructed. As the edge of the door rose, the live night air flooded in. It had all the smells of the roadside, hot tar and exhaust and a strange static charge.

When I went outside I felt strange under the lights, like a hermit crab out of its shell. So what now, I wondered? I couldn't go back to my post and leave the bays wide open and unattended. This was an area where, like water finding its level, lowlife crept out of the shadows and eased itself in the direction of any opportunity.

I took a washcloth and went around the fuel islands wiping road grease off the glass windows on the pumps. It wasn't a necessary job, but one that let me watch over my turf without drawing attention.

Thus occupied, I waited.

*   *   *

Someone had been stealing expensive cars to order, and somewhere in the service history of every one of the missing vehicles was a visit to Penry's Tire and Muffler Shop. None of the visits had been recent, which had made the pattern harder to spot.

Our guess was that someone had been copying keys and using a grabber to record keyfob security codes while each car was in the workshop. But we'd no idea who or how. If we were right, the thieves waited until the visit was all but forgotten, and then set out to collect. The method meant no hotwiring, no alarms to beat, no damage to the vehicle.

Worksheets carried the owners' addresses, so the vehicles wouldn't be hard to track down. Some cars had been stolen from off the street at night. A couple had been taken from locked but otherwise unprotected garages. Others with better security at home had been followed to parking lots and taken in daylight.

We didn't know where they went to. Some said the Far East, some even reckoned Japan. In some cases it was most likely that they'd be broken up for their parts.

All we knew for certain was that there was this one place that they'd all passed through.

I was feeling keyed-up at the prospect of a result. Even more enticing was the prospect of coming out from undercover and saying goodbye to the Ozone Motel, where every bedsheet had a readable history.

Something stroked the back of my neck when I saw a silver Mercedes coming down the road towards me. It was speeding. But it slowed before it reached the gas station, and came in without leaving the telltale rubber marks that would betray a stunt turn. It shot across the apron and entered the open workshop at such a speed that I fully expected it to come out the other side of the building in a shower of masonry.

No such thing happened, though. I'd been looking to see if Dave the mechanic had been behind the wheel, but it wasn't him. It *was* someone I recognised, though.

The driver was a soft-looking white boy with a knotted scarf covering his head.

Dave came in the following car, the knuckle-draggers' home-custom vehicle, with the other two boys. I realised with a shock something that had been staring me in the face; from the resemblance, Dave and the driver surely had to be brothers. I left the washcloth on the gas pump and went to meet them.

They'd done this before. They had a routine. The black car let Dave out on the forecourt and followed the Mercedes into the workshop, where the shutters were already beginning to descend.

Dave took me by the arm and walked me toward the lights of the store. 'You did good, John,' he said. 'It's John, isn't it?'

'What's happening?' I said.

'You must have worked it out by now. If you haven't, there's an empty place at the retard's picnic.'

'You're talking to a man on parole, here!' I said, playing the part. 'What are you trying to do to me?'

'Look, John,' he said. 'You have to understand this. Things happen. It's the way of the world. You understand what I mean?'

'I have no idea what you're talking about.'

'Let me put it another way. Nobody gave you any choices tonight. So nothing that happened here is your fault. So your conscience is clear and that means you should have no trouble keeping your mouth shut.'

'That's too deep for me,' I said.

'Let me explain it like this,' he said. 'You cause us a problem, we take you down with us. It's as simple as that. But you won't be making trouble, will you? Sit in your box and read your girlie book.'

*　　*　　*

And that's what I did, or at least I pretended to. I couldn't get to the pay phone because they'd have seen me through the open door. I ran the forecourt, took in some money, sold some stuff, watched a stand-up row between a Winnebago driver and his partner that almost ended with him driving off without her. One sobbing, mad-as-hell woman with mascara like a Zorro mask. Now, *there* was a complication that I didn't need.

All the while, I kept glancing toward the open doorway and trying to get some clue as to what they were doing through there. I didn't think they were chopping the Mercedes, that was too big a job to have done before morning. And it's mainly the newer vehicles that get broken up for their parts, in some cases bringing almost double the car's intact value. The most blatant scam I'd ever seen had involved a repair shop that would offer you a great deal to fix up your stolen, stripped and abandoned car when you got it back from the pound… as well they might, since the parts they put in were the same ones they'd taken out of it a few nights before.

No, I reckoned they were probably retagging this one… changing the number, switching the license plates, disguising it for resale. A retagged car can be hard to detect. You don't have to send them as far as Japan – I've even known of car dealerships that have been taken in. With a computer and a scanner you can fake all kinds of ownership certificates and registration documents.

After a while, Dave appeared in the doorway.

'Hey,' he said. 'John.'

'What?'

'Need you for something.'

'Can't leave the window.'

He looked toward the forecourt. 'Nobody's out there right now,' he said. 'Come on. What's the matter with you? I ain't gonna bite.'

Something wasn't quite right in his attitude. I'd sensed it, and he'd picked that up. I came out from behind my counter and followed him into the repair shop, wondering what I was going to find.

The Mercedes was on the hoist, about four feet off the ground and having its new plates fitted. The black car was in the next bay with its doors open and a radio playing. It wasn't playing music, though.

I said, 'Hey. You got a police scanner. They legal?'

Then two of them got hold of me and threw me against the shelves that lined the wall.

'Yeah,' one of them said as they picked me up off the floor, 'we got a scanner. And guess what it told us.'

Dave's brother, the one with the gun in his belt, didn't wait for me to answer but said, 'Everybody look out for three white guys in a black car, one with a concealed weapon. Reported from an undisclosed location by an undercover cop.'

'That could have been anyone,' I managed.

'An undisclosed location in the vicinity of Airline Drive.'

Oh, thanks a bunch, people, I thought.

'Okay,' I said. 'Don't make it worse for yourselves than it already is.'

One of them punched me and Dave said, 'Take him out.'

Dave's brother pulled the gun out of his belt and levelled it at my forehead, and I involuntarily screwed up my eyes.

'Whoa, whoa!' Dave called out quickly. 'I meant, take him outside. You do it here and they've got a crime scene. You know what that means. Someone shines a magic light and your name as good as shows up, written in brains.'

The one changing the plates stepped back from the car and pressed the control to lower the hoist.

'All done here,' he said as it descended.

'Okay,' Dave told the others. 'You heard me. Lose the cop.'

'You're too late,' I said. 'I already called this in.'

'No you didn't,' Dave said, and walked away from me as the others grabbed me by the arms and sped me over to the black car.

'You're dead,' one of them said close to my ear. 'What does it feel like?'

And I didn't get to answer because they thrust my head down and boosted me into the back, and then one jumped in on either side and held me in that awkward can't-breathe position whilst Dave's brother got behind the wheel and reversed us out of the bay. Dave had hit the red button to raise the shutters, and I heard our antenna twang as it caught on the way out.

They let me sit up after a while, but there wasn't much advantage to it. Nobody was going to see me through those tinted windows, and I didn't dare make a bid for attention because I could feel that one of them was holding a blade on me. It was pushing right into my side, threatening to cut me with every bump and turn.

We were still on Airline Drive, but this was no longer the lively part. This section was farther out of town, and all but deserted. Keep on going and you join the railroad tracks and pass factory after factory, each one visible through razor wire across an empty lot with parking for a thousand cars. All of them built in the boom years after the war, and most of them finished off by the recession.

Awfully quiet.

As these places went.

The boy with the knife leaned closer to me so that I could smell his stale breath, and he jabbed me with the point as he spoke.

'Feel it?' he said, and got some pleasure out of my involuntary jump.

Between them they had me pinned. My arms were behind me and my knees were jammed up against the seats in front. Dave's brother at the wheel glanced back over his shoulder and said, 'Get his clothes off.'

'There's no room,' the knuckledragger without the knife said.

'I don't mean like, undress Barbie,' Dave's brother said. 'Just cut them. I'm gonna find some gravel.'

'Why?'

'I saw this biker once, okay? It was hotter than hot and he was riding with no shirt on. He wiped out on a bend and hit the dirt on this gravel road. You could see his skin all flayed out on the ground where he'd gone along. He was like meat.'

'Did he die?'

'He wanted to.'

I started to speak and got chopped in the throat, which silenced me pretty well. I was thrust forward so that my face slammed into the seats, and the shirt was cut off my back. They dropped the window a few inches to stuff it out, and the wind ripped it away. They stamped on my feet to lever my shoes off. My socks went with them and everything followed my shirt.

'He's panting like a dog, back here,' one of them commented in a voice of wonder.

When my head came up again we were no longer on Airline Drive, but some back road that I didn't recognise.

'Where are we heading?' the kid with the knife said.

'Other side of the railroad tracks,' Dave's brother said. 'There's a dirt road I remember. It's long and straight. Hard clay topped off with black cinders. The track workers and linesmen use it. If throwing him out doesn't do the job, we can always drag him a little.'

There was nothing I could hang onto. Nothing apart from the short end of the seat belt that I could feel underneath me. It was just a few inches of webbing with a buckle on it but I managed to loop it around my wrist a couple of times. But what was I thinking of? I was sitting right next to a boy with a knife. One stroke of the blade and he'd have me cut loose in a second or less.

'Get him ready,' Dave's brother said.

'He's ready now.'

I could see the railroad. We were going to go under it. The street narrowed to a single car's width and passed under a trestle that sat on big stone blocks, one massive column to either side. The blocks had been painted with yellow and black diagonal stripes. Dave's brother had his foot right down, and wasn't slowing.

'Hey,' one of the others said nervously.

'Don't distract the driver,' Dave's brother said, and he leaned back in his seat and started to steer one-handed just to make a point.

Right then it was as if someone pulled a flare in the car.

It was blindingly bright. The boys screamed curses for about one full second. I felt the knife go in about half a centimetre as my captor flinched, and twisting myself away from the point is probably what saved me. The screaming stopped abruptly when the car hit one of the supports.

The shock drove the breath out of me, just as it did with everyone else. I've never felt anything like it. Everyone in the car suddenly seemed to turn boneless and to bounce like a ragdoll. The boys to either side of me went face-first into the fancy custom racing headrests on the seats in front of them and then rebounded, their faces destroyed. Dave's brother slammed into the wheel and carried on over it and through the windshield, not stopping until he met the wall.

The car half-spun and then there was a second shock as its rear end hit the other support. For a moment I thought it was all over, and then we bounced off something else, and then it was.

I somehow ended up lying across the empty front seats, covered in windshield glass, my arm twisted around and stuck through the gap into the rear of the car. The belt strap was still around my wrist. My shoulder hurt and I couldn't feel my fingers.

As I levered myself up, the glass fell from me and the air sparkled. The car was still flooded with that incredible light. I thought I could hear a train passing overhead; but no, it wasn't a train.

Dave's brother was gone. He was out on the road somewhere, all messed up. Which I count as a kind of poetic justice. The boy with the knife had stuck it in himself. The other one would survive, although it would be discovered in the Emergency Room that he'd bitten off most of his tongue. They'd look for the piece at the scene and not find it.

My bruises would come later. Right now, apart from the place where I'd been stuck with the point of the knife, I seemed to be unmarked.

'Well,' I rasped, as the air glittered and the roar grew louder overhead. The knife boy stared back at me, unseeing. 'You wanted to know what being dead felt like? Well, now you do.'

Except I don't think that I actually managed any sound.

I climbed out through the open space where the windshield had been. A hurricane wind was beating down on the neat circle of light that was being cast around the wreck. The mess was breathtaking. You could hardly even tell it had been a car.

Shirtless and barefoot, bleached in the candlepower, I screwed up my eyes and looked up into the searchlight beam from the spotter-helicopter overhead. Its beauty overwhelmed me. I couldn't take it for too long before it started to become a physical pain. Then, when I lowered my eyes, I found that I'd been all but blinded to the night.

But I could still hear. I could hear the pulsing of police sirens as they approached from the distance, guided by radioed directions from above. Responding to their sound, I started to walk toward them.

The ground cut at my feet, but I felt nothing. The cold wind of the downdraft poured over my skin but again, I felt nothing. Nothing save the sense that I had walked whole out of disaster and that I was, indisputably, blessed.

The helicopter moved and the searchlight tracked me. It swung away from me once, to check for movement back at the wreck, but it was back on me again within seconds. The sirens were louder now, and I was beginning to see the approaching headlights. Both cars stopped before me and I could see officers jumping out. One of them was my 'parole officer'. Except, of course, he was no such thing. His name was Danny Fialka and he was a fellow policeman. Some of the patrolmen were drawing their sidearms and shouting for me to get face-down on the ground, but Danny waved them away.

'Are you hurt, John?' he said.

'I think my shoulder's out,' I said.

I felt a blanket being put around me. He got me into one of the cars and then he called for someone to find me something to wear. I could see the wreck from here. Our people were clustered around one side of it. They'd found the live one and were calling for assistance. I could see others over by the pillar, shining their flashlights down onto the concertina'd remains of Dave's brother.

Danny was crouching outside the open door.

I asked him how the 'copter found me.

'It was the shirt,' he said. 'Lying on the road back there like a big yellow flag. They followed the rest of your clothes till they found you.'

'But who told them to come looking?' I said. 'I never got a chance to call anyone.'

'No, but you managed to set off the alarm,' Danny said.

'What alarm?'

'The silent alarm. The one with a phone connection that puts on a light in the despatchers' room.'

'I didn't trigger that,' I said. 'I turned it off.'

That's what I'd thought, but it turned out I was wrong. I hadn't disabled the panel after all. When I'd walked into the repair shop, it had sent off a signal. Silent alarms got lower priority than emergency calls, so it had been some time before anyone realised its significance.

The cause of my salvation was a simple one. I'd got the right digits on the keypad, but the wrong movie.

Did *you* know there was a movie called *12:01*? I didn't. But you can bet I do now.

The Perfectionist

Peter Lovesey

The invitation dropped on the doormat of *The Laurels* along with a bank statement and a Guide Dogs for the Blind appeal. It was in a cream-coloured envelope made from thick, expensive-looking paper. Duncan left it to open after the others. His custom was to leave the most promising letters while he worked steadily through the others, using a paperknife that cut the envelopes tidily.

Eventually he took out a gold edged card with his name inscribed in the centre in fine italic script. It read:

> *The most perfect club in the world*
> *has the good sense to invite*
> *Mr Duncan Driffield*
> *a proven perfectionist*
> *to be an honoured guest at its annual dinner*
> *Friday, January 31st, 7.30 for 8pm*
>
> *Contact will be made later*

He was wary. This could be an elaborate marketing ploy. He'd been invited to parties in the past by motor dealers and furniture retailers that turned out to be sales pitches, nothing more. Just because no product or company was mentioned, he wasn't going to be taken in. He read it through several times.

It has to be said, he liked the designation 'a proven perfectionist'. Couldn't fault their research. He was a Virgo, born under a birth-sign known for its orderly people, strivers for perfection. To see it written down as if he'd already achieved the ideal, was specially pleasing. And to see his name in such elegant script was another fine touch.

Yet it troubled him that the club was not named, nor was there any address, nor any mention of where the function was to be held. Being a thorough and cautious man, he would normally have looked them up before deciding what to do about the invitation.

The phone call came about eight-thirty the next evening. A voice that didn't need to announce it had been to a very good school spoke his name.

'Yes.'

'You received an invitation to the dinner on January 31st, I trust?'

'Which invitation was that?' Duncan said as if he was used to getting them by every post.

'A gold-edged card naming you as a proven perfectionist. May we take it that you will accept?'

'Who are you, exactly?'

'A group of like-minded people. We know you'll fit in.'

'Is there some mystery about it? I don't wish to join the Freemasons.'

'We're not Freemasons, Mr Driffield.'

'How did you get my name?'

'It was put to the committee. You were the outstanding candidate.'

'Really?' He glowed inwardly before his level-headedness returned. 'Is there any obligation?'

'You mean are we trying to sell something? Absolutely not.'

'I don't have to make a speech?'

'We don't go in for speeches. It isn't like that at all. We'll do everything possible to welcome you and make you feel relaxed. Transport is provided.'

'Are you willing to tell me your name?'

'Of course. It's David Hopkins. I do hope you're going to say yes.'

Why not? he thought. 'All right, Mr Hopkins.'

'Excellent. I'm sure if I ask you – as a proven perfectionist – to be ready at six-thirty, you will, to the minute. In case you were wondering, it's a dinner jacket and black tie affair. I'll come for you myself. The drive takes nearly an hour at that time of day, I'm afraid. And it's Dr Hopkins actually, but please call me David.'

After the call, Duncan in his systematic way tried to track down David Hopkins in the phone directory and the Medical Register. He found three people of that name and called them on the phone, but their voices had nothing like the honeyed tone of the David

Hopkins he had spoken to.

He wondered who had put his name forward. Someone must have. It would be interesting to see if he recognised David Hopkins.

He did not. Precisely on time, on the last Friday in January, Dr David Hopkins arrived, a slim, dark man in his forties, of average height. They shook hands.

'Is there anything I can bring? A bottle of whisky?'

'No, you're our guest, Duncan.'

He liked the look of David. He knew intuitively one of the special evenings in his life was in prospect.

They walked out to the car, a large black Daimler, chauffeur-driven.

'Luxury.'

'We can enjoy the wine with a clear conscience,' David explained, 'but I would be dishonest if I led you to think that was the only reason.' When they were both inside he leaned across and pulled down a blind. There was one on each window and across the partition between the driver and themselves. Duncan couldn't see out at all. 'This is in your interest.'

'Why is that?'

'We ask our guests to be good enough to respect the privacy of the club. If you don't know where we meet, you can't upset anyone.'

'I see. Now that we're alone, and I'm committed to coming, can you tell me some more?'

'A little. We're all of your cast of mind, actually.'

'Perfectionists?'

He smiled. 'That's one of the attributes.'

'I wondered why I was asked. Do I know any of the members?'

'I doubt it.'

'Then how -'

'Your crowning achievement.'

Duncan tried to think which achievement could have come to their notice. He'd had an unremarkable career in the civil service. Sang a bit with a local choir. Once won first prize for his sweet peas in the town flower show, but he'd given up growing them now. He could think of nothing of enough merit to interest this high-powered club.

'How many members are there?'

'Fewer than we would like. Not many meet the criteria.'

'So how many is that?'

'Currently, five.'

'Oh – as few as that?'

'We're small and exclusive.'

'I can't think why you invited me.'

'It will become clear.'

More questions from Duncan elicited little else, except that the club had been established for over a hundred years. He assumed – but had the tact not to ask – that he would be invited to join if the members approved of him this evening. How he wished he was one of those people with a fund of funny stories. He feared he was dull company.

In just under the hour, the car came to a halt and the chauffeur opened the door. Duncan glanced about him as he stepped out, wanting to get some sense of where he was. It was dark at this time, of course, but this was clearly a London square, with street lights and a park in the centre and plane trees at intervals in front of the houses. He couldn't put a name to it. The houses were terraced, and Georgian, just as they are in almost every other London square.

'Straight up the steps,' said David. 'The door is open.'

They went in, through a hallway with mirrors and a crystal chandelier that made him blink after the dim lighting in the car. David took Duncan's coat and handed it to a manservant and then opened a door.

'Gentlemen,' he said. 'May I present our guest, Mr Duncan Driffield.'

It was a smallish anteroom, and four men stood waiting with glasses of wine. Two looked quite elderly, the others about forty, or less. One of the younger pair was wearing a kilt.

The one who was probably the senior member extended a bony hand. 'Joe Franks. I'm president, through a process of elimination.'

There were some smiles at this that David didn't fully understand.

Joe Franks went on to say, 'I qualified as a member as long ago as 1934, when I was only nineteen, but I joined officially after the war.'

David, at Duncan's side, murmured something that made no sense about a body left in a trunk at Brighton railway station.

'And this well set-up fellow on my right,' said Joe Franks, 'is Wally Winthrop, the first private individual to put ricin to profitable use. Wally now owns one of the largest supermarket chains in Europe.'

'Did you say 'rice'?' asked Duncan.

'No. 'Ricin'. A vegetable poison.'

It was difficult to see the connection between a vegetable poison and a supermarket chain. Wally Winthrop grinned and shook Duncan's hand. 'Tell you about it one of these days,' he said.

Joe Franks indicated the man in the kilt. 'Alex McPhee is our youngest member and our most prolific. Is it seven, Alex?'

'So far,' said McPhee, and this caused more amusement.

'His skene-dhu has more than once come to the aid of the club,' added Joe Franks.

Duncan wasn't too familiar with Gaelic, but he had a faint idea that the skene-dhu was the ornamental dagger worn by Highlanders in their stocking. He supposed the club used it in some form of ritual.

'And now meet Michael Pitt-Struthers, who advises the SAS on the martial arts. His knowledge of pressure points is unrivalled. Shake hands very carefully with Michael.'

More smiles, the biggest from Pitt-Struthers, who squeezed Duncan's hand in a way that left no doubt of his expertise.

'And of course you've already met our doctor member, David Hopkins, who knows more about allergy reactions than any man alive.'

With a huge effort to be sociable, Duncan remarked, 'Such a variety of talents. I can't think what you all have in common.'

Joe Franks answered, 'Each of us has committed a perfect murder.'

Duncan heard the statement and played it over in his head. He thought he'd got it right. It had been spoken with some pride. This time no one smiled. More disturbingly, no one disputed it.

'Shall we go into dinner, gentlemen?' Joe Franks suggested.

At a round table in the next room, Duncan tried to come to terms with the sensational claim he had just heard. If it was true, what on earth was he doing sharing a meal with a bunch of killers?

And why had they chosen to take him into their confidence? He could shop them to the police and they wouldn't be perfect murderers any longer. Maybe it was wise not to mention this while he was seated between the martial arts expert and the Scot with the skene-dhu tucked into his sock.

The wine glasses were filled with claret by an elderly waiter. 'Hungarian,' Joe Franks confided. 'He understands no English.' He raised his glass. 'At this point, gentlemen, I propose a toast to Thomas de Quincey, author of that brilliant essay *On Murder, Considered as One of the Fine Arts*, who esteemed the killing of Sir Edmund Godfrey as 'the finest work of the seventeenth century' for the excellent reason that no one knew who had done it.'

'Thomas de Quincey,' said everyone, with Duncan just a half-beat slower than the rest.

'You're probably wondering what brings us together,' said Wally Winthrop across the table. 'You might think we'd be uncomfortable sharing our secrets. In fact, it works the other way. It's a tremendous relief. I don't have to tell you, Duncan, what it's like after you commit your first, living in fear of being found out, waiting for the police siren and the knock on the door. As the months pass, this panicky stage fades and is replaced by a feeling of isolation. You've set yourself apart from others by your action. You can only look forward to keeping your secret bottled up for the rest of your life. It's horrible. We've all been through it. Five years have to pass – five years without being charged with murder – before you're contacted by the club and invited to join us for a meal.'

David Hopkins briskly took up the conversation. 'It's such a break in the clouds, that discovery that you're not alone in the world. To find that what you've done is valued as an achievement and can be openly discussed. Wonderful. After all, there is worth in having committed a perfect murder.'

'How do you know you can trust each other?' Duncan asked, without giving anything away.

'Mutual self-interest. If any one of us betrayed the others, he'd take himself down as well. We're all in the same boat.'

Joe Franks explained, 'It's a safeguard that's worked for over a hundred years. One of our first members was the man better known as Jack the Ripper, who was in fact a pillar of the establishment. If *his* identity could be protected all these years, then the rest of us can breathe easy.'

'That's amazing. You know who the Ripper was?'

'Aye,' said McPhee calmly. 'And no one has ever named the laddie.'

'Can I ask?'

'Not till you join,' said Joe Franks.

Duncan hesitated. He was about to say he had no chance of joining, not having committed a murder, when some inner voice prompted him to shut up. These people were acting as if he was one of them. Maybe, through some ghastly mistake, they'd been told he'd once done away with a fellow human being. And maybe it was in his interest not to disillusion them.

'We have to keep to the rules,' Wally Winthrop was explaining. 'Certain information is only passed on to full members.'

Joe Franks added, 'And we are confident you will want to join. All we ask is that you respect the rules. Not a word must be spoken to anyone else about this evening, or the existence of the club. The ultimate sanction is at our disposal for anyone foolish enough to betray us.'

'The ultimate sanction – what's that?' Duncan huskily enquired.

No one answered, but the Scot beside him grinned in a way Duncan didn't care for.

'The skene-dhu?' said Duncan.

'Or the pressure point,' said Joe Franks, 'or the allergy reaction, or whatever we decide is tidiest. But it won't happen in your case.'

'No chance,' Duncan affirmed. 'My lips are sealed.'

The starters were served, and he was pleased when the conversation shifted to murders in fiction, and some recent crime novels. Faintly he listened as they discussed *The Silence of the Lambs*, but he was trying to think what to say if someone asked about the murder he was supposed to have committed. They were sure to return to him before the evening ended, and then it was essential to sound convincing. If they got the idea he was a mild man who wouldn't hurt a fly he was in real trouble.

Towards the end of the meal, he spoke up. It seemed a good idea to take the initiative. 'This has been a brilliant evening. Is there any chance I could join?'

'You've enjoyed yourself?' said Joe Franks. 'That's excellent.

A kindred spirit.'

'It's got to be more than that if you want to be a member,' Winthrop put in. 'You've got to provide some evidence that you're one of us.'

Duncan swallowed hard. 'Don't you have that? I wouldn't be here if you hadn't found something out.'

'There's a difference between finding something out and seeing the proof.'

'That won't be easy.'

'It's the rule.'

He tried another tack. 'Can I ask something? How did you get onto me?'

There were smiles all round. Winthrop said, 'You're surprised that we succeeded where the police failed?'

'Experience,' Joe Franks explained. 'We're much better placed than the police to know how it was done.'

Pitt-Struthers, the strong, silent man who trained the SAS, said, 'We know you were at the scene on the evening it happened, and we know no one else had a stronger motive or a better opportunity.'

'But we must have the proof,' insisted Winthrop.

'The weapon,' suggested McPhee.

'I disposed of it,' Duncan improvised. He was not an imaginative man, but this was an extreme situation. 'You would, wouldn't you?'

'No,' said McPhee. 'I just give mine a wee wipe.'

'Well, it's up to you, old boy,' Winthrop told Duncan. 'Only you can furnish the evidence.'

'How long do I have?'

'The next meeting is in July. We'd like to confirm you as a full member then.'

The conversation moved on to other areas, a lengthy discussion about the problems faced by the Crown Prosecution Service.

The evening ended with coffee, cognac and cigars. Soon after, David Hopkins said that the car would be outside.

On the drive back, Duncan, deeply perturbed and trying not to show it, pumped David for information.

'It was an interesting evening, but it's left me with a problem.'

'What's that?'

'I, em, wasn't completely sure which murder of mine they were talking about.'

'Do you mean you're a serial killer?'

Duncan gulped. He hadn't meant that at all. 'I've never thought of myself as one.' Recovering his poise a little, he added, 'A thing like that is all in the mind, I suppose. Which one do they have me down for?'

'The killing of Sir Jacob Drinkwater at the Brighton Civil Service Conference in 1995.'

Drinkwater. He remembered being at the conference and the sensation of the senior civil servant at the Irish Office being found dead in his hotel room on the Sunday morning. 'That was supposed to be a heart attack.'

'Officially, yes,' said David.

'But you heard something else?'

'I happen to know the pathologist who did the autopsy. A privileged source. They didn't want the public knowing how Sir Jacob was killed, and thinking it was a new method employed by the terrorists. How did you introduce the cyanide? Was it in his aftershave?'

'Trade secret,' Duncan answered cleverly.

'Of course the security people in their blinkered way couldn't imagine it was anything but a political assassination. They didn't know you had a grudge against him dating from years back, when he was your boss in the Land Registry.'

Someone had got their wires crossed. It was a man called *Charlie* Drinkwater who'd made Duncan's life a misery and blighted his career. No connection with Sir Jacob. Giving nothing away, he said smoothly, 'And you worked out that I was at the conference?'

'Same floor. Missed the banquet on the Saturday evening, giving you a fine opportunity to break into his room and plant the cyanide. So we have motive, opportunity.'

'And means?' said Duncan.

David laughed. 'Your house is called The Laurels, for the bushes all round the garden. It's well known that if you soak laurel leaves and evaporate the liquid, you get a lethal concentration of cyanide. Isn't that how you made the stuff?'

'I'd rather leave you in suspense,' said Duncan. He was thinking hard. 'If I apply to join the club, I may have to give a demonstration.'

'There's no 'if' about it. They liked you. You're expected to join.'

'I could decide against it.'

'Why?'

'Private reasons.'

David turned to face him, his face creased in concern. 'They'd take a very grave view of that, Duncan. We invited you along in good faith.'

'But no obligation, I thought.'

'Look at it from the club's point of view. We're vulnerable now. You're dealing with dangerous men, Duncan. I can't urge you strongly enough to co-operate.'

'But if I can't prove that I killed a man -'

'You must think of something. We're willing to be convinced. If you cold-shoulder us, or betray us, I can't answer for the consequences.'

A sobering end to the evening.

*　*　*

For the next three weeks he got little sleep, and when he did drift off he would wake with nightmares of fingers pressing on his arteries or skene-dhus being thrust between his ribs. He faced a classic dilemma. Either admit he hadn't murdered Sir Jacob Drinkwater and was a security risk to the club; or concoct some fake evidence, bluff his way in, and spend the rest of his life hoping they wouldn't catch him out. Faking evidence wouldn't be easy. They were intelligent men.

'*You must think of something,*' David Hopkins had urged.

Being methodical, he went to the British Newspaper Library and spent many hours rotating the microfilm, studying accounts of Sir Jacob's murder. It only depressed him more, reading about the involvement of Special Branch, the Anti-Terrorist Squad and MI5. 'The files remain open' the papers said. Open to whom? With all that high security involvement how could any ordinary man acquire the evidence the club insisted on seeing?

More months went by.

Duncan weighed the possibility of pointing out to the members that they'd made a mistake. Surely, he thought in rare optimistic moments, they would see that it wasn't his fault.

He was just an ordinary bloke caught up in something out of his league. He could promise to say nothing to anyone, in return for a guarantee of personal safety. Then he remembered the eyes of some of those people around the table, and he knew how unrealistic it was.

One morning in May, out of desperation, he had a brilliant idea. It arose from something David Hopkins had said in the car on the way home from the club. '*Do you mean you're a serial killer?*' At the time it had sounded preposterous. Now, it could be his salvation. Instead of striving to link himself to the murder of Sir Jacob, he would claim another killing – and show them some evidence they couldn't challenge. He'd satisfy the rules of the club and put everyone at their ease.

The brilliant part was this. He didn't need to kill anyone. He would claim to have murdered some poor wretch who had actually committed suicide. All he needed was a piece of evidence from the scene. Then he'd tell the Perfectionists he was a serial killer who dressed up his murders as suicide. They would be forced to agree how clever he was and admit him to the club. After a time, he'd give up going to the meetings and no one would bother him because they'd think their secrets were safe with him.

It was just a matter of waiting. Somebody, surely, would do away with himself before the July meeting of the club. Each day Duncan studied the *Telegraph*, and no suicide – well, no suicide he could claim as a murder – was reported. At the end of June, he found an expensive-looking envelope on his doormat and knew with a sickening certainty who it was from.

The most perfect club in the world
takes pleasure in inviting
Mr Duncan Driffield
a prime candidate for membership
to present his credentials after dinner on July 19th, 7.30 for 8 p.m.

Contact will be made later

This time the wording didn't pamper his ego at all. It filled him with dread. In effect it was a sentence of death. His only chance of a reprieve rested on some fellow creature topping himself in the next two weeks.

He took to buying three newspapers instead of one, still with no success.

Mercifully, and in the nick of time, his luck changed. News of a suicide reached him, but not through the press. He was phoned one morning by an old civil service colleague, Harry Hitchman. They'd met occasionally since retiring, but they weren't the closest of buddies, so the call came out of the blue.

'Some rather bad news,' said Harry. 'Remember Billy Fisher?'

'Of course I remember him,' said Duncan. 'We were in the same office for twelve years. What's happened?'

'He jumped off a hotel balcony last night. Killed himself.'

'Billy? I can't believe it!'

'Nor me when I heard. Seems he was being treated for depression.'

'I had no idea. He was always cracking jokes in the office. A bit of a comedian, I always thought.'

'They're the people who crack, aren't they? All that funny stuff is just a front.'

'His wife Sue must be devastated.'

'That's why I'm phoning round. She's with her sister. She understands that everyone will be wanting to offer sympathy and help if they can, but for the present she'd like to be left to come to terms with this herself.'

'OK.' Duncan hesitated. 'This happened only last night, you said?' Already, an idea was forming in his troubled brain.

'Yes. He was staying overnight at some hotel in Mayfair. A reunion of some sort.'

'Do you happen to know which one?'

'Which reunion?'

'No. Which hotel.'

'The Excelsior. Thirteenth floor. People talk about thirteen being unlucky. It was in Billy's case.'

Sad as it was, this *had* to be Duncan's salvation. Billy Fisher was as suitable a 'murder victim' as he could have wished for. Someone he'd actually worked with. He could think of a motive, make up some story of an old feud, later.

For once in his life, he needed to throw caution to the winds and act immediately. The police would have sealed Billy's hotel room pending some kind of investigation. Surely a proven perfectionist could think of a way to get inside and pick up some personal item that would pass as evidence that he had murdered his old colleague.

He took the five twenty-five to London. At this time most other travellers were going up to town for an evening's entertainment. Duncan sat alone, avoiding eye contact and working out his plan. First he needed to find out which room on the thirteenth floor Billy had occupied, and then devise a way of getting in there. Through the two-hour journey he was deep in concentration, applying his brain to the challenge. By the time they reached Waterloo, he knew exactly what to do.

A taxi ride brought him to the hotel, a high-rise building near Shepherd Market. He glanced up, counting each set of windows with its wrought-iron balcony outside, and thought of Billy's leap from the thirteenth. Personally, he wouldn't have gone so high. A fall from the sixth would have killed anyone, and more quickly.

Doing his best to look like one of the guests, he stepped briskly through the revolving doors into the spacious, carpeted foyer and over to the lift, which was waiting unoccupied. No one gave him a second glance. It was a huge relief when the door slid across and he was alone and rising.

So far, the plan was working beautifully. He got out at the twelfth level and used the stairs to reach the thirteenth. It was now around seven-thirty, and he was wary of meeting people on their way out to dinner. He paused to let a couple ahead of him go through the swing doors. They didn't turn round. He moved along, looking for a door marked 'Staff Only' or something similar. There had to be a place where the chambermaid kept her trolley, and he found it just the other side of those swing doors.

At this time of day the rooms were made up and the maid had gone off duty. Duncan found some worksheets attached to a clipboard hanging from a nail in the wall. All the thirteenth-floor rooms were listed, with ticks beside some of them showing, presumably, those that had needed a complete change of linen and towels. On the latest sheet, number 1307 had been struck out and marked 'not for cleaning'. No other room was so marked. He had found Billy Fisher's hotel room. Easy as shelling peas.

He took a look at the door of 1307 before returning to the lift. No policeman was on duty outside. It wasn't as if a man had been murdered in there.

Down in the foyer, he marched coolly up to the desk and looked at the pigeon hole system where the keys were kept. He'd noticed before how automatically reception staff will hand over keys when asked. The key to 1307 was in place. Deliberately Duncan didn't ask for it. 1305 – the room next door – was also available and he was given it without fuss.

Up on the thirteenth again, he let himself into 1305, taking care not to leave fingerprints. His idea was to get out on the balcony and climb across the short gap to the balcony of 1307. No one would suspect an entry by that route.

The plan had worked brilliantly up to now. The curtains were drawn in 1305. He didn't switch on the light, thinking he could cross to the window and get straight out to the balcony. Unfortunately his foot caught against a suitcase some careless guest had left on the floor. He stumbled, and was horrified to hear a female voice from the bed call out, 'Is that you, Elmer?'

Duncan froze. This wasn't part of the plan. The room should have been unoccupied. He'd collected the key from downstairs.

The voice spoke again. 'Did you get the necessary, honey? Did you have to go out for it?'

Duncan was in turmoil, his heart thumping. The plan hadn't allowed for this.

'Why don't you put on the light, Elmer?' the voice said. 'Now I'm in bed I don't mind. I was only a little shy of being seen undressing.'

What could he do? If he spoke, she would scream. Any minute now, she would reach for the bedside switch. The plan had failed. His one precious opportunity of getting off the hook was gone.

'Elmer?' The voice was suspicious now.

In the civil service, there had been a procedure for everything. Duncan's home life was similar, well-ordered and structured. Now he was floundering, and next he panicked. Take control, something inside him urged. Take control, man. He groped his way to the source of the sound, snatched up a pillow and smothered the woman's voice. There were muffled sounds, and there was struggling, and he pressed harder. And harder. And finally it all stopped.

Silence.

He could think again, thank God, but the realisation of what he had done appalled him.

He'd killed someone. He really *had* killed someone now.

His brain reeled and pulses pounded in his head and he wanted to break down and sob. Some instinct for survival told him to think, think, think.

By now, Elmer must have returned to the hotel to be told the room-key had been collected. They'd be opening the door with a master key any minute.

Must get out, he thought.

The balcony exit was still the safer way to go. He crossed the room to the glass doors, slid them across and looked out.

The gap between this balcony and that of 1307 was about a metre – not impossible to bridge, but daunting when you looked down and thought of Billy Fisher hurtling towards the street below. In his agitated state, Duncan didn't hesitate. He put a foot on the rail and was up and over and across.

Just as he expected, the doors to 1307 were unfastened. He pushed them open and stepped inside. And the light came on.

Room 1307 was full of people. Not policemen, nor hotel staff, but people who looked familiar, all smiling.

One of them said, 'Caught you, Duncan. Caught you good and proper, my old mate.' It was Billy Fisher, alive and grinning all over his fat face.

Duncan said, 'You're …?'

'Dead meat? No. You've been taken for a ride, old chum. Have a glass of bubbly, and I'll tell you all about it.'

'Wondering where you've seen them before?' said Billy. 'They're actors, mostly, earning a little extra between engagements. You know them better as the Perfectionists. They look different out of evening dress, don't they?'

He knew them now: David Hopkins, the doctor; McPhee, the skene-dhu specialist; Joe Franks, the trunk murderer; Wally Winthrop, the poisoner; and Pitt-Struthers, the martial arts man. In jeans and T-shirts and a little shame-faced at their roles in the deception, they looked totally unthreatening.

'You've got to admit it's a brilliant con,' said Billy. 'Retirement is so boring. I needed to turn my organising skills to something creative, so I thought this up. Mind, it had to be good to take you in.'

'Why me?'

'Well, I knew you were up for it from the old days, and Harry Hitchman – where are you, Harry?'

A voice from the background said, 'Over here.'

'I knew Harry wouldn't mind playing along. So I rigged it up. Did the job properly. Civil service training. Got the cards printed nicely. Rented the private car and the room and hired the actors and stood you all a decent dinner. I was the Hungarian waiter, by the way, but you were too preoccupied with the others to spot my false moustache. And when you took it all in, as I knew you would – being such a serious-minded guy – it was worth every penny. I wanted to top it with a wonderful finish, so I dreamed up the suicide, and' – he quivered with laughter – 'you took the bait again.'

'You knew I'd come up here?'

'It was all laid on for your benefit, old sport. You were totally taken in by the perfect murder gag, and you were bound to look for a get-out, so I fabricated one for you. Harry told you I'd jumped off the balcony, but I wasn't the fall-guy.'

'Bastard,' said Duncan.

'Yes, I am,' said Billy without apology. 'It's my second career.'

'And the woman in the room next door – is she an actress, too?'

'Which woman?'

'Oh, come on,' said Duncan. 'You've had your fun.'

Billy was shaking his head. 'We didn't expect you to come through the room next door. Is that how you got on the balcony? Typical Duncan Driffield, going the long way round. Which woman are you talking about?'

From the corridor outside came the sound of hammering on a door.

Duncan covered his ears.

'What's up with him?' said Billy.

A Nose for Murder

David Williams

'Oh ... thith is Mrs Friston. I'm...I'm so sobby to trouble you. Is ... is Doctor Prickle available by any chance?' pleaded the diminutive Cynthia, and then blew her sore nose very gently. Timid of voice, and slight of figure, she was palpably short of the ability to muster even a justified modicum of self-assurance on the telephone. After all, she was one of the doctor's private, fee-paying patients. Her frequent recourse to his ministrations, usually over quite minor ailments, provided him with a satisfying contribution to income for the very minimum of effort.

In youth, Cynthia had sometimes been charitably described as elfin. At 58, she was an irredeemably plain matron, if a very rich one. She could have afforded to take more care than most women in disguising the ravages that time was exerting on her face and figure. Instead, she was content to let the years take their inevitable toll, as she put it, never troubling about her clothes either, but wallowing in the comforts of her large home and four acre garden, and the attentions of a handsome husband who was five years her junior, and who, despite one puerile weakness, suited her admirably. She only regretted that there had been no children of the twenty-three year marriage.

'My dear Cynthia, what can I do for you? Are you unwell?' George Rickle was invariably ready to indulge one of his affluent patients, as now, at 5.30 on a Friday evening – or, come to that, at 5.30 on a Saturday morning, if needs be. It was this, and his being a fine physician, that had endeared him to so many of the wealthy inhabitants of Woodlake, an 'exclusive', leafy commuter village in rural Berkshire.

An hour's drive to the south-west of London, Woodlake was 'self contained', with its desirable residences, a golf course, a pretty church, and a large supermarket, all within easy reach of the motorways and Heathrow Airport.

'I'm afraid you'll think I'm becombing a hypochondriac,

George.' Cynthia was as careful of her health as she was careless of her appearance.

'Nonsense. D'you want me to pop over?'

'Oh…oh, dow. Certainly noth. It's just that I have this…this heavy spring cold.' It was early March.

'I can hear it in your voice. Lot of colds about, of course,' the doctor put in sympathetically.

'I know. I thig I picked it up in the golf club at didder on Wednesday.'

'Ha, so it's a cordon bleu virus?' the speaker chuckled. Incidentally, his own practical definition of 'exclusive' required that no top-class property in the area was offered for sale at less than two million pounds.

'My…my breathing's blocked all the time, and my dose is so sore from wiping. I was in the chemist's this afternoon. Miss Jones, you know, the nice pharmacist, she said I should take a Rhine-Off capsule every twelve hours. So I bought a pack. I haven't taken any yet. I've always been wary of magic remedies. Is this one quite safe?'

'Perfectly. It was good advice. Rhine-Off is one of the slow-release de-congestants. Won't cure your cold, but it'll stop those nasty symptoms. Quite harmless, so long as you don't take it for too long. Swallow one capsule now with water.'

'I'd hoped you'd say that. I have the capsule with a glass of warda beside me. I'll take it now.' She imbibed, swallowing loudly for the doctor's benefit.

'Good for you, Cynthia. That'll see you through the night. Take another capsule when you wake. If that doesn't do the trick, give me a call tomorrow or Sunday. Paul's all right is he?'

'Yes. He hasn't caught my cold. I hope he won't. He's not cubbing home this evening. Flying to Glasgow for a two-day company seminar.'

'But you're not going with him?' Rickle's voice was registering proper concern.

'Doe, doe. It's strictly business.'

'Good. Try to stay at home in the warm for a bit. Have a couple of early nights.'

'I will. Thank you so mudge. I'm very grateful.'

'No trouble at all, Cynthia. Good-bye.' After putting the telephone down, the good doctor logged on his laptop a £40 minimum consultation fee with Mrs Friston, before resuming his study of the stock-market report on the internet.

*   *   *

It was seven o'clock and very dark when Major Paul Digby Friston arrived, in icy rain, at the tree screened, marital home. As he had hoped, he hadn't passed another moving car or pedestrian since entering the village. He found his wife watching television in the snug. Although she had changed into a nightdress and frumpy negligee, she had not gone to bed. Her husband had phoned, shortly after she had spoken to the doctor, to say that he would drop by at the house on the way to Heathrow after all.

The London office of the financial services company which employed Friston was on the north-west side of the city. Cynthia guessed that he was coming home only to please her, after already cramming too much into a long, tiring day. His action showed that he hated their not being together at weekends as much as she did – or nearly as much. It was bad enough that he sometimes had to see clients in the evenings, or at their own homes on a Saturday or a Sunday – not quite as often as her naughty Paul would sometimes have her believe, but then we all had our foibles, and she indulged him as she would a small child.

It wasn't as if her Paul absolutely had to work. She had money enough for them both. In truth, his contribution to the cost of their lifestyle was miniscule. Selling insurance for a small salary, plus commission, which was basically what he did, was not a massive source of income. It was simply that, as he put it to her, he was an old fashioned husband who felt an obligation to help support his wife in a material way as best he could. It was a matter of self-respect. She admired him for that, but looked forward to the time when he had promised he would retire – in eighteen months, when he would be 55, and all hers.

'You needn't have come home,' she half admonished, after he kissed her on the cheek.

'I did, my precious. I'd forgotten to pack my razor. And, of course, there was the little matter of seeing you.' He gave her a winning smile to match the understated compliment.

'And I love you for it. You look tired, darling.'

'I am, quite. Needs must where the devil drives, of course,' he sighed, and this time a stoic look accompanied the comment.

Paul Friston cut a tall, elegant, upright figure, with his dark hair, strong chin, aquiline nose, and an appraising gaze that in Victorian fiction made women ready to surrender all. Surprisingly, he had gone through life convinced that he had exactly that effect on the opposite sex – a conviction, it has to be said, that'd had its owner's expectation fulfilled too often for him to stop believing in it.

Expensive schooling had failed to gain Friston a place at a university, but he had been lucky to find his feet in the army instead, and at a time when recruitment had been at an all time low. After officer training, he had scraped a commission, and been accepted by a lesser regiment, but one where his prowess at cricket had tipped the scales for him. It was this sporting reputation that had sustained the young officer's advancement up to the rank of captain. Thereafter his military career had stuck. Written appraisals by a succession of commanding officers had deplored his lack of leadership qualities, especially in the areas of initiative and rapid tactical reaction. He had been asked to leave the service at the age of 36 with the retirement rank of major – but happily for him, this was after he had bowled over Cynthia and married her.

Friston would have preferred a more glamorous partner, but a man couldn't have everything, and none of his other girlfriends then, or even later, owned a fortune nearly as large as Cynthia's.

The major had maintained his military title because, he said, it was good for business. The real reason was that he felt it added to his swash-buckling image. His dedication to his dull, mousy wife had, from the start, been maintained because it provided him with the wherewithal for sustaining a lifestyle given to the pursuit of other women. His frequent absences from home seldom had anything to do with business: they had everything to do with the availability of current seducible lovelies. Despite that, he had never considered himself to be truly unfaithful because his attachments never lasted, and, at bottom, he was so profoundly devoted to Cynthia's money.

What had been weighing on Friston's mind for some time was his retirement, promised in an unguarded moment, but proving to be a vow which Cynthia reminded him of almost daily, and clearly meant him to keep. And the prospect was not just untenable: for the last several months it had become unendurable for three reasons.

Retirement at home with Cynthia would be impossible.

Friston's attractiveness to desirable young women in the mass, as it were, had been losing its edge, though he hated to admit it.

For the first time in his life, he was hopelessly, passionately, madly in love with a paragon called Avril Trite – and his passion was returned in equal measure.

The third consideration made the second a matter of no consequence (except it provided a saving sop to his ego), and while it offered no solution to the Cynthia problem, in a vague sense, it simplified things – particularly in a man given to dangerous over-simplifications.

Avril Trite was a slim blonde, arresting rather than pretty, a little over medium height, an intelligent widow with a magnetic personality, and a recent, modest inheritance, following the death of her mother. At 33 she was distinctly older than Friston's usual conquests, but the way the two had fused from the beginning, mentally as well as physically, had persuaded him that overly young lovers had never provided him with the mature and thrilling satisfactions he was now enjoying. That this was mere sublimation might have been clear to a psychologist, but, again, the picture was even simpler for Friston. Avril had lifted a veil for him. He needed to make her his own, and no price was too high to pay for that.

Nevertheless, there still was a price – and its name was Cynthia.

Friston had first called on Avril, by appointment, one afternoon in early January, at her charmingly furnished, small apartment in Richmond, ten miles west of London, on the Thames. She had answered one of his company's advertisements. Her late husband, a drunkard, she explained, had left her nothing but debts which she had at last paid off. Now she needed advice on how to invest her mother's money for steady growth and income, which was precisely what Friston's company claimed it existed to do for people. Except that the sum proved to be even more modest than Friston had first imagined. The interest on it, whichever way the capital was invested, would scarcely be enough to meet the mortgage payments on the apartment. An interior designer, Avril worked from home, but commissions had recently been few.

A mutual sense of sympathetic understanding had developed

during the very first hour of the encounter. The way Avril had unburdened about her situation had prompted Friston to respond, without inhibition, in detailing his own 'desperations' (leading, in a calculated way, to his 'longings', his usual ploy), trapped in a marriage to a woman who adored him, but who offered him neither mental nor physical satisfactions. That the woman was rich had been volunteered in response to a seemingly quite incidental question from Avril.

Later, in the evening, the two had made love – a natural, pure progression in their short relationship, though the quality of the event had made it an astonishing one for Friston. Within a week he had totally determined to spend the rest of his life with Avril.

Divorcing Cynthia would have provided no material solution to her husband's problem, or rather to Avril Trite and Paul Friston's joint problem as it had become. Cynthia's fortune would effectively have remained hers. The consideration that if Cynthia should die first, then that he would inherit everything, was something Friston had hesitated openly to bring up – until Avril did. Soon after that, and following much, but not too much, agonising, it was Cynthia's early demise that the two lovers coolly chose not just to examine, but to initiate. For in the end there was no deep rationalizing, no profound justification. Their joint endeavours were focused solely on how doing away with Cynthia should be accomplished.

'You haven't told anyone I'd be coming home?' Friston enquired lightly, as he walked upstairs behind Cynthia on the way to their bedroom.

'No. No one's telephoned. In any case, you said not to mention it to anyone.'

He smiled. 'That was because I cancelled my last meeting. It was outside the office, and I had too much to do before I could leave. But I couldn't get hold of the client, so I left a message on his machine. He might have tried to call me back here. He has the number. Anyway, that's how I cleared the time to get home to you.' He moved ahead of her to make sure the bedroom curtains were closed before she turned on the lights.

'So thoughtful of you, my sweet,' she said, squeezing his hand.

'I was worried about that cold you were starting this morning.'

'Oh, it's gone. Quite…evaporated.' She didn't want to tell him about consulting the doctor over anything so trivial – and the

Rhine-Off capsule had already cured her sniffles.

'Good, but take it easy while I'm away. You haven't any dates tomorrow have you?'

'No, none. I shan't be seeing anyone, or going out. Just a quiet day here with a book.'

'That's fine. I told everyone I was getting the 8.15 Glasgow shuttle this evening,' her husband went on. 'Actually I re-booked onto the 9.15.'

She glanced at the time. 'So you can stay a little longer?'

'Not really. I'll have to be off again in a minute. I'll just get that razor from the bathroom.' In fact he had quite a lot planned for the next hour.

★   ★   ★

'I still can't get over it, Inspector. Still can't get over it,' Paul Friston repeated, motioning the policeman to a seat in the drawing room. It was just after nine on the following Tuesday morning, with sleet still falling heavily outside. 'I'm sorry I was so incoherent on Sunday evening. Did I give you adequate answers to your questions?'

'You did, sir. As I told you, I held over some routine ones, and that's why I'm here now. Routine questions and a few that have come up in the course of the investigation.' Detective Inspector Gordon Miler seated himself gingerly on the edge of the green velvet armchair as though afraid it might fall apart under his imposing frame. Too late, he wished he'd opted for something more robust. It was not that he was overweight, not for his height and width. He was just an all-round commanding size. In his late twenties, he wore an almost permanently earnest, encouraging expression, lit by wide-open, innocent blue eyes, which made it hard for some to credit his exceptional acuity.

Miler had admired this room on Sunday, as he had the rest of the house, including the bedroom where the Scenes of Crime team and the pathologist had each made tortuous examinations, finishing barely an hour ahead of Friston's return early that evening. Because of the time his journey had taken, the bereaved husband had been excused the sight of his wife's strangled and nearly frozen body crumpled on the floor before the open door to the balcony.

He had gone to the hospital mortuary on the following morning to make the formal identification.

'I'm sorry for the way the tragic news had to be broken to you, sir. But we thought the doctor would handle it best,' the policeman went on, producing a notebook from a side pocket of his grey tweed jacket.

'I'm not complaining, Inspector.' Friston had dropped into a chair opposite his visitor. 'George Rickle's an old friend. He showed that by coming here at midday on Sunday to see Cynthia was all right. As for his raising the alarm when he saw the balcony door was wide open.' The speaker paused, then let out a long breath before continuing. 'Well that was a merciful event. Otherwise I'd have been the one who found her. At least I was spared that. But it was still a terrible shock. To learn on the telephone your wife was done to death in your own home when you were seven hundred miles away, killed for the sake of some paltry jewellery. You feel so ... so utterly shocked, and ...yes, so bloody furious. That's what I am still. I just want to find the swine who did it and take him apart.' The speaker lowered his face into his hands.

'We're close to finding him, sir.'

Friston looked up almost too sharply. 'You're confident of that?'

'Pretty well, yes. Speed is all important at the start of a murder investigation, of course.' The inspector's countenance showed even greater earnestness. 'The first forty-eight hours are critical. It's also when the officer in charge gets the biggest allocation of personnel. I've had twenty-seven people on the case since Sunday night. That'll reduce if the trail cools. Except, don't worry, I won't let it.' He gave an embarrassed grin. 'If it was a burglar, who panicked when your wife woke up, and strangled her with the first thing handy, he's left clues which are being scientifically exposed right now.'

'The rope of the curtain tie-back being the first thing handy,' put in Friston. 'But why strangle her? Why attack her at all? He'd already got her jewels. Aren't burglars supposed to get the hell out if they're disturbed?'

'Usually they do, sir. But we don't yet know the full circumstances. Incidentally, was the bedroom balcony door always left open at night?'

'When I'm home, yes. My wife is...was a fresh-air fiend. I

implored her always to lock it when she was alone. I think she usually did, but having a head cold, well, that could have been why she wanted to keep the place well aired. George Rickle told me that with the body so cold, it'd be difficult to estimate the time of death.'

'Nearly impossible by normal methods, yes,' the inspector answered almost absently. It seemed he was more interested in the door to the balcony. 'We noticed the windows on either side of the door don't open, sir.'

'That's right, I'm afraid, so there's no other way of getting fresh air into the room, except less directly through the bathroom window. We'd always planned to have those windows changed, but never did.' He frowned. 'I'm afraid we've been backward in rejecting electric gates, and CCTV cameras. I know a lot of local residents have put them in, but more haven't. Like Cynthia and me, they've felt such devices reduce the rural atmosphere we've all worked hard to preserve in the area. Cynthia had even opposed increases in street lighting. Now it seems she's paid a high price for her country ways, as I have.' He sighed, adding in stoutish mitigation. 'Of course, we've had a burglar alarm for years.'

The policeman nodded. 'The alarm was armed downstairs when the uniformed police arrived on Sunday, sir.'

'Yes, Cynthia would have set it before she went to bed Saturday night. But only on this floor, not upstairs.' He frowned. 'So, common burglars are less careful than premeditated murderers?'

'Yes, sir. And impulse murders are sometimes easier to solve than the planned kind. Unless something happens to upset the plan.' Miler's study of Friston lingered for a moment, before he looked down again at his notes. 'Now, could we just deal with those follow-up questions I mentioned, sir?'

'Of course, Inspector, fire ahead please.' Friston was content with the officer's plodding pace. He wondered what the other twenty-six members of the team were finding to do.

'Right, sir. You flew to Glasgow on Friday evening?'

'Yes. For a two-day staff seminar at a hotel. I have the details here.' He produced some typed sheets from a document case and passed them to the inspector. 'God, if only I hadn't needed to be there,' he completed.

Miler glanced at the top sheet. 'But you didn't leave for the airport from here, sir?'

'No. I drove there direct from our London office. I caught the 9.15 shuttle from Heathrow.'

'So the last time you saw your wife?'

'Was here after breakfast on Friday,' the other man supplied. 'I talked to her on the phone later in the day.'

'From the office, sir?'

'Yes.'

'On an office phone, or your mobile?'

'Er … on my office phone.'

'At what time would that have been?'

Friston shrugged. 'Six-fifteen, or thereabouts. Does it matter?'

'We've got a print-out from British Telecom, and from all the mobile operators, covering calls made to and from the house at the weekend, sir. We're needing to account for the lot.'

'I see. Well, I rang her again on Saturday from Glasgow, on my mobile. That was at the end of the morning session at…at 12.35. You should find that on the print-out. I wanted to know how she was feeling.'

'And she was all right, sir?'

Friston gave a pained smile. 'She was fine. Just…just fine.' There was a catch in his throat on the last word.

The policeman paused sympathetically before asking. 'Did she tell you she'd rung Dr Rickle about the cold, sir?'

'No, but he told me so here on Sunday night. Something about her taking a pill to stop her nose running.'

'Yes. We have a problem with those Rhine-Off capsules, sir. It seems your wife bought a twelve pack at the local chemist's on Friday afternoon, and took one capsule after consulting the doctor. She'd never taken the product before.'

'That's what Rickle told me.'

'Had you ever bought Rhine-Off capsules, sir?'

'No, never.'

'So apart from what your wife bought, there wouldn't have been another pack in the house?'

'I suppose not, no. What are you getting at?'

'The pack is in the bathroom cabinet, sir, and there's only one capsule missing.'

Friston's eyebrows lifted. 'So she only took one. The stuff worked, or else the cold wasn't as bad as she thought.'

'Dr Rickle said the cold was a very bad one, sir, judging from your wife's voice on the phone Friday evening. He'd suggested she took one capsule straight away, and another first thing in the morning. How did her voice sound when you spoke to her?'

'On Friday evening pretty normal. On Saturday the same.' The speaker paused, then leaned forward with a confiding look. 'This is difficult to admit, inspector, but my darling Cynthia was a bit of a hypochondriac. She'd often start on a long course of medicine for a supposed ailment which would be completely gone next morning. That cupboard is full of practically unused nostrums. I know George Rickle says her nose sounded bunged up, but she could easily have been exaggerating on the phone to justify calling him. She was like that.'

'I see, sir. Perhaps…' The policeman paused as both men heard the ring of the doorbell. 'I'll answer that, sir. I'm expecting one of my sergeants.' He left the room and didn't return for over two minutes. When he did re-appear, he was accompanied by a tall, dark-haired young woman, smartly turned out in a black wool trouser suit over a white polo-necked sweater. Her brisk step was as firm as the searching look she fixed on Friston.

'This is Detective Sergeant Kim Bevan, sir, who's one of my assistants on the case,' the inspector explained, while the sergeant, without waiting to be invited, seated herself on the end of a sofa close to her boss, setting a large black leather shoulder bag down beside her.

Friston had stood up when the woman entered. After acknowledging her with a smile he had resumed his seat before she announced. 'When a Mr Arthur Pristable heard of your wife's death yesterday, Major Friston, he got in touch with us. He's an ex-policeman, now a private investigator who's been retained by your wife for the last three years. The arrangement was handled through Ms Rachel D. Smythe, your wife's business accountant. Mr Pristable's bills were paid through her.'

'Did you know anything about this arrangement, sir?' the inspector put in.

Friston cleared his throat. 'No. So are you going to tell me about it?'

On a nod from Miler the woman detective continued. 'On your wife's instructions, relayed through Ms Smythe, Mr Pristable, or one of his partners, has followed you when you called on single and sometimes married women in various parts of South East England, but mostly in the London area.'

'I find that difficult to credit.'

'The reports are very detailed, sir,' the sergeant responded.

'H'm. I'll take your word for that, for the moment.' Friston grunted. 'Oh dear. So my poor darling Cynthia suspected I was having affairs with my clients, did she? In my sort of work, of course, one always runs the risk that one's spouse can put the wrong interpretation on things. Strange that she never confronted me with her fears.'

The woman officer cleared her throat. 'According to Mr Pristable, and confirmed by Ms Smythe, sir, your wife didn't just suspect, she was convinced you'd been having affairs ever since you married her. It seems she didn't mind about them, so long as they didn't go on too long. Actually, when they were happening, she thought you were more attentive to her. It appears from Mr Pristable's reports, sir, that the affairs never did last long.'

Friston emitted a loud and exaggerated guffaw. 'I must say, if you believe all that you're as gullible as Pristable and Rachel Smythe, and, sadly, my dearest Cynthia. But she was right that I didn't have long affairs. You see, I never had affairs of any kind.' He sighed. 'I mean, how could any of them possibly know whether my calls on women clients were strictly business or some kind of amorous adventure. Especially if they happened behind closed doors. How did this Pristable know a client's partner wasn't present? And all because poor Cynthia had developed another of her fixations. You know she had them in other contexts too? But I'm damned if I'm going into all that now.'

'Your wife insisted to Ms Smythe that she usually knew when the alleged affairs were happening, sir,' said DS Bevan. 'This was partly because you often told her you'd spent the night away in one place when Mr Pristable had reported you were somewhere else. Also the visits seldom happened entirely behind closed doors. There were sometimes restaurants and hotels involved.'

Friston looked ruffled. 'Really, this is too stupid. And anyway, what's it got to do with my wife's tragic death?' He switched his gaze to the inspector. 'I mean, is this nonsense what your army of detectives is engaged in when it's supposed to be catching my wife's murderer?'

'I'm afraid there's rather more to it than you've heard already, sir,' said Miler, whose tone and general demeanour had become a lot sharper.

'We believe you're familiar with a lady called Mrs Avril Trite, sir,' put in the sergeant, who had been distinctly sharp from the start.

'Yes, she's a valued client,' Friston answered stiffly.

'So valued that in the last eight weeks, between you, you've made forty-eight phone calls to each other on your mobiles, in addition to the twenty-five you've made to the lady on your office phone.'

'I've told you, Mrs Trite is a client. I've had to confer with her a lot over the…the disposition of her financial holdings. But what right have you got to delve into my private affairs, or hers? Your job is…'

'Our job is to leave no stone unturned in finding your wife's killer, Major Friston,' the inspector interrupted. 'Those were your exact words to me as we parted here on Sunday night. We are trying to follow your wishes.'

Friston sighed testily. 'So are you suggesting that my business relationship with Mrs Trite has something to do with my wife's death? If you are, ludicrous as that is, perhaps I should send for my lawyer.'

'We're not suggesting anything yet, sir,' put in the sergeant. 'Only asking you to answer some questions that are causing us problems. From the private investigator's reports it seems that you've been conducting an affair with Mrs Trite. Since we know…'

'And if I deny…' Friston tried to interrupt.

'I was going to add, sir,' the sergeant insisted, 'that we have sworn evidence you've spent six nights at Mrs Trite's flat since January 8th last, and visited her there at least twelve times at different hours of the day over the same period, as well as taken her to restaurants. Since we have a list of the visits, with dates and times, it'd be better if you admitted the relationship so we can get on to more pressing matters.'

Friston looked from the sergeant to the inspector, then back again. 'Very well. The lady and I have been seeing each other. But what the devil has that to do with Cynthia's death?'

'Thank you, sir.' The inspector sounded relieved. 'We'll come to that in a moment. First, I have to tell you the pathologist's report suggests that your wife died on Friday evening.'

The other man looked surprised. 'But that's impossible. I spoke to her myself on the phone, Saturday lunchtime.'

'So you said, sir. You also told us you were never here on Friday evening. That you went straight from the office to the airport.'

'That's right.'

'Except that the tape from a neighbour's CCTV gate camera shows your car leaving this road at 8.19 on Friday evening, in time for you to catch your Glasgow flight. Were you in the car, sir, or was someone else using it?'

Friston shifted in his chair. 'It must be a mistake. Which neighbour?'

'It's a Mr Elder's house, sir.'

'The Elders have a gate camera? I didn't know ... but ... but that's three hundred yards from here. How could ...'

As Friston floundered, sweat breaking out on his forehead, the inspector provided. 'The camera swivels, sir. It covers the whole area around the gateway every sixty seconds, and happened to pick up your car.'

There was silence for several seconds before Friston straightened in the chair and, looking the inspector in the eye, explained. 'All right, I did pop home for a few minutes. To see Cynthia was all right. But I'd told clients and people in the office on Friday that I had to leave as early as I did to catch my plane. I decided on the way down on Sunday to stick to that story. It was silly, probably, but I didn't want to admit to such a trivial but possibly embarrassing fib, commercially, I mean.'

'Not even in the circumstances, sir?'

'You're right, of course,' Friston admitted heavily.

It was the policeman's turn to pause, pointedly lengthening the silence that had followed. 'Incidentally, sir, that gate camera also picked up a car rented by Mrs Trite driving toward your house on Saturday at 12.16 pm. That was fifteen minutes before you telephoned from Glasgow. Would she have rented a car because her white, soft topped Porsche is too memorable, especially in daylight?'

Friston, clearly thrown by the information, ran a hand up and down the sleeve of his cashmere sweater before replying. 'Yes, well that visit could easily be explained. My wife and Mrs Trite had become friends. It's often the way, isn't it? A friendship can develop between a man's wife and his er …'

'His mistress, sir?' Kim Bevan supplied in a wooden voice.

'If you insist. Except Mrs Avril Trite and I never suspected Cynthia knew about our…brief infatuation. We had Mrs Trite to lunch here early in February. I'd mentioned her off and on, as a decorator client, and Cynthia wanted to meet her. They took to each other. Perhaps Avril had promised to drop in for a snack lunch on Saturday. To keep Cynthia company. I believe her car's been in for repair. That would account for the rented one.'

'You didn't mention any of this before, sir?' questioned the sergeant.

'Because, as I said, it's only a possibility. You must ask Mrs Trite.'

'If the pathologist's report is correct, sir, your wife was lying dead in the bedroom upstairs when Mrs Trite arrived on Saturday. It seems she must have let herself in, switched off the alarm, answered your call at 12.35, re-set the alarm, and left, establishing for the record that the phone was answered by your wife.'

'Except I don't accept any word of that … that scenario.'

'Mrs Trite does, sir,' the sergeant continued icily. 'She insists she thought your wife was out, that she let herself in with the key you'd lent her. She answered the phone and you were the caller. When your wife didn't return, she just left the house, thinking she'd got the day wrong, or that your wife had forgotten she was coming.'

The colour drained from Friston's face. 'When did you see Mrs Trite?'

'Early this morning, sir. I left her half an hour ago. She doesn't want to be involved in a possible murder investigation. Perhaps she hasn't mentioned it to you, but her husband's death three years ago involved a police enquiry after a coroner's court returned an open verdict on the cause of death. It seems he was very wealthy. The enquiry was later shelved because of insufficient evidence. It can be re-opened, of course.'

Friston swallowed awkwardly. 'Very well. I admit Cynthia wasn't in when I rang on Saturday. Mrs Trite happened to be there. We thought it…it must have been that Cynthia had gone out, forgetting the appointment. I'd given Mrs Trite a key so she could get in on…on another occasion, when…when Cynthia was away. I'd given her the alarm code then as well. Didn't she tell you that?'

The sergeant shook her head. 'It must have slipped her mind, sir.'

'That's it, yes.'

'The fact remains, Major Friston, the forensic evidence firmly indicates your wife died on Friday evening.'

'The evidence can indicate whatever it likes, sergeant, but the inspector just told me the time of death was almost impossible to estimate. I'm sure Cynthia must have been alive on Saturday, unless you can prove otherwise. Did Mrs Trite tell you she had gone up to the bedroom when she was here, and found it empty?'

'She said she didn't go upstairs at all, sir.'

Friston's jaw stiffened. 'I expect because she was sure Cynthia was out. The reason I said I'd spoken to Cynthia on the phone was to avoid exactly what's happening now, with you trying to prove I couldn't have spoken to her because she was dead. That implies I had something to do with her death, which is monstrous. I'm aware the police always suspect the husband in these cases, but this time you're very wrong. I know in my heart that Cynthia was alive on Saturday, and the sooner you get back to accepting that, the sooner we'll catch the real villain.' Breathing heavily, the speaker fell back in his chair.

DS Bevan glanced across at the inspector who nodded again slowly.

'I'm afraid the forensic report did more than merely indicate the death occurred on Friday evening, sir,' the sergeant said. 'You see, there's the evidence of the Rhine-Off capsule.'

'What evidence?' Friston demanded testily. 'We know she took one capsule. So what?'

'And we know when she took it, sir. At six on Friday, while she was talking to the doctor. If she'd lived until the same time on Saturday, or even until midday, there'd have been no trace of the undissolved ingredients in her body.'

'Who says so?'

Miler cleared his throat. 'The Home Office Pathologist who did the post mortem examination, sir. A very conscientious, highly qualified lady. A slow acting decongestive is itself a kind of clock, with its granules arranged to dissolve at different intervals at normal body temperature.'

'My wife had a cold, probably a high temperature so...'

'Exactly, sir,' the inspector interjected. 'If anything that would have reduced the time it took for the medication to dissolve. Instead, the pathologist found particles of it in the lower bowel. If your wife had lived for twenty-four hours those substances would have dispersed or been passed through the body. The manufacturers confirmed as much last night. So, according to the pathologist's best calculations, your wife was strangled at between seven and eight-thirty on Friday evening. And in view of the unsatisfactory account you have given us of your own movements that evening, I'm afraid I have to ask you to accompany us to the station for further questioning.'

A staggered Friston was barely taking in the words.

Later, in his cell, after he had been charged, he didn't hold it against Avril for lying to prove she hadn't been involved. He even accepted the new possibility that she might have murdered her husband. What he firmly could not credit was that the only real love of his life could have had that same fate in mind for him, once she had married him, and Cynthia's fortune. But then, Major Friston had always suffered from an excess of conceit – and a shortfall in rapid tactical reaction.

Due North

John Harvey

Elder hated this: the after-midnight call, the neighbours penned back behind hastily unravelled tape, the video camera's almost silent whirr; the way, as if reproachful, the uniformed officers failed to meet his eye; and this especially, the bilious taste that fouled his mouth as he stared down at the bed, the way the hands of both children rested near the cover's edge, as if at peace, their fingers loosely curled.

He had been back close on two years, long enough to view the move north with some regret. Not that north was really what it was. A hundred and twenty miles from London, one hour forty minutes, theoretically, by train. Another country nonetheless.

For weeks he and Joanne had argued it back and forth, reasons for, reasons against, two columns fixed to the refrigerator door. *Cut and Dried*, the salon where Joanne worked as a stylist, was opening branches in Derby and Nottingham and she could manage either one she chose. Derby was out of the question.

On a visit, Katherine trailing behind them, they had walked along the pedestrianised city centre street: high-end fashion, café latté, bacon cobs, Waterstone's, Ted Baker, Café Rouge.

'You see,' Joanne said, 'we could be in London. Chiswick High Road.'

Elder shook his head. It was the bacon cobs that gave it away.

The empty shop unit was just off to one side, secluded and select. *Post no Bills* plastered across the glass frontage, *Sold Subject to Contract* above the door. Joanne would be able to hire the staff, set the tone, choose the shade of paint upon the walls.

'You know I want this, don't you?' Her hands in his pockets as she pulled him back against the glass.

'I know.'

'So?'

He closed his eyes and, slow at first, she kissed him on the mouth.

'God!' Katherine exclaimed, whacking her father in the back.

'What?'

'Making a bloody exhibition of yourselves, that's what.'

'You watch your tongue, young lady,' Joanne said, stepping clear.

'Sooner that than watching yours.'

Katherine Elder: eleven going on twenty-four.

'What say we go and have a coffee?' Elder said. 'Then we can have a think.'

Even a casual glance in the estate agent's window made it clear that for the price of their two bedroom first floor flat off Chiswick Lane, they could buy a house in a decent area, something substantial with a garden front and back. For Katherine, moving up to secondary, a new start in a new school, the perfect time. And Elder … ?

He had joined the police a twenty-year-old in Huddersfield, walked the beat in Leeds; out of uniform, he'd been stationed in Lincolnshire: Lincoln itself, Boston, Skegness. Then, married, the big move to London, this too at Joanne's behest. Frank Elder a detective sergeant in the Met. Detective Inspector when he was forty-five. Moving out he'd keep his rank at least, maybe push up. There were faces he still knew, a name or two. Calls he could make. A week after Joanne took charge of the keys to the new salon, Elder had eased himself behind his desk at the headquarters of the Nottinghamshire Major Crime Unit: a telephone, a Rolodex, a PC with a splintered screen; a part-eaten Pork Farms pie collecting dust in one of the desk drawers.

Now, two years on, the screen had been replaced, the keyboard jammed and lacked the letters R and S; photographs of Joanne and Katherine stood beside his in-tray in small frames. The team he'd been working with on a wages hi-jack north of Peterborough had just brought in a result and shots of scotch were being passed around in polystyrene cups.

Elder drank his down, a single swallow, and dialled home. 'Jo, I'm going to be a bit late.'

A pause in which he visualised her face, a tightening around the mouth, the corners of her eyes. 'Of course.'

'What do you mean?'

'It's the end of the week, the lads are raring to go, of course you'll be late.'

'Look, if you'd rather…'

'Frank, I'm winding you up. Go and have a drink. Relax. I'll see you in an hour or so, okay?'

'You're sure?'

'Frank.'

'All right. All right. I'm going.'

When he arrived home, two hours later, not so much more, Katherine was closeted in her room listening to Pharoahe Monch and Joanne was nowhere to be seen.

'*Decapitate his ass!*' confronted him when he stepped inside his daughter's room. '*Smack him, slap him in the back of the truck.*'

'Dad!'

'What?'

'You're supposed to knock.'

'I did.'

'I didn't hear you.'

Reaching past her, he angled the volume control of the portable stereo down a notch, a half-smile deflecting the complaint that failed to come.

'Where's Mum?'

'Out.'

'Where?'

'Out.'

Cross-legged on the bed, fair hair splashed across her eyes, Katherine flipped closed the book in which she had been writing with a practised sigh.

'You want something to eat?' Elder asked.

A quick shake of the head. 'I already atc.'

He found a slice of pizza in the fridge and set it in the microwave to reheat, opened a can of Heineken, switched on the TV. When Joanne arrived back, close to midnight, he was asleep in the armchair, unfinished pizza on the floor close by. Stooping, she kissed him lightly and he woke.

'You see,' Joanne said, 'it works.'

'What does?'

'You turned into a frog.'

Elder smiled and she kissed him again; he didn't ask her where she'd been.

Neither was quite in bed when the mobile suddenly rang.

'Mine or yours?'

Joanne angled her head. 'Yours.'

Elder was still listening, asking questions, as he started reaching for his clothes.

★   ★   ★

Fourteen miles north of the city, Mansfield was a small industrial town with an unemployment rate above average, a reputation for casual violence and a soccer team just keeping its head above water in Division Three of the Nationwide. Elder lowered the car window a crack, broke into a fresh pack of extra-strong mints and tried not to think about what he would find.

He missed the turning first and had to double back, a cul-de-sac built into a new estate, just shy of the road to Edwinstowe and Ollerton. An ambulance snug between two police cars, lights in the windows of all the houses, the periodic yammering of radios. At number seventeen all of the curtains were drawn closed. A child's scooter lay discarded on the lawn. Elder pulled on the protective coveralls he kept ready in the boot, nodded to the young officer in uniform on guard outside and showed his ID just in case. On the stairs, one of the Scene of Crime team, whey-faced, stepped aside to let him pass. The smell of blood and something else, like ripe pomegranate, on the air.

The children were in the smallest bedroom, two boys, six and four, pyjama-ed arms outstretched; the pillow with which they had been smothered lay bunched on the floor. Elder noticed bruising near the base of the older boy's throat, twin purpling marks the size of thumbs; he wondered who had closed their eyes.

'We were right to call you in?'

For a big man, Saxon moved lightly; only a slight nasal heaviness to his breathing had alerted Elder to his presence in the room.

'I thought, you know, better now than later.'

Elder nodded. Gerry Saxon was a sergeant based in the town, Mansfield born and bred. The two of them had crossed paths before, swapped yarns and the occasional pint; stood once at the Town ground, side by side, as sleet swept near horizontally goalwards, grim in the face of a nil-nil draw with Chesterfield. Elder thought Saxon thorough, bigoted, not as slow-witted as he would have you believe.

'Where's the mother?' Elder asked.

Lorraine Atkin was jammed between the dressing table and the wall, as if trying to burrow away from the pain. One slash of a blade had sliced deep across her back, opening her from shoulder to hip. Her nightdress, once white, was matted here and there to her body with stiffening blood. Her throat had been cut.

'The police surgeon …?'

'Downstairs,' Saxon said. 'Few preliminaries, nothing more. Didn't like to move her till your say-so.'

Elder nodded again. So much anger: so much hate. He looked from the bed to the door, at the collision of bottles and jars across the dressing table top, the trajectory of blood along the walls. As if she had made a dash for it and been dragged back, attacked. Trying to protect her children or herself?

'The weapon?'

'Kitchen knife. Least that's what I reckon. Downstairs in the sink.'

'Washed clean?'

'Not so's you'd notice.'

There were footsteps on the landing outside and then Maureen Prior's face in the doorway, eyes widening as she took in the scene; one slow intake of breath and she stepped into the room.

'Gerry, you know DS Price. Maureen, Gerry Saxon.'

'Good to see you again, Gerry.' She scarcely took her eyes from the body. The corpse.

'Maureen, check with Scene of Crime. Make sure they've documented everything we might need. Let's tie that up before we let the surgeon get to work. You'll liaise with Gerry here about interviewing the neighbours, house to house.'

'Right.'

'You'll want to see the garage next,' Saxon said.

There were two entrances, one from the utility room alongside the kitchen, the other from the drive. Despite the latter being open, the residue of carbon monoxide had yet to fully clear. Paul Atkin slumped forward over the driver's wheel, one eye fast against the windscreen's curve, his skin sacking grey.

Elder walked twice slowly around the car and went out to where Saxon stood in the rear garden, smoking a cigarette.

'Any sign of a note?'

Saxon shook his head.

'A note would have been nice. Neat at least.'

'Only tell you what you know already.'

'What's that then, Gerry?'

'Bastard topped his family, then himself. Obvious.'

'But why?'

Saxon laughed. 'That's what you clever bastards are going to find out.' He lit a fresh cigarette from the butt of the last and as he did Elder noticed Saxon's hands had a decided shake. Probably the night air was colder than he'd thought.

* * *

There was no note that came to hand, but something else instead. Traced with Atkin's finger on the inside of the misting glass and captured there by Scene of Crime, the first wavering letters of a name — *C O N N* and then what might have been an *I* trailing weakly down towards the window's edge.

Mid-afternoon the following day, Elder was driving with Maureen Prior out towards the small industrial estate where Atkin had worked, Head of Sales for Pleasure Blinds. Prefabricated units that had still to lose their shine, neat beds of flowering shrubs, no sign of smoke in sight. Sherwood Business Park.

If someone married's going over the side, chances are it's with someone from where they work. One of Frank Elder's rules of thumb, rarely disproved.

Some few years back, close to ten it would be now, his wife Joanne had an affair with her boss. Six months it had gone on, no more, before Elder had found out. The reasons not so very difficult to see. They had just arrived in London, uprooted themselves, and Joanne was high on the speed of it, the noise, the buzz. Since having Katherine three years before, she and Elder had made love less and less; she felt unattractive, oddly sexless, over the hill at thirty-three. And then there had been Martyn Miles, all flash and if not Armani, Hugo Boss; drinks in the penthouse bar of this hotel or that, meals at Bertorelli's or Quo Vadis.

Elder had his fifteen minutes of crazy, smashed a few things around the house, confronted Miles outside the mews apartment where he lived and restrained himself from punching him in his smug and sneering face more than just the once.

Together, he and Joanne had talked it through, worked it out; she had carried on at the salon. 'I need to see him every day and know I don't want him any more. Not turn my back and never know for sure.'

Elder had told Maureen all of this one day: one night, actually; a long drive down the motorway from Fife, the road surface slick with rain, headlights flicking by. She had listened, said very little, a couple of comments only. Maureen with a core of moral judgment clear and unyielding as the Taliban. Neither of them had ever referred to it again.

Elder slowed the car and turned through the gates of the estate; Pleasure Blinds was the fourth building on the right.

Constance Seymour read the sign on the door. *Personnel.*

As soon as she saw them, her face crumpled inwards like a paper bag. Spectacles slipped, lopsided, down on to the desk. Maureen fished a Kleenex from her bag; Elder fetched water from the cooler in a cone-shaped cup. Connie blew her nose, dabbed at her eyes. She was somewhere in her thirties, Elder thought, what might once have been called homely, plain. Sloped shoulders, buttoned blouse, court shoes. Elder could imagine her with her mother, in town Saturdays shopping arm in arm, the two of them increasingly alike.

The eyes that looked at him now were tinged with violet, palest blue. She would have listened to Atkin like that, intense and sympathetic, pained. Whose hand would have reached out first, who would first have comforted whom?

Maureen came to the end of her expressions of condolence, regret.

'You were having an affair with him,' she said. 'Paul Atkin. A relationship.'

Connie sniffed and said yes.

'And this relationship, how long …'

'A year. More. Thirteen months.'

'It was serious, then?'

'Oh, yes.' Her expression slightly puzzled, somewhat hurt. What else could it have been?

'Mr Atkin, was there … was there any suggestion that he might leave his wife?'

'Oh, no. No. The children, you see. He loved the children more than anything.'

Maureen glanced across, remembering the faces, the pillow, the bed. Killed with kindness: the proverb eddied up in Elder's mind.

'Have you any idea why he might want to harm them?' Elder asked.

'No,' she gasped, moments ahead of the wash of tears. 'Unless … unless …'

*   *   *

Joanne was in the living room, feet tucked beneath her, watching TV. Katherine was staying overnight at a friend's. On screen, a bevy of smartly-dressed and foul-mouthed young things were dissecting the sex lives of their friends. A laughter track gave hints which Joanne, for the most part, ignored.

'Any good?' Elder asked.

'Crap.'

'I'm just going out for a stroll.'

'Okay.'

'Shan't be long.'

Glancing towards the door, Joanne smiled and puckered her lips into the shape of a kiss.

Arms swinging lightly by his sides, Elder cut through a swathe of tree-lined residential streets on to the main road; for a moment he was distracted by the lights of the pub, orange and warm, but instead walked on, away from the city centre and then left to where the houses were smaller than his own and huddled together, the first part of a circular walk that would take him, an hour or so later, back home.

Behind the curtains of most front rooms, TV sets flickered and glowed; muffled voices rose and fell; the low rumble of a sampled bass line reverberated from the windows of a passing Ford. Haphazardly, dogs barked. A child cried. On the corner, a group of black youths wearing ripped-off Tommy Hilfiger eyed him with suspicion and disdain.

Elder pictured Gerry Saxon leaning up against a darkened tree, his hands trembling a little as he smoked a cigarette. Almost a year now since he had given up himself, Elder fumbled in his pocket for another mint.

He knew the pattern of incidents similar to that at the Atkins house: the man — almost always it was the man — who could find no other way to cope; debt or unrequited love or some religious mania, voices that whispered, unrelenting, inside his head. Unable or unwilling to leave his family behind, feeling it his duty to protect them from whatever loomed, he took their lives and then his own. What differed here was the intensity of the attack upon the wife, that single fierce and slashing blow, delivered after death. Anger at himself for what he had done? At her, for giving cause?

A cat, tortoise shell, ran two-thirds of the way across the road, froze, then scuttled back.

'She was seeing someone, wasn't she?' Connie Seymour had said, voice parched with her own grief. 'Lorraine. His wife, Lorraine. Paul was terrified she was going to leave him, take his kids.'

No matter how many times he and Maureen had asked, Connie had failed to give them a name. 'He wouldn't tell me. Just wouldn't tell. Oh, he knew all right, Paul knew. But he wouldn't say. As if he was, you know, as if he was ashamed.'

Maureen had got Willie Bell sifting through the house to house reports already; tomorrow Matt Dowland and Salim Shukla would start knocking on doors again. For Karen Holbrook the task of contacting Lorraine Atkin's family and friends. Elder would go back to the house and take Maureen with him.

Why? That's what you clever bastards are going to find out.

Joanne was in the bathroom when he got back, smoothing cream into her skin. When he touched her arm, she jumped.

'Your hands, they're like ice.'

'I'm sorry.'

The moment passed.

In bed, eyes closed, Elder listened to the fall of footsteps on the opposite side of the street, the window shifting uncertainly inside its frame. Joanne read for ten minutes before switching out the light.

*　*　*

They found a diary, letters, nothing of real use. In a box file shelved between two albums of photographs, Maureen turned up a mish-mash of guarantees and customer instructions, invoices and bills.

'Mobile phones,' she called into the next room. 'We've had

those checked.'

'Yes,' Elder said, walking through. 'He had some kind of BT cell phone leased by his work, she was with — who was it? — One to One.'

'Right.' Maureen held up a piece of paper. 'Well it looks as if she might have had a second phone, separate account.'

'Think you can charm some details out of them, recent calls especially?'

'No. But I can impress on them the serious nature of the situation.'

*   *   *

'You sure you want to do this alone?' Maureen said.

They were parked in a lay-by on the road north from the city, arable land to their left shading into a small copse of trees. Lapwings rose sharply in the middle distance, black and white like an Escher print.

'Yes. I think so.'

'You don't want...?'

'No,' Elder said. 'I'll be fine.'

Maureen nodded and got back into her car and he stood there, watching her drive away, rehearsing his first words inside his head.

It was a square brick-built house in a street full of square brick-built houses, the front of this one covered in white pebble dash that had long since taken on several shades of grey. Once council, Elder assumed, now privately owned. A Vauxhall Astra parked outside. Roses in need of pruning. Patchy grass. Close against the kitchen window, a damson tree that looked as if it rarely yielded fruit.

He rattled the knocker and for good measure rang the bell.

No hesitation in the opening of the door, no delay.

'Hello, Gerry,' Elder said. 'Late shift?'

'You know,' Saxon said. 'You'd've checked.' And when Elder made no further remark, added. 'You'd best come in.'

It was tea or instant coffee and Elder didn't really want either, but he said tea would be fine, one sugar, and sat, mug cradled in both hands, in the middle of the cluttered living room while Saxon smoked and avoided looking him squarely in the eye.

'She phoned you, Jerry. Four days ago. The day before she was murdered. Phoned you when you were on duty. Twice.'

'She was upset, wasn't she? In a real state. Frightened.'

'Frightened?'

'He'd found out about us, seen us. The week before.' Saxon shook his head. 'It was stupid, so fucking half-arsed stupid. All the times we … all the times we saw one another, we never took no chances. She'd come here, afternoons, or else we'd meet up miles away, Sheffield or Grantham, and then this one bloody Saturday she said let's go into Nottingham, look round the shops. He was supposed to be off taking the kids to Clumber Park and there we are coming out of the Broad Marsh Centre on to Lister Gate and they're smack in front of us, him with the little kid on his shoulders and the other one holding his hand.'

Saxon swallowed down some tea and lit another cigarette.

'Course, we tried to pass it off, but you could see he wasn't having any. Ordered her to go home with them there and then and of course when they did there was all merry hell to pay. Ended up with him asking her if she intended leaving him and her saying yes, first chance she got.' Saxon paused. "You'll take the kids", he said, "over my dead body."

'She didn't leave?'

'No.'

'Nor try to?'

Saxon shook his head. 'He seemed to calm down after the first couple of days. Lorraine, she thought he might be going to get over it. Thought, you know, if we lay low for a spell, things'd get back to normal, we could start up again.'

'But that's not what happened?' Elder said.

'What happened was, this idea of her taking the kids, he couldn't get it out of his head. Stupid, really. I mean, I could've told him, a right non-starter.' Saxon looked around. 'You imagine what it'd be like, two lads in here. Someone else's kids. Place is mess enough as it is. Anyway …' Leaning forward now, elbows on his knees. '… you know what it's like, the kind of life we lead. The hours and all the rest of it. How many couples you know, one or both of them in the Force, children, how many d'you know make it work?'

Elder's tea was lukewarm, tannin thick in his mouth. 'The last time she phoned you, you said she was frightened. Had he threatened her or what?'

'No. I don't think so. Not in as many words. It was more him coming out with all this guff. Next time we're in the car I'll drive us all into the back of a lorry. Stuff like that.'

'And you didn't think to do anything?'

'Such as what?'

'Going round, trying to get him to talk, listen to reason; suggesting she take the boys away for a few days, grandparents, somewhere like that?'

'No,' Saxon said. 'I kept well out of it. Thought it best.'

'And now?'

'What do you mean, and now?'

'You still think it was for the best?'

The mug cracked across in Saxon's hand and tea spilled with blood towards the floor.

'Who the fuck?' he said, on his feet now, both men on their feet, Saxon on his feet and backing Elder towards the door. 'Who the fuck you think you are, coming in here like you're some judge and fucking jury, some tin-pot fucking god. Think you're fucking perfect? That what you think, you pompous sack of shit? I mean, what the fuck are you here for anyway? You here to question me? Arrest me? What? There was some fucking crime here? I committed some fucking crime?'

He had Elder backed up against the wall, close alongside the door, the sweat off his skin so rank that Elder almost gagged.

'Crime, Jerry?' Elder said. 'How much d'you want? Three murders, four deaths. Two boys, four and six. Not that you'll be losing much sleep over them. I mean, they were just a nuisance, an irrelevance. Someone to mess up this shit heap of a home.'

'Fuck you!' Saxon punched the wall, close by Elder's head.

'And Lorraine, well, you probably think that's a shame, but let's face it, you'll soon find someone else's wife to fuck.'

'You bastard!' Saxon hissed. 'You miserable, sanctimonious bastard.'

But his hands fell back down to his sides and slowly he backed away and gazed down at the floor and when he did that, without hurrying, Elder let himself out of the house and walked towards his car.

*   *   *

He and Joanne were sitting at either end of the settee, Elder with a glass of Jameson's in his hand, the bottle nearby on the floor; Joanne was drinking the white Rioja they had started with dinner. The remains of their take-away Chinese was on the table next door. Katherine had long since retreated to her room.

'What will happen?' Joanne asked. It was a while since either of them had spoken.

'To Saxon?'

'Um.'

'A bollocking from on high. Some kind of official reprimand. He might lose his stripes and get pushed into going round schools sweet-talking kids into being honest citizens.' Elder shook his head. 'Maybe nothing at all. I don't know. Except that it was all a bloody mess.'

He sighed and tipped a little more whiskey into his glass and Joanne sipped at her wine. It was late but neither of them wanted to make the first move towards bed.

'Christ, Jo! Those people. Sometimes I wonder if everyone out there isn't doing it in secret. Fucking one another silly.'

He was looking at Joanne as he spoke and there was a moment, a second, in which he knew what she was going to say before she spoke.

'I've been seeing him again. Martyn. I'm sorry, Frank, I ...'

'Seeing him?'

'Yes, I ...'

'Sleeping with him?'

'Yes. Frank, I'm sorry, I ...'

'How long?'

'Frank ...'

'How long have you been seeing him?'

'Frank, please ...'

Elder's whiskey spilled across the back of his hand, the tops of his thighs. 'How fucking long?'

'Oh, Frank ... Frank ...' Joanne in tears now, her breath uneven, her face wiped clear of colour. 'We never really stopped.'

Instead of hitting her, he hurled his glass against the wall.

'Tell me,' Elder said.

Joanne foraged for a tissue and dragged it across her face. 'He's

... he's got a place ... up here, in the Park. At first it was just, you know, the odd time, if we'd been working late, something special. I mean, Martyn, he wasn't usually here, he was down in London, but when ... Oh, Frank, I wanted to tell you, I even thought you knew, I thought you must ...'

She held out a hand and when Elder made no move to take it, let it fall.

'Frank ...'

He moved quickly, up from the settee, and she flinched and turned her face away. She heard, not saw him leave the room, the house, the home.

★   ★   ★

It wasn't difficult to find out where Martyn Miles lived when he was in the city, a top floor flat in a seventies apartment block off Tattershall Drive. Not difficult to slip the lock, even though stepping across the threshold set off the alarm. 'It's okay,' he explained to an anxious neighbour, 'I'll handle it. Police.' And showed his ID.

He had been half-hoping Miles would be there but he was not. Instead, he searched the place for signs of what? Joanne's presence? Tokens of love? In the built-in wardrobe, he recognised some of her clothes: a dove-grey suit, a blouse, a pair of high-heeled shoes; in the bathroom, a bottle of her perfume, a diaphragm.

Going back into the bedroom, he tore the covers from the bed, ripped at the sheets until they were little more than winding cloths, heaved the mattress to the floor and, yanking free the wooden slats on which it had rested, broke them, each and every one, against the wall, across his knee.

Back in the centre of the city, he booked into a hotel, paid over the odds for a bottle of Jameson and finally fell asleep, fully clothed, with the contents two-thirds gone. At work next day, he barked at anyone who as much as glanced in his direction. Maureen left a bottle of Aspirin on his desk and steered well clear. When he got home that evening, Joanne had packed and gone. *Frank — I think we both need some time and space.* He tore the note into smaller and smaller pieces till they filtered through his hands.

Katherine was in her room and she turned off the stereo when he came in.

Holding her, kissing her hair the way he didn't think he'd done for years, his body shook.

'I love you, Kate,' he said.

Lifting her head she looked at him with a sad little smile. 'I know, but that doesn't matter, does it?'

'What do you mean? Of course it does.'

'No. It's Mum. You should have loved her more.'

*   *   *

Two weeks later, Joanne back home with Katherine and Elder in a rented room, he knocked on the door of the Detective Superintendent's office, walked in and set his warrant card down on the desk, his letter of resignation alongside.

'Take your time, Frank,' the Superintendent said. 'Think it over.'

'I have,' Elder said.

Weasal and the Fish

Peter Turnbull

See me, I can't make relationships. I didn't make a relationship with my mother so I can't make relationships with anyone. I know that 'cos I read my file, like I'm entitled to. See, one of the other lassies in here said you can read your file, Freedom of Information or some such. So I read my file. I managed to learn to read and write before I started to dog school, before I went to live in the drainage duct with the glue sniffers and the alckies and the smack heads. So I read that I can't make relationships because of my old woman, but see her, who *could* make a relationship with her. I mean who'd *want* to? So that was what she wrote, the dark haired woman that I saw once soon after I came here, and asked me stupid questions like, what would I do if I saw a battleship going down the motorway? Daft cow. I mean, what would you do? Then she showed me these inkblots and asked me what I saw in them? So I told her what I saw. In one I saw a cave man battering a cave woman stupid with a club, a big club, giving her a real hiding, and in another I'd see a man getting burned at the stake, and in another there was this wee infant surrounded by wolves. Then she showed me drawings, real neat ink drawings full of detail and asked me what was going on in the picture? One was of this lad up a tree and this lassie running along a path beneath the tree. She showed me this picture and asked me what was happening? Obvious I thought. So I said the lad's going to shin down the tree and run after the girl and murder her. So they fixed me up with Cathy, my counsellor, big motherly-type, big spectacles like a moth on her face. Want to crush the moth. Me and Cathy talk to each other twice a week, about me, about my feelings, but I go along with it, invent feelings. But see me, really I don't have no feelings. I don't have no feelings at all. I mean, what are feelings? And the dark haired woman was wrong. I can make relationships. I can. I made a relationship with Weasal. We had a relationship. We were together for a week.

See the things I liked about Weasal. Still like. See him, he wanted me, seemed to, just me. He wasn't interested in the other stuff not like the other guys, not Weasal, he just wasn't interested. I liked him for that. I mean, I would have let him if he had wanted to but he just didn't. And he didn't drink. All the other guys just existed to get pure blitzed, so they did, but not Weasal. He didn't like the drink and I liked that. I don't like drink. I don't like the people who do it. Weasal didn't drink. I like that in a man. And the other think I liked about Weasal is that he killed people.

See, when I met Weasal I was with a group of lassies passing a bottle of 20/20 around. Except I didn't drink but I was sitting with them. We were in Bridgeton, down the east end, on a bench in a wee park when Weasal came along the road. One of the lassies says 'he's called Weasal, he's off his head. He's a pure headbanger, so he is'. But he looked all right to me. He came up and stood in front of us and all the lassies went quiet like they were feared of him. So he just stood there, hot day, shirt sleeves, blue sky above the red tenements, they orange buses whirring up and down the road. And Weasal standing there, so he looked at me and he says 'you're not on the bevy then, hen? So I said 'no', said I didn't take it. Then he smiled at me and said 'coming with me then, hen?' So I stood up and went with him and he said 'what's your name, hen?' So I said 'The Fish', they call me 'The Fish'. He didn't say anything but he didn't call me 'The Fish'. I liked him for that too. He just called me 'hen', made me feel ordinary. I liked being ordinary. So we walked on and he said 'where do you live?' I said 'the street, and the drainage duct when it's wet'. Then he said 'want to earn some money?' I said 'All right'.

We walked on, seemed to be just cruising round Bridgeton and Weasal said 'See that shop?' I said 'Yes'. It was a totty wee shop, a Daily Record sign above the window, a narrow door, the sort run by Asians. We walked past it and into the next close and stood at the turn of the stair just out of sight of the street and see Weasal, he pulled a plastic bag from his pocket. There was a wig in it, a long blonde-haired wig, and a pair of spectacles and he put them on too. Then he pulled a length of metal from his trousers, shiny, chrome-plated. It was about eighteen inches long and it had a fair weight to it, I could tell by the way Weasal slapped it in his palm. Weasal told me to go back to the shop and buy a copy of the Record. He gave me the money, told me to come back to where we were standing and tell him who was in the shop. So I did. Came back and told Weasal that the only guy in the shop was an Asian guy. Tall, but getting on. No customers, least when I was there. Weasal said 'nice' and he said 'wait there' then he left the close with the bit of metal shoved in his trousers. Seemed to be gone a wee while but he came back and put the wig and spectacles and the length of metal into the plastic bag and gave the bag to me. He told me to walk slowly, really calm like to the end of the street and wait for him. So I did. He also told me not to look at folk. So I didn't. Then Weasal joined me and we heard a klaxon and an ambulance passed us and stopped outside the shop. 'Found him then' said Weasal. We walked into another close and went under the stair and Weasal emptied his pockets; paper money, stamps, envelopes, a ballpoint pen. 'He went down easily,' said Weasal. 'I wasn't being fooled so I gave him a couple more until he started to groan. Can you write, hen?' I said I could. So he gave me the ballpoint and told me to write 'Begg' that was his real name, 'Begg', initial R. *R. Begg.* That was his real name. Then he told me to write, 14, Caledonia Road, Calton, Glasgow. He said I had to write that name and address on each envelope and stick a stamp on each envelope. So I did what I was told, sitting there under the stair, addressing each envelope and sticking a stamp on each, first class stamps I remember. Then he handed me the money and said, 'Count it', so I did. One hundred and ten pounds. He kept the ten pounds back and put the rest in an envelope and sealed it. Then we went out into the sunshine and put the envelope into the first postbox we saw. 'Don't want to get caught with it,' he said. I was learning from him. Then he said 'You still with me, hen?' I said 'Aye, I was, I was still with him'. So then all that day it was the same sketch. We found a wee shop, no customers, found a close nearby, Weasal changed into his disguise, went to the shop, came back with pockets full of paper money and blood on the end of the length of metal. I put the money in an envelope while Weasal got out of his disguise and we'd walk into the sunshine and pop the envelope into a postbox. Then look for another shop. All round the east end we did that, Calton, Bridgeton, the air was full of klaxons, the cops were looking for a guy with glasses and blonde hair. If they saw us they went past, because Weasal had short hair and no glasses and I was with him. They were looking for a guy alone, not a guy with a lassie. We got good at it. So good Weasal didn't have to tell me what to do. We did about ten shops that day, all the while the cops buzzing about like a nest of hornets.

We walked to Calton, a lad with his lass, me and Weasal, and we passed a couple of cops and they didn't give us a second glance even though Weasal was walking with a stiff leg because he'd got his club shoved down his trousers. We got to Caledonian Road, got to number fourteen and went up the close. The door with 'Begg' was one up. 'Begg' was written on a bit of paper stuck to the door. The nameplate proper was 'McPherson'.

Inside it was a tip so it was, but it was better than the drainage duct. Weasal gave me the ten-pound note he'd kept back from the first shop he raided and sent me out for a pizza. That night we watched TV. It was an old black and white set and the aerial was a coat hanger stuck in the back. Weasal slept on a mattress in the bedroom and I curled up on the couch. Before we went to sleep I asked him what sort of flat it was and he said it was a squat, so I said 'oh', like I knew what a 'squat' was. Weasal said he heard the old woman who rented the flat was in hospital so he moved in. When the old guy across the landing asked him who he was Weasal said he was the old woman's nephew and was looking after the flat. After that they didn't bother him. Anyway we had to leave because the gas and electricity were going to be cut off. I liked the way he said 'we'. Made me sleep well that night so it did.

The next morning Weasal said we couldn't go to Edinburgh because he was known to the polis there. He said we couldn't stay in Glasgow because he'd done some things. He said what we did the day before was nothing, nothing. He said he'd got victims in this town and he'd left his fingerprints all over the tills he'd robbed. He said he'd done that deliberately, on purpose. So the police would know who he was. I didn't know why he did that but I knew by then that Weasal knew what he was doing. And as we were talking the postie arrived and all these envelopes went 'flop', 'flop', 'flop' on the hall carpet, it was all the money Weasal had stolen the day before, arriving for us. That was pure dead brilliant. Weasal asked me to count it. I did and it came to one thousand, two hundred and thirty pounds. Weasal said 'We can go a long way with that money, hen'.

'Out of Glasgow?' I asked.

'A long way out of Glasgow' he said.

I told him I'd never been out of Glasgow. Then I made us both some coffee. We hadn't any milk so I went out and bought some. The nearest newsagents sold milk and there was the Record, with Weasal's E-fit on the front page and a write up. Two of the shop-pies Weasal had battered were still out cold and on the critical list. So I went back and told Weasal, I also told him his name was in the paper Begg a.k.a. Weasal and a police photo of him without the wig and glasses – which it was. So he said 'We're going now.'

There was this thrill. I've never felt it before. It was like I was somebody, life felt more real, the sky was bluer, the colours everywhere were stronger, I felt bigger. I knew then that Weasal was the best thing that had happened to me. I still think that. I always will.

★   ★   ★

We went by bus to Kilmarnock. Weasal carried a shoulder bag with him. It's a nice wee town. Weasal gave me some money to buy some clothes and a bag to carry them in. We went into a pub and while Weasal had an orange juice I went to the women's toilets and changed into my new clothes. I left the old ones shoved down the toilet, so I did. We walked out of the pub and Weasal said that we keep going, that's what we do, we keep going and if we want something, we take it. Just like that. I asked if we were going to sleep rough. He said 'No'. He said we stay in folks houses. He said he would show me how it's done. Then I asked him what was in the bag he carried?

'A gun,' he said, 'and some bullets. About fifty. I bought sixty bullets but shot ten off at a quiet place, getting to know the gun.'

We walked on. Weasal said he was sorry it was summer. Too much daylight he said. Autumn's best for badness said Weasal. Dark nights and it's dry. In the summer there's too much daylight, in the winter it's too wet and slushy, but autumn, those few weeks when it's dark and dry. See, that was my Weasal. I couldn't think like that, I just couldn't.

Killing someone wasn't as bad as I thought it would be. Fact is, it was fun. I felt really … I don't know, really *someone*.

The first thing we had to do was sight up a house. We walked out of Killie under the railway bridge and got out into an area of fancy private houses. Weasal wanted a house with a car in the drive and one which looked like the owner was old. It's not easy sighting up a house in the suburbs, you can't wander about looking at houses, that gives the game away. You have to walk looking dead ahead and sight up houses from a distance, then a quick glance while you're passing. Weasal found three or four which he reckoned were o.k. and out of them settled on one. I remember it well, a white painted bungalow, with neat gardens and a small white car in the drive. Weasal said that the car was an old woman's motor and the garden was a pensioners, too neat for a working person. It was an old woman's house who has a guy come and do the garden.

Then we had a stroke of luck. It's just the way it happened. We were walking past the house when the old woman came out of her house with a shopping bag. She got into her car and drove out of the drive and down the road. Weasal said to keep walking because she's got a rear view mirror and we didn't want her to see us loitering about her house. When she had turned the corner, Weasal went back to the house crunching on gravel as hard as he could and rang the front door bell. Later he told me that if someone had answered he would have asked them if 'Joe' was at home and then kidded on he had mistakenly come to the wrong house. We went round the side of the house to where the woman had come from. Weasal said if she let herself out of the back door, she'd likely let herself in there. So we waited in the back garden, squeezed between a garden shed and a privet hedge. We made a bit of noise because a cat appeared at the window and then went away again. We sat there and waited. Weasal said she'd gone with a shopping bag, so she was away to get her shopping, so she'd be back soon. We just had to sit and wait. So we did. I liked that, the garden, the silence, the flowers. She had trees round her garden to keep her garden private I should think. Suited us, meant we couldn't be seen. The woman came back after an hour. We heard the car. Weasal said to keep quiet and he took the metal bar from his bag. I kept still, I was calm, sort of peaceful inside. We heard her walk round the back of the house, just one set of footsteps, then we heard keys rattle in a lock, then the woman said 'Hello, Pixie Puss'. Called her cat 'Pixie Puss'. Then Weasal struck. Moved fast. I heard a dull 'thud', as he hit the woman with the iron bar. Then he hit her again and again. Then he called me. 'Come on, hen.' So I joined him. We were standing over the woman, her blood was on the kitchen floor. We closed the back door. Weasal said to look round the house, make sure it was empty. I did and it was. Back in the kitchen I asked if the woman was dead and Weasal said she was. She was the first dead person I'd seen. Apart from the blood, she looked as if she was asleep. We took some cans of food from her larder and then pushed her in there.

We spent the rest of the day in her house. We both had a bath and then a good sleep. When we woke it was dark. Weasal shut the curtains and put on the lights. Weasal went about touching things but told me to find a pair of gloves and wear them all the time. He said they could have his prints but not mine. I made us a meal, just stuff from cans, while Weasal searched the house for cash. He found twenty pounds but it was better than nothing. And we'd washed and rested. That was the main thing. Before we left the house, Weasal made me do a weird thing. He made me take the woman's lipstick and write a message on her dressing table mirror. I had to write 'Please stop me'. So I did. 'Please stop me'. Later that night, near midnight, we shut off all the lights and opened the curtains so the house would look normal in the morning and took the woman's car and drove away. It was nearly out of fuel so Weasal said we had to stop and buy some. He said each time we stopped we had to fill up so that way we'd keep down the times the car was caught on the cameras the garages have. We saw a filling station and Weasal stopped the car and told me to get out and walk beyond the station and wait for him on the other side. That way it would look like he was alone. So I did. He put his wig and spectacles on and drove into the forecourt of this filling station which was all lit up like a spaceship, so it was. I waited for him like he told me to and he drove up and picked me up and we drove towards Ayr. Folk went to Ayr for their holidays and I'd heard it was a fun place but I never did see it, 'cos Weasal pulled up and stopped. He looked around the car and saw that the wee woman had a road atlas in the back seat and he picked it up and said, 'Do you know how to read a map?' So I said 'I knew fine how to read a map.' So he said right, which way's north from here?

'Just follow the signs to Glasgow' I said.

'No.' He was getting angry. 'Tell me to go left or right or straight on. Understand?'

'Aye.'

'And I don't want to go anywhere near Glasgow. All right!'

'Well, we're too late for the ferry across the Clyde' I told him. 'So it'll have to be the tunnel.' So he reckoned that that was fine. Told me to tell him the way to the tunnel. So I did, saying, 'turn around and back to Killie.' Then it was left or right, or straight on until we got to the tunnel and went through it. We got onto the Expressway and I took him out towards Crianlarich, up the side of

305

Loch Lomond. I remember how it gleamed in the moonlight.

We drove all night. Weasal was a good, steady driver, not too fast, not too slow. We drove to Fort William and stopped. It was about three in the morning, beginning to get light, but still and quiet. Weasal said we had to get out of the town because a night cop might clock us. He said we looked suspicious and they could stop us for that. So he drove out of the town and turned left and asked me where the road went to. So I looked at the map and said Mallaig. I'd heard of Mallaig as a place for a holiday too, not as nice as Ayr, but folk went there, or they caught a ferry from there, or such like. I never got to Ayr and I never got to Mallaig. Weasal drove up a side road and stopped beside an old building. It looked eerie in the half light.

We sat there. Didn't feel tired. One or two cars went by as the morning went in, folk driving to Fort William for a day's work. At eight o'clock we went back to Fort William and split up for an hour. I ate breakfast in a cafe. I met up with Weasal at the car. He'd got a can of spray paint and had fastened a Union Jack to the car aerial. He'd got the flag from a wee gift shop, the sort that sells daft wee plastic models of the Loch Ness Monster. Then we drove back to beside the old building which looked like it had been a school house. There was no reason why we should have gone there, it's just that we knew it was there, so we went. Weasal spray-painted the car blue. Didn't look like the colour blue it was supposed to be but it wasn't white any more. Weasal said that soon the cops would be stopping every white VW Polo in Scotland on account of the wee woman's body would be found today, stuffed in her larder with her head battered in, and her car noticed missing, and him in disguise buying fuel for the old woman's car at the filling station, that would be on film, that would. So we spent the day lying in the heather while the paint dried on the car. When we were lying there Weasal said only one thing. He said the Union Jack was to make folk think that we were bastard English. Only the bastard English would fly a Union Jack, the Scots would fly the St Andrew's Cross. So we had a blue Polo with a bastard English flag on the aerial. Weasal said that that might stop a cop being suspicious. That was Weasal, he thought of everything. When the paint was dry, we drove back into Fort William. 'Same sketch as Killie,' Weasal said. 'Find a likely house, batter our way in, rest up, then leave after dark.'

* * *

The first time Weasal gave me a hiding I deserved it. And it wasn't a proper hiding not like I remember my dad giving my mum before he left for the last time. He just couldn't take it anymore and when she came home with another good drink in her 'cos she'd spent all the 'social' money on booze. So he gave her a real kicking. I mean he put her blood everywhere. Then he picked me up and put me in a taxi and took me to the Welfare people and carried me into their office and sat me on the receptionist's desk and ran back out and went away in the taxi and I never saw him again. They put me in a foster home and I stayed for four days. It was on the fourth day that I lit a fire in the living room, anything I could find to burn, paper mostly, didn't get a proper hold 'cos the family dog started yapping and the foster mother came in and screamed then poured water over it. Then I was put in a children's home, then another, each one harder than the last 'cos I was a 'behavioural problem'. That's what they said. Anyway, Weasal didn't give me a doing like my dad gave my mum. Slapped my head a couple of times. That was all.

After we met up again in Fort William, we went to another café to get off the street. I sat opposite him and then I saw his eyes. Really beautiful eyes. I mean eyes I like, steely, cold, but not just that, it was like looking into two endless tunnels when you looked into his eyes, two bottomless wells, they just go deeper and deeper and deeper and you can't tell if there's any feeling in them at all. But it's there 'cos he could get angry so he could. But the other thing I liked about his eyes, one was blue and the other was green. So I said that. I said, 'Weasal, one of your eyes is green and the other is blue' and he said 'Hey!' and grabbed my arm and pulled me out of the café. I knew folk were looking at us but that didn't bother Weasal, he slapped me around the head, right there in the café. He bundled me into the Polo and we drove off. I never mentioned his eyes again. But I sometimes wonder if me mentioning his eyes set him off so he killed the woman? I don't mean the old woman in Killie. I mean the other one, the one that was built like a Highland cow, the second one we did.

It happened like this. We'd been hanging around F.W. all day, meeting up and then separating for an hour and as it was getting dark Weasal said we needed to hide. He also said we needed to change the car. So we set off to cruise around the town. F.W. isn't a big place, smaller than a Glasgow housing scheme, so we got to know it well. Nothing for us in the council schemes, or the bought houses so we moved a wee bit out of the town and we found a house standing in its own grounds, stone built with bay windows. Weasal liked it because it had no gate and a grass driveway. Weasal said that they hadn't invented house breakers in F.W. so that's how folk could live with no gates and a grass drive. There was no car in the drive but Weasal said we couldn't have everything. I waited by the house trying to get the measure of it on the sly, while Weasal went into F.W. to get the Polo fuelled up. He wanted to get his photo taken by the filling station camera but not in disguise. So he looked different than he looked when he got the car filled up in Killie and anyway the car was now blue. He reckoned that would fool the cops long enough for us to get out of the town. When he came back I told him a light had gone on in the house and I saw an old woman once or twice moving about. But she wasn't a small woman, she was built like a prison warder. I didn't see anyone else. I saw her when she was closing her curtains and she saw me, and her, the look she gave me, like I was a bit of dirt, me, I've had that look all my life. I really wanted to be there when Weasal beat her head to pulp with his length of shiny metal.

'Just one person and the curtains drawn,' Weasal smiled. 'That makes it easier. But there could be more than one person, we'll have to take that chance. The good thing about my situation is that I can't get any deeper. I am at rock bottom. Doesn't matter how many folk I kill, they can only throw the key away once.'

'And me' I said, 'I'm in deep too. I'm in with you Weasal.'

'No, hen' he said. 'I need you, but you'll never be in deep. I'm going to make sure of that.'

Made me feel warm inside that did. I've never been needed before. But I was needed then.

When it was dark, we went back to the house. Got close to it. No alarm. No dog. Heard music playing, fancy stuff, classical, violins and that. Weasal said the only thing we had to worry about was if the woman had a chain on the inside of her door but he said it was unlikely because no alarm and no dog meant she was unlikely to have a chain. Me, I knew she wouldn't have a chain, see that big old cow of a woman, glaring at folk with an 'I'm the boss' attitude, I knew she'd swing her door open demanding to know who was knocking on her door at that time of night. Which is exactly what happened. It was then that Weasal pulled the trigger. Just once. But it was enough. I felt really good to see that little hole in her forehead. It felt good to see her fall backwards into her own hallway. That was sweet, when I thought of that dirty look she gave me, that was a sweet sight to see her dead. Weasal didn't hesitate, went straight to the phone in the hall and knocked it off its hook. 'If there's anyone else in the house, they can't use an extension now' he said. Then he said 'Don't worry about the gunshot, it wasn't as loud as it sounded.'

We pulled her away from the door and then shut it. She was too heavy to move so we left her in the hall. Weasal told me to go from room to room, make sure she was alone in the house. I did and she was. Her house had five bedrooms. Five! But only one bed was made up. All the other beds were not. And the air in the other bedrooms was musty. So no one would be coming home there that night and me and Weasal could relax. That's what I thought but when I went downstairs, I saw Weasal standing over the woman's body saying 'This is bad, bad, bad. This is wrong, shouldn't do this … wrong …bad … bad …bad boy. Very bad boy.' But it didn't seem wrong to me. Nothing wrong at all. The only thing I was sorry about is that she didn't see me, she didn't know I was a partner of Weasal's. I thought that next time Weasal drills a nasty who deserves to die, I'll make sure they see me standing there, smiling.

We freshened up in her house. We ate her food. We watched her TV but when the news came on Weasal turned the TV off and said it was time we slept. We shared her bed, lying side by side. But Weasal didn't touch me. I loved him for that. And when he saw my body without clothes, because we'd both washed our clothes and left them drying on a radiator, he didn't bat an eyelid. I loved him for that as well.

So the next morning, when the clothes were dry, I crept out of the house, leaving Weasal snoring and I went to a newspaper shop and bought a copy of the Record. I was learning from Weasal and so I acted natural and pretended I wasn't really interested in the headlines. I didn't react 'cos people always look at me and also I knew Weasal wouldn't want me to react. So I bought a Record and went back to the woman's house without looking left or right. I went into her kitchen and made a cup of tea and read the paper.

We'd made the headlines, me and Weasal. The woman in Killie had been found and her white VW Polo was noticed to be missing, the paper gave the registration number, but then Weasal had repainted it and stuck an English flag on the aerial so I reckoned we'd be alright for a while yet. Anyway, I read about me and Weasal and what we'd done. The woman in Killie was called Bush, Sonia Bush, she was 66 years old and a retired school teacher. Her son was travelling up from London to sort things so that was alright. There was a street map of Killie showing where her house was and one or two folk were quoted as saying what a nice woman she was. See that helped no one. Being nice wouldn't help you if you messed with me and Weasal when me and Weasal were travelling. Then I got onto the bit about Weasal. They knew it was him 'cos he'd left his prints everywhere. His real name was Rory Begg, 28 years old, a.k.a. 'Weasal' because of his small build and staring eyes between a pointed nose. He'd been in the State Hospital since he was 16 until a year ago when he was discharged as 'incurable'. So they let him out. Just like that. Lucky me though, I mean, without Weasal where would I be ? I'd be in the drainage duct with the rest of them. Thanks be to Weasal. Then it said he had an accomplice because Weasal had left a message for the cops in lipstick on the woman's mirror, but Weasal was known not to be able to read or write or count.

That's when I knew why he needed me. He needed me to count the money, he needed me to read the road signs 'cos all he knew was his left from his right from straight on. And he needed me to write the messages for the cops. So he was a totty wee guy, so he had different coloured eyes, so he couldn't read or write or count numbers. But he never called me 'Fish' and he could kill people. What more could a lassie want?

When Weasal woke up and came down to the kitchen I told him I'd been out and that we'd made the headlines in the Record. He threw a blue one and he gave me a real hiding, right there in the kitchen, fist, boot, slap. I was screaming … blood everywhere … seeing double. When he'd calmed he said he didn't want to know. He didn't want to know what the cops knew. I couldn't understand that, I may be big and stupid but I would want to know what the cops knew, I would have thought the whole idea was to keep going for as long as we could. It would help if we knew what the cops knew, I would have thought. But Weasal knew best so I went along with what he wanted. I washed the blood from my mouth and nose and then we ate some food. Before we left the old woman's house, Weasal took me upstairs and he made me write a message on the woman's dressing table mirror, just like I'd done in Killie. This time I had to write 'Catch me quickly. I'll be doing it again'.

We drove from F.W. to Inverness along the banks of Loch Ness. I looked for the monster but I never saw anything, just a lot of water and a boat or two. I enjoyed the drive, I was learning about Scotland, the green and the blue, the hills and the valleys and the lochs. I grew up in Glasgow, I never left the city until I chummed up with Weasal. I never knew why guys in kilts came on the TV and sang songs about Bonnie Scotland until I took that drive with Weasal. Now I know. Towards the end of the journey we saw a cop car at the side of the road. Weasal said to hold the Road Atlas up in front of my face so we'd look like bastard English. See me, it was the first time I ever wanted to be a bastard English but it worked because the cop didn't pull us. But Weasal wasn't happy, he said that we couldn't go on depending on a colour change of the car so we had to ditch it and steal another. See him, see Weasal, there were times I couldn't fathom him. First he acted like he wants to be caught, then he doesn't.

We got to Inverness and Weasal parked up as close as he could get to the town centre without worrying about parking restrictions. We were sitting there as a cop drove past, he slowed to look at us and then speeded up. Weasal said, 'That's it.' We got out of the car and split up. We agreed to meet at the bus station an hour later. We did that and took a bus north. Weasal said he wanted out of Inverness fast. So we took the first bus north, into the Black Isle.

The end, when it came, came quickly. Very quickly. We were in the Black Isle, it was night. We were walking. We were tired and hungry. We saw a campsite but walked past. It was well turned midnight by the time Weasal saw what he wanted. It was a camper van, parked up a lane, a long way from anywhere. The light in the van was switched on. We crept closer and heard two people talking, a man and a woman. They were having an argument.

Weasal said we had to kill them. It's wrong he said, but we had to do it. I asked him if I could do it? Weasal looked at me. It was the only time I ever saw emotion in his eyes. He looked worried, I mean worried for me. Then he said, 'All right hen, all right, you can do it. But I'll kill the guy, you can kill the girl.' That suited me. I thought then that that would suit me fine, especially if she was a slim bitch, like those girls at school, like them, that day in the shower when I slipped and went on my back. I've always been big, I can't help it, I'd be slim if I could, but lying there, struggling to get up and all those slim girls standing round me giggling. One said 'She looks like a beached whale' and then they all started chanting 'whale, whale, whale...' Then that was my nickname for a few days until they hit on 'Fish' instead and finally they settled for 'The Fish'. See me, I hated those girls. I pure hated them. Hate, hate, hate to kill. I started dogging school then and went to live with the glue sniffers in the drainage duct. I was with them for a few days until Weasal came along and I went with him 'cos he called me 'hen' like I was normal and I read the road signs for him, and I counted the money for him. Oh, yes, and I wrote messages with lipstick for him.

Anyway Weasal knocked on the door of the van, gun in hand. The couple stopped arguing and the guy opened the van door. The one thing he shouldn't have done and it was the one thing he did do. But my Weasal didn't hesitate. Up comes the gun and the guy's flung backwards into the camper with a bullet in his head. I took the gun from him and I went into the van, and oh, it was lovely, this woman, slim and slender, just like the girls in the shower that time. She wasn't one of them, but she was close enough for me. She wasn't laughing, sort of whimpering, like a dog that wants something. All the while Weasal was saying 'Do it, do it, don't hesitate ... no .... this is wrong ... this is wrong ... stop me, stop me ... stop me ...' But me, I thought, see me, this isn't wrong. It's so good, it can't be wrong ... and I shot her in the chest. She slumped back and started to make gurgling sounds so I shot her again. And again. Weasal took the gun from me and wiped my prints off it. We stayed all night in the van, him in the driver's seat and me in the passenger seat, and the dead couple behind us. We sat there until well after dawn and all night Weasal kept saying 'No ... no ... no ... wrong ... wrong ... this is wrong, wrong ...' But he reloaded the gun anyway.

About nine in the morning Weasal started the camper and drove off, out of the lane. He struggled at first. He said it was a bitch to drive but eventually he seemed to get the hang of it. Then he laid a hand on my leg and said 'I shouldn't have got you into this … I shouldn't, but I've worked out a way to get you out.' And I put my hand on his. We came to the main road, green fields all around, a wide blue sky. He said, 'Will you do what I tell you to do?' I said I would. At the main road he stopped and put on the handbrake. He waited as a few cars passed us going south towards Inverness or north, deeper into the Black Isle. Then he saw a truck moving slowly south. He said, 'This will do.' He told me to get out and pull the body of the guy out of the van and onto the grass verge. So I did. He got out too and went round the van and pointed the gun at me while I was doing what he told me to do. I saw the truck driver's face as he passed, wide-eyed, open mouthed. Then he looked straight ahead and speeded up.

We turned north then, towards Cromarty and drove through this lush green countryside. I'll never know why they called it the Black Isle. It's not black, it's green. And it's not an island. Weasal saw a house by the road and a guy sitting in the front garden on a bench. Weasal said 'Same sketch.' He told me to pull the woman from the back of the camper and dump her body on the verge. I did so and all the while he held the gun on me. As we drove off I saw the guy stand up from the bench and run into his house. I glanced at Weasal and he was smiling. I knew he knew what he was doing. Weasal always did.

★　★　★

The Fatal Accident Inquiry was told that four bullets hit Weasal but I only heard three. I suppose two were … what's that word … simul-something. Anyway, I swear to God I only heard three.

Looking back, the first sign of the end was when there was no traffic coming towards us. None behind us either. Next thing was a police helicopter flying above and behind us. Weasal saw it and smiled. From then on he never stopped smiling until he died. And he was relaxed. Totally relaxed. We cleared a crest of the road and in front of us was a roadblock. One car and one van. Blue lights revolving and headlights on. Cops with guns and body armour. Weasal slowed. I remember the green fields around us, the blue sky, no other roads leading off. Just a straight road to the road-block and the helicopter above us. I knew, I just knew that the cops would be behind us as well. Weasal stopped short of the roadblock, about the length of two buses. Weasal got out and walked round the back of the van and round to my side and told me to get out. So I did. Then he pulled the gun and stood behind me and walked towards the roadblock. The cops kept yelling that they were armed police and he was to drop the gun but that didn't bother Weasal. They yelled at him to 'let the girl go'. Me a girl? Like I was slim and slender. Funny that. Then he stopped us from walking. He just said 'stop' so I did. He stood at the side of me, gun by his side. I remember a bird singing. He lifted the gun and pointed it at my head. At the inquiry they said he was shot four times, but like I said, I only heard three shots. I remember, someone had hold of me and was saying, 'Alright hen, you're safe now.' I didn't give anything away but inside I was all smiles.

They decided I had no case to answer about they murders. See, they had people who'd seen Weasal batter me in a café in F.W. And I still had bruises from where he'd given me a kicking for bringing a copy of the Record to the woman's house, and two folk had each seen me unloading a body at gun point, like two different times, one witness to each time, and the cops said I was being ordered about by Weasal who was holding a gun on me. But they did decide I was a danger to myself, couldn't let me go or else I'd be back in the drainage duct. So I got a one year residential supervision order. So I'm in here, attending the Christian Union like a regular gaol house convert, and once I volunteered to unblock the toilets when it was the caretakers day off – I did well for myself there. I'm really smoothing my way through here, talking to the dark-haired woman who asks me what I see in drawings and speaks to me about battleships and motorways. And I talk to my counsellor, with the big glasses like a moth that I want to squash, who says she's fond of me and that I have to like myself more. I think a lot about Weasal. I think what he taught me, about disguise and fingerprints. I learned all that. And I learned that I can kill, and I learned I like it, killing people. I like it. Anyway, I keep all that to myself, and I keep myself to myself. I do what I'm told when I'm told and I don't make waves. That way I'll slither out of here. Got my twelve month review soon. I reckon I'll be out then. I'll be 16. Just turned.

The Rightful King of England

Amy Myers

Were the English *all* completely mad? Auguste Didier, safe in the comfort of knowing he was half French, fumed as he ran through the gardens of Stalisford Place, hunting for their owner, the host of this crazy assembly. It was only because Sir Henry Arthur was a member of Plum's Club for Gentlemen, for which Auguste was chef, that he had found himself agreeing to cook the feast for this day. This was partly, he conceded, because Sir Henry had ordered a medieval banquet, preceded by a lighter luncheon. Now the highlight of the evening's dinner would be ruined for the eccentric baronet had vanished; his guests were growing hungry and somewhat concerned. They had every reason to be, in Auguste's opinion. All the members of Plum's were strange in their behaviour, but Sir Henry outstripped them all. Perhaps he had set off to blow up the Houses of Parliament?

There was no sign of him in the main garden and Auguste had hardly expected there to be. If he was here at all, he would no doubt be found admiring the scene of his coronation which had taken place earlier that afternoon. Auguste cautiously went through the opening in the tall yew tree hedge that surrounded the Tudor knot garden. Jig-jagging grass paths divided the jig-jagging borders of herbs, laid out to an ancient turf maze plan, and leading eventually to the centre to which the eye of the onlooker was taken.

Auguste's immediately was. His quest was over.

There, by the sundial, lay sprawled the body of the Rightful King of England.

*   *   *

'Didier,' Sir Henry had roared in appreciation at luncheon that day. 'After I'm crowned, I'll dub you knight for this. Howdyer like that?'

Auguste had bowed his head in apparent gratitude at the tribute

315

from this soon-to-be-crowned king of England.

'You can't dub him anything, Henry.' Enid Arthur was a female version of her brother. She looked some years older, had a snappier tongue and, if Auguste guessed right, saw no reason that women should not have equal rights to the monarchy. 'He's a citizen of France, and you know what they do to aristocrats. He'll poison you before the day's out.'

Auguste tried to keep his smile pleasant.

'Goddamit, I'll be crowned king in half an hour,' Sir Henry roared at his sister, 'I'll do what I blasted well like. Be silent or I'll have your head off. What do you say to it, Ruggles?'

Charles Ruggles, a stalwart Scottish gentleman in his early thirties was, Auguste had gathered, special advisor on constitutional law to the present royal family, and had presumably been dispatched by the Prince of Wales, on behalf of his elderly mother Queen Victoria, to dissuade Henry from his rash venture. Nevertheless, Auguste was somewhat puzzled, since Ruggles bore little resemblance to any lawyer he'd ever met. Paid assassin came more to mind from the man's build and silent watchfulness.

'I doubt if the law would uphold your beheading your sister, sir,' Ruggles diplomatically replied.

'Not that, you fool. What about knighting a Frenchman?' Sir Henry growled.

'There are precedents' Professor Launcelot Arthur intoned gravely. He was, Auguste had been told, Sir Henry's cousin and, as the nearest male relative, was next in line for the throne. 'When I was digging in Egypt –'

'I,' glared Enid, 'am not a mummy.'

'Launcelot,' his wife Jane came in weightily to support him, '*knows* about these things.' From the accounts of her exploits in the Press, she was a formidable woman. While her husband ferreted underground in Egypt, his wife donned thick bloomers and boots and strode up mountains. They looked at least ten years younger than Sir Henry, and therefore could probably look forward to some years wearing the crown. Auguste caught himself impatiently – twenty-four hours in this household were affecting his own brain.

Launcelot looked smug at this tribute. 'I'll make you an Order of the Blue Lotus, Didier, when I'm king. Ever tried cooking with blue lotus?'

'No, sir,' Auguste murmured, trying to inch slowly backwards out of the dining hall. 'Thank you, sir.'

Enid snorted. 'You won't cook for us again. I don't trust foreigners with our food.'

Auguste decided it was time to put an end to this charade. He ignored the slur and addressed his host from the doorway.

'You're most kind, Sir Henry, but I seek no knighthood. My reward is in giving pleasure to those who eat my cuisine.'

It was a well-used phrase, though he meant it, and usually had its effect in extracting him from awkward situations. Not this time.

'Tell you what,' Sir Henry offered, inspired. 'You can lead the coronation procession, Didier. Old Venables won't mind, will you?' He turned to his least objectionable guest.

The Reverend William Venables, rector of Stalisford, whose living was in the gift of Sir Henry, hastily shook his head. 'No, sir.' To him would fall the honour of crowning the new monarch, but his silence and woebegone face suggested he was not looking forward to it, and would be only too glad to cede this function to Auguste as well.

'Thank you, Sir Henry,' Auguste muttered in resignation.

'Bang the gong, then, there's a good chap,' Sir Henry boomed. 'Time to get going.'

Demoted from knight to butler, Auguste crossly went into the passageway to obey. It appeared the gong was the arranged signal for the entire staff of Stalisford Place (twenty-eight indoor and fifteen outdoor) to form a corridor outside the front entrance of the house. At the end of it, the 'Royal' Golden Coach (one of Sir Henry's carriages smothered in gold paint) awaited its owner. The procession now approached. Sir Henry, bearing a look of the utmost gravity and clad in a coronation robe of purple velvet edged with white fur, climbed into the coach alone. It was Auguste's lot to walk before the two horses, whose breath was increasingly close behind him as if they could not wait to get back to their stables. Enid followed the coach with Charles Ruggles, Launcelot and Jane strode behind, and the long robes of the Reverend Venables flapped miserably around his legs as he brought up the rear. The carriage set off at a slow, dignified pace round the house to its rear and then took the long, winding path down to the knot garden.

Amy Myers

There Sir Henry stepped down in regal fashion from the carriage and marched along the twisting grass paths to the centre mound of the garden. The rest of the party fell in behind him, picking their way cautiously over the narrow paths. The shadow on the sundial proclaimed it was about two-thirty, and the engraved motto on its side: 'How quickly the pleasant days have passed away'. Personally Auguste couldn't wait for this one to end. It was too high a price to pay even for the pleasure of presenting dressed 'peacock', flower garden salad and cheese curd tarts.

Two of the gardeners were standing ready for the signal to reveal the sundial's recently discovered treasure. Auguste had not seen it, but it was on this that Sir Henry's claim was based and which Ruggles was to inspect. Sir Henry climbed on to his throne, placed at the sundial's side. Originally a humble wooden chair, for this day of glory it had been painted gold, adorned with golden cushions and surmounted by a cloth of gold embroidered King Henry IX.

'Get on with it,' Sir Henry impatiently ordered his men, who were labouring to pull the entire sundial aside to reveal an ancient box which it had been concealing within its hollow centre.

'I'll tae a wee look at that.' Charles Ruggles strode forward.

'Doubtful of my claim, are you?' Sir Henry growled. 'No need. The marriage was legal all right, and here's the proof.'

Suddenly Auguste ceased to think of this as a boring farce. It had become all too real, and there were some intense passions at stake. This dotty family, craning eagerly towards the box, really believed in its heritage. Even in its age-worn state, the lid still boasted the initials MA, for Lady Margaret Arthur, daughter of the Earl of Stalisford.

'Come here, Didier,' ordered the king-to-be. Auguste's heart sank. He had hoped to be able to melt into the background like butter in a hot sauce. 'Open the box and give Venables the crown.'

Genuinely curious, however, Auguste obeyed. The crown within the box gleamed, for it had already been cleaned and replaced for the occasion. It was hardly a rival to King Edward's crown, being little more than a diadem, but it was undoubtedly gold. Next to it, lying on a velvet cushion was a ring, a woven circle of golden strands, with a sapphire and ruby set into it.

'The Ring of Kingly Dignity. Part of my regalia.' Sir Henry's eyes gleamed.

'Where's the proof of the marriage?' Charles Ruggles asked quietly.

'Get out the register, Didier.'

Venable showed somewhat more interest as Auguste lifted out the decaying volume from the bottom of the box. The parish priests of Stalisford had been unusually zealous in obeying the edict from King Henry VIII to keep registers of births, marriages and deaths. The registers from mid-1540 onwards had been impeccably maintained, but the register from 1538, the year of the edict, to the early part of 1540 was missing from the church records – if, of course, it had ever existed. It had, and here it now was, a trifle sorry for itself, but still clearly legible. Auguste watched Sir Henry gleefully turn the pages and give it to Charles Ruggles.

'Here you are, complete with the tick to show royalty's involved. November 14th 1538: Henry Tudor to Margaret Arthur, and in the same handwriting a note, Daughter of the Earl of Stalisford to Henry VIII of England.'

'I should have succeeded after Edward VI died,' his descendant claimed, 'and before those women robbed me of my throne.'

'You weren't there at the time,' Enid pointed out. 'And why shouldn't women come to the throne?'

'If I'd been king then, I wouldn't have had all these executions for a start. Except for you, maybe,' her brother snarled. 'If you look at the end of the register, Ruggles, you'll find their son's baptism: Bedivere Tudor, 16th September '39. And Margaret's death three weeks later.'

Auguste knew that every year, Sir Henry celebrated the day on which by his rights he should have succeeded to the throne, the day of Edward VI's death, 6 July 1553. This coronation, however, was taking place in early June, and no doubt this was an added reason for Ruggles' presence since Queen Victoria's Golden Jubilee would be taking place very shortly.

'Any objections, Ruggles?' Sir Henry boomed. 'You've no need to worry. I'll see Victoria's treated well. She can keep Osborne and Balmoral, if she likes. I'll take the Palace and Windsor.'

'No objection, sir,' Charles Ruggles replied.

'I'll be Your Majesty in a few minutes,' Henry chortled proudly. 'Let the coronation proceed. Step forward, Venables.'

Auguste had gathered that the coronation service as held in Westminster Abbey was an extremely long process, and had been fearing that that evening's feast would be kept waiting for many hours. He need not have worried. The king-to-be had written his own service.

Two musicians, whom Auguste recognized as underfootmen dressed in doublet and hose for the occasion, stepped forward with lutes, while two trumpets sounded a fanfare outside the garden; between them to the best of their ability given this inadequate orchestra, they played 'The Arrival of the Queen of Sheba', 'The Hallelujah Chorus' and 'Greensleeves' in strict rotation over and over again.

The Reverend Venables cast a look of desperation at Auguste, stepped forward and began to babble.

'Speak up!' Jane Arthur roared. 'Launcelot is the heir, after all.'

'Not before I'm dead,' Enid snarled. 'I come next, don't I, Mr Ruggles?'

'I think constitutionally –' Ruggles began hesitantly.

'I don't think constitutionally,' she snapped. 'I think equality.'

'I'd make a better monarch,' Launcelot said belligerently.

'And so you shall,' his wife said fondly. 'You're a lot younger than Henry. You'll rule for years.'

'Do you mind waiting till I'm dead?' Henry hissed. 'I haven't even been crowned yet.'

Venables cleared his throat, and began again to read from the long parchment declaration he had been handed.

'Our new king presents his right to rule the kingdoms of England, Wales, Scotland and Ireland, and the countries of the British Empire. In 1537 the dearly beloved wife of his ancestor Henry VIII, Jane Seymour, died after giving birth to the future Edward VI. Henry mourned her fully six months, but reluctantly realized that it was his duty to marry again; the babe was sickly and he had no other male heir. When he fell in love, however, it was with Lady Margaret Arthur, daughter of the Catholic Earl of Stalisford. Henry truly loved Margaret but was forced to wed her in secret. The newly formed Church of England, which he himself had so recently created in order to divorce his Catholic wife, could hardly countenance another Catholic wife so soon after its establishment, and most certainly not any heir she might bear.'

'Hurry up,' interrupted Sir Henry.

Venables cast him a scared look and doubled his pace: 'In the unlikely event that his son Edward died without issue, the country would accept his Catholic elder sister as monarch, because she was born before he had created the new church, but they would not accept Bedivere. The church would be doomed. Alas, Margaret too died in childbirth in October 1539. Henry, while sincerely mourning Margaret, realized it was his duty to marry again. Four months later he married the Protestant Anne of Cleves, but as is well known he did not live with her. And why not? Not, as tradition says, because she was ugly, but because he remained devoted to the memory of Margaret. It sincerely grieved him to condemn to death for religious reasons the Earl of Stalisford and the priest who had performed the marriage ceremony in 1538. When Henry later married again for love, he honoured the memory of Margaret by placing a crown and a ring where earlier they had hidden the register containing the truth of their marriage. It was then that the sundial gained its loving inscription: How quickly passed the pleasant days. Henry loved her so much he wanted Margaret's child or children's children to inherit when the country was ready for a Catholic ruler again. He has waited many years, but now, thanks be to God, who works in mysterious ways, his dream has come true and the descendants of Bedivere Tudor will sit upon the throne of England.'

This did not seem to reflect the King Henry VIII known to history, Auguste thought, but perhaps there had indeed been a nicer side to his nature than wife-butcher.

The Reverend Venables then shook out another huge parchment roll on which was a family tree proving Arthur's descent from Margaret Arthur.

'And what's more,' Henry shouted in defiance of all coronation etiquette, 'I didn't get the name Arthur by accident. Lady Margaret was descended from the great king of England.'

'That's how I came to be Launcelot. I shall be,' said the professor in some awe, 'King Launcelot I of England.'

'I'll be Queen Enid first,' snapped Enid.

'And I *am* King Henry IX,' roared the pending king. 'Put that crown on, Venables.'

'I crown thee King of England, in the eyes of God, the present so-called Royal family, your dearly beloved family here assembled, and the people of this nation.' The Rector picked up the diadem and nervously placed it on the new king's head, as Ruggles stirred uneasily.

'I canna think –'

'Be quiet,' Enid snapped. 'We all have to shout God Save the King now.'

A weak chorus ensued, with the musicians and gardeners looking uncertain as to whether they were of sufficient rank to join in.

'You canna claim Scotland,' Ruggles pointed out. 'It wasn't united with England then.'

'It is now,' Sir Henry retorted. 'I'm emperor of half the world.'

'What about Egypt?' Launcelot asked eagerly. 'I'd like to be king of that.'

'We don't formally rule it,' Ruggles murmured.

'If I have anything to do with it, you'll have it, darling,' Jane declared.

'Anoint me, Venables,' snarled Henry.

'No sir,' Venables quavered. 'I cannot do that. This is not holy oil.'

'That should have come before the crowning.' Ruggles seemed to be getting into the spirit of the thing now, to Auguste's amusement.

'This is my service, not yours. Bless the oil then, Venables, and then dab it on.'

Venables, clearly expecting his head to be removed with a garden scythe, bravely replied again, 'No, sir.'

'All right,' Henry glared. 'Then put the Kingly Ring upon my finger, give me the orb and sceptre, and then everyone can pay me homage. You too, Didier.'

To Auguste, a farce should stuff a goose, not provide antics on a summer afternoon. This additional service would be reflected in the size of his bill.

Hitherto he had assumed that the gardeners were leaning on sticks, but now he saw, as they hastily pushed them into Venables' arms for onward passage to the new king, an iron sword obviously removed from the ancestral collection in the smoking room, and what seemed to be a poker with an improvised orb of paper surmounted by a cross stuck on its end. It made a strange contrast with the undoubtedly genuine golden crown, but after Venables had clasped the ring upon his finger, the new monarch received them eagerly enough.

'Enid,' barked her new monarch, 'you begin the homage.'

She walked forward, glaring at her brother. 'I do thee homage, King Henry, but only until women have their due rights. I am, after all, the elder of us.' She extended her hands clasped palm to palm, and her brother snatched them firmly with his – after a short delay to tuck the orb and sceptre behind him. She was followed by Launcelot and Jane carrying out the same ritual.

'Ruggles,' the new king then demanded.

'As a solicitor, working for the other side, so to speak,' he replied hastily, 'I must remain an onlooker.'

'Damned traitor,' Henry muttered. 'Didier?'

'I'm half-French, sir.'

'Then the other half can blasted well pay me homage.'

In the interests of his bill, Auguste forfeited his pride. After all, as Ruggles must know perfectly well, this man was hardly going to raise an army and march on Buckingham Palace. He extended his hands, and two palms clapped them triumphantly inside his, grinding them so hard the ring dug into Auguste's hand. It seemed a small price to pay for the sake of keeping his host happy for the dressed peacock.

*   *   *

After the body of the new king had been removed, Auguste still lingered in the knot garden. Shaken himself, he was appalled that the shock of this death was producing not sorrow from the late king's subjects, but squabbling over who should be his successor. Ruggles too was lingering, perhaps to see fair play as Enid, Launcelot and Jane pitched fierce battle. The death had been attributed by the Arthurs to a fit brought on by over-excitement, but the doctor had not been convinced. It was in his opinion a case of acute gastric fever, brought on by adulterated food. All eyes had centered on Auguste, whose luncheon was the obvious suspect. He had had a few well chosen words with the doctor, pointing out that a sole au Chablis, roast chicken and strawberry bavarois were unlikely to produce such symptoms, and that in his experience of working with Inspector Rose of Scotland Yard further investigation at least through the coroner and probably by the police might be an excellent idea, especially since it was a diplomatically sensitive gathering. The Kent police had duly arrived and had now left.

There were factors at play here that Auguste did not quite understand and if Sir Henry had indeed been murdered (or rather assassinated since he claimed to be a king) then he had to find out how this had happened very quickly, if he were to avoid the Tower of London as his next residence.

The first step in his own interest would be to alert Egbert Rose to the strange situation at Stalisford Place. After the telephone call he returned briefly to the kitchen to prevent any further disposal of the remains of luncheon, and to scale down the planned feast for something more suitable to the occasion. He bade a regretful farewell to the dressed peacock, then set off to inform the company that dinner would be served in half an hour and to make discreet enquiries as to what had happened during the afternoon. On the way to carry out this mission, he met Charles Ruggles in the corridor whom he buttonholed for his support.

'They're all off their trolleys,' was Ruggles' surprising response, 'but I agree there's something odd happening, so you can rely on me.'

Legal advisers to royalty would not ordinarily go out of their way to collaborate with chefs which further confirmed Auguste's suspicions, which he had shared with Egbert Rose.

'You work with Mr Lewis, do you not?' he asked Ruggles.

'Who?'

'The Prince of Wales' solicitor,' Auguste replied innocently.

'Ah.' Ruggles laughed. 'So you think I'm not a lawyer by profession, but a paid assassin, Mr Didier. Wrong. When the Prince's secretary received the letter from Sir Henry informing him of this charade, it was decided that someone should come down to investigate. With the Queen's Jubilee so shortly due we wanted no disturbance, or dare one say, assassination attempt. The timing seemed too close for coincidence.'

In the drawing room the battle was still in full flow when they entered, and only the mention of dinner brought a brief pause.

'Mr Didier tells me that it's possible that if they find evidence of gastric fever poisoning in Sir Henry's body,' Ruggles informed them blandly, 'Scotland Yard might become involved.'

'Really?' Enid was delighted. 'Henry would have liked that honour.'

'He's trying to distract attention from his cooking,' snapped Jane. 'Don't be a fool, Enid.'

'*Queen* Enid, if you don't mind. I am now Queen of England.'

'Nonsense,' said Launcelot roundly.

'Speaking for the Prince of Wales –' Ruggles attempted.

'Former prince,' Jane pointed out.

'Very well, let us agree on Regent of Wales, while you are settling the constitutional position here. We should be clear as to where Sir Henry was this afternoon in case it transpires that murder was involved.'

There were surprised looks but no one seemed disposed to disagree with this. 'We were all here of course, save Mr Venables and Mr Ruggles,' Enid said. 'Henry was planning to rule with me as I was next to succeed.'

'Like the Egyptians,' Launcelot observed.

'I thought they married their sisters?' Jane muttered.

'It's immaterial,' Enid began, but was interrupted by Auguste's gentle:

'Were you all here all the time?'

'At one time or another,' she airily replied.

'The coronation ended about three-thirty,' Jane said. 'We all came back to the dining room then.'

'Sir Henry too?'

'Certainly,' said Enid vigorously. 'Henry was with us for about an hour, then he said he did not feel well, and would go for a walk in the gardens. We realized he wished to be alone to ponder the great responsibilities of state.'

'And no one saw him again?' Ruggles asked.

'Where were you?' Launcelot asked quickly. 'Venables went home, but you weren't with us at first either. You didn't join us for another half hour or so. *And* you went out again ten minutes ago.'

'Your first point isn't relevant, since Sir Henry was here, and the second was a mere call of nature. Hardly enough time to reach the knot garden, poison Sir Henry and return here.'

'And what about you?' Auguste asked the new queen and her dissident relations-in-law. 'Did you remain together all this time? Were there any more –' he paused delicately – 'brief absences?'

'Certainly I went to the water closet,' Enid informed him loftily, 'but that absence too failed to give me time to poison my brother.'

'This,' proclaimed Jane, 'is ridiculous. Any poison reacting on Henry so quickly would have been given to him at luncheon-time.'

'But a murderer could not count on knowing who was to be served and with what,' Auguste pointed out.

'Precisely. That is why,' Enid snapped, 'it is clearly the food at fault. Did I not warn poor Henry that you would poison him before the day was out?'

Auguste struggled for calm. 'No one else has fallen ill,' he commented reasonably.

A pause in which all four considered this point.

'The drinks?' Launcelot ventured.

'No,' Auguste said. 'Sir Henry sat at one end of the table. Anyone reaching over to put anything in his wine would have been noticed. The risk was too great.'

'It still looks uncommonly as though you are the murderer, Mr Didier,' Enid said gleefully. 'Only you or one of the other servants could have leaned over my poor brother to drop poison in his food or wine without causing comment.'

'Unless all three of you acted together,' Ruggles suggested to her.

This caused uproar. 'A typical suggestion from a representative of the Saxe-Coburgs,' snarled Launcelot.

'I think you may safely assume, Mr Ruggles,' Enid put on her best queenly voice, 'that we are too divided over our future to conspire together. Scotland Yard – if it becomes involved – will leave empty-handed or with you in handcuffs, Mr Didier.'

*   *   *

The dinner safely served, Auguste walked into the gardens to get away from the gloomy atmosphere of the house. It was dusk and the scent of the roses was strong. It was hard to realize that unnatural death had taken place here earlier this day, and harder even to imagine that a murderer might be sleeping within those walls tonight. So far as he could see, there had been no opportunity for any of the three Arthurs to poison Sir Henry, assuming the poison used caused a fairly quick reaction. That left Ruggles – and yet he, as Egbert Rose had just confirmed, was with Special Branch, who had no need to murder to achieve their ends. A gentle tap on the shoulder and a threatening letter from solicitor George Lewis would have sufficed.

He wandered into the knot garden. The orb and sword lay discarded by the sundial, and the box had been thrown carelessly to one side. The crown, he knew, was in Enid's keeping, but to his surprise, the register still lay in the box. Venables had clearly been too overwrought to take it with him, but who, Auguste wondered, had replaced it so neatly in its former home?

For a moment Auguste speculated with the idea of Venables as a murderer. After all, a mad rector would match a mad lord of the manor. He dismissed the idea, and opened the register, turning to the page where the marriage was recorded. With a sense of inevitability, he saw that it was now missing, as were the other two relevant pages; they had been roughly torn out, and were nowhere to be seen. Ruggles' mission was now quite obvious. He or Venables had to be the murderer, if murder it proved to be – and of the two ... But how had he done it, and why?

Auguste went to sleep that night, his brain buzzing with possibilities that rapidly turned into improbabilities. Ruggles may have torn out the register pages, but that would remove the reason for any murder. Without such evidence, Sir Henry's antics would be foiled.

In his dreams, Auguste ran round and round the labyrinthine paths of the maze, but never reached the centre. Each turn of the path produced a different thought. What had poor Queen Margaret felt about her wedding remaining a secret, as she was hidden away to bear her child? What had Henry VIII's thoughts been as he added the crown and ring to the concealed register after her death? And at whose hand had the descendant of Bedivere's line met his death, probably by arsenic, the favourite poisoner's weapon of past and present.

Round and round Auguste ran on the grass paths in his dreams, until at last an idea emerged out of the ghosts of the past.

In the morning he telephoned Inspector Rose once more.

'I've had the scientists' post mortem report. They were at it all night. Arsenic,' Egbert Rose informed him. 'You can start looking for your murderer before we arrive.'

'You will need to check, but I believe I have found him.'

'Good. Who?'

'You could say all of us.'

'*What!* Trust you to make it difficult.'

'The idea came from the Medicis who had interesting methods of poisoning their victims in order to leave a trace so delicate it would not be noticed. This was one of them. I believe you will find a needle point contained in the ring on Sir Henry's finger with a mechanism triggered by pressure on the hands – such as that caused by the friction involved in acts of homage at a coronation ceremony. We all killed Sir Henry, but we were guiltless of intent.'

'So whose intent was it?'

'The murderer was King Henry VIII of England. He of the Seven Wives.'

Marbles

Marion Arnott

15 March

Cold and overcast. My records show that this is the thirty-third consec-
utive day without sunshine. But overnight the daffodils opened in the
bed by the gate and in the afternoon the wind shredded the clouds and
I saw patches of blue sky. When we went for walkies, Lukey and Razz
snuffed the air and barked. Spring is on the way and the little sillies feel
the excitement. My new neighbour has moved into the house across the
street. I saw the removal van and heard a dog bark. I hope it's not a
bitch to disturb the peace of Lukey and Razz.

Eight serious in the office today. No. 6 was especially difficult: an Irish
whisper, fast, low and hard to make out. Her silences grew longer and
longer and I heard an old story in them. I am filled with foreboding.

Miss Buchan's pursuit of Ken was the talk of the street. She had
lived there for years, keeping her dogs in luxury and herself to herself, and if it wasn't true that she never spoke to anyone, it was true
that she was careful to whom she spoke. Or she was until Ken
moved into the house opposite.

Mr Ross saw the beginning. 'Would you look at Miss Buchan?'
he said, and nudged his neighbour, Mrs McCabe, who was beside
him at the bus stop. 'She's blushing.'

Mrs McCabe looked and sure enough, Miss Buchan was,
though Mrs McCabe thought that the crimson was more like slap
marks than blushes, which was more fitting somehow than that a
sallow middle-aged woman should colour up like a girl. 'What
brought that on?' she asked.

Mr Ross smirked. 'Our new neighbour. See him going past her
house?'

Mrs McCabe knew that there was nothing unusual about that
woman looking through people, although she was more inclined to
blame standoffishness than trance states; less usual was Miss

Marion Arnott

Buchan's present motionlessness: she was still standing with her hand frozen in a half wave.

Mr Ross suggested that she go and ask if Miss Buchan was all right, but Mrs McCabe refused. She didn't like talking to Miss Buchan because the effort made her queasy. 'It's those fishy eyes,' she explained, 'big and grey and empty, always wander, looking past you, beside you, through you, anywhere but at you. Makes me seasick. Anyway, it would be a waste of time to ask. All she ever says is "Hello" and "Lovely weather, isn't it?" and after that you're on your own.' Mr Ross knew exactly what she meant.

The pair was saved from further worry when Miss Buchan exploded into her customary frenetic gawkiness and dashed across the road in pursuit of her dogs.

'Daft biddy!' Mrs McCabe snorted. 'Didn't even notice she'd dropped their leashes.'

'Still blushing like a kid,' Mr Ross laughed.

He fancied himself a student of human nature and entertained his neighbour all the way into town by insisting they'd just witnessed love at first sight. He called it 'Last Chance Syndrome', the old maid's complaint, brought on by the arrival of an eligible widower of clean habits.

18 March

Cold and overcast with not a patch of clear blue anywhere. My new neighbour has a golden retriever, a bitch called Cara. He called her to him and I turned. I don't know when I last turned at the sound of a human voice, but I was compelled. Such a voice he has, such a smile, such a face – unforgettable. 'Cara!' he called. 'Carissima mia!' It struck a chord in me. Italian is such a romantic language. All day I could hear his pleasant golden voice: 'Cara mia, cara mia, marissima,' as if he were calling me to him.

No. 6 hasn't rung again – that's three days now. She is absent, yet with me; detached, yet joined. Perhaps she won't call again and I'll never know why. My phone mate says he doesn't understand my calm. Calm! Strange how little of oneself appears on the surface but when I consider my phone mate, I can see that's for the best. He specialises in screechingly audible compassion. It can be very wearing.

19 March

Heavy sleet today, but K went twice to the park, and so I did too. Cara has a tartan coat to keep her warm. He went through the swing park, along the beech walk, then round the pond. Pets' Corner was quiet with no children about. He stood for a long time at the fence. Cara barked when she caught the smell of the animals, which made Lukey and Razz bark too. I kept them on the leash but they struggled frantically to get to Cara. I was exhausted by the time I got home, what with restraining the dogs and keeping up with K. He walks very fast.

The office was quiet today. No.6 still absent although her whispery voice runs constantly through my head and, worse, her devastating silences. I took my knitting to give myself something else to think about – Lukey and Razz shall have a woolly coat each – but a new voice filled my head. 'Cara Carissima' it said, and it was never silent.

It occurred to me that K might go to the park when I am not there to see; I have asked for a change from the afternoon to night shift. I asked quickly before I had time to think about it. Night shift means going outside in the dark, which I have always feared, but it means I shall be available all day.

Mr Ross was not the only one who noticed the effect Ken had on Miss Buchan. Whenever Ken took Cara to the park, which was often because for all his seventy years he liked the exercise, she shot out of her front gate like a gawky rabbit from its hole, dragging her spaniels after her. At one time or another, everyone saw her following him along tree lined paths, stopping when he did, walking on when he did, occasionally glancing sidelong at him when she thought he wouldn't notice. Young Susan Hay in particular, from her vantage point in the smoking den behind the hydrangeas, enjoyed the show. 'Sub-til, very sub-til,' she said to her friends every time Miss Buchan slipped furtively by; and every time she said it, they all ducked down and giggled.

Of course, Ken did notice, he couldn't help but notice, but if he nodded in his friendly way, she only flushed an ugly plum colour and, with a smile thin as a splinter, sidled away down the path as fast as she could go. 'Now, that's what I call playing hard to get,' Susan Hay drawled, and her friends laughed till they choked on their smoke rings.

Marion Arnott

28 March

Milder today. The first green buds are unfurling on the trees. There is such a stirring in the air; all around the park a stirring and a movement. Lukey and Razz love all the extra walkies. If I so much as look out of the window, they think we're off to the park again.

He went past the swings today and into the walled garden. He is very spry for his age and could pass for much younger. 'Age cannot wither him nor custom stale his infinite variety.' My father said that about my mother every year on her birthday, except of course he said her instead of him, but it described K just as well.

The park was deserted – it was very chilly – and so there was no one for him to stand and chat to. That was a relief as I didn't feel like loitering today. He stood by the pond for a while, watching the swans, while I sat in the shelter watching him.

He's what my mother used to call a gentleman of the old school. His shoes are polished like mirrors, a sure sign. She thought you could tell a lot about a man from the condition of his shoes: dull leather signified a lack of character. Mother read shoes the way other people read teacups, palms, minds. She would think well of K's shoes, although she would have advised against leaving off his coat so early in the year – 'ne'er cast a clout till May be out' – but I'm glad it's off.

Coat. I mentioned the coat. I can't believe I did that after more than a week of avoiding it, but there it is in black and white. It crept in; it made itself heard. Objects have their little ways, and it's foolish to pretend that they are powerless, like prayers and curses, unless they are put into words.

3.30 a.m.

I must give it words. A record is pointless if things are missed out. His voice was the first thing I noticed, then his face and smile, then just as I was adjusting to all that, as if that wasn't enough to cope with, on the nineteenth of March he appeared in the herringbone coat and I was overwhelmed by it and pitchforked into the past, to another time and another place.

I smelled Ovaltine, malty and hot, and in my mouth there was sweetness and crunchy bits – Mummy didn't always dissolve the granules properly. 'Mummy, Mummy, it's got bits in it' – I heard myself say it – and she came and fished them out and licked them off the spoon, laughing. I heard her, I saw her, clear as day and solid as Lukey and Razz beside me. Her hair gleamed in the yellow kitchen light and I thought my heart would burst. She laughed, popped the spoon into the pocket of her floral apron, and turned away. 'Mummy' I said, but she had gone.

'Mummy,' I said. Perhaps I spoke aloud, perhaps I was only remembering – the distinction isn't always clear – but the longing for her to turn back was real. We might have talked; after all if she could laugh, a few words shouldn't have been impossible. But she was gone, the street was empty, and I was alone.

My heart did burst then – a tidal wave of longing broke through its walls, swept me along, and deposited me on the hearth rug, the red and royal blue one she liked so much. I lay on the rug reading my comic and sipping Ovaltine. The heat from the fire burned my cheek. I heard the ash sigh and fall into the grate, and the clock on the mantelpiece ticking like a big brave heart.

It was cold outside, colder and snowier than it ever gets now. Mummy stuffed my wellingtons with newspaper and set them to dry on the hearth. I was drowsy with heat and then Daddy swept into the house in a flurry of snowflakes. It was cold outside, but before he closed the door, I glimpsed the snow, white and ghostly, lying thick on the hedge. He spread his herringbone coat, zigzagged with black and grey, over a chair at the fireside.

I learned to count on that coat; all the bones slanting one way were even numbers and the opposite ones odd. 'I'll give you a shilling if you can count all the herringbones,' he used to say. He only wanted peace to read his paper. I never got the shilling, except once. I was only six. I missed rows and had to start over, or else I fell asleep and woke up with his coat spread over me. I loved its heavy weight and scratchy warmth. And then he'd give me a threepenny piece for counting so well.

Words cannot describe how it felt to see them again, to be on the rug counting bones while Daddy lit his Senior Service and Mummy smiled in the yellow light. I was happy and quiet inside and so very glad to be home again.

It was a shock when the rain came on and I found I wasn't home at all but standing in the street. I looked up the road and K had clean got away.

I ran all the way to the park. I was breathless and staggery-legged before I found him trotting Cara up and down the walled garden. He nodded and said hello. I have noticed before his compulsion to talk to me – strange considering that I can be of no interest to him – but the compulsion is there. It connects us.

Marion Arnott

I didn't answer; what could I have said? For me, it was enough that we were alone together in the garden. I couldn't take my eyes off his herringbone coat. It drew my eye and I followed it all the way down the beech walk and back to the crescent.

I mustn't risk visiting Mummy and Daddy again, which is a shame because the best time of my life was when we were all together under the ticking clock with Mummy humming along to the radio. But it would be selfish to go back now. The connection with K has been made – he feels it, I feel it – and I mustn't be distracted again because that's how K got out of sight last week. What if I hadn't found him again? So I'm glad that he's left his coat off so early in the year.

Ken gave up making friendly overtures. With a laugh, he told Mrs McCabe that he was losing his touch. Mrs McCabe sniffed and said he should consider himself privileged because at least he wasn't entirely beneath her notice, but later, when she was chatting to Mrs Ross, she said that the old man was hurt because he liked to get along with everybody.

And he usually did. Within weeks of moving in, he had progressed from nodding acquaintance to first names with all the park regulars who stopped to pat Cara, a friendly animal, and as Ken was quick to reassure anxious mothers, good with children. He was a thoughtful man too. He creosoted Mrs Campbell's fence for her, just walked into her garden with the tin in his hand, claiming he had creosote going to waste. 'Dirty job for a woman,' he told Mrs Hay and Mrs Ross, 'and she's got enough to do since her husband left.'

He was always doing something for somebody. The hard thing about retirement, he said, was filling his time, and so he would happily sit in for plumbers and electricians to help out neighbours who were at work, or pop down to the shops for the elderly, which made everyone smile because some of the elderly were younger than he was. But then, Ken was very unelderly, straightbacked and lively with thick strong hair, even if it was white. He showed none of the old man's sourness when children were noisy or kicked footballs into his hedge. It was more his style to join the kickabout. 'Keeps me young,' he said, puffing only a little after an hour in goal for the Campbell children.

But his spry friendliness never won a word from Miss Buchan

and, in the end, he gave up. Oddly, abandonment made her heart grow fonder, as Mr Ross insisted on putting it. By the summer, she had stopped slipping and sliding away from his smile. When he stopped to chat with anyone, she hovered just within earshot, hanging on every word. She never spoke herself, but everyone could see she was listening patiently, waiting for Ken to walk on so that she could be alone with him in her own peculiar way.

Susan Hay thought the whole performance was a scream and one bright Saturday morning, she couldn't contain herself. 'You're winning, Ken,' she said sepulchrally from the depths of the smoking den. 'She's getting keener.' Ken parted the bushes and peered in. 'Mesdames Anonymous all present and correct, I see,' he said sternly. 'OK, who's going to do an old man a favour and take Cara for a run round the park?'

The dog barked and thumped her tail on the path. The girls scrambled out of the bushes and ran away squealing with Cara at their heels. Ken took a seat on the bench next to Mrs Ross and Mrs McCabe. 'Best way to exercise a dog,' he said and settled comfortably on sun-warmed wood. The three chatted idly until Mrs McCabe nudged Ken. 'Your shadow's here,' she said, then smiling boldly, called out, 'Good morning, Miss Buchan.'

Miss Buchan, visibly flustered, retreated down the path. Ken said, 'Don't stare at her, Jean. It agitates her,' but Jean McCabe, who prided herself on her sense of humour, amused herself by staring Miss Buchan right out of earshot. Miss Buchan kept a sidelong eye on the threesome, but they all pretended not to notice. 'Never knew a woman so timid in all my life,' Ken said.

'Bloody snooty, you mean,' Mrs McCabe said sharply.

'No, she's just lonely and doesn't know how not to be,' Ken said. 'It takes people different ways.'

There was a respectful silence. Ken had told them more than once about the loss of his dear wife and how loneliness had driven him to leave their old home. She had haunted every corner of it, the top of the stairs, the little passageway leading from the kitchen, everywhere really, and he hadn't minded that, but he minded the black sorrow when he realised she wasn't really there. It was like losing her all over again.

The silence was broken by Susan's Hay's little sister, Ailie. She came trotting down the path, tearful and sniffing, and squeezed on the bench between Mrs Ross and Ken. 'Did they leave you behind again?' Ken said kindly.

She slipped her hand into his and nodded. 'They said I have to wait with you 'cos my legs are too short and fat to keep up.' She stretched the pink corduroy legs out for inspection. Mrs Ross clucked soothingly and admired the sparkles in her new blue jellies, but Ken only laughed and said long legs were more trouble than they were worth. His friend Skinny Lizzy had legs which wouldn't stop growing no matter how hard she tried to stunt them. When she was seven, she had to tie them in reef knots before she could fit in her bed, but by the time she was twelve, only a round turn and two half hitches would do the trick. And by the time she was sixteen, the driver wouldn't let her on the bus, because when she sat down, her knees touched the roof and showed her knickers, which caused a public scandal.

When Mrs Ross told her husband about it later, she was still bewildered by what happened next. She was laughing at Ken's daft story when she noticed Miss Buchan circling closer and closer to the bench, moving so fast that no matter where Mrs Ross looked, she could see her out of the corner of her eye. Then Jean McCabe grabbed Ken's arm and said she was sore laughing. Miss Buchan heard and straightened up then, glaring like a wild thing.

She stepped up to the bench, her mouth opening and closing soundlessly like a goldfish. Ken said, 'Are you all right, Miss Buchan?' It was obvious that the woman wanted to slide out of sight, but she stood her ground, and just when it seemed that something was going to happen, Cara came bounding up, Ailie squealed for a ride on her back, and whatever it was that might have happened, didn't. Then Susan arrived and made some catty joke about Miss Buchan's old brown anorak and Miss Buchan exploded.

'Susan Hay,' she said, and her voice came out all squeaky. 'Susan Hay – ' For once in her life Susan shut her cheeky mouth because Miss Buchan was heading right for her. Susan's friends stopped laughing – the woman looked deranged – and Susan was as close to nervous as that wee madam was ever likely to get. But all Miss Buchan did was squeak: 'Susan Hay, I wore pink once,' which made the girls giggle. 'Susan Hay!' Miss Buchan yelled. 'Susan Hay!' The woman was fish-eyed and floundering and absurdly falsetto, which reduced the girls to helpless hysterics. 'You silly girl. You nasty silly girl!'

Susan shrieked with laughter. 'Oooh, pretty in pink. Pink to make the boys wink. Pretty as this were you?' And she turned and waggled her backside at the woman, her skirt so short that everyone got an eyeful of shocking pink and scarlet love hearts. Ken told her to behave herself, really sharp he was, and she turned sulky. Miss Buchan turned and fled into the walled garden.

Mr Ross was unimpressed by his wife's tale, because he had been expecting a major drama. All the story did was prove what he had always said: Susan Hay was long overdue a good skelping, and Miss Buchan was mad as a hatter.

But Mrs Ross lay uneasy that night, remembering Miss Buchan's fuse had been lit when Jean took Ken's arm. And then Susan's pink knickers. Jealousy. It wasn't right. It wasn't healthy.

3rd June

… and he patted Ailie's arm and said, 'And so, little Caracarissima, don't pine for long legs. Remember Skinny Lizzie,' and they all laughed, and suddenly I was at the bench and I don't know how I got there or what I intended, but they stared at me, all of them at the same time, I cannot bear being looked at. As for Little Miss Lovehearts and Spite, I wanted to say, 'Fuckdoll! Do you think K is interested in your underwear? Stupid fuckdoll! That's what you are in your scarlet and pink, a stupid little fuckdoll!'

But I couldn't possibly say anything like that – Mummy would have been shocked rigid. I don't even like writing it down, but a record must be true or there's no point – so I said the first thing that came into my head. I said, 'I wore pink once.' Such a meaningless, ineffectual thing to say!

They think I'm mad! Someone muttered something about my losing my marbles. Susan's and Mrs McCabe's sneers don't matter, but Mrs Ross looked frightened – as if there was anything to fear from me! – and K's pity was unbearable. It's not how things should be – our connection was tainted by it.

Apart from anything else, the incident made me lose track of him. By the time I came out of the garden, he was turning out of the park gates with Ailie riding on Cara; I could see her fat little legs thrust out on either side. In a second they were out of sight. They could have gone anywhere.

Marion Arnott

It was selfish to indulge my temper and draw attention to myself after all these weeks of going unnoticed.

How odd it is that after years of wishing that I could be seen and not overlooked, of wanting someone to look me in the face and put out a hand and say, 'Everything's all right,' it should happen today. Everyone noticed me, and K, metaphorically speaking, put out his hand to me. It was unbearable. Now I want only to be invisible, to be everywhere K is, near him and watching over him.

2.30 a.m.

Not much going on at the office tonight. A few drunk pranksters wanting to talk filth. We don't get many of them in the daytime, but at night they come out like moths. There was nothing too upsetting, which was just as well, because K was running through my mind. How organised he is: Cara draws people to him and K charms them into staying. I have lived here for years and never made a friend, but K is sociable. Today fifteen people stopped to pat the dog: six children and nine adults. Cara offers her paw to anyone who passes and K performs the introductions: 'This is Cara, mia carissima.' This community socialising didn't happen in the spring – too cold to linger, I suppose, even for a lovely dog and a warm, golden voice.

I have nightmares that as summer goes on, more and more people will flock round him and that everything will get out of control. How will I manage to stay close then?

4.45 a.m.

Confession. I won't sleep while this is on my conscience. Something happened at the office tonight. I was thinking about Ailie's pink corduroy and Susan Hay's pink and scarlet. I was thinking about them, the innocent and the coarse, how innocent the shell pink, how coarse the pink and scarlet, and was remembering when I wore pink.

A drunk woman phoned in, wanting to know if we could send someone round to rescue her cat from the garage roof. Well, really! I know what the training manual says, and I'm always patient and polite, but this was too much. The woman demanded to know what the sodding Samaritans were for if it wasn't to help people and people's sodding cats too. 'Fuckdoll!' I hissed without thinking. She became aggressive, but I don't have to put up with that sort of thing and I hung up.

All the way home, I worried about it, because the words popped out

all by themselves – I had no say in them. I think it happened because
she interrupted my visit to the past. But would it have happened if No. 6
had called? Would I have hissed her whispers into silence? Surely not!
But the words erupted before I knew it. How can I be sure?

I had to remind myself over and over that No. 6 hadn't in fact called
and that I had not driven her away. The thought calmed me, the thought
and the night, which was pretty with stars and warm moonlight. I am
getting used to the night, am even beginning to like it. The dogs are com-
pany and we roam cool and airy and free, three capering shadows in the
shining dark.

K's windows were in darkness when we passed and the darkness in
them was thicker and heavier than the night, as if it was more than an
absence of light. The thought sent me running for home and I am very
angry with myself.

Susan Hay was at her garden gate with a gang of rowdy boys. The
sight of me scurrying up my garden path set them off laughing and jeer-
ing, but Mrs Hay called Susan in and the boys ran up the road whoop-
ing like wild Indians. They left Coke cans lined up along Mrs Hay's
wall, and those cardboard boxes for pizza. They wouldn't dare do that
in daylight, but night is an invitation to be bold – now that I'm a night
traveller myself, I understand that. Even I could be daring in the shad-
ows, and should be, to make up for the scurrying.

And why now? Why shouldn't I caper a little?

Every lover needs a little luck, as Mr Ross said when he told the
tale of how Ken and Miss Buchan eventually got together. Miss
Buchan's share came in the form of a neighbours squabble.
Several neighbours mentioned in passing to Mrs Hay that Susan
and her friends had been rather noisy the night before. Mrs Hay
was apologetic and promised to speak to Susan, but she drew the
line at apologising to Ken. Susan denied absolutely that she had
scattered empty cans and pizza boxes around Ken's front garden,
and although Mrs Hay was the first to admit that Susan was no
angel, she was no liar either. But in the end, Mrs Hay had to eat
humble pie.

It was the queerest thing, she told Mrs Ross later. She was
weeding her front garden when Miss Buchan sidled up to her gate
and mumbled that she had seen Susan and her friends with cans
and boxes the night before. When questioned, Susan had lied.

'What Coke? What pizza?' she'd said. 'Where would we get the money for that?' And that was something else she'd be looking into, Mrs Hay told Mrs Ross grimly. In the meantime, Susan was grounded for a month.

Mrs Ross told Mrs McCabe all about it, and they were jointly astonished, not by Susan who came as no surprise, but by Miss Buchan. That was the second time she'd volunteered to speak in two days. 'The power of love,' Mr Ross said. 'She couldn't let the desecrators of darling Ken's garden get away with it.'

He was less amused by what happened next. Two days later, when he and Jean McCabe were on the way to the bus stop, they saw that Ken's garden had been trashed. Flower heads littered his lawn and the contents of the wheelie bin had been dumped on his doorstep. Worse, his front door had been spray-painted. GRASS, the uneven letters read. Miss Buchan's door had been similarly treated.

'That Susan Hay wants a good thrashing,' he said, and they hurried on by since there was nothing they could do.

7 June

Action is good for me. Today was a beautiful sunny day and everything about it was fresher and brighter than usual – sunlight dazzled green and gold through the treetops and haloed the cool clean shadow below. I was reminded of a poem Daddy used to like which ended 'annihilating all that's made to a green thought and a green shade.' Green thought and annihilation. Health and destruction. It's a strange combination which I never understood before.

K was stopped a dozen times in the park – much headshaking about headless roses, spray paint, and the young of today and their general horridness. When I came close, the little crowd around him parted like the Red Sea and our eyes met. 'Miss Buchan,' he said. 'How are you?' There was concern in his voice; I heard it, warm and real, and I froze like a rabbit caught in headlights. They were all looking at me, willing me to speak, but I only nodded and hurried on. His audience was disappointed: he and I are fellow victims, after all, and should share the experience.

I suppose you could say the experience was mutual. Is it ever possible for two people to share an experience in exactly the same way?

He went round the pond three times today. Mrs Hay was there with Ailie. I did my best to avoid her, although I do feel some guilt that

Susan is being blamed. I have to remind myself that she is not a very nice little girl. Then Mrs Hay saw K. Ailie went running to him. Mrs Hay pulled the child away from Cara and complained noisily about K sending the police to her door, insisting that Susan had nothing to do with the vandalism last night. K said that either Susan or her friends were the obvious suspects, but then Mrs Hay spotted me. 'Miss Buchan,' she screeched. 'Did you tell the police that Susan – '

She blocked my path and I couldn't get by. I hate confrontation – I could feel myself shrivelling inside. I blurted out that I had said nothing and squeezed past her.

K followed me, hauling on Cara's leash, calling after me. He jogged at my heels all the way home and caught up with me at my garden gate. 'Couldn't you have backed me up?' he said, without so much as a hello or a good morning. 'It stands to reason that Susan – '

He must have seen my agitation, because he spoke more gently. 'Were you afraid, Miss Buchan?'

I managed a nod – I could not speak for my heart throbbing in my throat. He patted my arm. 'There's nothing to worry about,' he said. He was smug. It made me angry and I found my voice.

'Do you really think so?' I said. 'I've read about this sort of thing. Gangs get it in for someone and run campaigns against them.'

He smiled reassuringly, pityingly. A flame of anger scorched me. There's no room for pity between K and me. That's not how things should be.

'Susan and her friends won't want any more police attention,' he went on. 'They've had their fun.'

He was certain, smug, secure. My thoughts were green and ready to annihilate.

'Are you sure it was Susan?' I said. 'I saw a crowd of boys in the street last night, not the same ones as before. These were older. They hang around here at night, sitting on people's walls, breaking twigs off hedges.'

He said I mustn't let my imagination run away with me.

'But I had a good view of them,' I said. 'These boys – young men really – were very tough-looking.'

He seemed a little uneasy as I closed my gate, which was a small triumph.

Marion Arnott

1 a.m.

A distressing night at the office. There was a report on an inquest in the newspaper: a middle-aged Irish woman dead of an overdose, a nonsense note in her hand. 'Just taking the pins out,' was all it said. The coroner could make no sense of it. 'While the balance of the mind was disturbed,' he decided, and wrote her off.

It was No.6. She often spoke to me about being pinned to life like cloth to a pattern. Pinned all round, she said, and cut to shape, someone else's shape, and she couldn't find her own.

Now she has taken out the pins and drifted shapeless into the dark, airy and free at last. Her name was Theresa. I cannot silence the whisperings in my mind. Sometimes the whispers are hers, sometimes mine. Women whisper to themselves or to strangers on the phone. And sometimes to dolls.

My doll was Louby Lou. 'Louby Lou, Louby Lou, what can we do?' It was when the pins were going in and the cloth cut to shape.

3 a.m.

I've been trying to remember the Louby Lou song.

> *'Here we go Louby Lou*
> *Here we go Louby Light*
> *Here we go Louby Lou*
> *All on a Saturday night.'*

I think that's right but it doesn't matter. I have to stop singing now – it makes Lukey and Razz whine. Anyway, I'd rather hear Mummy singing. I can hear her in my head. I like to think that, since I haven't visited her for a while, she has come in search of me.

We sang the song through twice. Louby Lou couldn't sleep unless she had her song twice. She had been my doll forever. Her long floppy legs hung permanently from the crook of my arm, and like me, she wouldn't eat vegetables. I told her she would be able to see in the dark if she ate up her carrots, and that brussel sprouts would make her big and brave, but she wouldn't touch them. Mummy said there was nothing for it but to set a good example and eat them myself. And I did, especially the carrots, so that I could be sure the dark round my bed was empty, but it didn't work; I was never sure, have never been sure. I still have to have a light on at night. Still. And the sprouts didn't make me big and brave. I stayed as floppy and useless as Louby Lou. I could tie her legs round the bedstead about her head and poke her with pencils and she just lay there, curled upwards, floppy and silly and ugly.

Once I pulled and Louby came away from the bedstead minus a leg. Mummy had to untie it because I couldn't get the knot out. Louby's sawdust spilled all over my quilt and I screamed because I thought it would turn red like blood. Mummy said not to be silly and made me scrape it up with a soup spoon. I didn't let the stuff touch my hands, sure it would feel slimy like people's insides. Mummy sewed her leg back on, but it was skinnier than the other one after that and hung crooked.

'Her legs will fall off if you're not more careful,' Mummy said, 'and she'll be spoiled forever.'

'The dolls' hospital could fix her,' I said. Mummy shook her head and showed me the seams at the top of Louby's leg.

They were gappy and the pink cloth was shredding. I screamed because sawdust trickled on to my arm. Any minute it would turn red and slimy. I knew it would. I knew. Spoiled forever. Forever and ever. I screamed and screamed.

For months I dreamed of twisted ruined legs endlessly leaking crimson slime. No matter how kind I was to Louby, I still dreamed. Even when I kept her legs dangling straight, even when I dressed her in her favourite pink satin dress and red satin shoes, the dream still came.

I pestered Mummy to make us more clothes. Louby would feel better then. Her clothes were identical to mine, made from leftover scraps. All that summer, Mummy's dressmaker's shears crunched through paper patterns and stiff starched material – yellow gingham or pink cotton or fine green twill – and the room filled with the warm smell of new cloth. I was always impatient to see the shape Mummy had given the material and used to tear the pattern pieces off quickly and let them drift to the floor, not understanding that the pattern was what mattered, that the cloth followed it, that it couldn't do anything else.

People are like cloth: nothing in themselves, and before they know what's happening, they're folded and sheared and snipped into shape. Theresa, poor Theresa, knew all about that.

But I won't think about Theresa, not now. K is more to the point. He has kept his lights on all night. He's not so smug and certain now; he's learning that lights won't help him know who's out there watching.

It's dawn now and his lights are feeble and thin, fading into the rising sun. I've always hated the loneliness of that sight, but hated darkness *more. Not now though: Tonight's dark was friendly and intimate. His lights reached across the street to mine and made a shining rope which bound us together.*

This afternoon he asked, 'Are you alright, Miss Buchan?'

Tonight I would answer, 'Cara carissima, I haven't felt so right in years.'

6.30 a.m.

Mummy is shouting and wakes me up. Her face is too close. There's lipstick on her teeth. 'What are you doing? Elizabeth, stop it!'

I sit in a puddle of pink satin and the shears are in my hand and the cloth crunches into shimmering strips. She shouts stop it stop it but I crunch and crunch and when she snatches at the shears I stab them into her hand. Mummy, I didn't mean it, I didn't mean it.

Blood drips on pink rags and down her floral apron and I scream and she slaps and swings me up by the arm and shouts, 'What are you doing? Wicked girl, what are you doing? Your party dress! And Louby –'

I kick her shin and shout that Louby is silly and floppy and ugly and now she's dead and better dead. My kicking foot catches Louby's head and sends it spinning across the floor. Sawdust leaks everywhere and gets on my shoes and socks. I try to shake it off – I have to get it off – and I scream and scream that nobody can fix her now, nobody, nobody, nobody.

I hide behind the sofa, but she comes after me and her face is screwed up tight and scary.

Mummy, I didn't mean it. I didn't mean it.

The neighbours where outraged by the vandalism suffered by Ken and Miss Buchan. Mrs Ross suggested setting up a Neighbourhood Watch scheme, but the organisation seemed out of all proportion once Ken had tidied his garden and Miss Buchan had repainted her door. The only legacy of that night was the bad blood between Ken and Mrs Hay. The neighbours blamed Mrs Hay for that. She couldn't get over having the police on her doorstep. If she and Ken met in the street, she ignored him. If Ailie went running to pet Cara, Mrs Hay called her back. It was sad to see the dog's excitement when she saw Ailie coming, and their mutual disappointment when she turned away. The old man's pretence at not minding was pitiful.

Mrs Hay's stock fell to an all time low when Susan buried the hatchet. She stopped at the bench in the park and told Ken straight that she'd nothing to do with the mess in his garden or the paint on Miss Buchan's door. 'Honest,' she said. Ken nodded, and the next thing Susan was away up the beech walk with Cara and soon things were back on their old footing. Ailie even got her rides on the dog's back, although she always got off before they came in sight of her house.

17th June, 3 a.m.

I saw Ailie in the park today, riding on Cara's back, laughing and giggling. I had thought that particular game was over for good. Mrs Hay wouldn't like it, but youngsters today don't care what their mothers like, even children as young as Ailie. Their mothers are to blame – they don't supervise their children enough; they don't ask enough questions. Yesterday Ailie dawdled at K's gate and put little heaps of dog treats along the wall for Cara. Then she walked to the corner and watched till K let the dog out. Cara stood up on her hind legs and wolfed down the treats while K stood at his window gently smiling; when Ailie crossed the road, she wriggled her fingers at him behind her back. They are in a conspiracy, K and his little caracarissima. The affection between them is palpable.

My first impulse was to tell Mrs Hay, but that would only drive Ailie underground and me out into the open. Besides, Mrs Hay is an aggressive woman and would shout. I'm not sure I'm up to that.

K is feeling smug and secure again. Tonight his house was in darkness for the first time since June 7th. Our rope of light is severed and I am alone.

5.30 a.m.

I was startled awake by a voice singing 'Here we go Louby Lou, what are going to do?' It was a relief to wake and find no one there, then a shock to realise the voice singing was my own. It was shrill and crazy. Or was it? Isn't it rational to ask what's to be done when something must be?

Without thinking, I snatched up the phone and dialled his number. I let it ring and ring until the light went on in his bedroom. His shadow was huge on the blind. I rang off without answering, then when his light went out, I rang twice more, and the second time, when he shouted at me to piss off, I hissed at him: 'Ssss … Ssss,' like a snake. I surprised myself because I hadn't meant to say anything, only let him know he had company, but his coarseness provoked me. 'Ssss … Ssss.' He swore a lot, but he was afraid. I could hear it. After that, he kept his bedroom light on and put Cara out into the garden, as a watchdog, I suppose. That makes me smile. Cara standing guard! Cara who offers the paw of friendship to all comers!

He isn't so safe and smug now. We shall keep company till daylight and that's some satisfaction. But it isn't going to be enough.

People noticed that Ken was tired looking and sometimes missed his morning walk in the park. He told everyone that he wasn't sleeping well, and left it at that, but Mrs Ross, gently questioning, managed to draw out of him that he was being plagued by prank phone calls. The old man tried to laugh it off, said he wasn't worried, but the deep shadows under his eyes told a different story.

She decided to let Mrs Hay know what was happening, without making any direct accusations against Susan. Sometimes a word in the right ear… Mrs Hay flew off the handle immediately and demanded to know if Ken was insinuating that her Susan was involved in this. Mrs Ross assured her that he had done no such thing and then went home, terribly afraid that she might have made things worse, and resolving to keep her mouth shut in future. For once, she agreed with Jean McCabe: the young today were getting out of hand and it was time something was done about it. She couldn't think what though.

It was Jack Ross who advised Ken just to leave his phone off the hook. 'As long as they get a reaction, they'll keep it going,' he said. Ken was staunchly indignant because he didn't want to be seen to be giving in to bullies, but in the end, he'd agreed there was no fun in an engaged signal and no shame in depriving young morons of their fun.

15th July

I am shut out. The phone sits on my table, helpless, useless, empty of me, empty of him. I remind myself that I am not powerless, that his lights burn through the night because of me, that he is deprived of Cara's company at night because of me, that he looks haggard because of me. But I cannot reach him. I can only see his lights and feel the rope that binds us together.

We were company for one another! It's not fair - he can shut me out and I can't shut him out; I cannot silence his pleasant golden voice!

But Caracarissima isn't so easily excluded.

Half the street was roused in the middle of the night – police cars are noisy – but had to wait till the next day to find out what had happened. Except for Mrs Ross who had been a witness. She had been up with the baby, walking the floor, when she heard police radios crackling. She looked through the slats of her blind and saw a Panda car outside Ken's house. The surprising thing was that when Ken opened his door, Miss Buchan was there beside him.

Mrs McCabe's eyebrows defied the law of gravity when she heard that. 'So that's where she goes at night, is it?' And she roared with laughter. 'Sly bitch! Oh, God, it's disgusting!'

'Don't be silly, Jean,' Mrs Ross said, wishing she'd never mentioned it.' 'She was passing by– '

'Must have been,' Mrs McCabe sniggered. 'I don't suppose he asked her over, not when he can have his pick of the geriatric ward. That sly biddy has been hell-bent on getting her foot in his door since he moved in. The thing is, does she know what to do now she's there?'

'It wasn't like that,' Mrs Ross said stiffly, remembering Miss Buchan's pale, haunted face, 'although if it was, that's their business. But she was only trying to help.'

'Heard it,' Mrs McCabe chortled. Mrs Ross, who was still upset by the night's events, and didn't much like Jean McCabe anyway, stalked off, and Mrs McCabe had to wait to hear the full story from Mr Ross at the bus stop. Which was fine by her, because there was nothing prissy about Jack Ross.

It turned out that when Miss Buchan was out prowling with Lukey and Razz, she saw the shadows moving in the dark alley beside Ken's garage. Her dogs had barked like mad things, and the shadows, which turned out to be flesh and blood and thug-sized, ran down the path and pushed her to the ground. Five or six of them, Miss Buchan had said. She had knocked up Ken and together they had found obscenities, real filth, scrawled all over his garage wall. And worse, sheets of loft insulation material soaked in paraffin pushed against the wooden door. The police had reckoned

Marion Arnott

Miss Buchan had disturbed the thugs in the nick of time.

Mrs Hay was incandescent with rage when the police turned up on her doorstep again: she was quick to tell everyone that no accusations had been made, as obviously Susan wasn't thug-sized, but everyone heard her yelling at her daughter – 'If you know anything, if you or any of your friends...'– and exchanged knowing looks. Everyone except young Mrs Ross, who wasn't sure what to think. She had been walking the floor with Baby Angela for an hour before the police arrived and had heard nothing: not Lukey and Razz barking; not half a dozen thugs pounding along the quiet street; not Miss Buchan's screams when she was pushed. She'd heard nothing at all until police radios cracked the darkness apart.

Of course, Baby Angela had been teething and whiny and perhaps she'd been too distracted to notice. But every time she closed her eyes that night, she thought of lit fuses burning sparky paths around Ken, and Miss Buchan's wandering grey eyes refusing to meet hers.

16th July
I could not go to the office tonight. I am confused. I know I'd have been useless. I almost lit the fire last night, almost, and then realized it might carry to Mrs Ross's house next door. Baby Angela sleeps in the side bedroom – the smoke might have gone into her tiny lungs. I was paralysed by the thought of the choking, the closing of the throat, the fighting for breath. I felt it all so vividly that I could not breathe myself and had to sit down on the path till I was calmer. Cara came nosing over and I had to give her more biscuits to keep her quiet. My only comfort was that although I appear to have lost half my marbles, I still retain my community spirit.

I had to adjust my plans to fit the circumstances – after all, my aim was not to watch K's garage burn. Or perhaps it was. I'm not sure what I planned. I was in a fit of night anger at the time, there was a burning in my head, that's all I can say. But when my sense of civic responsibility overcame me, I was still able to salvage something from my shadow capering. I rang K's doorbell. I knew I had done the right thing when from behind his front door, he quavered, quavered, 'Who's there?'

He sounded old and nervous which was very satisfying. I led him straight to the graffiti and saw his reaction first hand. The colour drained from his face – even in the moonlight I could see his pallor – when he saw it and smelled the paraffin. I exclaimed in terror, 'Arson! Dear God, that could just as easily have been your front door, and if it had caught, and if I hadn't happened by – '

'Now, now, Miss Buchan, don't get carried away.' But his face was bone white.

We waited for the police in his front room. He fussed over me, courteous and gallant, eager to soothe me after my encounter in the dark, desperate that I should not leave him alone. And so once again we were company for one another and found mutual comfort. His hand trembled as he poured the tea, whether from fear, or from emotion over the loss of his dear wife, which he insisted on telling me about when he saw me glance at the wedding photograph on the wall, I really couldn't say.

I was rescued from this mawkishness by two charming policemen who escorted me home once I had made my statement. They checked all my doors and windows – infuriatingly slowly – and so it was some time before I was alone with K again.

He had opened his blinds, but soon went round and closed them again. I understood at once. If the blinds are closed, he can't see who's outside – anyone could be creeping closer, like a cat padding towards its prey; but if they are open, anyone outside could see in and know exactly where he is and how he looks when he's afraid.

He kept all his lights on all night and our old togetherness was renewed. We kept company until the sun came up, one at either end of a glittering rope.

My heart ticks brave and steady as a big loud clock.

17th July, 9 a.m.

Woke up choking on anger and fear. It was Lukey who roused me, whining for his breakfast. There was fog. I was lost in the fog and crying, 'Daddy! Daddy!' It's confusing to wake from sleep but not the dream. The fog was all around, cotton wool thick and smoky, filling my mouth and ears and nose; even when I slipped on my dressing gown to go downstairs, the November fog followed me, shredding and thickening and wrapping itself round me. Figures loomed in front of me and disappeared as suddenly, leaving muffled hacking coughs behind them to die in the fog. The yellow light from shop windows is blurred and dimmed and I'm choking and spluttering, there is something in my mouth, I put my hand to my mouth and it's my red woollen scarf. Everything is all right, it's only my scarf.

Marion Arnott

November, Daddy and I are going to buy fireworks. Mummy has put a handkerchief over my mouth and nose and ties it in place with my scarf. This is to stop the fog getting into my chest. The red woolly pixie hood is to protect my ears – my ears are a big worry in the winter. It has been dark with fog all day, and she's not keen on my going out in it; neither am I, it's spooky out there, but when Daddy says, 'Come on, Little Red Riding Hood, time for sparklers and Catherine wheels and rockets,' I'm not afraid any more. He takes my hand and tucks it in his pocket and everything is all right.

We wade through fog like heavy dry water and here's the shop. I can just see the orange masked guy in a barrow at the door of the shop, slumped to one side, grinning. We buy two boxes of fireworks, dark blue, the lids bright with red and yellow flames, huge boxes, and Daddy has to carry them in front of him when we head for home. He is right in front of me in the fog, tall and solid, and I hang on to the tail of his herringbone coat and trot behind. But his steps are too long. I can't keep up, I stumble and let go. He doesn't notice and strides on. 'Daddy! Daddy!' I stand still. That's what you do when you get lost, you stand still and Mummy and Daddy will come and find you. But no one comes. I hear harsh winter coughs but can't tell where they are coming from. I squawk, 'Daddy! Daddy!' but the sound is deadened by my hankie and scarf. I turn around and round and can't see anyone, and then suddenly he's there, a huge shadow looming ahead. He doesn't see me and strides past, but I grab the tail of his coat and tug. He stops and turns and bends down with his hands on his knees. 'Hello!' he says. 'Who can this be?' His voice is warm and golden, but he isn't my Daddy. 'Hello,' he says again. I step back and something cold presses against my leg. I squeal. The warm voice says, 'Sit, Cara.'

Cara sits, but she's still as tall as I am. The man laughs. 'It's all right. She's good with children. Friendly.' He laughs again. 'My goodness! What big brown eyes you have, Little Red Riding Hood!' I laugh too because he knows my Daddy's joke and everything is going to be all right.

Cara was friendly., I wonder how many Caras there have been over the years? Caras-good-with-children, come-into-my-garden-Caras, come-and-play-with-me-Caras. The nice big man and his dear wife never chase you away. 'I don't mind kids round the place,' he told Mummy. 'We've never been blessed ourselves. It's nice to watch them play.'

Something cold presses against my leg. Cara? No. Lukey, the little silly. He was getting impatient for his breakfast. I was in the kitchen with the tin in my hand. I must have been there for half an hour. I don't remember going in to the kitchen, but I must have.

18th July

K and I met in the park today. He was sitting on a bench in the swing park with Mrs Thompson. I sat as close as I could get. Children were queuing up for rides on Cara – Ailie, and the Campbell children, the little girl who lives round the corner, others I didn't know. Too many to keep track of. Mrs Thompson was entranced. She likes to see children at play, she said. K made the children come and say their names. He gave them sweets if they would tell a joke or do a handstand. They all showed off like mad, even Cara. She stood on her back legs, balancing a sweet on her nose till K called 'Snap, Cara!'

It was like a circus round the bench with K as ringmaster and Cara the focus of all eyes. He spoke to me several times, but I have no small talk and he soon forgot I was there. I mentioned that the children were tiring Mrs Thompson, but she said that she didn't mind, and laughed till the tears came when Ailie tried to balance a square of chocolate on her nose for as long as Cara could. Cara and Ailie: two well trained little bitches sitting up pretty together, although Cara's the better performer – she's been doing it longer. Lukey and Razz were wild to join in, but on principle, I have never taught them tricks. I told Ailie to pat them and she did, but only out of politeness. She couldn't wait to go back to Cara and K.

I heard him tell the little Campbell girl that he would take her to nursery in the morning when her Mum was at the dentist. Good old K, ever helpful, ever obliging, ever there or thereabouts.

I can't be everywhere. I must be more constructive, more rational. What have phone calls and paraffin and graffiti achieved?

Cara is the big attraction.

Ailie's screaming brought everybody running. The poor little mite could hardly speak for crying, Mrs Ross told her husband later. And it was a terrible sight which had upset her. Cara was lying on the front lawn, writhing and twisting, and there was bloody froth at her mouth and nose. She whined and snapped at anyone who came near her. It was heart rending, and almost a relief when her eyes

351

glazed over and she died. Some kind of fit, the Rosses concluded, and so did everyone else.

Ken was a solitary and pathetic figure when he went walking in the park. He seemed to age overnight, Mrs McCabe said, and predicted knowingly that he'd go downhill quickly now. Old people were like that.

Ken was the centre of attention for days. All his neighbours expressed their sympathy, even Mrs Hay. Ailie and Susan were heartbroken, she said, and Ailie had had to be kept off school for two days. She described to Mrs Ross how the old man's eyes had filled with tears when she told him that. 'They're good girls,' he had said. 'Always kind to Cara.'

The peace between Mrs Hay and Ken lasted until the results of the autopsy came through. Cara had died of rat poison, ingested with dog treats. Unbidden to everyone's mind came the vision of Ailie heaping treats along Ken's wall. No one seriously suspected her, but the culprit wasn't a hundred miles away, and if it wasn't Susan herself who had poisoned the dog, then those friends of hers who'd been causing trouble – well, she ought to be made to name them. First vandalism and funny phone calls, then arson, and now a poisoning. Someone really twisted was on the loose.

20th July

Mrs Ross is still looking at me strangely. She seems always on the verge of saying something, but I hurry on by. It's a pity, because she is the nicest of my neighbours. Not that we've ever talked much, but I've seen her on a bench in the park with Baby Angela. The baby bounces up and down on her lap, crowing and waving her fists, and Mrs Ross laughs and blows kisses on her cheek. They are lost in their own private world.

That was my world once, mine and Mummy's. I have a photograph of her sitting on a sunny sea wall. I am standing on her lap, wearing a knitted hat with rabbit's ears. She has turned me to face the camera, but she is looking at me. Her cheek is pressed against my fat baby face and the wind is blowing strands of her hair around our heads. Any moment I am going to bounce and crow and she will laugh. That was our world when everything was all right. Left to ourselves, it would have been like that forever.

I remember the long narrow skirt she's wearing – it was cobalt blue with covered buttons at the vents – and the clatter of her tall spiked heels.

I was only a year old, but I remember. Children suck up memories like sponges – the feel of things, the colours, the patterns, the rattle of high heels, the things they don't understand and save for later.

I cannot put Cara's agonies out of my mind. She took a long time to die. I had thought it would be unpleasant but quick. The little girl Ailie cries herself to sleep at night. I can hear her through the wall. Susan too. The sound of little girls weeping is unbearable. It has made me cry for the first time since I was little.

I met K in the park and offered my condolences. To my horror, the tears sprang to my eyes. He reached out and patted my arm. 'You're a dog lover too,' he said. 'I know you understand.'

And I do. With a dog along, a walk in the park is a delight; without, it is a dull and pointless exercise. I would never set foot in the park if not for Lukey and Razz. I don't expect K will for much longer. I think he might be persuaded to move house at the very least to stay out of the park.

He is concerned for my two little sillies, what with a mad poisoner at large in the area, and advised me not to let them out of my sight. He threw a stick or two for them, but his heart wasn't in it. We took the bench outside the walled garden. People stopped to enquire after him, but no one stayed long. It is easy to discourage people. I've been doing it all my life – a look, a silence, a hint of impatience, and they're gone. Children need a little more encouragement. 'Don't startle the dogs,' I said. 'They're not used to children. They might bite.'

We were soon left in peace together. He treated me to a long lecture on dog training, and insisted that I had a responsibility to make Lukey and Razz safe for children, who can't help being attracted to dogs. I assured him my sense of responsibility to the community was alive and well, that I do my best to keep children away. Then he said he couldn't go on calling me Miss Buchan and asked my name.

'Theresa,' I told him. It seemed a fitting memorial somehow.

I can still feel the pressure of his fingers on my arm.

The neighbours shared many a joke about the geriatric Romeo and his scrawny Juliet. They courted on the hoof, strolled round the pond, accompanied by the sharp excited barking of Luke and Razz. Mrs Ross and Mrs McCabe saw them often in the park and passed them smiling, Mrs Ross indulgently, Mrs McCabe with sly malice.

'What does he see in her?' Mrs McCabe said once.

'Well, they're company for one another,' Mrs Ross said vaguely.

'Company? She walks him like she walks her dogs. Never talks to him, never smiles, just steers him three times round the rose beds, down the avenue, and home again.'

Once on that subject, Mrs McCabe was apt to go on and on. Mrs Ross scarcely listened. The truth was, she too often wondered what the attraction between Ken and Miss Buchan was. Jean McCabe was wrong about one thing. Miss Buchan did in fact talk to Ken, but Mrs Ross didn't much like what she talked about. Ken was still in a fret about a story Miss Buchan had read in the paper: a pensioner harassed for months by teen thugs, his windows smashed, his house broken into, and finally a murder. It was extraordinarily tactless of Miss Buchan to tell him about these things.

3rd August

I did not anticipate this. He has taken to calling round when it is time for the dogs' walkies. He is chatty and charming, as if there were only one interest in his life – getting to know me. It's Theresa this and Theresa that, and many helpful offers to walk the dogs for me if he thinks I look tired. He is pitiful sometimes. 'I miss Cara,' he says often, and asks to borrow my animals with tears in his eyes. I understand: a man alone in the park, chatting to children, draws attention; a man with dogs is unre-markable. But I won't lend him my dogs: a man with dogs and a mid-dle-aged spinster has his style cramped. And so I must put up with his company and he with mine. Another shared experience.

He wants to train Lukey and Razz. It was Ailie started him off on that. She stopped to chat and asked him if he'd teach them to balance chocolate on their noses. He said that trick took time to learn and that they had to be trained every day. She promised to meet us in the park as often as she could. They ignored me entirely, made their plans without consulting me. I told Ailie I could see her mother coming and she shot off. But she'll be back. She's a very determined little girl. I was sharp with K and said that training living creatures to behave in a way not natural to them degraded them. There was a burning in my head and I couldn't stop. 'Some people find fulfilment in exercising power over animals – even over other people,' I said. 'I disapprove.'

He laughed. 'Theresa, it's as much fun for the dogs as it is for their owners. They like it.'

My head burned and burned. 'Like it! How do you know that? How do you know what it feels like to be made to perform? To be made to do things, to curry favour, to fawn? To be laughed at and giggled over? You cannot possibly know how that feels!'

I took one of my spasms and had to clench my jaw to stop my head jerking. 'You will not train my animals,' I said through gritted teeth.

'There's no need to get so agitated, Theresa,' he said. 'If you're so dead set against it, then of course I won't.'

I wanted to walk away, to leave him standing and never speak to him again, but I was brought to my senses by Ailie, who came galloping up, gap-toothed and grinning, to say that the ice cream van was at the gates, and that it would be lovely to have an ice lolly. The Campbell children were lurking a few feet behind her, shy and hopeful. I had to stay then and apologise for being so sharp. I had to go to the van with them. He bought us all a treat, the children and me. I had to eat ice cream. I had to watch Ailie putting out her tongue and licking her ice lolly. I wanted to be sick.

'Ailie, go and play with your friends now. You're making a nuisance of yourself.' She stared me out, pert and mutinous, and my voice rose, I couldn't help it. 'Will you do as you are told!'

She eyed K and licked raspberry slush from her lips. Their twinkling eyed silence bordered on insolence, but after a long moment, she turned and ran off, crying, 'I'll see you tomorrow!'

'You don't like children much, do you?' he said kindly.

'I don't dislike them. I don't know any,' I said.

'Their friendship is a privilege,' he said. 'You should make friends with Ailie. She's a lovely child.'

Cue for more mawkishness: his dear wife and the sorrow of her life – childlessness. And another rendition of how she haunts him in all the old familiar places. 'We were never blessed,' he said and my head spun. 'Theresa, you've gone quite pale. Would you like to go home? I could take Lukey and Razz for their run.'

'We'd best both leave,' I said and with some inspired prevarication, got him out of the park.

Everything is getting out of control.

Marion Arnott

4 a.m.

I've given up on sleep. I'll only dream. I'd rather be awake: remembering isn't as bad as reliving.

Never been blessed, he said. That was how they always put it, K and his dear wife, whenever they came to visit. The first time I heard it was in my mother's kitchen, in the yellow light, that time I got lost in the fog. 'We've never been blessed,' he said, with a casual smile and a glance in my direction. I was on the red and blue rug with Cara, running her silky ears through my fingers. It was good to be safe home with Mummy, good to see Daddy's relief when he arrived and found me there, good to see them all so friendly, fun to hear Daddy and K thrilling over the boxes of fireworks. 'You're like a couple of kids, Mummy said. 'Even Elizabeth isn't so excited.'

I was more interested in Cara. I was afraid of dogs, but K said Cara liked me, he could tell. And she did. She sat with her head up and her chest thrust out, panting, while I ruffled her fur and tugged her ears. It was a perfect night: I had had an adventure and been rescued; I had been comforted with Ovaltine and was swaddled in the warmth from the coal fire and the quiet laughter from the tea table. Cara gave her paw to everyone and was fed scraps; I counted bones on Daddy's and K's coats and K gave me a whole shilling. And when the evening was over, it didn't really end: K was to bring Cara and his wife to our bonfire and we were going to roast potatoes and melt marshmallows on sticks.

6 a.m.

She haunts me too, K's wife, with her moth pale face and ruby lipstick. I visited their house often, to see Cara. They lived just round the corner from my school. Mummy hoped I wasn't making a nuisance of myself, but they liked having a child around the place, not having any of their own. Yes, K's dear wife haunts me in all the old familiar ways, in all the old familiar places, on the stairs, in the passage leading from the kitchen, at the bedroom door with the clothesline in her hand. 'Do you learn knots at the Brownies?' she said. 'Come on, I bet I can tie you up so tight that you can't escape.' She was hopeless at knots – they fell off when I giggled and tugged. She swore to learn harder ones for the next time I came. K, leaning on the doorpost, laughing. 'Time for tea,' he said. 'We've got trifle tonight. She's better at that than knots.'

Lots of knot games. Other games too: tiddlywinks, ludo, snap, nets of twinkling marbles. Kid's games. I won sixpence every week. But knots were my favourite. Loops and whorls of rope, complicated arrangements, impossible bonds from a book about Houdini, but they always fell off. Tell Mummy you're learning knots for your Brownie badge.

It was spring before she learned the knots to keep me tied. 'Come round in your party frock before the birthday tea. We have a present for you. And we'll take a photo.'

Me and Louby Lou in pink satin and red shoes. Photos. Flash. Flash. 'I've learned the knots,' she said with a giggle. Into the bedroom with the brass bedstead. 'But you don't want your pretty frock crushed.'

Pink silky slip and matching knickers with rosebud trim, a present from my Gran. This is a special knot, a round turn and two half hitches. Wrists. Ankles. Bedstead. A cry of protest. Too tight. K shaking his head, what a baby, what a big baby you are. Skinny Lizzie, she says, and prods. Slip pushed up. Do you know what Apache Indians do on their birthday? They paint themselves. Ruby lipstick. Colouring in. Flash. Flash. Flash. Photos. K's funny smile. Slimy stuff on my tummy.

Mustn't tell. Mummy would die if she knew what a bad girl I was. I'd get taken away. Anyway, I have to be trained before I'm eight or it's too late, I'll never be a real woman.

There's a lot to learn: how to please, how to look pleased, how to sound pleased, how to guess his mood and not make him angry, how to sit up pretty, say I love it, love him, over and over, so I can be his carissima. Poke and prod. No tears, don't tell me you don't like it, stupid wee fuckdoll.

Flash. Flash. Flash. Photos.
Photos. Flash. Flash. Flash.

9 a.m.

'I disapprove,' I said to K yesterday. The harshest words I've ever said to him. As always, I am futile, useless, powerless. I was patterned too young, pinned all round, I'll never be any other way now.

Is it possible to decided to be braver?

Mrs Ross had another uneasy night. She had overheard Ken and Miss Buchan talking at the ice cream van. Ken had given out goodies all round – those kids knew a soft mark when they saw one – and then he and Miss Buchan had drifted nearer to the bench where she and Angela were sitting. Miss Buchan said she'd heard noises from his garden a couple of times this week, but since nothing happened, she hadn't wanted to worry him about it. But there were some tough looking young men with motor bikes by the park gates who seemed familiar, and they were staring at Ken. One of them was coming over. It might be an idea to leave the park.

Mrs Ross had looked up from Angela then, and was shocked by Miss Buchan's ghastly yellow colour. The next thing, Ken was escorting her to the side gate at a rapid trot. The biker had come towards Mrs Ross and she had felt a chill of fear – all that leather and long greasy hair, Miss Buchan's sallow terror – but he only went to the van and asked for six cornettos. And when Angela threw her fluffy duck out of her pram, he stooped and picked it up for her. 'There you are, little pretty,' he said, and placed it carefully on her coverlet. He had quite a nice smile really.

Mrs Ross lay awake thinking about Ken. He had developed an old man's stoop which hadn't been there in the spring, and he had a habit of continually looking behind him. It was no wonder he was nervy with Miss Buchan harping on about thugs and helpless old people; she didn't seem to realise she was actually making him more nervous. Jean McCabe had been right about Ken going downhill – but even she hadn't thought of Miss Buchan giving him a good hard push.

Mrs Ross had asked Jack if she should drop a hint to Miss Buchan about being more careful about what she said. Jack had only laughed. 'Old people enjoy their miseries,' he said. 'It makes them feel close to each other.'

5th August

The same policeman turned out as last time. Had I seen anything? Heard anything? Only the breaking glass, I said, and then the police sirens. I told them I was impressed by how quickly they'd turned out. I could see they were pleased. I don't expect they get much appreciation. They said they'd been keeping an eye on the street in view of the recent problems.

That was unwelcome news – I hadn't noticed them about the place. I must be more careful. It would have been undignified to be caught tossing a brick through a neighbour's window.

I don't know why I did it. It was an impulse born of opportunity. I was sitting thinking things over, remembering, and then saw that K had gone for a bath in the middle of the night – the bathroom window had steamed up. He must have taken my advice about letting a bath soothe and relax him. It was easy to get at the rear kitchen window through the gap in the hedge.

The police said K was in a dreadful state. And so he was. Quite pale and trembly. I made him a cup of tea with a shot of brandy in it. He said it was good of me to come over. 'You've been right all along about this, Theresa,' he said.

'It's the times we live in,' I said and swept the broken glass off the sink unit. He tells me he's buying another dog on Saturday. Another Cara – he can't see past golden retrievers: reliable and safe around children. He thinks the new dog will be nearly as good as I am at alerting him to the presence of strangers. Then his eyes filled with tears. He's missing Cara, he says. And with apologies to my good self, he's going to teach the new one tricks. It will be fun for little Ailie.

I have sat here for hours, listening to the ticking of my heart, louder and louder, braver and braver. I must be braver.

Mr Ross had a friend who worked for a home security firm. He managed to get Ken a good deal on an alarm system and a dusk-to-dawn light. He was amused to see that Miss Buchan was the first to be invited in to see the new fixtures and fittings.

'Maybe he's trying to tempt her to move in. Home security is all he has to offer,' he laughed.

7th August
Fort K was in darkness. I called in on my way from the office. 'I just wanted to check you were all right when I saw the lights were out,' I said.

I was inside in a minute. He said he didn't need lights now that he had an alarm system so sensitive that nothing could penetrate it.

'If you're sure,' I said, 'but there were three figures at your gate when I turned into the street. Oh, they weren't doing anything – only hanging around. They made off when the dogs barked.'

We went out and inspected the gardens. There was nothing amiss of course, much to K's relief. 'You must have scared them off before they had the chance to –' He broke off with a catch in his voice. 'Where do you work anyway? You keep such odd hours.'

'The Samaritans,' I said.

'I should have guessed. You're certainly my Good Samaritan.'

We had tea and brandy. After three, he confided that dusk is when the terror begins.

'I can imagine,' I said 'Yes, when night falls. The dark always feels so full of things, doesn't it?'

He was very sorry for himself. I wanted to tell him about real terror, how it lives on in a series of flashlit scenes, Skinny Lizzie blanched and petrified in white edged photos. Terror began when I was seven and he was thirty and it has never stopped. I have no pity for him: I have spent my life with Hell at my heels. And now he has Hell at his. I think there is fairness in that.

He walked me to the door. I said I'd left my scarf on the sofa. He went to fetch it. I noticed that he has developed a shuffling walk. While he was gone, I scattered marbles all over the step. Little glass ones with coloured twists in the middle. Kid's game. It took him five minutes to find the scarf which I'd hidden under a cushion.

'Don't forget to switch on the alarms when I'm gone,' I said. 'Those men might be back.' I listened to him lock up when he'd shut the door. Two deadlocks. Two bolts. As if terror can be kept out. Silly man – terror comes from within. Always.

By the time I went to bed, the lights were on in every room in his house. He's under house arrest, shut in by keys and bolts and locks and bells. And he still doesn't feel safe.

We were company for one another all night, as we have been since I was seven. His lights and mine joined together and made a long glittering rope which bound us together.

Mrs McCabe and Jack Ross saw the ambulance on their way to the bus stop. Someone had booby trapped Ken's front steps with marbles and sent him crashing down on to the concrete path. He suffered a broken hip, wrist, and collar bone. And a fairly serious concussion. Jack Ross was furious – his friend had assured him that a field mouse couldn't slip past those alarms. He felt responsible somehow.

Mrs Ross stopped worrying about Miss Buchan's treatment of Ken. While he was in hospital, she was a model neighbour, visiting him twice a week and minding his house and garden for him. As she said to Mrs McCabe, it was surprising how alike the two of them actually were – always ready to help out a neighbour in trouble. She reckoned Ken has brought out a hidden side in Miss Buchan. Mrs McCabe only snorted.

1st September, 3 a.m.

They're keeping K in for another week. I never dreamed that my marbles would be so spectacularly successful. He has lost weight and his air of nattiness – doesn't shave, slouches like an old man. He doesn't talk about coming home any more either – he feels safer in hospital. I promised there was nothing to worry about, that I'd keep an eye on him and his house. 'I'll always be there for you,' I said. He could not speak for emotion.

I dreamed of Mummy last night. She was tight-lipped the way she used to be when I did something horrible: that time with the scissors, the times with the matches, the tantrums. Doctors couldn't help. ECT couldn't help. She got resentful when I didn't respond to treatment. So did the doctors. Well, they didn't understand what they were treating me for. Nor did she. I never forgave her for not knowing, not understanding. We were not on speaking terms when she died.

She was tight-lipped in my dream, but I spoke to her anyway. It's time we made up.

'Mummy,' I said. 'I've done something right.'

'Have you, Elizabeth?'

Her voice was cold the way it so often was, because of the things I said, the things I did. She came towards me, her high heels clicking. Then she frowned and turned away.

'Mummy!' I was shrill and desperate. 'Mummy!'

All of a sudden I was little again. She came back and bent and scooped me up in her arms. She took me to the window. It was snowing outside, more heavily than it ever does now.

'Watch for Daddy, Elizabeth. He'll be coming round the corner any moment.'

We peered through swirling white together. 'And what have you done that you're so pleased about?' she said.

'I helped my friends, Ailie and Theresa.'

'I haven't met them, have I?'

'No. We played marbles together.'

'That's nice. Oh, look. There's Daddy.'

And he came swinging round the corner and as usual his eyes went straight to our windows and he smiled and waved. In a moment, we were all together again and it was so lovely to be home.

Nicholas Royle

If Birmingham was the Venice of the Midlands, in Sir Reginald Hill's appropriated phrase, what did that make Venice? The Birmingham of the Veneto? From where I was sitting, sipping a glass of prosecco at a café terrace overlooking the Grand Canal, I couldn't see it catching on. The bright sunlight and fresh breeze turned the broad expanse of waters into an inverted version of the Aertex ceiling in my Yardley flat, white and choppy. I tried to picture the Grand Union Canal at the end of my road, midway between Acocks Green station and the Swan Centre in Yardley, and found that I could do so all too easily. Tench-green, oxygen starved and barely two rod-lengths across, it would have a job making it on to the World Heritage list. To be fair, though, I'd seen canals in Venice that were not dissimilar. Only the setting was markedly different.

This was my last night in La Serenissima – the most serene republic – my last night of a week-long visit that I had nearly cancelled. Only two things had stopped me: firstly, the fact that the travel company offered no refund in case of cancellation and, secondly, Martin Weiss.

I left the café terrace and headed back towards the hotel to shower and change before dinner.

Martin Weiss was a friend from schooldays. In fact, although he and I had been at school together in Acocks Green, we hadn't been particularly close. But then we found ourselves attending the same college at London University. Anything to get out of Birmingham, had been pretty much my approach to further education, whereas Martin, if our conversations in the union bar were anything to go by, missed the Midlands and looked forward to going back as soon as he'd completed his degree, if not sooner. It seemed to me the particular area of London in which we'd chosen to study, the East End, was not much different from Birmingham anyway. Urban deprivation, a deprived community, the subtle yet constant threat of violence: Martin should have felt at home.

For the first few months, Martin and I saw little of the neighbourhood, in any case, as we spent most of our spare time in the union building. I would be reading, either set texts or potboilers, but I made little progress owing to Martin's constant interruptions as he showed off his talent for solving the *Daily Telegraph* crossword. Martin didn't read the *Telegraph* (I don't think he read a paper at all; he got it for the crossword), but that didn't stop the Labour Club types who controlled the union glaring at him disapprovingly. He made no effort to justify his choice to them.

'The *Guardian* crossword's too fucking hard,' he confided. 'Now, what about three down? 'Bubblegum, chewed, loses fellow but gains one in country.' Seven letters.'

'I struggle with the quick crossword,' I said.

'It's easy. Look.' He pointed with his pen. ''Bubblegum, chewed', i.e. anagram of bubblegum, but minus a word meaning 'fellow'. That's 'bub'. Then you add 'i' – that's 'one' – and the answer is the name of a country. Belgium. See, piece of piss.'

'You're not just a pretty face, are you?' I said, smiling at him.

There was no warmth in his hazel eyes as he replied sharply, 'Fuck off back to GaySoc.'

The college had a good reputation for science-based courses, but I was doing English, while Martin was doing – or, closer to the truth, not doing – history of art. He didn't last long. A term and a half into the second year, Martin vanished for two weeks, then reappeared, not as a remorseful student begging the vice-dean to let him stay, but as the featured artist of a one-man show at a scabrous basement gallery in Bethnal Green. His blurry photographs of East End murder sites, under the title 'Echoes of the Past', showed that he had, after all, found something to hold his interest in Whitechapel: the district's lasting association with the crimes of Jack the Ripper.

The show was both an inauspicious debut into the art world and his 'Goodbye, I'm off' note to the corridors of academia. He wasn't seen on the Mile End Road again, although the college paper was the only journal to include a review of 'Echoes of the Past'. A rather overlong, not entirely uncritical but largely positive write-up, it marked my own first appearance in the world that would later claim me for one of its own, newspaper journalism. In particular, I praised the cryptic captions Martin had given his photographs: each, like a crossword clue, had to be worked out, making you think about the pictures.

When I eventually left college with my predictably average degree, it was back to Birmingham that I went, working for a spell as a sub-editor on the *Post,* then as a reporter on the *Evening Mail.* Gradually, telescoping a series of various staff positions, freelance gigs and 'rest periods', we return to the present day, which sees me employed as a crime reporter on a launch project for a rival publisher to the bunch that owns the *Post* and the *Mail.* A new daily paper for the West Midlands, it's likely to ditch into Edgbaston Reservoir within a year of launching, if we even get that far; but it seemed like a golden opportunity in the final dismaying weeks of 2001, when I was staring out the window cursing the name of Patricia Cornwell.

If it hadn't been for Cornwell, I would have been getting on with my book. For about eighteen months, I had been writing this book, on spec, entitled *The Art of Murder,* and had just reached the chapter about the Victorian painter Walter Sickert, in which I would explore the conspiracy theories that placed him at the centre of the Jack the Ripper case. Whether you buy the Sickert-as-Ripper theory or not (and I didn't), the work of the founder of the Camden Town group is full of interest for those drawn to the representation of murder in visual art, with paintings such as *The Camden Town Murder* and *L'Affaire de Camden Town* indicating his own close interest in the subject. The chapter on Sickert was always going to be the beating heart of the book, but then Patricia Cornwell tore it out with her widely reported act of monumental stupidity. By buying up thirty-two of Sickert's paintings and having one ripped asunder in the hope of finding evidence to back up her 'one hundred per cent certain' view that Sickert and the Ripper were the same man, she had rather taken the wind out of my sails.

I remember emailing Martin Weiss on the day the story broke. I asked him if he'd seen it. He emailed me back and said he had, but added, 'So what?'

'Well, it's obviously a publicity stunt,' I emailed back. 'Guess what her next book's going to be all about?'

The phone rang. It was Martin.

'Listen,' he said, without preamble. 'She won't be the first person to argue in print that Sickert was the Ripper. Nor will she be the last.'

'Well, I might as well cancel my trip to Venice,' I grumbled. Sickert had lived in the Italian city, producing numerous pictures of its people and places.

'Bollocks,' snapped Martin. 'Fuck Patricia Cornwell. She doesn't own Sickert and Jack the Ripper or the right to conjecture over any links between them. Of course you should still go.'

* * *

As I showered in the hotel, I thought of Martin back in Birmingham. We hadn't seen that much of each other since college, despite my occasional promptings that we should get together. I missed his company, but he had his own circle of artist friends, or so I presumed. It was Martin, though, who put me on to Sickert, sending me a series of postcards of his work: *Ennui, Sunday Afternoon, Mornington Crescent Nude.* He had emailed me a web address, which turned out to be a Masonic site with an endless screed devoted to the Sickert/Ripper theory, and the seed for my book idea was sown.

I tried to maintain contact with Martin, sending him a long, chatty email when I started researching the book and asking what he was working on, but he didn't reply. Months later, I received another Sickert card in the post: *La Hollandaise,* another downbeat nude, a prostitute perhaps, on the back of which Martin had scrawled a note to say he was working on a big project that required all his energy. It would be the making of him, he wrote. I took the hint and got on with my research into Sickert, and the material for the other chapters, on my own.

For all its licentious reputation over the years, even earning the soubriquet Sea-Sodom from Lord Byron himself, Venice these days is rather tame and a man may have to travel away from the centre of things to satisfy his carnal desires, especially if those desires are of a homosexual nature. I selected a restaurant in between San Marco and the Rialto bridge, so that I could cruise Il Muro in search of a potential livener. The guidebook said there might not be that much action out of season, but it was even quieter than I'd feared, and I ended up eating on an empty stomach.

From the restaurant it was a short walk back to the Rialto, and thence to the hotel, but there was always a chance I might get lucky.

I didn't. I got unlucky.

As I approached the rio di San Salvador by the calle dell'Ovo, I noticed a large crowd gathering on the bridge. With my reporter's instinct, I eased through the crows to the front. As long as you're polite and don't push too hard, no one really minds, especially in a country like Italy, where queuing is hardly a way of life. When I reached the parapet, I saw the humped shape in the water, the dark hair floating like seaweed. A police launch was just arriving and so I witnessed the body being pulled out of the water. She looked about twenty-five, still clothed, and couldn't have been in the water more than a day, although her face was a waxy grey under the harsh spotlight. Her eyes, thankfully, were closed. Mine were not, and even when I did close them later that night in the hope of finding some relief in sleep, I couldn't banish the image of her grey face, water trickling off the end of her nose back into the canal, drop by sickening drop.

There were even more upsetting images of the dead girl in the papers when I got home. They showed a pretty, lively 23-year-old management trainee called Hannah Power, from Balham in south London, who had gone to Venice with a group of girlfriends and never come back. Initial reports indicated a high level of alcohol in the bloodstream, so it was assumed she had simply strayed, slightly drunk, too close to the edge of a canal. According to her friends, she had left the bar they'd been in just to get some fresh air. When she did not reappear and then later failed to show up at their hotel, the girls raised the alarm, but by then it was too late.

Fortunately, I didn't have much chance to dwell on my memory of that last night in Venice. At work on the Monday morning, we were summoned to a meeting in McCave's office – James McCave was the editor – and told to prepare a dummy issue of the paper to an unpopularly tight deadline. The launch date had been brought forward by three weeks. We weren't told why.

With three days to go to the deadline, a new story broke. I was the crime reporter and this story wasn't a crime story, at least not yet; but the news guys couldn't keep up with the stories they were already chasing, so I volunteered, as my desk was pretty clear. I don't really know why I volunteered. Well, I do, but I don't, if you see what I mean. I'll tell you what I mean. The story was that of a Birmingham girl who had fallen into a canal in Amsterdam and drowned.

I should have realised when volunteering for the story that it would mean interviewing the grieving parents, but for some reason that didn't occur to me, not until the news editor gave me that specific instruction as he handed me a Post-It bearing the dead girl's name, Sally Mylrea, her parent's names, Bob and Christine, and their address on the Old Birmingham Road beyond the Lickey Hills. I was to get a cab, the news editor said, adding that I should make sure I got a fucking receipt.

'You want me to go now?'

The news editor, a hardbitten, hot-metal throwback called Paul Connelly, happened to be not very tall and suffered from Small Man Syndrome. Actually, it was the rest of us who suffered as he strutted about the office cursing and scolding whoever was daft enough to get in his way. 'No, I want you to go next fucking week,' he retorted. 'Of course I want you to go fucking now.'

As I walked out of the office, the last thing I felt like doing was finding a cab to take me to see Bob and Christine Mylrea. I wasn't a parent so I could only imagine what they might be feeling. It was a bright January morning, almost lunchtime. Our office was located between Brindleyplace and the Vyse Street cemetery, which meant that most lunchtimes I would end up sitting in one or the other eating my sandwich in silent contemplation. That day in particular I could really have done with some time to sit and think. I find it impossible to relax stuck in the back of a taxi.

On any other day, on any other mission, it would have been good to get out of the city. The long straight run down the Bristol Road past Longbridge, the hills ahead full of the vague promise of wind in the hair, a spring in the step. But today I was rooted to the back seat of a Cavalier, dreading the moment when it would pull up by the side of the road and the driver would turn round to demand his fare.

The dreaded moment arrived. The Mylreas lived within yards of the Gracelands garage; its zoot-suited mannequin loiterers out front and lifesize Elvis on the roof seemed, for once, like a bad joke in poor taste. I paid the man and stepped out of the car, only remembering as he U-turned in the garage forecourt and headed back up the hill that I had forgotten to ask for a fucking receipt.

As I arrived, a photographer was leaving. Bob and Christine were standing at the front door holding a framed graduation picture of their daughter. Dazed, they invited me in and the three of us sat in an isosceles triangle formation in the front room; Bob and Christine, red-eyed, taking up their expected positions next to each other on the low-backed, high-cushioned sofa, while I perched on the edge of an armchair opposite them, notepad on my knee. As soon as I offered my condolences, the tears began welling up in Christine Mylrea's eyes. She lowered her face and her husband did the talking in a cracked voice, but I couldn't look away from the grieving mother, her tears dripping off the end of her nose, reminding me of the water that trickled off Hannah Power's nose as she was hoisted out of the rio di San Salvador.

*　　*　　*

Sally Mylrea's death didn't strike me as anything more sinister than a macabre coincidence – there had been no evidence that she was pushed or that she might have jumped, and trace elements of cannabis and alcohol in her blood were hardly surprising, given where she'd gone on holiday – until a month later.

Our dummy issue had been well received and we were starting to gear up for the actual launch. My piece on the Mylreas, onto the end of which I had tacked a brief, factual mention of Hannah Power's death in Venice, earned me a nod of acknowledgement from James McCave (and a disguised snort of derision from Paul Connelly). In a brief lull before the intense pressure of the next few weeks, I took a couple of days off, intending to decorate the grottiest parts of my flat. I lived in a modern conversion above a tools reclamation workshop (and if you know what one of those is, you're one step ahead of me) at the bottom end of one of the short ladder of streets that runs between the Yardley Road and the canal. The view from the back of my flat (my living room/study) was of Yardley Cemetery, while from the front (my bedroom, where decoration was most urgently needed) the vista was dominated by the green ribbon of the canal.

I wandered down the road to get a paper. As I was walking back, my eye fell on a story on page four: 'Canal death treated as suspicious,' ran the headline. 'The body of Marijke Sels, 25, was recovered from the Regent's Canal in London's Camden Town yesterday. Ms Sels, a student from Amsterdam enrolled at London University, is believed to have drowned, but the police are treating as suspicious certain marks found on her body, which could possibly have resulted from a struggle. Police are appealing for witnesses.'

Decorating forgotten, leave cancelled, I was at my desk inside half an hour.

Paul Connelly spotted me. 'What the fuck are you doing here?' he enquired.

I showed him the story.

'Don't waste your time,' he muttered.

'They must be related,' I persisted. 'The three deaths: Hannah Power, Sally Mylrea, Marijke Sels. It's too much of a coincidence. There must be a common thread.'

'Of course there's a fucking common thread. They're all dead. Now stop wasting your time. Since you're here, you might as well do something useful. Sub that.'

He dropped a galley on my desk and stalked off. I wasn't a sub, but nor did I fancy a four-hour-wait in A&E with a broken nose, so I had a look at what he'd left me. It was copy for a canal walk, the first of a weekly column 'by our environmental correspondent Julie Meech'. This had run in the dummy so shouldn't have needed subbing; but again it didn't seem my place to point this out, so I read it, marked up a few little things and scrawled Connelly's initials in the right-hand corner before sticking it in the internal mail.

I spent the rest of the day digging up everything I could find on the three dead girls. Apart from the fact that they were all around the same age, nothing seemed to link them. I lay in bed that night unable to sleep as I turned the girls' names over and over in my head and etched their grainy newspaper faces swim past me into the murky depths. A phrase from Julie Meech's canal walk kept coming back to me: the Inland Waterways Association. Writer and stillwater enthusiast Robert Aickman had co-founded (with LTC Rolt) the Inland Waterways Association in 1946, Meech had written, to promote the restoration of his beloved canals and encourage more people to use them.

I got out of bed and walked to the window. I'd taken the curtains down in preparation for the now-abandoned decorating. The link between the three girls was staring me in the face. The canal. There was no other common thread. Whether they fell or they were pushed, the three had died in canals. One in Venice, one in Amsterdam and one in London. Gazing out into the darkness, I was struck by another thought, which hit me like a hammer in the back of the head.

There was no reason to assume that the killing of the Dutch girl was the end of it.

In fact, as I realised as I hurried to work the following morning, there was one very good reason why it wasn't the end of it.

If the news editor had been anyone other than Paul Connelly, I would have gone to him – or her – with my theory. You could argue I should have gone straight to the police. But I waited, and while I waited I did some research. Using the phone book, the A-Z and the internet, I scoured Birmingham for Italian communities or associations. I discovered that part of Digbeth had become a thriving Italian quarter following an influx of migrant workers from southern Italy more than a century ago. Whether their legacy amounted to more than a couple of Italian restaurants in the area was unclear, but even if it did, what good would that do me? What did I think I was going to do? Distribute flyers? Stand outside with a sandwich board? No. What was the point of working for the press if you didn't use it as it was meant to be used?

Assuming the intervals between the other deaths had set a pattern, I had at least a week before the final piece of the puzzle was slotted into place.

I wrote my article, describing the pattern I believed had been set and issuing the warning I thought necessary. I emailed it directly to McCave. Half an hour later the phone rang. I was to see the editor in his office.

'What's this?' he asked, waving a printout of my story.

'I'm completely serious about it,' I said.

'So I see. Why didn't you follow procedure and send it to the news editor?'

I looked at McCave as if seeing him for the first time. Broad-shouldered, straight-backed, he looked at home in his tailored suit.

There was a tiny shaving cut just below his left ear.

'He seems to have a bit of a downer on me,' I said.

'He's got a downer on everybody, but he's good at his job. Pull a stunt like this again and you'll be looking for a new one. Is that clear?'

'Yes.'

'Close the door on your way out.'

* * *

Close the door on your way out. So people actually said that.

My piece appeared in the launch issue. I had no illusions about why McCave had ordered Connelly to run it: it was bound to generate publicity and McCave was gambling that it'd work for us rather than against us. Connelly had barely looked at me over the last four days, which I found more alarming than his usual confrontational methods of intimidation.

The reception was mixed. Briefly, I'd stated the facts. Hannah Power, from London, had been found dead in the rio di San Salvador in Venice. Sally Mylrea, from Birmingham, had drowned in the Keizergracht in Amsterdam. Marijke Sels, from Amsterdam, had been pulled out of the Regent's Canal in London. While the possibility remained that one or two or even all three of the deaths were accidental, if you considered the details, the coincidence seemed too unlikely; and once you factored in the evidence of assault in the Marijke Sels case, it became almost impossible not to conclude that all three girls had been murdered, presumably by the same person, who we should be expecting to strike once again. The missing piece in the jigsaw puzzle he (again, a presumption) was assembling would be the drowning of a Venetian girl in a canal in Birmingham.

The police didn't waste any time in calling to say they were dispatching two detectives to interview me at the office. The Heart of England tourist board were not best pleased, faxing the ad sales director to complain that this had set them back years. And readers – in their dozens – emailed, telephoned and even turned up in person at the Frederick Street offices to report suspicious sightings of strange men by canals throughout the Birmingham area.

I'd half expected to hear from Martin Weiss, so when I didn't I emailed him and later called; but if he was there, he didn't pick up.

I did, however, get a card the following morning. It was another of Martin's trademark Sickert postcards, *Nude on a Bed*, which showed a woman sitting on the edge of an iron bed with her hands clasped behind her head. On the back, Martin had written: 'Nice tits. I hope your bosses appreciate your "news story" as much as I did.' Unable to work out if he was taunting me – the pointed reference to the model's breasts seemed uncharacteristically vulgar – I slipped the postcard into my inside pocket and it went home with me at the end of a long day of police interviews and difficult phone calls, as many from cranks as from anxious Italian parents. What could I tell any of them that I hadn't put in my piece? Everything I knew for sure was there, and most of what I suspected. Should I have told them of my vague suspicions regarding an old friend? Such thoughts would have seemed monstrously fanciful with no real evidence to back them up.

The evidence arrived the next day in the shape of another postcard. Again it was a girl on a bed. Lying back, one leg on the floor, the other hanging in the air. As with one or two of the Camden Town paintings, it was impossible to say if she was asleep or dead. The title was the one I should have been expecting if I'd done my research thoroughly: *Fille Venitienne Allongée*.

On the back, in Martin's handwriting: 'Four down. Birmingham noir (10)'.

I took it straight to the photocopier, then to Connelly.

'Fuck's that?' he asked.

'Look,' I said, turning it over. '*Fille Venitienne Allongée*. Venetian girl lying down. It's a direct reference to my piece.'

'I can see that,' he said icily. 'What about the fucking crossword clue?'

'Bournville?' I suggested hesitantly.

* * *

When I got to the stretch of the Worcester and Birmingham canal that passes through Bournville, alongside the railway line that runs right past the Cadbury factory, it was like a film set. Police cars, ambulances, reporters, TV crews, lights, lines and lines of police tape strung up like bunting between the trees, and crowds of onlookers.

I bitterly regretted that I was too late, but I was glad of one small thing: that I was too late to see the girl's limp body emerging from the dark water in the arms of a police diver. I saw the pictures later, but they didn't have the same power that seeing her in the flesh would have had.

I often go back there. Some kids have built a rickety stepladder up the side of a tree, leading to a couple of strategically placed sheets of hardboard where you can sit quite comfortably. It doesn't look new and has probably been there for years. It's as good a place as any to sit and brood. I tried to work out how far in advance Martin had planned everything. Did he only get the idea once I became interested in Sickert and decided to go to Venice, or had he been planning it from the moment when he first introduced me to the painter's work?

I don't know, but I remember his telling me he was working on a big project. So this was it. Right from the beginning, since his photographs in the Bethnal Green gallery, he'd been drawn to the overlap between violent crime and visual art. His series of murders, perfectly constructed, deftly executed, had been signed just like a painting. The police investigation proved that he'd flown to Venice while I was there and that he'd returned to Birmingham via Amsterdam. Apart from that, they were no nearer catching him than I had ever been, in any sense of the word.

The canal at Bournville is quite beautiful, especially at dusk. Sometimes I sit there for hours, until the sky turns purple, over the chocolate factory, and I wonder about Martin, still out there somewhere. Is that it? Has he finished? Or will there be more? I realise that asking *Why me?* implies a solipsistic attitude when the tragedies affected so many lives, but I can't help wondering if the responsibility for the murders should really be all Martin's. Clearly, he used me because he knew I would be interested. He engineered things in such a way that I was bound to be interested. He wanted the world to hear about his work, just as it gets to hear about the work of any great artist, and I could be relied upon to make sure of that. But was I not also being punished, or at the very least put in my place?

Sally Spedding

The mist still lay low enough to seal all the penitent but imperfect souls close to the winter earth. Including herself, thought fifteen-year-old Eira Williams, for her guilty pleasure in leaving the constraints of home.

Named after the snows that linger like shreds of sail cloth on Capel Ffin, she was now just as pale, just as frozen after a long day on the road, and let Fly the head drover's dog lick her face. He reeked of cow dung but no matter, with his tongue like hot bacon on her cheek and his ribby warmth enough to keep her from death, she gripped his collar as if he was the only rock back in the flooded river Bran.

All she could see were his two front paws, white as ladies' gloves. The rest so blurred that the girl come to work at Castle Ashby House in Northamptonshire couldn't see where her bed for the night and the coat she'd sleep in began.

That garment was her father's most prized possession, specially cleaned of straw for the morning the porthmon Moses Richards called to add her to his herd of Pembrokeshire Blacks strung out along by Gallt y Mwyn like lumps of coal and impatient to be off.

'Don't ever be parted from it,' Evan Williams warned. 'The Saesneg will sell anything my girl.'

'Oh Evan, don't,' pleaded Mrs. Williams. 'It'll do her good to see the world and get fattened up with the rest of them. Won't it, cariad?'

Eira nodded, aware that Moses' twin kept his piggy eyes on her all the time.

'You forgotten about Non Jenkins then?' the farmer persisted, buttoning up his daughter with the best boars' teeth on the best 'brethyn cartref', rough on her throat but heavy as a shield against his fears, so she could at least smile a farewell to them both and wave once they'd merged into the drizzle.

*   *   *

But Eira heeded him nevertheless, and the coat stayed on her back for all of the three weeks. Through Sennybridge and the joining with Llew Lewis's drove of Shorthorns. Through Aberhonddu, Hereford and places she couldn't pronounce, as west became east with the weather grown cold as prayers of the dying. However, those weren't the only changes.

By the time they'd reached Northamptonshire she knew Aaron Richards had a mind to make her his woman. She could tell the way he fixed on her and worked his tongue round his lips whenever she caught his eye. Twice she'd fought him off. And twice he'd returned for more. So now with night falling, Eira made sure she was settled well away from him and Gwallter Jones in the dark bank above Sulgrave Lane.

Suddenly a whistle, and the dog leapt from her lap. Moses Richards was swearing that God must have dropped his guard and let Satan take his place.

'Those who blaspheme on All Souls will have their hearts bound with flax,' she whispered, then sat bolt upright, her ears tuned to a blur of sound which gathered momentum like the worker's chants in the forestry.

But this was no singing.

'Haiptrw Ho!' boomed through the mist, alerting her to the hedge. She clung to the pleached hawthorn as the panic swell grew closer, thundering down to the deep end of the world, choking the narrow lane with the Pembrokeshire Blacks in front taking low branches on their shoulders.

Then the Shorthorn bullocks sensing freedom, pressed the leaders up the banks until the way ahead was clear. Eira felt them on her coat and prayed aloud until it was the only sound in the curdling stench of blood and scouring. Next, out of the haze, boots pounding like a drum roll. Her voice locked in terror. They were leaving her behind. Even Aaron Richards. Even the dog.

Her teeth juddered in the silence as she slithered down the gulley. Ox blood hung in the air, stiffening her coat. Suddenly a hand to end it all came stinking on her face, flattening her nose.

'No need to call out, Miss Snow. Ye'll be all right now.' The twin who'd crept back from the others tried to hold her close. This ugliest of God's works with the scurvy and breath worse than the pig floor at Nant y Ffin would never touch her again as long as she lived. 'Better come with me if you want to get where you're intended.' His nails reached her bones like the vermin traps up on the Moel Pregethwr. 'We got them all in, thank the Lord. Went sweet as lambs at the end…'

Sweet as lambs. Eira shivered, plotting furiously how best to escape. The only weapon was her voice, so she set her jaw and took in a great gulp of air. But Aaron Richard's hand was there again.

'Castle Ashby's two days from here. How'll you manage that?'

'I'm not going.'

Just past Southam, when his eyes had gone straight through her clothes, she'd decided to find a return party to take her home. Capability Brown or no Capability Brown, she wasn't going to be a sitting duck in the pretty winter gardens just for his pleasure. She heaved and sicked up.

'Brwnt gast!'

The blow sent her to his feet, and once more in darkness, Death's finger beckoned.

'Aaron?' his twin bellowed. 'What you a doin' of? Jones and Lewis here's on their own!'

Eira sensed her captor's indecision. Subservient to his brother who by being married held the Drover's Licence – the upper hand, and on a night such as this, a warm bed. She took the advantage and ran up the lane as Moses' threats continued.

'At Maidford, I'll see you get nothing! And nothing means nothing!'

Her heart like a hammer, Eira waited for the man's next move, but only sighs of the long-dead reached her as she dodged loose stones, the strewn limbs of ash and beech and pools of dung.

At the crossroads to Moreton Pinkey the sign lay broken. Nor was there any moon or stars to set north or tell the time. Was it still night or dawn? Without birdsong who could say? Only those above it all whose vision lay unclouded by matter knew the answer, at least that's what The Wizard of Cwrt y Cadno had said when they'd called in for his rinderpest cure.

How she longed for their gift now, turning as though in a solitary game of Blind Man's Buff, in a strange country with neither coin nor candle to her name. She thought of twp Non Jenkins from

Siloh. Sold with the milk near Banbury and found on St.Swithin's day in two forage bags. Better she'd been taken by footpads – at least she'd have a chance...

Then Eira shut her eyes and for the second time, cocooned in blood and ordure, she huddled by a clump of ivy to sleep.

* * *

Fly was limping and whining in turn. He'd slunk away from the men arguing at breakfast as to what had started the stampede, and who should go for the smith in Culworth. At least half the herd needed re-shoeing and most had lost what little condition they'd had. It wasn't until Moses Richards had shaken out his napkin and blown his nose that he realised their one dog had gone.

Too many smells, new distractions, and the brown half-breed instead of keeping straight, took the hidden turning up to Capswell Lodge.

* * *

The dowager Lady Dunbarnie felt a draught from outside and something brush her skirts. Being of an affectionate nature she leant forwards to acquaint herself with the visitor, still keeping her considerable weight on her stick.

Fly cowered under her petticoats until he was lifted from his sanctuary and held aloft by a young man dressed more for the city than larks in the country.

'I recognise this whipster, Mama. He's with those Taffies.' Michael Macgregor's grin widened. 'Time for a clean up, my friend, and none too soon at that.' Still dangling the dog he went through from the kitchen to the scullery where he broke the ice on the bucket with his heel.

His mother heard the pathetic howling and covered her ears, wishing not for the first time she was deaf as well as blind, and wondering out loud why her youngest wasn't bettering himself like William up at the locomotive works in Newcastle, or James just qualified as a physician in Edinburgh.

How the male blood thins and sours, she thought, ringing for Agnes to come and stir the fire. Maybe if Michael had come first, and maybe if Lord Dunbarnie had lived they could have stayed in

Kirkcudbright and things would have been different…

'Always so many maybes, don't you agree?' To the maid who could never look at her employer's face.

'That's life, innit?'

The dowager's eyeless pinpricks stared in her direction.

'You know my one regret is that I never had a daughter. Someone to fuss over me, to take care of things…'

'So you keep saying, Ma'am.'

'Tell me, Agnes,' she began, settling herself at the kitchen table, 'just what would you advise?'

'You mean, about producing one, Ma'am?' The old Dame was well past anything like that. Barren as the sow strung up in the barn. But Capswell Lodge was full of goings–on. Some too strange for words…

'Whatever.'

The old retainer studied the flames then quickly tucked her sixth finger into her palm when she heard Dunbarnie's tread on the flags.

'My grandmother said to eat apples. Red ones, and four a day for the first month…' She babbled.

'Mama, this simpleton talks such utter bunkum,' shouted her son from the adjoining scullery. 'I don't know why we don't just send her back to the hole in the ground and hire someone whose opinion we can respect.'

Agnes Larter scurried out but not before noticing his dirty boots and the wet dog, barely alive at the end of old twine as he dragged it back into the kitchen. He kissed his mother's scented cheek leaving her to fret over the possibility of sparks.

'Training,' he lied, 'and this Welsh runt had better learn new tricks or he'll be vittles for the hounds.' He kicked his haunches for good measure as the dowager's stick quivered in anger.

'I don't know where you come from, sometimes, Michael MacGregor. Perhaps if I could summon the Devil, he'd tell me.'

Her son chose not to hear. Instead let his helpmeet guide him back through the grounded clouds.

* * *

Eira woke too quickly and knew she wasn't alone.

'Fly?'

But the stranger hauled him away.

'What sort of name is that, pray? I can think of a dozen better for such a mistake.'

'Who are you?'

'Just show me your pockets.' The young man from Capswell Lodge squatted beside her. Beer, and the smell of carbine didn't go with the clothes, but he was more handsome than anything her side of the Aust. 'You're with the Sennybridge' lot aren't you?'

She paused, unsure of his tone. That name where the droves of Blacks and Shorthorns had converged now seemed far away...

'I might be, I might not.'

'A girl with spirit. Hey ho.'

'I'm not a girl. I'm a young lady, and sir, you'll do me the honour of addressing me so.' Her words surprised her, altering her colour. Even though she'd played Lords and Ladies countless times with her cousins Mair and Owen, using stones for cups and bracken for fans, this was different.

'Well if I might enquire of your Ladyship why she's so covered in manure with no silver in her hand?'

Eira fell silent with the shame of her filthy clothes, the mess of her hair and even as the mist became fog she could see all too vividly the mud walls of Nant y Ffin, the midden, the feeble fire. She unbuttoned her coat and hefted it over into the next field.

'That's better.' His fingers took hers. The gentleness of it bought a smile and he thought her exceptionally pretty, unlike the plate-face from Siloh. Just what his Mama had always wanted, but what a pity the old mare would never be able to see her...

They walked arm in arm, with the dog close at heel – the night demons fading as an easy ambience settled on their conversation. Past the great elm swathed in mistletoe where his shot had seen off the herd, back to his secrets and the light still guttering in the window.

Acknowledgments

MARTHA GRACE by Stella Duffy © 2002 by Stella Duffy. First appeared in *Tart Noir*, edited by Stella Duffy and Lauren Henderson. Reprinted by permission of the author.

SAINT NICKED by Ian Rankin © 2002 by Ian Rankin. First appeared in *Radio Times*. Reprinted by permission of the author and his agent, Curtis Brown Ltd.

ALICE OPENS THE BOX by Denise Mina © 2002 by Denise Mina. First appeared in *Tart Noir*, edited by Stella Duffy and Lauren Henderson. Reprinted by permission of the author.

SLAUGHTER IN THE STRAND by Edward Marston © 2002 by Keith Miles. First appeared in the *Mammoth Book of Comic Crime*, edited by Maxim Jakubowski. Reprinted by permission of the author.

24 HOURS FROM TULSA by Martin Edwards © 2002 by Martin Edwards. First appeared in *The Mammoth Book of On The Road*, edited by Maxim Jakubowski and M. Christian. Reprinted by permission of the author.

SEDUCED by Jerry Sykes © 2002 by Jerry Sykes. First appeared in *Shots* online. Reprinted by permission of the author.

GOING THROUGH A PHASE by Robert Barnard © 2002 by Robert Barnard. First appeared in *Ellery Queen Mystery Magazine*. Reprinted by permission of the author.

BRAND NEW BOYFRIEND by Carol Anne Davis © 2002 by Carol Anne Davis. First appeared in *Tourniquet Heart*, edited by Christopher C. Teague. Reprinted by permission of the author.

EXIT, PURSUED by Simon Brett © 2002 by Simon Brett. First appeared in *Much Ado About Murder*, edited by Anne Perry. Reprinted by permission of the author and his agent, Michael Motley.